© 2005 by Andrew Brown

About the Author

YXTA MAYA MURRAY is the author of *The Queen Jade* and *The Conquest* (a Barnes and Noble Discover pick). In 1999 she was the recipient of the Whiting Award for Fiction. She teaches law at Loyola Law School in Los Angeles, where she lives.

the
KING'S GOLD

ALSO BY YXTA MAYA MURRAY

The Queen Jade

The Conquest

What It Takes to Get to Vegas

Locas

the
KING'S GOLD

AN OLD WORLD NOVEL OF ADVENTURE

YXTA MAYA MURRAY

HARPER

NEW YORK • LONDON • TORONTO • SYDNEY

HARPER

HarperCollins books may be purchased for educational, business, or sales promotional use. For information please write: Special Markets Department, HarperCollins Publishers, 10 East 53rd Street, New York, NY 10022.

FIRST EDITION

Rebus by Yxta Maya Murray
Map of Italy and calligraphy hand-lettered by John Del Gaizo
Book designed by Joy O'Meara

Library of Congress Cataloging-in-Publication Data has been applied for.
ISBN 978-0-06-089108-4

08 09 10 11 12 OV/RRD 10 9 8 7 6 5 4 3 2 1

To my father, Fred MacMurray,
and
Edward St. John

The [Aztecs] shouted to Cortés a great fury, inquiring why he wanted to destroy their gods. . . . Some of [the divinities] were in the form of fearsome dragons . . . and others half-man half-dog and hideously ugly.

So the door to [Montezuma's treasure house] was secretly opened, and Cortés went in first with certain captains. When they saw the quantity of golden objects—jewels and plates and ingots—that lay in the chamber they were quite transported. . . . A number of soldiers had loaded themselves with this treasure, and some had paid for it with their lives. Cortés now proclaimed that a third of it must be returned to him, and that if it was not brought in it would be seized. Cortés gained some of it by force. But as nearly all the captains and the King's officials themselves had secret hoards, the proclamation was largely ignored.

—BERNAL DIAZ, *The Conquest of New Spain* (1570)

Alchymy . . . proposes, for its object, the transmutation of metals, and other important operations.

—SAMUEL JOHNSON, *A Dictionary of the English Language* (1755)

He no longer saw the face of his friend Siddhartha. Instead he saw other faces, many faces, a long series, a continuous stream of faces—hundreds, thousands, which all came and disappeared and yet all seemed to be there at the same time, which all continually changed and renewed themselves and which were yet all Siddhartha. . . . He saw all these forms and faces in a thousand relationships to each other, all helping each other, loving, hating and destroying each other and become newly born.

—HERMANN HESSE, *Siddhartha* (1951)

BOOK ONE

THE TOY
OF DOOM

I

I first realized that I was changing from a sedentary, word-mad bibliophile into a genuine biblio-*adventurer* on the Sunday evening a dark and dangerous man showed me that priceless piece of treasure.

It was a bright warm June in Long Beach, in 2001, the year of our Lord Sir Arthur Conan Doyle, in the moments before I was to lay my hot hands on this prodigy. At seven p.m., the California sky loomed clear, sapphire, cloudless; down below, the city's shining boulevards teemed with slim-limbed soccer players and beach sylphs. Despite the example set by this rabble of healthy humanity, however, I had ensconced myself in my scrumptiously tome-spangled adventure-and-fantasy bookshop, the Red Lion.

I, Lola Sanchez, am small, tawny, librarianish, and blessed with extravagant Maya bones. Ox-eyed, tiny-busted, with nice, sturdy legs, I will also allow that I looked particularly fetching on this night, as I had dressed in a hand-sewn violet gown designed after the description of priestess robes in *The Mists of Avalon*. After checking my cell phone for "texts," I dusted a little, admiring the sparks shed by my wee diamond engagement ring. I then plumped the plush red-wine-colored leather chairs that waited for the fundaments of Sherlock Holmes fans and the devotees of Bram Stoker. By these thrones stood a small cherrywood table upon which I had placed a heavy lead-crystal decanter of sherry and a plate of homemade Gruyère puffs. Richly colored kilim rugs, imported from the black sands of Arabia, glimmered on the oak floor. All of this lavish scenery set the stage for the real stars of the store, which of course were *the books*. My splendid first-edition octavos and fabulously grotty pulps towered in their cherry shelves, their covers illustrated with square-jawed portraits of "dark horse" adventurers—Allan Quatermain, "Indy" Jones, Dirk Pitt, Professor Challenger, Gabriel Van Helsing.

I stocked my shop with such an old-fashioned collection because I have a personal weakness for these sorts of knuckle-dragging raiders. I'm intrigued by pulp heroes because my biological father happened to be one such dinosaur. Not that I'd ever *met* the man. Nor, I thought, would I probably have liked him if I *did*, as he apparently had been a hateful brute, and nothing like my adopted father, a gentle neurasthenic to whom I am slavishly devoted. Nevertheless, like many others of my generation (in 2001 I was thirty-three) I was born to a departed, prodigal dad. Instead of popping Xanax, I simply tended to linger over my *King Solomon's Mines* and my *Lost Worlds* a bit too much, like a strange readerly version of Antigone.

And yet all my fan-girldom did not prepare me for that trio of X-Men-looking boys who suddenly came rap, rap, rapping at my glass door!

"Hello? Ms. de la Rosa?"

The three strangers stood right below the Red Lion's sign. Through the door's glass window I could see that the first fellow was light-haired and thick as an ox. The second was red-haired and fox-wiry. The third man regarded me with such dark and dramatic intensity he seemed to blot out the other two as if by eclipse, and I noticed also that he held a small, silk-wrapped parcel in his strong-looking hands.

This Third Man dressed with a Londoner's restraint, wearing a rich black three-piece suit, but he had glowing eyes that are meant to transfix women from behind a silk vizard-mask. His face had sharp cheekbones and swarthy skin; his hair was short and black and soft. His brow brooded in a sardonic mood that matched the curl of his mouth.

He, and his friends, came in.

"May I help you?" I asked, the standard question.

"Yes, I believe you may," he answered in Spanish, with an accent that I recognized immediately as Guatemalan.

"We sell adventure and fantasy books here," I said automatically, switching tongues. "Used editions, mainly. That is, used, but first to seventh editions in *spectacular* condition—"

He rolled his eyes to the ceiling. "I have no interest in fiction. The business that draws me to this store tonight is of a much more . . . practical nature than that of fantasy."

A cold finger seemed to touch my heart when he said that.

"Oh—*pretty* ring." He glanced down at the diamond-glow wavering above my knuckle. "But . . . enough with the pleasantries! Let's get right to business, shall we?" He held up the parcel so that its white wrapping caught the lamplight, rustling the papers inside a little, and this did snag my attention. "For I've traveled such a very long way to see you."

"From where, Mr. . . . ?"

"My name is Marco. And I've been everyplace . . . Prague . . . Zurich . . . lately, Florence and—Antigua."

"Yes, your accent is Guatemalan. My sister's from there, so, I'm familiar—"

"And your father as well, no?"

I folded my hands in front of me. "I'm sorry—do you know my family?"

"*Everyone* knows your family," he said smoothly as he walked around the store, looking at the books with more than a little interest. "That's why I'm here. I just happened to come into the possession of a very interesting document—a sort of puzzle, you might say. Really intriguing, as it may involve money. A great deal of it, Miss de la Rosa."

"Actually, my name is Sanchez. Lola Sanchez."

"Ah, sorry." He gestured with the hand carrying the parcel, so that it dangled in front of me, like a bright fishhook or a mesmeric charm. "But you *are* related to Tomas de la Rosa, no? The great—but *dead*—archaeologist? And—more famously—the war hero? If you're not a de la Rosa, please excuse me, I seem to have made some mistake, and though I would always like to remain in the company of an attractive woman such as yourself, I am on a schedule and would have to take my leave."

"Oh! Agh! We couldn't have that," I exclaimed, quite stupidly flattered.

"You see, because what I have here is a very, very, *very* old piece of writing. It's rather important to me. And I heard that the daughter of de la Rosa—"

"My sister's name is Yolanda de la Rosa—"

"No, no, no, not that grubby one, with the hat? The tracker? I was definitely instructed to find a more refined lady named Lola. Whom I was told had inherited her father's talents."

"Who said that?"

"Oh, this shabby member of the criminal element whose path I happened to cross in Antigua. A *fence*, I think is what they're called. One Mr. Soto-Relada, a purveyor of— What does he

call it? 'Difficult-to-obtain wares.' He's the one who brought this
fascinating antique to my attention. Mr. Soto-Relada worked for
your father too, from what I understand. He says you're the next
best thing to Tomas—"

"Soto-Relada? Never heard of him. He worked for de la
Rosa—doing what?"

"Helping him . . . *discover* antiquities. You know, the dug-up
ruins, the potsherds, the bits of jade and crockery that made your
father so notorious—along with his 'political work.' Oh, I *do* admire Tomas de la Rosa—as all we Guatemalans do. It's sort of
a national religion—except among the military, obviously. Who
haaaate him. But, yes, your father was quite the genius, quite the
darling. Wasn't he? Though now, sadly, *mortuus*, as they say in Latin.
Buried in Europe, I understand."

"In Europe?" I tilted my head.

"Yes. Italy. I have it on very good information—"

"Tomas de la Rosa died in Guatemala, in the jungle."

Marco boggled at me. "Who on earth told you that?"

"Everyone knows it," I said, flustered. "I mean, we don't know
exactly where he was buried. We looked, two years ago. My family. But we were told he was killed by soldiers."

"He was a civil war casualty."

"The fascists murdered him," I said bluntly. "He's one of the
disappeared."

"It *was* sad. Such a loss, a talent like his. Though I hope you
don't mind my saying that perhaps his skill was not irreplaceable—
as I mentioned, my associate told me that this Lola de la Rosa lady
was supposed to be something of an expert in code-breaking.
Who knew how to read in several languages? I'm looking for a
girl who has an interest in old texts. Paleography."

The white parcel shone in the bookstore's gloom.

"Paleography," I said.

Behind me, the redheaded fox-faced man and the ox-built blond remained perfectly impassive, only remaining standing by the door like two huge stumps.

"Yes, the interpretation of antique documents," this Marco went on. "In particular, documents that other people have difficulty deciphering. You're so modest. You say you went looking for your father in our jungles—but what you *did* find was that relic, no? That Queen Jade hullabaloo that everyone was shrieking about? The jade that turned out to be something or other else . . . a woman . . . some sort of mummy, from what I heard. Though . . . you ran into a bit of trouble, or something. Some loony Colonel Victor Moreno and his Lieutenant . . . something or other, chased you through the Guatemalan swamps. They wanted blood vengeance for de la Rosa's war crimes. Yes? Because he killed that boy in '93? And then these soldiers shot at you like maniacs, from what I hear. But you managed to execute them, rather violently? The colonel was beaten to death, wasn't he? *Yes*, that's it—Colonel Moreno was torn to pieces, his chest caved in, his face black, bleeding. His insides hemorrhaging. It left an ugly mess, I hear. They say his son went insane at the funeral . . . What was his name?" Marco furrowed his brow. "I can't remember. Anyway, the stories of your derring-do as they've come down to me have been quite colorful. From what I understand, despite all that drama, you still kept your head, and stumbled across one of the most remarkable archaeological finds of the century, really."

"Well, hmmm, bah—" I said, reddening. "Look, the truth is . . ."

I stammered and gabbled for a second, but the truth *was* that this Marco person had just given me a nearly perfect rendition of my recent family history. I *did* have a heinous jungle adventure two years back. And, unfortunately, it passed much as he described:

In 1998, my mother, the archaeologist Juana Sanchez, disappeared into the Guatemalan rain forest, supposedly on the trail of an archaeological relic known as the Queen Jade, but actually searching for the body of my recently deceased biological, and aforementioned, father, the archaeologist and Marxist rebel Dr. Tomas de la Rosa. Besides achieving fame for his archaeological discoveries, de la Rosa had also for many years operated as a political insurgent, by fighting military dictatorship in Guatemala's civil war (1960–1996). The nadir of his guerrilla efforts had occurred in the war's early years, when he crossed into an army camp disguised as an old woman, planting a bomb that killed one Serjei Moreno. This victim had been the nephew of a major architect of military oppression, a genocidal man-monster named Colonel Victor Moreno. Despite this crime, and though my mother had long been the paramour of the museum curator Manuel Alvarez, she had fallen into de la Rosa's bed in '68, conceiving me. And even when Tomas dumped her, and Manuel took her back and adopted me, she'd never fallen out of love with that heartbreaker. Multilingual, subversive, and a crack scientist, de la Rosa amounted to a sort of Byronic Che Guevara, with some Louis Leakey mixed in. Thus, when she received word in '98 that junta forces had killed Tomas and then buried him in the Guatemalan swamps, her lasting obsession with the man led her to embark on a dangerous quest. A devastating hurricane called Mitch tore over Central America in the very days that she set out to find the grave of her old lover—which she never found.

Moreover, she had been lost in that deluge. Soon after we discovered her disappearance, I; my sister, Yolanda (de la Rosa's other, legit daughter); Manuel; and my now fiancé, Erik Gomara, had ventured out into the jungle to search for her. Tracking her down required the decipherment of an intricate Mayan text that she had been using as a guide, but before we finally found her, injured in the burial ground of a Maya queen, we were intercepted. Colonel Moreno and his henchman, an insane butcher named Lieutenant Estrada, had chased us through the jungle. Moreno ordered Estrada to kill us in revenge for his nephew, Serjei. This unstable assassin, however, had been made so mad by Colonel Moreno's military "training" that he wound up bludgeoning his mentor before our eyes—ripping apart the man's body with his bare hands much as Marco recounted; later, the lieutenant drowned himself in our presence. As might be imagined, this series of catastrophes had taken its toll on my family: a temporary split up of Manuel and Juana, a deepening grief for Yolanda (made worse by her move to suburban L.B.), a rash of nightmares for Erik. For my part, I'd developed a fascination for my dead and vanished father. However, I never mentioned my fixation to anyone—particularly Manuel—and had resolved to quietly deal with this neurosis by stocking those expensive books about mad, bad, and dangerous to know swashbucklers. And that is why, also, I now said to Marco:

"The truth is, I'd rather not talk about all that, if you don't mind."

"But you *were* there," he insisted. "You found the Queen Jade. And had that tiff with Colonel Moreno? That is, the *former* Colonel Moreno."

I waved off the reference, closing the subject. "I did some deciphering, but my fiancé and my mother did most of the archaeological work—"

"Still, you *are* the one I'm looking for, aren't you?" His smile turned warmer. "How lucky for me that you're so . . . charming."

"And who are you, exactly?" I asked.

"A playboy, I think, is what most people would call me. Lived in Europe for many years, and have quite recently begun dabbling in politics. And now"—he raised the parcel even higher, so that it was above my eye level—"archaeology, it seems. You see, I was hoping that you might be able to aid in the deciphering of this riddle I've brought you—which perhaps is also a map. If the document I'm holding here is authentic, then it is *very valuable*: Supposedly, the thing was written by a member of the Medici family—some scrofulous and suicidal Florentine alchemist named Antonio Beato Cagliostro Medici who went to Mexico with Hernán Cortés—you know, in the sixteenth century—"

"Oh. Yes! I've read about him—the Italian conquistatore, soldier of Cortés—"

"Right, old Hernán, who rabbled around the Aztec city Tenochtitlán, with his mercenaries . . . and then they smashed it all to pieces and took that emperor's gold."

"The Emperor Montezuma."

"Yes, *him*. The big king—the big old failure—probably the most embarrassing figure in all of Latino history! I'm sure you've heard the story of how Montezuma handed over all his gold— scads and scads of it—to Cortés, who claimed he was a god or something colossally moronic like that."

"That's a fairly simple version—the Europeans were carrying smallpox and syphilis and had these big, sharp, basically omnipotent steel weapons that they were swinging around like Musketeers—"

"And blah blah blah blah blah *blah*. Yes, right. Poor, poor losers. Poor, poor *us*! Crushed to pieces by Whitey. Still, it's a fascinating story. How a handful of bandy-legged, scurvy little Anglos toppled one of the greatest kingdoms in the world. And, again, *took all that gold*—and no one really knows what happened to it."

"A huge amount of the treasure just disappeared, according to the histories."

"The histories that *we've* read, that is. But what if there were another, secret story, about what happened to the gold? What if . . . we could find out where it . . . was?"

Again, he dangled the package, back and forth, back and forth.

"It may just be a matter of solving a little puzzle, if I'm right," he went on. "Rather a *nasty* puzzle, though, I'm afraid. Possibly dangerous. In this letter, Antonio Medici claims *he* stole Cortés's or Montezuma's gold, brought it to Italy, and after probably spending part of it, hid the remainder in some kind of trap that he'd set for his nephew Cosimo I, the duke of Florence. Cosimo was a disgustingly successful warmonger, empire-builder, destroyer of Siena, abuser of the weak and the stupid—you know the type. He apparently wasn't very *nice* to Antonio, who I think might have been considered a weakling, or what we'd called disabled. Antonio suffered from a 'condition,' it seems."

"Yes—the Condition—Antonio's disease. No one really knows what it was, exactly, though there are rumors—"

"Of werewolfism, yes. Whatever it was, he tried to cure it with alchemical potions. It was probably some sort of mental illness, but there were those stories that he turned into some savage black dog, if you can believe it—"

"Certainly, I can—Renaissance Florentines were incredibly superstitious."

"Yes. Well. Whatever he was, man or superman, he was *smart.* In these papers, Antonio claims that he drew a map to the gold's Italian location, a map that I would very much like to study . . . though I can't find it. And there are clues in this letter, as well— it's some sort of suicidal treasure hunt—but I can't seem to figure them out. I wonder if *you* could—after authenticating the letter first, that is. You see, there's so much work to be done." He turned and called out: "Do you think she could help us, Blasej?"

"If you think so, sir," the sinewy redhead replied in Czech-flavored Spanish, as he still stood by the door.

"And you, Domenico?"

"He thinks the same, sir," the redhead answered.

"Christ, he can speak for himself, can't he?"

"I wouldn't know anything about it, Marco," the blond answered brusquely.

"Mmmm. It would be too bad if she weren't up to the task that's in here." Again, he slightly crumpled the papers, making a delicious sound.

I touched my engagement ring, a little anxiously, but took a step forward, closer to him.

"Oh, here she comes—it looks like she wants to give it a try." Marco retreated a step as he put the package behind his back. He drew back another step. "I think we've got her attention, boys."

I stood right in front of him, peering around his body to see the bait. Reaching across his ribs, I grasped it, though he held on tight, smiling down at me.

"Let me see," I said. "Oh—come on, ha, ha—no, *give it here*."

"Gotcha," he murmured.

Pulling the package from him, I ripped slightly at the envelope, which was wrinkled and fragile, like a cocoon. The papers crackled under my touch. I saw a papery glitter within.

Inspired by the Wonka-like shimmer of the text in the envelope, and the stranger's stories, I began to claw the thing open.

Inside, concealed in layers of pearl-colored tissue and tucked within two hard cardboard squares, I found a small cache of fold-ed papers. One thick new cream sheet doubled over an enclosure of pale onionskin papers that looked very old and delicate. I spread these out.

A short note had been printed by laser jet on the cream paper. The black ink characters sunk into the plush stock. The writing on it was in Spanish.

The translucent onionskin papers bore a message handwritten with a whorled, jewel-cutter's perfection that marked them as antique. The letter also was affixed with a broken gold wax seal that bore the heraldic mark of a wolf rampant.

The ink on these opened pages, once ebony, had faded to dove gray, and the letters were formed in the enduring and beautiful Roman italic. Here, the writing was in Italian, but I am fluent in that language and have some facility in translating it.

A hot excitement rushed through me as I held onto that jewel, whose hand-ductus, or penmanship, revealed the care I have seen only from the hands of Renaissance calligraphy masters.

Even as those strangers stared down at me, I was snared, just by that inkling, just by the sight of that ancient and mysterious text.

"I had a feeling you'd find this interesting," the man said, laughing in a low voice as my eyes ravished the letter.

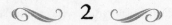

2

Señor Sam Soto-Relada
Dealer in Used Goods
11 Avenue and 11 Calle, Zona 1, Via Corona
Ciudad de Guatemala, Guatemala,
502–2–82–20–099
Dear Sir or Madam,

Please enjoy this *rare letter* in fine health.

Having any problems with the item? Any questions? Feel generally befuddled or confused? Feel free to call at ANY TIME. And remember that Soto-Relada is your go-to guy for any and all "hard to obtain" goods!

Yours truly,
Sam Soto-Relada

[Translated from old Italian by Lola Sanchez, with a smidgen of poetic license.]

June 1, 1554
Venezia

My dear nephew Cosimo, Duke of Florence,

I write this missive in response to your call for funds, on the eve of your quite stupid battle against Siena. Your appetite for shaking spears baffles me, as this is a war I have told you I find in bad taste. Or I would have told you so, if you had ever deigned to allow me an audience. When did we last meet, before you Exiled my wife, Sofia the Dragon, and me? It was in the 1520s, I believe, just after I returned from America, in the few months when I was still allowed to feast at our family's palazzo. The dining hall was so lovely, I remember, full of mysteries and hints of treasure—with its friezes of golden girls, its secret passageways, its fresco of The Rape of Proserpine, and that gew-gaw I commissioned, namely Pontormo's gorgeous map of Italy. On those evenings, after dining in your grudging company, I was permitted the indulgence of retreating to my laboratory, to conduct my Experimental searches for the Cure to the Condition—all such small familial pleasures denied to me since I have become your outcast!

I find it impressive that after this ill treatment, you still have the liver to beg a war chest from me.

As I take the destiny of the Medici more seriously than your idiocy, however, I have decided to honor your request. Our family Name requires it. After all, there was much wisdom to that old saying of the poet Plautus: Nomen atque Omen—one's name is one's omen.

I thus send along with this letter six coffers of silver, three hundred soldiers, and the pledge of my own sword.

Yes, Cosimo, I myself shall be on the field of Siena in a fortnight's time; I do not intend to pay over my lucre without watching with my own eye how it is spent.

And, along with my silver, I give you also two more gifts:

My first favor is a prophecy: I expect to die in this war. Now that my lady Sofia has been taken from me by brain fever, I lack the will to survive a battle—though I do intend to take many enemy lives before I depart from this world.

As for my second Sacrifice, I vest to you all my Fortune. You certainly recall my venture with Hernán Cortés, when I was a stripling and ran off to the Spaniards' Americas in search of their King's Gold. When I returned to Italy—with the corpse of that tiresome slave I starved to death—you had already heard all the Rumors about me: That I was filthy with Montezuma's filched treasure; that I was Different from before. But all of this was a preamble to your idiotically mispronouncing my Secret name, and then casting Sofia and me from the City.

"Some call you il Lupo, but I see you for what you really are. Darken not my door again, Versipellis," I recall you jabbering.

"I am no Versipellis, my Lord!"

"Do not lie to me!"

"Nay, nay, but these plaguey stories are mere slanders. I am no monster! I have no gold! I am only your same poor, penniless Uncle, dependent upon the Goodwill of the House of my fathers, the Medici," I wailed, weeping, as your Guards dragged me away.

Well, Cosimo, you will now be happy to learn that I lied.

I do own a vast, bloodstained, and secret treasure, which I bartered for my soul in Tenochtitlán, and have kept hidden from the world all these years. I leave it to you. I bequeath my Yellow Mettle with a condition, however. You must first solve my Puzzle:

Included in this letter are Two Ciphers that reveal the hiding places of four Clues I have scattered through your rival city-states, and that will lead you to the Fortune. One of these Ciphers is a riddle, and the other, as you see, is a map (or at least, you shall see it should you be able to look up from your feasting and banqueting, and pay nominal attention to what I am telling you).

Does that sound easy enough? Two more things:

Should your brains prove less thick than I expect, and you do find the clues, know that they are not in sequence, and must be recombined by you to spell a secret countersign that will win you your Treasure. Moreover, I have, of course, fitted each of the Clues' Secret hiding places with the most extraordinarily Deadly Traps that will surely kill you in manners that are as clever as they are supremely painful.

I do all this in the greatest hope that your greed will give me ample opportunity to wreak my vengeance from the grave.

Here is The Riddle:

TO FIND MY YELLOW METTLE

IN CITIES FOUR SHALL YOU STRIVE.

OF YOUR TRUE WORTH THE TESTS WILL TELL:

DIE POOR, OR SURVIVE YOUR PRIZE.

IN CITY ONE FIND A TOMB

WHERE UPON A FOOL WORMS FEED

ONE HAND HOLDS THE TOY OF DOOM

THE OTHER GRIPS YOUR FIRST LEAD.

IN A SHRINE AT CITY TWO

A SHE-WOLF TELLS MORE THAN I

FOUR DRAGONS GUARD THE NEXT CUE

READ THE FIFTH MATTHEW OR DIE.

CITY THREE'S INVISIBLE

WITHIN THIS ROCK, FIND A BATH

BURN LOVE'S APPLE, SEE THE CLEW

THEN TRY TO FLY FROM MY WRATH.

FOUR HOLDS A SAINT FROM THE EAST,

A NEIGHING, SHAPE-SHIFTING WRETCH.

ONCE HE WAS CALLED NERO'S BEAST—
HEAR HIS WORD AND MEET YOUR FETCH.

I have said I am sending you two Ciphers in this letter. The second is a Map, which I also enclose. I certainly do hope that you can discern it, and understand my joke.

Good-bye for now, nephew
I'll see you soon in Siena.

Antonio Beato Cagliostro
MeDici

3

The redhead and the blond stayed silent by the door as Marco observed my puzzling over this astonishing letter's dates, its wordplay, and its strange, last page with the signature.

"This is fantastic—if it's real," I gasped. "I'll need a verified sample of Antonio's handwriting to compare the slant, the letter height, rhetorical style . . ."

Marco bent over my shoulder, his cheek briefly touching mine, though I was too caught up to yet worry about personal niceties. "But what about the riddle? All that business about She-Wolves and Fools and Invisible Cities?"

"I don't know yet. I'd have to do research, but, oh. I could start *tonight*—"

"So you have no idea at all, really."

"No, no—I have *tons* of ideas. Like, look at this." I ran my thumb against the gorgeous calligraphy. " '*Darken not my door again*, Versipellis.' *Versipellis*. That's what Cosimo, the Duke of Florence, said to Antonio. This is the first written confirmation I've ever seen that the Medici did in fact believe that Antonio was a supernatural creature. *Versipellis* was the Italian word for werewolf. It's Latin for 'skin-changer.' "

Marco nodded. "So I've learned."

Beep beep.

Both of us started at this sound. It was my phone, ringing from my purse. I looked up. "Oh—gosh—I forgot." I suddenly frowned, touching my hand to my forehead.

"What's wrong?"

"Oh, dear. Before I get too deep into this, I've just got to rearrange some plans."

I gave him the letter and ran over to the sales counter to grab my bag. Once I had my little red Nokia in hand, I saw this message from my sweetheart, Erik. Apparently he was getting peckish for the fancy French dinner that we'd agreed to eat out that night:

```
baby i want u n love you n am also really
really hungry
```

I rapidly typed out:

```
want u too but cant do dinner new client
wants me to resrch medici papers n aztec
gold
```

I sent that message, and then, as an afterthought, also quickly sent a second:

```
he also says tomas dlr wuz buried in italy
not guat u ever heard that be4
```

Marco visibly stiffened as I worked the keypad. I thought I saw him shoot a glance at the redhead and blond who remained standing like sentries by the door. "Who are you calling?"

"My fiancé. We're getting married in two weeks, June 16—
and we'll be making some last minute plans at dinner tonight—"

"Oh, two weeks, that's awfully soon."

I nodded. "Tell me about it, we still haven't agreed on the music." I raised the phone so that he could get a good look at it. Recall that this was 2001, and I'd only had the technology for about a month. "But look at this. Text messages. They're amazing! I just got the service—you can type messages on your cell!"

Rolling his eyes, Marco muttered: "We've had those in Europe already for two years. God, get me out of this backwater. And—look—I don't have that much time, Lola. Let me be clear: What I'm conducting right now is an *interview*. Mr. Soto-Relada told me that you would be very helpful in cracking this thing, and if you are, then I'm ready to bring you onto the project. I want to take you to Florence, so that you can authenticate the letter. We'll be going to the Palazzo Medici Riccardi. You were saying you needed Antonio's writing samples? They have archives that will be very useful—old examples of his writing style. And then we'll also have the advantage of working with Dr. Isabel Riccardi, the Antonio Medici scholar."

"Oh my God!" I gave a little leap. "Dr. Riccardi! I've read her book—*Antonio Medici: Decorator and Destroyer*. And I *love* Florence, I think. I love reading about it, I mean."

"But if you'd rather just e-blabber on your little phone, then perhaps I should take my leave—or, dare I say it, maybe you're not quite the expert that Soto-Relada says you are."

"No, no, no. Here, hold on. I do know about him . . . let me just think. Okay. Okay: Antonio Medici." I shoved my phone in my pocket and squeezed my eyes shut, remembering. "One of the lesser lights of the Medici family. Born in, what, 1478. He . . . had an earlier career as a kind of scientist—he performed

experiments on people, I think, living people, in Florence. Not
like da Vinci and his corpses. He was a monster, really, a vivi-
sectionist. This is where the werewolf rumors got started. After
that, he became bored with domestic victims and went abroad.
To Africa, was it? Algiers? He became a kind of conquistatore,
but with a scientific bent. Let's see . . . around 1510, he's in Timbuktu, slaughtering Muslims. He did a lot of alchemical research,
plundering their alchemical labs. He also kidnapped at least one
African man, and made him into a slave. I don't know the slave's
name. After that, maybe not surprisingly, Antonio signed on with
Cortés. He sailed to the Americas, assassinating hundreds of Aztecs in Tenochtitlán—and I *have* heard stories that he stole Montezuma's gold. But, after he returned to Florence from Mexico,
the only thing I know is that he killed that slave of his—there's an
awful tale about Antonio starving the man with some sort of gold
mask that blocked or muzzled his mouth. A torture killing. Like
something out of *The Man in the Iron Mask*."

"Yes."

"But that was his last murder for a long time. After Mexico
he—"

"Changed."

"That's it. He underwent a conversion, after he married. A
woman called . . . the Dragon? That was his nickname for her,
Sofia Medici. She encouraged him to become an arts patron and,
as you were saying, an alchemist. Though he did have troubles:
Cosimo exiled Antonio and his wife for unknown reasons—
alluded to in this letter—and they spent the rest of their lives
traveling through Siena, Venice, other parts of Italy. Antonio led
an uneventful life, at least compared to his earlier slasher days—
that is, until this war, the one he's writing about in this letter.
He died in it, the Florentines' 1554 battle against the Sienese.

He became confused during the battle, didn't he? Because of the smoke? He killed hundreds of his own men, with some kind of alchemists' weapon, some sort of explosive—a huge bomb."

Marco blinked at me for several seconds in astonishment, then said: "Well, I have to hand it to him. Mr. Soto-Relada did say you were a brainy one."

I wrinkled my brow, smiling. "Sorry, how does this Soto-Relada person know me? And did you say he was a *fence*?"

"That old schemer? Yes, Soto-Relada makes it his business to get his hands on all kinds of naughty commodities, including your address. As I said, he worked with your father, and had scads of information about Tomas and his family. He assured me that you would be worth the trouble."

"Worth the trouble." I laughed, unsure as to his meaning.

"Yes. I'm just saying that I'm glad I took his advice and took the time to chat with you. Before I . . . did anything else. How did you know all that just off the top of your head?"

I cast my hand around the store. "Reading—reading—you know."

"Yes, actually, I do. But in my research, *I* haven't had any luck finding the map Antonio describes in the letter. No chart or atlas that fits Antonio's description has ever been recovered. Mr. Soto-Relada says it's been lost. But, it's settled. You're hired! I have flights booked for all of us to Italy tonight. On British Airways. Flight 177—first class, of course."

"*Tonight?*" I began walking around the bookstore, trying to organize my thoughts. "That sounds sort of sudden."

"We actually should get along. Assuming you have your passport . . . ?"

"I do—it's in my back room, in my files—" I guffawed abruptly at his lunatic suggestion. "But I can't. I'm getting married in four-teen days."

"Oh, we'll just be in and out in a day, two days. You can still come back in time for the ceremony. Unless you're not interested."

Marco held up the letter's translucent onionskin pages. They glittered in the lamplight, and I caught again the strange, elaborate signature page. I attempted to think logically despite my overwhelming desire to snatch those papers and parse Antonio's puzzle until either my head fell off or I solved it.

"Oh," I breathed. "Maybe I *could* go, for a little while. God, what am I even *saying*?"

My Nokia suddenly beeped again. I plucked the phone from my pocket and saw these two messages from Erik:

```
wat r u tlking about crzy grl aztec gold
is long gone

              . . .

i just asked ur sis about tdlr being
buried n itly she freaked
```

Wildly, but also half as a joke, I typed out:

```
sory gng to florence tonite with client
flt 177 british air 2 go find mntzumas
gold staying at palazzo medici riccardi
he's a handsum guy mayb u shd come too n
make sure i behave self

              . . .

no u r not

              . . .

am so u shd come unless you dont mind me
eating pasta w mr tall dark n handsum

              . . .
```

```
grrrrr u r making me jelus need to make
love to u right away
            . . .
sory leaving now see u when i get back
hope we don't have to put off weding
            . . .
u r nuts we r geting maried
```

My last line *was* actually intended as a tease, since I was so scorchingly in love with Erik Gomara that I would never postpone our nuptials. But before I was able to send off a "JK" Marco interrupted: "Writing about dinner plans again?"

I shook my head. "I'm sorry—that was rude of me to just keep you standing there. I was telling Erik about the letter."

Marco's mouth twisted. "I wish you hadn't done that."

"Oh, you don't have to worry about him. Erik's very discreet." This actually was not true at all. "And he's really good at code breaking. In fact, I think we should bring him in on this project. He did incredible work the year before last, in the jungle—like we were talking about."

"Yes, we *were* talking about that, weren't we? What happened in the jungle?" Marco looked down at the phone in my hand. "Say, that *is* a cunning little device, now that I take a better look at it. May I?"

"Sure."

Marco took the Nokia from me and threw it over his shoulder. "Blasej."

The redheaded man caught it neatly with his right hand. He put it in his pocket, without making eye contact with me.

"My phone," I said.

"Oh, he's just checking it out."

"I need that."

"You won't in Italy," Marco assured me. "Domestic lines don't work over there."

"What's going on? This is weird—"

Before I could object any more, however, Marco startled me by leaning over and breathing in sharply as he sniffed my hair with his slender nose.

I stepped back. "What are you doing?"

"What is that I smell? Perfume?" He sniffed again, beneath my ear. "Hmmmm, beautiful." And then, in a very low murmur, I heard: "And I thought the de la Rosas stank—"

"What the hell did you just say?"

I skittered quickly away from him and over to the far wall, by the Red Lion's history section.

"Your perfume, it's lovely." He laughed. "As are you, for that matter. It's really such a surprise."

I hesitated for a second. He was a *freak*. "I think you should go."

"*Go?* Why?"

"I heard what you said."

Marco lowered his eyelids and smiled. "I don't mean to offend. But . . . it's just that the de la Rosas don't have the best reputation, do they? As we were discussing, there was that very *dirty* business you were involved in a couple of years back, in the jungle. Colonel Moreno, and all that?"

"Like I said before, I'd rather not discuss that subject—"

"What, Colonel Moreno? Yes, it *is* unpleasant. As is the fact that your father bombed that army base in—what?—1993. And murdered Moreno's nephew."

"Did you come here tonight to talk about de la Rosa or the Medici?"

"They're connected, actually." He grinned.

I gawked at him. "What do you mean? How?"

"Oh, I don't want to get ahead of myself. Let's see, where was I? De la Rosa murdered Serjei, and then Colonel Moreno wanted his revenge. Oh, I know—Moreno *was* crazy. A Central American Stalin! Once the war was over, he wanted to breed a society of warrior-aristocrats, and to that end was a fanatic for clan honor, reprisals. Thus he went after you, de la Rosa's daughter. Agh, the Morenos! Can't get over their grief. They're so *emotional.*"

"Emotional?"

Marco did not seem as nearly harmless as he did just a minute before. He no longer seemed like a flighty playboy at all. Rather, he moved stealthily toward me as he talked. "Yes, they can't seem to get over their sorrow. That's why he didn't stop hunting de la Rosa after the bombing—and put out a death warrant on the entire de la Rosa family, in fact. Which is why you had that trouble in the jungle, yes? While you were searching for your father's grave? But you took care of it. When the army showed up, you defended yourself and your family by killing the colonel."

I shook my head. "Is that what people are saying? Because I didn't kill anyone. Moreno ordered Estrada—one of his men, a lieutenant—to shoot us; it was terrible."

"Yes, it *must* have been. Hideous!"

"But Estrada lost his mind when the colonel told him to do that. He killed Moreno instead. We just . . . watched."

"Oh, is that all?" Marco said, in a low, soft voice. "You just stood by, while a man was beaten to death?"

A deep beat of silence passed here.

"And it remains true, doesn't it," he went on, "that the de la Rosas are the reasons why the Morenos suffered such unforgivable losses. I mean, if Tomas had been, say, strangled in his cradle—and you had never been born—then today, the Morenos would still be one, big *adorable* family."

I had my back to the bookshelf, and my pulse rattled in my throat. Marco stepped very close to me. He was a good foot taller than I am, and he drew so near that I could smell the spice on his skin. I could also see the tears suddenly welling up in his black-shadowed eyes.

My heart began beating irregularly. "Who are you?"

A tear rolled down Marco's face. He had turned very pale. "Oh, God."

"Yes, I suppose I've shown my hand, haven't I?" he asked. "It's a family trait. I can't seem to control my grief."

"What are you—his—the colonel's—"

"I'm Victor's only son, Lola."

The tears fled down his cheeks and, appalled, he wiped them off. The salt water clung to his hands, wet and shining. Flicking his wrist in disgust did not help, and he quickly resolved his conflict by putting his glistening fingers on my face and so anointed me.

"Get away—get out of my place," I barked.

His hands were on my jaw and my throat, caressing my skin as he rubbed in the tears. "Oh, I will, but with *you*, of course. You little mongrel. You little bitch." From the trembling of his mouth I saw that he was trying hard to master himself. "You should be happy that I'm inviting you along, Lola. I see now that Soto-Relada was right, about your value. In helping me find this gold. Yours *was* a nice little performance." He squeaked out, in a tinny voice: " 'Versipellis, it's Latin for skin-changer.' Because if your wits had been a hair duller, then . . . well, I would have had to leave you in the same condition that you left my father."

I snatched the letter out of his grasp, kicked him, and ran past him, shrieking.

"Help me! Someone help me!"

But I am no natural sprinter, or fighter. Marco grabbed me brutally around the waist. We went tumbling down to the rugs on the floor, knocking over the table so its sherry bottle poured down in a red, staining splash, like blood. I madly scrambled away, holding up the letter to protect the pages from the wine. Marco snatched hold of my neck and yanked back, hard.

"No!"

"Blasej," he barked.

The redhead moved forward and with one lunge had me in his huge and bulbous arms. The blond had grown excitable from the violence and breathed hard while looking around for something to trash. He walked over to the bookshelves and began tearing the volumes out, throwing and gruesomely breaking three precious octavos against the walls.

"Don't hurt the books, you ass!" Marco hissed.

The blond stopped, his arms hanging at his sides, and looked at the redhead.

"Cool out," Blasej said.

The blond nodded. "Yeah, sorry, boss."

"Christ. Go get her passport, in her file cabinet—it's probably in the back room."

"Okay."

"Get her up!"

The redhead hauled me to my feet and half-carried, half-dragged me out into the street. It was twilight now, and Sunday. Since bookselling isn't the most lucrative business, I had stationed the Red Lion in a barely trafficked, low-rent, dead-end road in an "up and coming" business district. This same street was thus empty of any possible good Samaritan as I was tossed into the backseat of a silver four-door Mercedes.

"Help! Help!"

Marco muffled my mouth and sat on me while I struggled.

"Dammit. What a mess." He surprisingly started to laugh. "Lola. Lo-la. My filthy little floozy. Calm down. It'll be better that way. Look, I *know* I got upset, and we haven't really gotten off on the right foot, and I want to snap your neck and everything— and *might*—but if you just listen to me, you'll be begging to come along on this little vacation." He turned his head to Blasej. "Or maybe I should just drug her?"

I began to scream inside the car, and as all the windows were rolled up, my shrieks stabbed into our eardrums.

"Ah, ah, help!"

The men covered their ears, yelling, until Marco closed his fingers over my throat.

"Gag—gaaaaa—" I wrenched his arm off me, biting his hand.

"Shit!"

He gave me a good, stunning slap. And then another.

"Go. *Go.* Move!"

I held my burning face in my hands. The car roared off through the darkening streets, as we sped toward the Long Beach Airport.

4

The streetlights flickered in the windshield as we passed through Long Beach. We reached the airport terminal in twenty minutes. At the car park, an automated machine spit out a ticket; Domenico drove to the very last, nearly empty floor of the complex.

"Let me go." I still held Antonio Medici's letter in my grabby hands. "Let me out of here."

I looked around to see a man walking away from his car in the parking garage. As I tried to scream, Marco wrapped himself around my upper body. Almost like a lover, he twined his arms tight about my neck, whispering in a hoarse voice: "Lola, you'll understand what we're doing if you just *listen*."

"I don't talk to crazy, murdering—"

"Crazy. That's a little extreme." He lightly bit my cheek, to further pacify me. "Though, I have been going through *such* a hard time these past two years."

"Oh, my Lord—"

"Yes, after I flew out from France to Antigua for my father's funeral I just . . . drank. Floated around in the pool, chugging brandy, crying about my *papi*. He was *such* a bastard. But I *miss him*. I loved him." After a long, rough pause, he said in a calmer voice:

"Everyone did. They were all—my father's colleagues—telling me that I couldn't let his death go unavenged. I was supposed to kill you and your family, understand. All very Greek tragedy. And well within my training, as a long time ago, the colonel taught me how to be an excellent assassin."

"I'll bet."

"Oh, we had some jolly times in the war. But I was so depressed that I halfway didn't give a fuck if you all rotted or not. Your mother, Juana, your 'father,' Manuel . . . your sister, the unhygienic Yolanda, who's now living in the *suburbs*, I hear? And your fancy man, Erik. Because I had tried to *run away* from all this—violence. Killing. I went to Amsterdam, Paris, drank absinthe. Not that I exactly kept my hands clean in Europe, but I found that I no longer had my father's knack for . . . taking care of problems. Lost the stomach for it."

"It's easy, man," Blasej said. "Try it out on her. She'll be a pain in the airport—"

"I don't really think she *wants* to bring me out of retirement." Marco brought his face closer to mine. "I did make a mistake, showing you who I was. I lost my temper."

"You're kidnapping me!"

"What I'm doing with you remains to be seen, doesn't it?" He tweaked me on the nose, trying to smile. "Because I feel *so* very optimistic about your future. You see, I'm betting on you, Lola. I think you're going to pay off. And I *am* a gambler, aren't I, Blasej?"

Blasej threw up his arms. "You always take the table at Carlo, man."

"Well, we're back in Monte Carlo tonight. And I think I've got a winning hand."

"You can go f—" I blathered.

"Oh, *shut* up," he said fiercely. "And let me finish before you lose your ladylike manner. As I was saying, there I was, in Antigua, drunk, depressed—considering a pipe bomb for you or a shotgun for me. It was *very* bad. But then . . . something happened."

Marco knocked his head against mine again, waiting for me to guess.

Grudgingly, I rustled the pages in my hand. "You found the letter."

"Yes. I met Mr. Soto-Relada and well—there it is in your hot little paws. I've spent the last year and a half trying to crack it. I did make some progress. But not enough. And that just won't do. Because I *need to*. My father had a vision for the country, and if there is gold to be found, then, why, I can redeem myself. And finish his work—"

"Your father's vision," I spat. "He was a mass murderer. In the war—"

"As could you," he interrupted.

"As could I, what?"

"Finish *your* father's work."

"What do you mean?"

"I told you Tomas de la Rosa died in Italy, not Guatemala."

"Which doesn't make any sense. Everyone says he was buried in the jungle—"

"Of course it makes sense. Tomas de la Rosa was always a secretive bastard. Montezuma's gold? What lie wouldn't he tell for that?"

"I don't understand."

"He died researching *this*." Marco pointed at the letter. "Soto-Relada told me its provenance—which of course made it so interesting to me! I have the documents to prove his prior ownership. And I've seen his grave. I know exactly where he died, and how.

It's *very* interesting. Not exactly what you'd expect of a 'hero' like old Tom."

I just looked at him, silent and not breathing.

Marco began to pet my hair. "Look at her face." He tilted my chin so that Blasej could see me. "Look at that. I told you. She can't resist it. I *told* you she was bats. All the de la Rosas are!" He lifted the bangs from my forehead. "Yes, that's why I think that I'll be able to forego snapping your neck and otherwise mussing your hair, Lola. Because you're coming. Aren't you, darling?"

Marco's teeth were very white as he now truly smiled at me. He leaned away, unlatched his arms, and tugged the letter from my hands. Then he opened the door.

He and Blasej got out of the car. Domenico had been standing by the trunk with the luggage. Now he began walking swiftly out of the car park, muttering, "We're already late."

"Man," Blasej was saying to Marco. "This is stupid. She's a casualty."

"Blasej, don't be hasty. If she doesn't come with us, we'll visit her when we get back."

"Unless I call the police on you now, *you idiot!*" I yelled.

Marco continued smiling at me, walking backward, as I remained sitting in the backseat.

He held the letter by his fingertips, teasing me by shaking it back and forth. I could see the delicate paper, the gorgeous puzzle of it.

"Come on, poppet," Marco sang. "Come on, kitten. Go ahead. Call the police."

I stayed in the backseat, refusing to move, and chattering to myself: "No, no, no. Get a grip, Sanchez. Run away. 911. There's nothing here for you. All he's got is a . . . map to Montezuma's gold and maybe your father's—*agh!*"

He had been right about me. I couldn't resist it. A steady diet of Alexandre Dumas novels and a flaming Electra complex had twisted my wits. He talked about pipe bombs and slapped me? He qualified for a solid dose of Thorazine and probably double life sentences in federal prison? Didn't matter.

For another few minutes I stayed on the backseat, quietly cursing as I watched Marco flutter the letter at me. I stepped out onto the concrete. I slammed the car door shut.

"Told you," I heard him sing out.

I followed Marco Moreno out of the parking lot, my throat so tight I could choke.

"That's it, Lola . . ."

Two hours later, I was sailing over the wine-dark sea to Florence.

∽ 5 ∽

Hello! Handsome boy! And you must be Lola . . . what was it? De la *Rosa*, wasn't it?"

More than forty-eight hours after my abduction/ psychotic break, an enthusiastic woman in vibrant midlife greeted Marco, Domenico, Blasej, and me upon our bustling into the dream scape of the Palazzo Medici Riccardi. Sandwiched between the goons, my priestess gown was bunged up, and my hair exploded all over my head as I blinked derangedly at the art sparkling all around us.

We were in Florence, Italy. This was my first time. And I was discovering that Italy is so beautiful it can arouse the senses to a deliciously painful inflammation, even when those faculties have been dulled to near catatonia by exhaustion, terror, digestive troubles, and a hypnotic focus on historical puzzles.

In other words, I loved it, insensibly and irrationally under the circumstances.

But I am a hedonist and couldn't help myself. I loved Italy as soon we had endured two *insanely* delayed connecting flights (during which Marco's thugs monitored my every move), and stepped off the plane at the Leonardo da Vinci Airport in Rome. Enthralled by art, nauseated by fear, I gawked at the tiny streets,

the deathly mopeds, the streets littered with ancient monuments.
As I stared at the scattered fortunes of Roman public sculpture,
my "companions" dragged me to the Colosseum to barter with
a baggy-panted scoundrel for two small, cloth-wrapped items,
which I did not see but suspected might be pistols. Next, trips
were made to camping stores, to inexplicably purchase pulleys,
axes, and knives. Finally, we traveled to Tuscany. Now dazed
by the sight of the Duomo's miraculous red breast and a battalion of vendors hawking mini priapic *Davids*, I bumbled around
this Florentine palazzo. The fifteenth-century haven of the
Medici blooms with marble nudes and trompe l'oeil paintings of
satyrs and vixens. Scaffolded all around its exterior, the palace
gyrated with sexy workmen built like Atlas. Below their vertiginous heights our host, this round-hipped, red-spectacled man-
darin, whose hair matched her glasses, quick-footed through
the foyer alongside a dark-haired North African lady of about
twenty-one. This sylph wore a black dress cut with a stoical sim-
plicity, as well as a resigned look on her pretty, very serious face.

"I am Dr. Riccardi. Most welcome, most welcome!" the older
woman cried in English, grasping my shoulders with such force
my head wobbled precariously. "Marco said you would be arriv-
ing with him, Lola, you lucky thing." She peered over her glasses
at his immaculate shave, his smooth hair, and his wool and cash-
mere clothes. "How *are* you doing, dear?"

"Much better now that I'm finally seeing you, again, Isabel."
He grinned.

"Ooooh, you are wicked. Looking quite as dashing as I remember, isn't he, Adriana?"

"I—"

"This is my assistant," Dr. Riccardi said to me, gesturing at
the sylph.

"Hello—"

"And here are your two *friends*—the big, strong, silent types?"

Blasej and Domenico just stood there, huge and granite-headed, and said nothing.

"And that's all?" she went on, counting us. "I was expecting a larger group."

"Just us." Marco laughed. "What, did you think I'd bring an entire team of experts? I'm not one of your Getty friends, Isabel."

"No, but I thought—what was it—Adriana here was saying something about a phone call from a rather *voluble* young man—"

"He— I— We—" Adriana tried to explain.

"Yes, well, it must have been one of those ghastly telemarketers," Dr. Riccardi continued. "No matter. Because here *you* are, in the *flesh*, dear Marco. Please do forgive the scaffolding. Florence is constantly under repair, you see. No—but you barely notice, do you? My dear Signor Moreno. Always so focused, and still honking on about that letter—eight months you spent here, driving me wild with your questions."

"You were very helpful in my researches, Isabel—"

"Yes, *right*—which is why you've now dragged this lovely little creature back here with you?" She turned back to me. "So. Lola. Sweet, isn't she? Like Marco, you too have been bewitched by his little letter? He must have told you how it was written by Antonio Medici, and all that tosh about gold, and werewolves, and Montezuma, and I don't know what? He had me helping him research the thing last year—I quite admire you for putting up with this man. Seduced you into working night and day, I'll bet. He has that capacity, I'm afraid—"

I jabbered, "Actually, he kind of abducted me—"

"Hmmmm?" Dr. Riccardi goggled. "Oh, yes! Hilarious—he is a *beast*. But that's fine, the more the merrier. The palazzo was *made* for madcapping around the archives, so let's get you settled, come on—superb!" Dr. Riccardi walked speedily away. "Don't worry about your luggage! My girl will be happy to bring it up to the fourth floor, which is where your room is."

The young assistant cursed in several languages while struggling with the bags, even as Dr. Riccardi levitated out of the foyer and into the gloomy spectacle that is the palazzo. Domenico and Blasej stayed behind—Blasej to order Domenico around, Domenico to watch the girl at her labors rather than help—as Marco and I hurried into a network of gray-carpeted halls, passing inappropriately dressed German and American tourists and a series of tapestry rooms.

Dr. Riccardi flicked her hand at me as she vaulted past marble busts of severe-looking dead Italians. "I was very intrigued when Marco said he was going to whisk you down here to help him with his letter. To get a 'second opinion' I believe is what he said, though you don't have any formal training in paleography, or handwriting identification, from what I understand."

"No, I'm self-taught," I said in either Spanish, Italian, or Urdu, for all I know, as my synapses were still maxing from jet lag and anxiety.

"Oh! How rustic. Though I like to say that our archives are available to anyone with an academic interest in them—we're very democratic—as artifacts do belong to all of us, don't they? They're the property of the whole world—the future, no?"

"Honestly, Doctor, I think this letter might have been stolen."

"Don't mind her, Isabel," Marco said. "She's one of those radical political types."

"Oh, yes. Well. One can take the argument too far, can't one? Once I had a professor of archaeology—from Zimbabwe, of all places—try to *race* off with our collection of silver spittoons. All of it was certified as having come from the Medici coffers, without the slightest shadow of taint. Yet he was *screaming* that the silver had been melted down from the chests of King . . . King . . . Dakarai, that's it . . . and that he was going to bring that patrimony back to his home country." She was hurtling down another hallway. "He was from Oxford, too. I really did sympathize, after I recovered from the trauma. After all, there were a number of poxy thieves in the Medici family, simply pilfering the Africans."

"What happened to him?" Marco asked. "The professor?"

"Well, he went to jail, of course!"

I tried to keep up with her pace. "You said you studied the letter then, Dr. Riccardi?"

"Yes, *exhaustively*! But I won't influence your analysis with my opinion quite yet."

"I know of your qualifications." Despite a certain Patty Hearst–like flavor of this Italian boondoggle, I was still excited to meet this author. "I read your book, *Antonio Medici: Destroyer and Decorator*. It was very good. I liked how you mixed theory and scandal."

She smiled with uncontained satisfaction. "Oh, I like *you*. The book wrote itself, actually! You'll have noticed my focus on the last decades of Antonio's life, which were so compelling, at least from a decorative arts point of view—they don't get as much attention from his other biographers as his earlier . . . career."

"I wouldn't call genocide a career, Madam," I said frenetically.

"Yes, as a *conquistatore* Antonio Medici was guilty of many embarrassing crimes. My real interest in him, though, begins upon his

return from the Americas. That's when he became an arts benefac-
tor. He was a patron to the painter Pontormo, and the goldsmith
Benvenuto Cellini, who made for him these splendid exploding
safes. But while many of these wonderful objects survive, there
are very few documents, as Antonio heartlessly burned most of
his papers. I assured Marco that a personal record from the mid–
fifteen hundreds would be invaluable—most of the information
we have about him then is secondhand. So, when you're ready,
I will bring you to our archives, show you Antonio's letters—the
ones up until the fifteen twenties, that is, which is when our collection stops. You will be able to compare the scripts."

"Lola's made a study of the handwriting already, on the plane,"
Marco told her.

"It's very striking," I said, not mentioning that said study had
been interrupted by watching Blasej break my Nokia with his
bare hands while he explained how he'd similarly crack my clavi-
cle if I misbehaved. "In particular, the signature."

Dr. Riccardi stopped before a staircase and slapped her hands
around my arms. "Okay. You two are tired, maybe? We can let
you sleep for a while, before we begin to work. Or, I could have
Adriana bring you something up on a plate."

Marco turned to me, touching me on the elbow with such in-
congruous solicitude that I had a brief and painful image of Erik,
and backed away. "Are you hungry?"

I shook my head; on the plane, I'd drunk so much alcohol my
blood sugar had spiked.

"No rest for the fabulous," Marco observed to his friend.

"The sooner we get this done, the better," I said. "I'd like to
take a look at those archives now, if possible."

"Oh, my dears, *everything* is possible in Italy." Dr. Riccardi
began hurrying up carpeted steps, then maneuvered us down a

pewter-tinted corridor until we reached a large oak door. As she stood before the entrance to the collection, a mighty, mischievous librarian's pride glowed in her face. "As you are about to see."

And then she opened the door.

I gasped with delight at this revealed Eden. The Medici Riccardi library is frosted with gold, its shining walls studded with rare books. I had read that these were culled from the collections of Lorenzo the Magnificent, who had dispatched the librarian-hunter John Lacasis to the East, where he bought texts of Plato, Lucan, and Aristophanes that had been hand-copied in Arabic at Saladin's behest. This first floor boasted pearl-inlaid reading tables with gold chairs occupied by a smattering of scholars. Among the professors was one noble-looking man reading a tome with the aid of a large, bronze, face-obscuring magnifying glass. His most visible feature was his shoulder-length night-black hair, signifying that Ottoman or even Peruvian blood enriched his Florentine industry. The library was silent except for the rustlings of his turned pages. A fan-shaped but inaccessible window admitted a soft light onto these studies.

Dr. Riccardi walked toward this window and stopped at a shelf stacked with clamshell boxes bound in taupe silk. She pulled down two of them.

Inside the first was a pair of items: A beautiful antique leather book, tooled with blown roses, and also a large deck of cards bearing strange hand-painted signs. The card on the top bore an insignia of a red, golden-eyed dragon.

"Wrong box," Dr. Riccardi said, shaking her head.

"What are these?"

"The wife's belongings. We bought them at auction three years ago, at a very good price. A journal and occult cards. She— Sofia—was something of a spiritualist."

"Tarot cards," I said. "Rare ones, they look like. Hand-painted. They're fantastic—"

"Oh, ugh, not these again," Marco mumbled.

She smiled. "Yes, very good, Lola. The tarot was inherited by Sofia from her mother, along with, probably, her rather vivid imagination, revealed here in this journal. It's of decent interest to feminist historians—though, as you see, Marco did *not* think these ladies' things sufficiently important to study. He's a terrible sexist." She cheerfully criticized him as she took up the other box. "*This*, on the other hand, did earn his attention."

She lifted the cover of the second container, which held approximately eighty leaves of unfolded parchment that still bore their broken, wolf-shaped, gold wax seals.

"Antonio's letters—the seal's the same." I lifted into the light a missive from Antonio to Leo X, née Giovanni de' Medici, his second cousin and the pope. After examining it a second, I said, "Though the letter's much earlier than Marco's—it looks like it was written during an invasion of Africa."

"Yes." Doctor Riccardi squinted at the text through her red glasses. "This dates a decade and a half before he traveled to Mexico to catch up with Cortés. In his youth, Antonio did not intend to become an American conquistatore, but rather focused on . . . scientific experiments—"

"Vivisections," I said. "Of peasants, disabled people. The poor and mentally retarded."

"Yes! Thank you for being so hideously accurate! Anyhow, he later moved his operations to Africa—this was in the early fifteen hundreds. There, he dabbled with slavery, and also investigated the Moors' famous alchemical practices. He began searching for the secrets to immortality in metals as he once had in the human body. He became intrigued with the idea of the Americas, since

Europeans hoped—with great reason, as it turned out—that
they would be awash with precious metals. Thus, the venture in
Mexico with Cortés, after which he returned home to Florence,
killed one of his slaves in some sort of rage, and married. Upon
his exile, he devoted himself to the decorative and alchemical
arts, et cetera, et cetera." She adjusted her glasses, squinting at
the document I'd pulled from the archives. "This letter was written during his provocative Africa adventure. It's what we call his
'barking mad' phase."

December 3, 1510
Timbuktu, West Africa

To Giovanni, Holy Father, and our good Cousin in the World,

I understand that you are presently squandering the Church's coffers with your Debauchery. I write you this letter to order you to cease
your spending, as I shall need the Vatican's funding for my Expeditions
among the Moors, in the interests of my Philosophical projects.

Though both you and my Intended, Sofia, have oft criticized my
great Goal to cultivate a Stronger and More Select Society as that of a
Black Magician, I have only been a good student of Plato, aiming to
usher the World from the Era of Appetite into an age of Reason. First
came the necessary killings and autopsies I conducted of Criminals &
Madmen in order to fathom the structure of their benighted Brains.
Then, two years ago, I sailed here to Byzantium to discover the Moors'
alchemical secrets—Medicines—that would Cure this whole world of its
Superstition and Barbarism. Two years! That Remedy long eluded me!

Only now, after all this long time, have I struck upon the Solution
to this dark earth's Ills—yet I think it is one you will not like.

Last week, I followed the Spaniards into the City of Timbuktu, which had just been raided by Moroccans. As the Conquistatores went off to conquer a Mosque, I took six of my Florentine mercenaries through the ruins, maneuvering past the cracked battlements, torched libraries, dead bodies, until we saw a sign of life: A thin plume of the queerest blue-green smoke drifted from a little house's chimney.

Breaking into this lair, we saw small dark men bending over silver stills, and working with the aid of supernaturally bright torches. All about there were leather chests spilling forth with powders and marked with signs of the Philosophical Elements.

"My Lord Antonio," whispered one of my generals. "What kind of place is this?"

"An Alchemist's lab!" I shouted—such was my excitement.

The dusky men turned and roared with fury at the sight of us. One of the eldest stumbled forward, menacing me with his bony fists; this, despite the efforts of a younger, handsome lad to stand between us and protect his apparent Father.

"You are making the Universal Medicine here," I said in the tongue of Mali. "The Philosopher's Stone that can cure any disease—Death—Stupidity—Religion. I must have it—you must tell me your Secrets. In that way I will bring Light into this Dim world."

"We shall never tell you the Receipt of that great Potion," the brave old wizard said.

"What you will not give, I shall take." I brandished at him my sword.

"Oh, but I will give you something. I will give you the prize I award to all who attempt to conquer our City."

"And what is that?"

"Your death."

From a purse tied at his waist he plucked a handful of dripping, fetid, yet incendiary amber-colored Mud, which he hurled upon my person before igniting it with one of the torches blazing nearby.

I do not know of what infernal Drug that mire was made, but it took to fire in an instant, and my entire body became as one pure, killing light. That flame, moreover, only burned the hotter when my general poured his flask upon me, as the Savage's potion was not doused by water, but instead incensed. I tore off my clothes, rolling on the floor, as the Wizard's son hurried to sprinkle upon me a thick layer of salt. It was only by the Charity of that Moor that I did not die a Martyr's death.

But I still vowed to kill them all. Taking one of the torches, I brought it over to a Great Chest, which was marked with a devil-looking symbol I recognized, for Mercury:

I set light to the Quicksilver. A blue, stinking, foul Fume exploded and sixty souls fell dead, quivering, green-faced from their own infernal Poison. Close by, there were two additional barrels, each marked with different signs. One was for sulfur, shaped into a cipher that resembled the mark for Woman.

The other was for the salt the young Moor used to save me, a circle cut through by a bar.

I opened the box with the woman-like sign, touching the torch to the Sulfur. A column of killing fire burst open, as if I had just beckoned the Sun to come down from the heavens and do my bidding. The swarty

Magicians burned like straw men, and those who escaped the flame embraced the blades of my Mercenaries—save for the ash-pale son of the Wizard, who wailed to us Fluent Tuscan.

"You are stained by the color of cowardice, my son," I said. "You are weeping like a woman."

"What have you done?" he cried. "What is the true nature of Man, that he can commit such offenses against heaven?"

"A man is made of nothing else but reason."

"No, you have proved today that the real Soul of mankind is that of a beast."

The timid Moor's words struck me with a dizzy Revelation, even as I ordered him clapped with iron cuffs branded with the Medici device. "Perhaps we are both correct, but that man, in order to survive, transmutes so easily between Reason and Beast-Mind that the difference is impossible to detect." I laughed with delight at the idea. "You interest me, boy. What is your name?"

"Opul of Timbuktu."

"We are the same," I urged him, "surely you can see that."

"You are the opposite of me, my Lord." He made a strange sign with his left hand. "I am a poor alchemist but you—you are my reverse. You are an animal. You are what the Italians call il Lupo, the Wolf."

"A Wolf," I said, slowly. I was impressed by the trickery of his language. "You are too clever to die."

"He performs witchcraft," warned my general. "He is calling upon his Djinn, and cursing you with African sorcery, Sir Antonio. We must kill him to remove the jinx."

The slave bowed. "I only spoke of what I saw. All fear the Wolf, my Lord. As do I."

"What he says is true," I replied. "As the trickster Plautus writes, nomen atque omen—each man's true name is also his omen, his portent. And this Varlet has discerned mine. I have transformed into a Wolf, today."

"Mercy upon us," whispered my general, crossing himself.

But I did not fear strange signs or Moorish prayers. I have found that my new slave speaks several tongues, can write passably well, and though he swears he does not know either the secrets of the Philosopher's Stone or of this burning amber mud, I will convince him through such measures as are necessary to give over to me those receipts.

Yet these are not the only reasons I keep him alive. In truth, I find him most intriguing.

For he is the first to have discovered the truth about me.

Note my new seal, Cousin: I am a Wolf. And with the warlocks' secret fire, I shall achieve what I could not through all my hacking away at peasants & felons, for all my reading.

You see, I will usher the world into an Age of Reason.

But it shall be made for my Reason, and not that of any other.

Do you understand? Cease spending at once what shall be my money, which shall build the Grand Schools I will set up all over the world, like Alexander the Great, like Caesar.

If you do not, Beware.

Antonio.

"This doesn't look the same as your document," I answered to Marco's intense gaze, once I'd read this monomaniac's description of the flammable "amber-colored mud" that reminded me of naphtha—the ancient Moorish incendiary weapon, used most famously by Alexander the Great against the Indians, that is inflamed by water but doused by powders.

This recognition had only flitted through my mind for a moment: I focused less on the substance of the letter than the very look of it. I've studied the mysteries of penmanship—not only practicing calligraphy myself but reading everything from FBI manuals on the science of forensic handwriting identification to sixteenth-century tomes on occult graphology. Immediately I could see that the ductus, or pen angle, of this document's calligraphy differed from Marco's.

"Well, you mean the letters don't read alike." Marco impatiently slapped at the air with his long pianist's hands. "The tone of the thing, I mean, the literary style."

Dr. Riccardi leveled her glasses at us. "It is true that if your letter had been authored by Antonio after his return with Cortés's fleet, it would not *read* like this one—so savagely, that is. In his middle and late life, his character matured because of an illness, which he called *the Condition*. He also mellowed on account of his wife's beneficent influence—"

"Sofia," Marco and I both said at the same time.

"Yes. But Lola was speaking, I believe, of the penmanship?"

The noble-looking professor sat with his back to us while reading, grunting as if to communicate distaste at the volume of our conversation.

"Marco," I whispered. "Bring your letter out—I have to take a closer look at it."

He slipped the pages from the envelope; the transparent pages glowed like pearls.

I said, "The paper of Marco's letter is strange, now that I think of it. What do I remember about onionskin—it wasn't used much in the Renaissance, was it?"

Dr. Riccardi shook her head. "No, it wasn't. And it would be an odd choice of writing paper for Antonio to make. The Medici wrote on parchment, as in the other letters. This isn't onionskin, precisely, but rather a hemp fiber, which has been scraped so fine as to become transparent. And it became popular only in the seventeenth century, and then mostly with parvenu courtesans who absurdly thought it lascivious, as it resembled the fabric of their lingerie."

"But the real problem is the handwriting," I said. "In Marco's letter, the script is slightly more cramped, in the ascenders, the garlands. The difference is subtle."

Dr. Riccardi nodded. "It is actually quite glaring to my eye."

"Lola, don't make a snap decision, take *your time*," Marco ordered me, in a low voice.

By Antonio's letter to the pope, I placed the letter that Marco had purchased from Mr. Soto-Relada, which I quote again for clarity:

My dear nephew Cosimo, Duke of Florence,

> *I write this missive in response to your call for funds, on the eve of your battle against the Sienese . . . a war I have told you I find in bad taste. . . . When did we last meet, before you Exiled my wife, Sofia the Dragon, and me? It was in the 1520s, I believe, just after I returned from America, in the few months when I was still allowed to feast at our family's palazzo. The dining hall was so lovely, I remember, full of mysteries and hints of treasure—with its friezes of golden girls, its secret passageways, its fresco of The Rape of Proserpine, and that gew-gaw I commissioned, namely Pontormo's gorgeous map of Italy. . . .*

I ran my fingers over these lavishly inked words, which were like miniature black silk sculptures. "Oh, it could be a different author; look at the slant. Your letter's veers more to the left—it almost appears as if the writer's changed hands from one decade to the next. And the scripts, serifs, heights—they disagree."

Dr. Riccardi concurred. "And—here—the swashes on the *T*s are also different, and the *A*s are all hideously wrong."

Marco was not ready for that answer. "The seal *is* identical. What more do you need? That's a classic sign of authenticity! The second letter could have been written by a secretary."

Both Dr. Riccardi and I forcefully said no.

"The seals do match," I agreed. "But the Medici were crazy about the New Learning, humanism—they tried to model themselves after Cicero and his hand-lettered correspondence. A personal note, and one this important, to Giovanni de' Medici, and written in the italic script, would have been written by the author unless he were *dying*, probably."

"During the sixteenth century," Dr. Riccardi added, "the style of writing, the content of the letter, and the personal touch in correspondence were considered a mark of the man himself."

I held out the letter under the lights as Marco's hands clenched, and his mouth paled as he shot me a warning look. But I still gave my verdict.

"You've brought me here for *no reason*." I roughly pushed the pages of his document at him. "The letter's a forgery, Marco."

6

Marco thrust his letter once more into my hands.

"Look at it again," he demanded.

"I did look at it. I told you what I think."

"What you think is wrong!"

I pushed the pages back into their envelope, stuffing it into his blazer pocket. "I'm right. They're different—they weren't written by the same man."

"You're being sloppy. You can *do better* than this. Sloppy work always makes me lose my temper."

"The letter's a piece of trash, Marco—"

"No, no, no," Dr. Riccardi bubbled. "No scholarly lovers' spats—"

"We are *not* lovers."

"Those are the absolute worst. Come on now, kids, stop *biting* each other to death." We continued sputtering while the doctor wrapped us in her surprisingly strong arms, mashing our shoulders together and crooning, "I'm *sure* we can still make this trip worth your while. The evening isn't beyond repair, my darlings! I have a wonderful dinner planned for all of us."

She forcibly hauled us out of the library, reminding us that though the Palazzo Medici Riccardi serves as a museum, it still harbors a working kitchen whose chef can re-create the *tortellini en brodo* and *fritto di calamari* that delighted Cosimo I himself. Also, some of its grand bedrooms and dining halls remain in sumptuous order for the scholars and diplomats—and booksellers—who are "lucky" enough to spend a night or two there.

Adriana appeared in the darkling halls, as if on instinct or telepathic command, and was told in easy tones to "bring these nice people up to their room. They're having a kind of disagreement, so—I don't know—make them . . . *happier* or something."

After communicating a violent coded message to her employer with her eyes, the assistant's powerful little paws manhandled us up the stairs to an apartment designed for the fleshly pleasure of Florence's exacting duchesses. She tilted her head, expertly studying my plane-rumpled outfit. "Marco—that is, sir—and madam, will be advised that while staying in the palace you are expected to mind whatever manners you have been taught by the cavepeople who raised you . . . and to please dress appropriately for dinner. We do require that sir wears a tuxedo and madam favors more . . . suitable attire."

"I don't have anything else but this dress," I yammered, gesturing at my priestess gown, which now made me look like an ethnic extra in *Conan the Barbarian*.

"When sir made his arrangements, and explained that madam was from Long . . . Long . . . *Beach*, was it? We instantly took measures to take care of any sartorial dilemma madam might have. Please do look in the closet and you'll see we've provided more than suitable attire."

"Yes, and thank you, Adriana," Marco said, collecting himself enough to give her a smile.

Then she shimmered into the recesses of the palace.

"Why are your things here?" I said wildly, when I saw that

Adriana had stacked Marco's bags in my suite's closet. "Why does she think we're staying in the same room?"

Marco pulled out the golden-sealed letter from his pocket, his face dark red with anger: "You did a shabby job of it back there. This is the real thing! I know it! I'm not joking around about this, for Christ's sake."

"Are—we—staying—in—the—same—room?" I repeated, even louder. "With one bed?"

He gazed around the suite for the first time, the veins standing out in his temples. "It was the only way I could get any accommodations."

I stared at him, trying not to think what I was thinking about him, but thankfully he looked repulsed when he understood my fear.

"What? Rape? No—not in the cards, no, not part of the plan." He waved his hand at me as if I were ridiculous. "That's a bit too dirty for my taste."

"I'm glad to hear it."

"I am a gentleman. Sometimes."

"Last I heard, gentlemen didn't slap women around and threaten them."

"Who told you that lie? Gentlemen do all sorts of beastly things. But I don't do *that*." Marco regarded me with his hot eyes. Taking in my bush of a hairdo and near-screaming, he evidently determined that this conversation would yield only diminishing returns. "Fine. Look. I don't mean to push you into hysterics; it's not a very productive state of mind."

"I might find it very productive."

"I doubt that. And it doesn't really seem your way, hysteria. You're too smart."

"Just *go*. I've done what you wanted. The letter's a fraud.

I'm just hoping you aren't. You said you knew something about Tomas—about where he was buried. So tell me now. Because I'm leaving."

"Actually—no you're *not*. Because then you'd just get into a nasty squabble with Domenico, who will beat you, is that clear enough?" Marco said tiredly.

"You *are* disgusting," I fumed.

He fluttered his eyes, looking suddenly ragged. "Yes. It's a family trait, and if you're not careful, you'll bring it out."

"Poor you. *I* just inherited big hips and a flaming distaste *for being held hostage!*"

His features unexpectedly flared out into a half smile.

"Is something funny?"

"Oh, my goodness. Well, actually, sort of, yes. Look at you stomp around. Roar, roar, roar. You're like a tiny Genghis Kahn."

"I'm glad you're having such a party."

"All right. Let's calm down. Clean yourself up, killer. Chop chop. You heard our orders from Adriana regarding dinner."

"I'm not hungry."

"I don't *care*. Because, listen to me: There's something I want you to see downstairs, in the dining room. I think you'll find it interesting. It relates to the letter."

I hesitated for two beats but couldn't help asking: "The dining room? What's there?"

His dark eyes latched onto me, and he reached out to tweak my chin. "Ye-es. That's better. Curious Cat. *That's* the little freak Soto-Relada promised me. Don't worry. I'll show you when you get down there—you won't be disappointed. Just don't disappoint *me*."

He took care to leave the letter on the bed, then snatched up his bag and left the room.

I scanned the place to see if there was a way to crawl out of a window, or maybe I could just go running down the stairs and hope the ogres didn't see me escape. When I opened the door, though, I saw Domenico filling up the hall like a dam. This left me to the confines of the palatial suite with its barred windows, marble fixtures, large oak tester bed hung with green and gold tapestries—and two phones, one by the bed, the other by the bathtub.

I immediately called my fiancé, Erik, twice, but there was no answer. Sitting down on the bed while listening to the incessant *ring, ring, ring,* I nervously fondled the silk coverlet and its embroidery, then the shining envelope tossed there.

I looked down at it. It was a fake, as I'd said. It was a hoax. The different writing styles proved it. *There was no Aztec gold.* That I continued to entertain the possibility demonstrated that my intelligence had been eroded by far too much indulgence in Conan Doyle and Jules Verne. And even if the letter was beautifully executed, and had that matching wolf seal, these features certainly didn't mean anything—forgers had been known to do exquisite work before.

I should call my parents or Yolanda, I thought. I should call the U.S. Embassy.

But I am *perverse.* I picked the letter up. I slid the shining leaves of onionskin or hemp between my fingers, tilting the envelope.

Out slipped that little card.

Señor Sam Soto-Relada
Dealer in Used Goods
11 Avenue and 11 Calle, Zona 1, Via Corona
Ciudad de Guatemala, Guatemala,
502–2–82–20–099

Dear Sir or Madam,

Please enjoy this *rare letter* in fine health.

Having any problems with the item? Any questions? Feel generally befuddled or confused? Feel free to call at ANY TIME. And remember that Soto-Relada is your go-to guy for any and all "hard to obtain" goods!

Yours truly,
Sam Soto-Relada

What had Marco said about him?

That old schemer makes it his business to get his hands on all kinds of naughty commodities. He worked with your father, and had scads of information about Tomas.

My curiosity sizzled in me as I wandered around the room, twirling the card between my knuckles, wandering to the bathroom, drawing the bath water, reading the note over and over.

I inserted myself into the hot, foaming bath, touching the phone.

I dialed.

"Soto-Relada," a harried, sparrowlike voice answered. "Who is this, please? Rather busy here."

"Señor Soto-Relada . . . it's Lola Sanchez."

"Is this the police again? This is *harassment*—"

"What? No. It's Lola . . . de la Rosa . . . ?"

"What? De la Rosa? Did I hear that right? Oooooooo—yes—sorry—of *course*. Not Tomas's little girl."

"Yes, that's it. That's me. I guess."

"Oh dear— Hello, dear child! Well— What an honor this is— What a . . ."

"Sir, are you out of breath? Are you all right?"

"Just running around a little— Nothing to worry— Getting my exercise. *Wait*— You're in Italy, aren't you? This isn't collect— you are paying for this call."

"Um . . . no, but you aren't either—"

"Good. So! How's it going? Having any problems with travel arrangements or tragic sociopaths?"

"Marco Moreno, you mean."

"Isn't he a charmer? You two getting along?"

"*Why* did you say that I would help him with this Antonio Medici business?"

"What, haven't you guessed?"

"I don't see how—"

"To save your *life*, you little fool. He was going to make you into chicken cutlets!"

"You mean kill me."

"You'd be dead as King Tut right now if I hadn't told him to consult your brains rather than bash them, dearie! Oh, the Morenos are famous for it, slagging people. Didn't you know? After the colonel died, little Marco was just drunkenly racing around here, foaming about how he wanted to burn your father's bones, and bombing your family home, other unpleasantries—and . . . I'd heard how good you were at the ancient document-reading-thingum—so I thought, well, two birds, stone—whatever the saying is. Couldn't let Tomas's kid get creamed like a coconut pie—especially if she might be able to find this Montezuma whatsis. I just mean that I thought it would be terrific if you wouldn't get dead—and, at the same time, well, you might also help make me some money! By finding this gold what-have-you, the Aztec stash—"

"Marco said you knew Tomas."

"Did I 'know' Tomas—*hell* yes. An awful man. Good client—

terrible human being. But—it has to be said, a genius. An absolute
genius. Master of seven languages, disappearing acts, disguises,
political organizing, archaeology, and womanizing. *And*— An absolute ass. Look how he treated your mother, the fair Juana, whom
he abandoned to the spindly arms of that Manuel person, that
bald little curator—"

"My father—"

"And then we can't forget how he treated that daughter of
his—your sister."

"Yolanda."

"Yes, right. Yolanda. Yolanda de la Rosa. Oh, he was the *worst*
to her, your sis. Wasn't he? Always testing her mettle, as it were—
didn't he once drop Yolanda in the middle of the jungle when she
was twelve years old and tell her to find her way home? And he
was always disappearing—she'd hear reports of his death—and
then he'd pop right back up months later. Poor little cabbage. No
wonder she's so quirky. And she always wears that ghastly black
hat, doesn't she? Like her father did. I think she's touched in the
head."

All of this rather weird family history was, in fact, true, but
as I had a two-ton thug guarding my door and a possible maniac
returning to my room at any moment, it didn't seem an appropriate time to get into a lengthy discussion about the many foibles
of the de la Rosa clan.

"Yes, yes, but—hold on, Señor Soto-Relada, please—stop—
talking—for a second. I have a *lot* of questions for you. First,
about this letter—it's turned out to be a forgery."

A pause here, some panting. "Has it?"

"I was wondering if you had any more—"

"Now that's odd—"

"—information about it."

"Information? Do I have any? *No.* Though I can tell you that there was a time when your father was interested in it."

"Marco said the letter used to belong to Tomas."

"Yes, he bought it from me fourteen years ago! Old Tom spent a good amount of time trying to solve the thing, and was close to doing so—but then, you know, he went crackers and died. And so I . . . liberated the letter, if you will, from his estate, and sold it—again—to our friend, Moreno. I have a rather unorthodox business model, gets me into a lot of trouble—at the moment, in fact, I'm currently trying to avoid a date with . . . what do you *Yanquis* call it? The 'fuzz'?"

I was so galled I just clung to the phone with my mouth open.

"But why dwell on that nasty detail? On the other, much less self-incriminating subject, Tomas was like that—the crackers part—you must have heard. Something of a melancholic. Given to *moods.* Like the daughter. Yolanda. And his war—his experiences in it—did not help his sulks much. So it didn't surprise me much at all to hear that he might have died in Italy—it was just like him to race off and not say anything about it to anyone . . . wait, did you just hear something? A siren—something like that?"

"What? No."

"Are you sure? Someone hyperventilating on a megaphone?"

"You're saying he *did* die here, in Italy. How?"

"Oh—blagh—so you're saying you don't know. Well, I won't tell you. Look, I'm very sorry that your family has had things *so* hard, but you really should thank me, as you would be floundering around with the fishes if I hadn't recommended your talents to Sir Marco. And as to the letter—well, I'm sure it's not a forgery. Your father would not have been interested in it if it were. *And,* if you are a de la Rosa, then . . . well, you'll *figure it out.* The de la Rosas always do. That's what will keep you healthy with Mr. Marco. Figuring it out. What I'd do if I were you is spin out this treasure hunting business with your Latin phrases and witty perambulations and he's sure to remain your friend. Then, after you find the stuff, that is, the *gold,* find some clever way to slip him some particularly painful poison. And make sure to remember I get my percentage."

"Señor Soto-Relada—"

"Yes, excellent—very well then—look, I have to go. See, I *do* hear it. Oh, damn. Oh, my God, that's a siren—I see these flashing . . . red lights—must dash—good-bye, Lola—"

"Señor—"

"Mucho gusto!"

And with that, he clicked off the phone.

7

I scrambled out of the tub, redialing to no avail, and trying to piece together that baffling conversation while drying myself off with a towel. I had dabbed at my thighs and belly button when I recalled that I had nothing but that wadded up Kleenex-looking priestess gown to cover up my confusion. Adriana, however, had earlier mentioned something about providing me with dinner wear. I moved over to the suite's wardrobe, a delicately carved sixteenth-century affair, and opened it. Inside shimmered a selection of silk gowns adorned with tiny explosions of spiderwebby embroidery, crystal beading, ruches, Venetian laces.

"Oh my God!" I yelped, because I'm not made of wood. I had half slid into a bias-cut silk firecracker with a Marlene Dietrich décolletage when I heard brief knocking, then a rattling at the front door's lock.

Marco Moreno sauntered back into the room, dressed in a magnificent tuxedo. He coughed embarrassedly and turned away when he saw my frantic flashes of skin.

"Oh—you take a long time to get ready. Sorry."

"How did you get in here?" I hurriedly slipped the thing on.

He held up a key. "As you were shrieking before, it's my room too. Well, well! You were looking very road kill before, but you're *much* better now. Been enjoying yourself?"

I wasn't going to tell him about my conversation with Soto-Relada, and so only asked, "What do you think?"

"A little, actually, yes."

"Wrong." I turned my head, briefly. Out in the hall, I could just now hear the sound of a door opening, and also footsteps. A woman's low laughter. Adriana.

"But you've been looking at the letter again, haven't you?" Marco observed the pages scattered on the bedspread. "Any more thoughts?"

"Many."

"I'll just bet." He picked up the onionskin papers, brandishing them at me. "So, I'll give you another one, then: You diagnosed this letter as being a forgery. But have you considered the fact that sometimes people's writing just *changes*? You compared this letter to one that Dr. Riccardi showed you—the one Antonio wrote to Pope Leo X, right? That was written—what?—in the early fifteen hundreds, when Antonio had just sailed from Florence to Timbuktu. He was a young lunatic then, torturing Muslims, enslaving them, but that was all over by the time he married, left Florence, and then wrote *my* letter—"

"Tomas's letter," I corrected him.

Marco smirked. "In a manner of speaking, it *was* written by a different person! Antonio was over forty years older, a sick, tired, melancholy old man when he penned this letter that I'm holding. I once read that Shakespeare's signature would look different, just a little, mind you, but discernibly, every time he wrote it. Handwriting differences would be even greater in this case! *And* you forget that Antonio suffered an illness—"

I grudgingly nodded. "That letter was written when he was dying from the Condition."

"Exactly. He suffered from the Condition. No one knows exactly what the illness was, but couldn't it have been some sort of nerve damage, some sort of palsy, or even an injury to the hand, which would have altered the letter heights, the threads, the pen pressure?"

I considered this for a moment before conceding that what he suggested was possible. "You know more about this than I thought."

"It's become a consuming interest of mine."

"*Why?*"

"It seems as if I have found my calling."

"What—history?"

He hesitated, staring down at the letter. "Politics. It's something of an inheritance."

"I don't understand."

"It doesn't matter." He moved closer to me. "What matters is *this* right now. And I have seen your brain at work. You practically *ate* this letter when I first showed it to you. I thought I was going to have to give you a tranquilizer you became so excited. And in the Long Beach Airport—despite all your whingeing about calling the police, you chased me through the terminal like a little demented bloodhound. But I completely understand. I feel the same way. There's a *promise* in this writing, don't you think? Of something wonderful." He moved toward me again, and I took a step back, so that we were walking in a circle, the way wrestlers do before a fight. Soon my back was toward the front door, and he smiled at me with his white teeth. "Pretty Lola, I know you want to find out the truth. There are secrets here—I can *smell* them, can't you? There's something downstairs—in the dining room, as I said before. I can't put my finger on it. Something in this palace that's been bothering me for a year—"

"What?"

He was now very near, and shining-eyed. I remembered the old biblical tales of Lucifer and his beauty, his hissing seduction of Eve. Marco was an extraordinary shape-shifter to move so quickly between threatening thug and honey-tongued tempter.

His hand rested on my hand, gently, grazing my engagement ring with his fingertips.

"Don't touch me like that," I said, rattled.

Outside, I could again hear the sound of that laughter— actually, more like a shrieking—that punctuated the halls of the palazzo.

Marco smoothed out my fingers so that my palm opened, then laid the opal-colored pages in my grasp.

My fingers folded over the letter.

"Come on, look at it," he half-sang to me. "Really *study* it. After all, don't you want to show how you're better than him? Tomas, I mean? Soto-Relada told me he spent years trying to fig- ure out this puzzle. It must pique your interest—Tomas's failure. And the idea that you might have the chops to break a code he couldn't."

I didn't answer that. "In Long Beach, you *hit* me, Marco. You threatened my family. Now you've put a gorilla outside my door."

"Yes."

"I don't work that well when I think that people are going to hurt me if I displease them."

He kept his eyes intently on mine. "Actually, I'm becoming more and more convinced that you will please me, Lola."

"If you intended that to make me feel better—guess what? It *doesn't.*"

"Well," he said smoothly, "it's true. I'll confess that I wasn't quite sure what I would do with you once I got you over here. Drag you by the hair about Italy and make you figure this puzzle out for me, I suppose. Not very efficient. And not likely to end well. But, it appears you just might be smart enough to truly work with me on this letter, and not because I bully you. Which would require, of course, that I would be *stupid* enough to forget who you are." He brought his hand to his lips, briefly, and he seemed suddenly less bulletproof, less brittle, before he spread out his arms and laughed bitterly. "But it is possible that I could forget. After all, I am a man in grief, terrible, terrible grief, and am not seeing clearly."

He stared at me for a long time then. Or I, at him. At this moment he did not seem dangerous. He was weirdly, almost intimately sad, even seductive—in a Stockholm syndrome sort of way.

"Yes, after all—why not? Why fight? You could prove yourself to me now, if you wanted," he murmured, and I could feel his warm breath on my cheeks. He took my face in his palms, pushing back my hair. "Little beauty. Little nutter. We're not so very different, are we? But I want you to *work with me.* I know you're capable of more than that amateur show you put on in the library! I *dare* you. Show me that not all of the de la Rosas are trash. It would mean a great deal to your family. Maybe I'll give you a chance."

"Oh—you—*grrrrr!*" Holding the letter tightly, I furiously jerked my face out of his grasp. Marco kept hold of my arm as I blundered out of the suite's front door and faced the source of the laughter outside.

"Or, maybe *not,*" Marco said, over the din.

In the Persian-carpeted hallway, the formerly blasé Adriana was flushing crimson and spasming with hilarity. Opposite her stood a tall, stocky man in a crumpled, navy suit with stuffed pockets, and with wayward black and silver hair.

"You're really going to have to educate these Italians, Adriana, because the customs guy says to me, 'You're what—Latino? That's what? As in . . . Indian? As in Chief Running Bear or something? As in eagle feathers and nude dancing? I thought you were Chinese, boy, because of your, well, your *eyes*.' And I said, 'No, I'm Indian—Maya Indian—and my ancestors did wear feathers, in fact, particularly when they were performing these incredibly painful human sacrifices, especially on large-bottomed male Italian colonials, because their effeminacy pleased the harvest gods—Italians, to tell you the truth, a *lot* like you'—but he didn't think it was very funny, because he said he was going to put me in the airport prison—"

"I know, I know, they are blockheads," gasped Adriana, reaching out to dust off some lint from his lapel, before spotting me and composing herself.

"Who's that?" Marco asked from behind me.

Adriana patted down her hair. "Oh—yes. This lovely man says he is your . . . *fiancé?*" She rolled her eyes meaningfully. "Signorina de la Rosa?"

The guest turned around. The man's dark, exhausted glance first veered up to Marco and shot out little poisoned darts when he saw his hand on my arm. Then he looked at me, with his funny, handsome-haggard face.

"Hi . . . ," he said, bobbing his airplane-seat-mashed head back and forth and opening his arms. "Surprise, sweetie! What the hell are you doing here? Love you! Guess you didn't expect me to really come when you invited me on that text message thingie. Well, ha! Um—here I am!"

I rushed to Erik and nearly crushed him to pieces in my embrace.

8

"W hen did you get here?" I almost brutally squeezed
Erik around his big waist; his hands were very cold
as they moved through my hair.

"Rome, about two hours ago. After you texted me about this
'client' person, and Aztecs, and Tomas, I couldn't get a hold of you
on your cell. So I called up your parents and Yolanda, but no one
knew what was going on. Then I phoned *this* place—the palazzo—
you gibbered about it in your text. Adriana told me that you had
a room reserved here! So then I ran to the airport! And then I just
staggered around! I was trying to figure out what in holy hell was
going on—your flight had just left! You were gone! We had dinner
reservations! We were going to have lobster and pick the rehearsal
dinner DJ! And then I was sort of *upset* and then I kind of felt myself *floating* over to the ticket counter and babbling out *my fiancée's
in Italy*—and they put me on standby and—well—bam *bam!*" He
waggled his hands around his ears. "I just did it! Flew here like a
maniac! All very spontaneous, you know, and I was hoping it would
be romantic and not stalking—"

I started laughing. "Are you drunk?"

His thick black bangs stuck up all around his head, and his
beard-bristles sprang out from his thick jaw. "No, not very. Any-

more. But you know, coach is *such* hell and they've got this duty-free whiskey and I sipped like half a bottle while nibbling on . . . these—" From the depths of his bulging jacket pockets he began pulling out the treats he'd purchased en route: Tiny cans of gourmet nuts, Baci balls, little Parmesan cheese twists, a squeaky-new paperback novel, and a miniature bottle of L'Air du Temps for me. Even while a few stray Baci balls tumbled to the ground, however, his gaze moved up to Marco, who still stood behind me in the hall. "But I still didn't get drunk enough to survive the freaking Christian Slater movie they kept on playing over, and over, and blah, blah, and yadda, yadda, yadda, and what I'd actually really like to know is, *What the hell is this guy doing in your room?*"

If Erik Gomara, Ph.D., pitched a jealous fit at the sight of Marco Moreno, it was the first that I could recall in our two-year relationship. Healthy-bellied, with dark chocolate eyes, large pink ears, and a tall Diego Rivera frame, Erik usually proved too busy reading, teaching, writing, eating, or rigorously seducing me to bother with the annoyances of romantic rivals. Nor could there have been any, because he was fabulous. Erik was an archaeology prof at UCLA, along with my mother, Juana, and two years back, we had gotten together while searching for her in Guatemala. He had been born in that country, before immigrating to the United States and its Ivy Leagues, then carpet-bombing UCLA's humanities deans and female undergrads with his shaggy-dog sex appeal. When I'd first met him, he was as famous for his sophomore-deflowerings as his medal-winning digs in Maya burial sites, but it took only a couple shakes of the Sanchez hips—and the whole near-death experience in the Guatemala jungle—for him to make me the sole beneficiary of his extreme coolness. Erik had struggled with Colonel Moreno during our adventure in the rain forest, and also watched as Lieutenant Estrada had beaten that man to a dead bloody pulp. This tragedy had both bonded us and plagued him with bad nightmares. Still, we had settled into a very happy life, dividing our time between his apartment in L.A. and my family home in L.B. Our romance, moreover, was to very shortly detonate into a wild wedding. This was to be a one-week affair that my mother and father Manuel had organized, complete with mariachi bands, live cockatiels, bowling, and a tracking demonstration by Yolanda, who had dyspeptically agreed to take the wedding party on a scavenger hunt around the Long Beach suburbs. So it's understandable that he became agitated at the sight of Marco grabbing at me in a lavish penthouse, a mere twelve days before we were to exchange vows.

"Why is this guy in your room?" he repeated.

"Oh, they're *staying* together," Adriana helpfully offered, while kicking the dropped candies into a beautiful iron-wrought waste can. "Sharing a suite, you know. Most economical."

"No, we're not," I objected loudly. "That was a mistake."

"Mistake?" Erik asked.

"Why is our party being crashed by a sweaty chimpanzee, Adriana?" Marco smoothly asked.

"He said he wanted to surprise his fiancée," she replied.

Erik's face flushed red and white. "And who are you, bud?"

I still had the letter in my hand, and I waved it around. "Honey, let me explain. There's this letter—"

"Lord, Adriana, just get this person out of here—"

"I can't, Marco. I'm afraid Dr. Riccardi was more than welcoming. She thought his presence might be amusing—"

I said, "Erik, he came into the store, talking about gold and Tomas's grave, and Col—"

"Yeah—I got that part. I told your sister and she's *flipping out* about it. I'm surprised she's not here herself. Everybody at home wants to know what's going on. You're missing your dress fittings, the shower, the caterer, the music—"

"He basically abducted me, Erik. At first, anyway."

"Abducted you."

"Yes, that's what you call it when handsome men make you tart up in one of *my* red dresses and hurl you into suites that cost a thousand euros a night," said Adriana, drily. "Sir."

"What a wonderful way to put it," said Marco.

I said, "Seriously—listen—"

"Actually, why *are* you wearing that?"

Everyone was talking at once.

"You can interrogate her cleavage back in California." Marco eased a cigarette box from his tuxedo pocket, lighting up with a flick of his elegant hands. "Why don't you find a bowl of ranch dip dressing and stick your head in it, my good boy? Go suck on a chocolate. Though you're awfully amusing with your little cheese crackers and aroma of armpit, we are both very, very busy and can't be bothered."

"Will you shut up?" I hissed at him.

"I'm persuading him to *go*. Nicely, you'll note." Marco exhaled smoke through his nostrils before glancing over at Domenico, who still stood in the hall like a guard. "I could be ruder if you like, sweetheart."

Erik puffed up at Marco, in a he-man sort of way, raking his fingers through his hair before patting him in a hard and whapping manner on the shoulder. "I don't feel like we've been properly introduced. What's your name?"

"Marco Moreno." He smiled. "I can very easily ensure that you never forget it—"

"No, Jesus, don't do that," I said. "Okay, everyone stop acting manly right now!"

"Marco *Moreno?*" Marco's shoulder juddered back as Erik continued to smack him. He reached up and rapped on Erik's head with his knuckles. "Ring a bell? Moreno?"

"Stop whacking each other, sirs," Adriana commanded. "It's entertaining, but no one's fought at the palazzo since, ah, 1523, I think. Too many antiques. And besides, it's bad for the digestion. Would you like to a tour instead?"

"No, Erik has to look at *this.*" Again I tried to show him the pages in my hand, rustling them under his nose. "Here, just in case you see something that I didn't—"

But Erik roughly brushed Marco's lapel, so the man had to take a step back. "Hey. This is a *really* nice tuxedo. Does it wrinkle easily?"

"Honey," I said. "Stop."

"Gentlemen," warned Adriana.

Marco's face rippled with mirth. "Ha ha ha. Not at all. I'll give you the name of my tailor—as you'll soon need to be stitched up."

"Look, all of you, *do shut up,*" Adriana bassooned, so that we gave a little jump and quieted down.

"Even me, darling?" Marco asked.

"Especially you. Sir." She smiled again before pushing him down the hall, his cigarette smoke following him like the devil's gas. She maneuvered Erik after him, before propelling me toward the staircase. "I run this house, you see. My job is to make sure the doctor is happy. When she is not happy, she screams. This, I hate. And if you kill each other before dinner—and thus are not able to sit down for appetizers—what will happen? Unhappiness. The screaming. So, please . . . *move.*"

This sufficiently startled Erik and me so that we automatically followed her orders. Marco floated down the stairs, and we

followed him past more of the palazzo's marble nudes, Renaissance landscapes, and a spectacularly painted chamber tucked
into a side corridor.

"Here, *this* should divert you!" Adriana said. "This always
works! We have a very nice chapel, with a lovely mural. Look,
look, look. Pay attention. It has your friend in it; you'll love it.
No, don't stop mumbling at *him, sir*—up here! Recognize this?"

"What?" "What?" "What?"

We had been dragged to a small room ablaze with a green-
gold painted panorama showing nobles surrounded by slaves,
dogs, brilliant hills and trees. Adriana was frisking about, drawing our attention away from our argument by pointing up to this
mural of young handsome men riding muscular steeds in a kings'
processional.

"Points for who gives me the name of the mural." Adriana
waved her hands in the air. "Those of you who can't will immediately be branded a buffoon. Come on, come on."

"This is *absurd,*" said Marco.

"*Buf*-foon," answered Adriana.

"It's the Gozzoli mural," Erik said instinctively, confusedly,
his bangs waving like wheat above his ahead. "Um—Benozzo
Gozzoli. This is his *Procession of the Three Magi*. The progression
under the North Star. Gozzoli used Medici family members as
models."

"Yes. Excellent—especially for a big old sweaty chimp, isn't
it, sir?"

"Agh—"

"What year was it painted, sir?"

Along with a miasma of cigarette smoke, Marco puffed:
"Bagh—1459—"

"Buf-foon, incomplete answer."

"Oh—shit—the last of it was painted—"

"The latest scholarship argues 1497." Erik nearly hollered, unable to repress himself. "The last year of—"

"Gozzoli's life," rapped out Marco.

"And *whose* portrait do the scholars say was painted in that year?" She raised her eyebrows, barely wrinkling her perfect skin.

"Oh, *right.* I've read about this." That was me. I made my way to one particular portrait of a magus on a white horse; this was a darkly handsome, though severe-looking, person, wearing an embroidered green-and-gold coat and a gold-pointed headdress. The artist had taken great pains to render the subject as a dashing, bronzed Moorish prince. "This is our *man.*"

"That's Antonio Medici," Marco gargled. "When he was a youngster—nineteen years old—here, in Florence. He posed for Gozzoli as the Babylonian magus Balthazar. He's one of the three magi who visited the Christ child."

"That's it, sir," she said, clasping her hands. "You're back on track now. Here's your Signor Antonio, in the late fourteen hundreds, *long* before his rehabilitation. Look at him! Murderer of inmates and asylum patients at this age, later moving on to Ottomans in Africa in the fifteen tens, then Aztecs in the Americas in the twenties. Gozzoli said that painting him was like painting the devil. Still, he did make a good model for Balthazar. Some say that Antonio had a Sicilian mother—that's why he had such a temper. You know people will have their theories. But I'm just happy the historians are blaming him on the Sicilians and not on Algerians like me."

Adriana smiled, and I found myself almost liking her then.

"There now!" she piped. "You aren't ululating at each other anymore. This always works—I can't tell you how many times I've had intellectuals come steaming and barking in here and wanting to assassinate each other over . . . what . . . the provenance of some rubbishy potsherd or piece of dented silver. And then I bring them in here, give them a test—and my, you really are just a bunch of apple-polishing four-eyes after all these years, aren't you? Cool as fish now. Good for me. So! Now that I've gotten you all under control, it's time for dinner. I laid an extra plate for Dr. Gomara and whisked away the steak knives. No, you don't have to thank me. Come on, then, come on. Let's go."

We were commandeered back to the public areas of the palazzo, which were sparsely populated with antique-looking guards.

"Behave yourselves now—I'm warning you. Okay, super! See you in a bit." Adriana gave us a bow before melting away.

Our tense little trio stood at the entrance of the palazzo's opulent and gilded private dining room, where Dr. Riccardi bewilderedly attempted to engage the monosyllabic Blasej and Domenico in conversation. As I entered the room, I labored to give her a nonpanicked smile—that is, until my eyes turned up, up, up, to the salon's paintings, its gilding, its ceiling frescoes.

And here is where the day began to take an unexpected turn once again. The moment I entered the art-littered fantasia that was once the Medici dining hall, it was as if I experienced a mental *click*, some sort of uncanny déjà vu:

I knew I had seen this room before.

Or that someone had *told* me about this room before.

Gliding over the carpets, the glimmering wood, I had the strange sensation that someone—not Marco—had once whispered to me about this place. That it was full of—what? *Hints* and *mysteries*.

But what could that mean?

I grabbed Erik and hurried into the dining hall to find out.

9

My gaze flew above the forms of the impatiently waiting Dr. Riccardi, Domenico, and Blasej. All through the extraordinary room. The walls were striped with gilt friezes of ladies' faces, and beyond these glimmered a ceiling fresco showing a disturbing scene of a woman being spirited away by some sort of kingly figure. High on the west wall preened a huge Vasari portrait of Cosimo I. Right next to it shone a beautifully precise map of Italy, lavish with calligraphy and gold leaf, which looked quite old.

"Where have I seen this before? Or when have I *been* here before?" I asked, while Erik continued to question me with his eyes, while attempting to smash down his travel-grunged hair in preparation for an evidently expensive dinner.

"I told you, didn't I?" Marco replied. "The dining room."

"Yes—but where have I seen it?"

"What's that?" Dr. Riccardi raised her eyes from the monolithic Domenico and Blasej to the glittering ceiling.

Pointing at the pages I still held in my hand, Marco said: "You didn't see it, you *read* about it—*he* described it, very precisely. In Antonio's letter to Cosimo. Antonio begins recounting his life here in the palace, in the days before Cosimo threw him out of the city. He wrote about the dinners they had had here: *'When did we last meet, before you Exiled my wife, Sofia the Dragon, and me? It was in the 1520s, I believe, just after I returned from America, in the few months when I was still allowed to feast at our family's palazzo. The dining hall was so lovely, I remember, full of mysteries and hints of treasure—'"*

I said: "Yes, right—that's it—*'mysteries and hints of treasure.'* "

" *'With its friezes of golden girls,'* " Marco went on, " *'its secret passageways, its fresco of* The Rape of Proserpine, *and that gew-gaw I commissioned, namely Pontormo's gorgeous map of Italy.'* "

"Lola," Erik said. "I'm in the dark here—"

"Antonio made a clue of the room in the letter—it's subtle, but it's there," Marco pressed. "The question is, why?"

"Oh, you're not still chattering about *that*?" Dr. Riccardi said. "Ale! Ale! Marco, *you* talk to your friends. I'm finding it too difficult."

"I brought them only for you to look at, Isabel." Marco moved over to her and his hoodlums, who looked big and muscled and completely out of place in the delicate salon. "I thought you would find them invigorating."

"You *beast*."

"Who are *those* guys?" Erik touched his belly. "God, everybody works out a lot around here—"

"Honey—"

"And what were you talking about, being 'abducted'? A band of rabid Chippendales dancers busted into a used book store and kidnapped its owner to take you . . . to dinner?"

"Erik, there's a lot I have to tell you. About him, who he is."

"Marco Moreno."

"Let's have some wine," Marco was at this moment suggesting to the doctor.

"But before I do—and you freak out"—I pressed Antonio's

missive into Erik's hands—"please, just take a look at this letter. I'm hoping you can help me with it."

He took hold of the onionskin pages, inflating his cheeks. "Because I'm such a flexible guy, I'll put this whole Rico Suave–red dress–unexplained flight to Italy thing on the back burner."

"Just for a minute."

"Hmmm, all right. What have we got here. It looks . . . old." Erik glared down at the writing, then raised his eyebrows. "What—what *is* this?"

"It's a letter written by Antonio Medici—"

"Who you were just talking about—the psychotic one? The killer? The one who went with Cortés—"

"Yes."

"Oh—the *gold*. What you were texting me about—"

"There's a riddle, and Antonio says that he has a map to the treasure."

"To Aztec gold—*Montezuma's* gold," he rapped out.

"That's right."

He lightly ruffled the papers. "I don't see a map in here."

"Read it, read it, read it."

"Sit down, please," Dr. Riccardi was saying in Spanish as she stood by the huge walnut dining table, which was set with silks and silver. She puckishly managed to navigate me into a chair between Erik and Marco, with Domenico and Blasej opposite us. Taking her place at the head of the table, she breathed: "What's all this about you being Miss de la Rosa's fiancé, Dr. Gomara? Is it *true*? Am I in the midst of a scandal? Do tell."

"Of course not," Erik said in a big overly confident voice as he looked up from the letter.

"But you *did* fly out here the *instant* you heard that the lovely Ms. de la Rosa had arrived in Italy with another man?" she exclaimed.

"Basically."

Dr. Riccardi shrugged her shoulders and opened her mouth with delight at the idea. "Have you always been such a knight?"

"Actually, *no*."

"How intriguing! Ooo. You don't even have to *say*. It's written all over you. You were quite the Don Juan, weren't you? Before your fiancée *tamed* you?"

"I actually sort of chased her down like a crazy wildebeest."

"Excellent!"

"Let's just say that love changes you for the better," Erik suggested, rolling his brown eyes over at me.

Dr. Riccardi waggled her fingers at him. "Oh, Lord, who told you that? What a lot of twaddle. And on that note—" She raised her nose toward the door. *"Adriana! Adriana!"*

Now Erik began to study the epistle.

"Adriana!" she blared again. "Dr. Gomara, do they have you twiddling with that fake old letter too?"

"I guess they do. Beautiful paper."

She focused her red spectacles on Marco. "You *have* to give that thing up, dearest. It's contaminating people—look, *two* new converts to your conspiracy theory in just under a day."

"I didn't tell you to give him the letter," Marco said in a thin voice.

I ignored him. "But Dr. Riccardi, I recognize this room. Antonio—or whoever authored Marco's letter—wrote about it. When he described the dinners they had here, before he was forced from the city. . . ."

In about seven minutes, Erik had rapidly absorbed the contents of the letter with his typical Evelyn Wood speed, agreeing that "Antonio" had taken pains to write about the room's decor. "My Italian's not great, but I think I just saw what you're talking about; it's here:

When did we last meet, before you Exiled my wife, Sofia the Dragon, and me? It was in the 1520s, I believe, just after I returned from America, in the few months when I was still allowed to feast at our family's palazzo. The dining hall was so lovely, I remember, full of mysteries and hints of treasure—with its friezes of golden girls, its secret passageways, its fresco of the Rape of Proserpine, and that gew-gaw I commissioned, namely Pontormo's gorgeous map of Italy.

Looking up from the letter, he compared the text to the room itself. "So, he talks about a *'dining hall with its friezes of golden girls, its secret passageways.'* And on the walls there are these very pretty gilt friezes. Check." He raised his face to the painted ceiling. "And check, the fresco. Then: *'And that gew-gaw I commissioned, namely Pontormo's gorgeous map of Italy.'* " He turned to the west wall, admiring the gold-leaf adorned map. "Check. It's all here."

Dr. Riccardi waved us off. "Let's at least have a *drink* if we're going to belabor the forgery again. Hello there—*Adriana?*"

Dr. Riccardi's protégé entered, carrying a jeroboam of red wine and a plate of tidbits.

"Have you been squalling for me, Doctor? I can't hear you through the heavy doors."

"Don't blame good Renaissance architecture for your bad behavior. *Amuse bouche?*"

"But certainly."

"Not those nasty livers."

"You will *love* them."

Adriana filled all our glasses before sailing through the back door. Dr. Riccardi pursed her mouth before turning her attention back to us.

"Cheers, then," she said. "To—to—Antonio."

"To Antonio," Marco agreed, clinking glasses with the doctor.

"*Per Antonio*," Domenico said hesitantly. He glanced at Blasej, who shrugged and drank.

Erik's glass remained untouched as he read the letter one more time. "Okay, I have the basic idea here. Antonio claims that when he was in Mexico with Cortés, he stole Montezuma's gold. Very nice! And it's also clear that he hated Cosimo, duke of Florence, because he exiled Antonio for—something. Being a 'Versipellis.' What's that, skin changer? Um—'werewolf'?"

"Exactly," I said.

"But he's having his revenge, as he's *hidden* the gold here in Italy, with all of these hints as to its location. And he also made up a map." Erik leaned back in his chair and laughed, loudly, his belly shaking. "So—*wow*." His big shiny face had a slightly electrocuted but happy expression. "This could be—this might be—incredibly—"

"I know!"

"But there's no map here."

"Not that we can find, no."

Erik and I swiveled our heads around, studying the room. The gilt frescoes of the ladies' faces stared into the distance, and my eyes strayed over the well-fed face of Cosimo. I looked over to the splendid framed map of Italy. This was book-size, exquisite. The cartographer had drawn the long boot of the country with billowing pen strokes. Mountain ranges and lakes were illuminated with scarlet lacquers, a reddish leaf-gold, and woad blue. Masterful Carolingian calligraphy designated the ancient cities of Romagna, Pons Aufidia, Scylazo, Malfi. . . .

Dr. Riccardi said, "As I have explained to Marco a million times, that letter does *not* bear the writing of my Antonio *il Lupo*."

"Antonio the Wolf," Erik said, sipping his Chianti. "*Lupo* means 'wolf,' right? People called him that because they thought he was a werewolf—the Versipellis business."

Dr. Riccardi poured him more wine. "Yes, Antonio had some sort of revolting medical problem—*the Condition*—and in his early Florentine career, that, combined with his habit of murdering people, inspired a local myth that he'd been *hexed*. The story transformed into an absolute *epic* after the expedition with Cortés, when people began to claim that Antonio and an African slave man of his were cursed by Montezuma in Mexico!"

"The slave we read about in the letter to Pope Leo X?" I asked.

"We think so. Montezuma purportedly transformed Antonio into a werewolf, and the slave into a vampire. But what *really* happened is that Antonio was just a literal monster. After his return from the Americas, he famously tortured his slave in a Venetian dungeon, using a golden mask that covered the mouth and nose, leaving only little tiny pits for the eyes. They called it the Tantalus mask—you know, Tantalus was punished by the gods, who wouldn't allow him to drink or eat but paraded food before his eyes. In prison, the mask performed the same function: the slave could see the meals displayed before him but never taste them."

Erik shook his head. "Poor bastard!"

"*Poor Fool*," Dr. Riccardi corrected. "That's what Antonio called him, the slave. 'The Poor Fool!' Or, just 'the Fool.' "

Marco stiffened at this. "Poor Fool? I don't remember that nickname. And I've been studying this letter for over a year. How could I have missed it?"

"No? Oh, I thought I told you—it's all in Sofia's journals.

Anyway, the rumor is that Antonio had the Fool slave clapped in jail because he tried to steal from him. Tried to snatch his gold, precisely—that's the story that our forgers here are capitalizing upon. Legend has it that Antonio secreted scads of the stuff out of the jungle, which he wanted to use to fund a revolution in Tuscany, to develop some sort of class of, what did he call them—"

"Warrior-aristocrats." Marco pronounced these words so acutely I was reminded again of his father's dreams of military dictatorship, and shivered. "Antonio performed those human experiments in Florence, and fought the Moors for their alchemical secrets because he wanted to lift his people to a higher plane—a *stronger and more select society.* Isn't that what he planned for?"

"Yes, well, happily, he gave up his beastly little utopia. After the slave's death, Antonio turned over the proverbial leaf. He quite peaceably returned to Florence, and even seems to have paid penance by burying the slave in a tomb just off the Medici crypt, behind a stone marked with a crescent moon—which is the sign of Islam *and* of the vampire and werewolf in folklore, of course. A marvelously grand chapel was much later built right around it—the Cappella dei Principi at the Basilica di San Lorenzo. People say it has been stalked by an African vampire ever since. And there *have* been one or two squeamish incidents at the chapel." Dr. Riccardi now spoke in a mock-spooky sotto voce: "Involving grave robbers, who died hideously after trying to break into the slave's coffin. It was as if their blood had been *sucked* out of their bodies."

Erik had been looking at me, then at handsome Marco, before drinking extremely deeply from his wineglass. "I've read those stories. There's an old wives' tale about a vampire who flaps around that chapel in the terrible form of Antonio's slave.

He's seeking revenge for his murder. But now he's supposed to be white-eyed, teeth dripping with blood, and offering his victims jewels, precious objects. If you accept them, you won't only die, but also be doomed to leave a corpse that looks something like a fruit roll-up."

"Bad luck to talk about that," Domenico murmured, shifting in his seat and muttering a prayer or complaint against this distasteful subject.

Blasej gently gestured at him to relax. "It's okay, Dom. Eat your dinner."

"My, your fiancé does seem to know a lot about this history," Dr. Riccardi enthused over their voices. "Miss de la Rosa—or will it soon be Mrs. Gomara?"

"*Nomen atque omen,*" Marco recited, evilly.

I peered intently at him, suddenly struck by that quote.

Erik leaned across me, toward him. "Who *are* you, anyway?"

Marco precisely adjusted his cuff links. "Still haven't made the connection? My name, my name? Haven't you heard it before—say, two years back?"

"Last year?"

"He's the colonel's son, Erik, that's what I had to tell you . . ." I would have finished this sentence, but my words trailed off as my breath came out quick and shallow. "What did you say?"

"I was talking to your friend about my name—"

"No, Marco, *the Latin.*" I felt a sparkling sensation in my mind. "Say it again."

Marco lit another cigarette and shot his goons a look. "*Nomen atque omen,* it's one of Antonio's favorite sayings—"

"Erik, read that part of the letter to me again. Where he writes that Latin bit."

He wrinkled his forehead at me. "Did you just say something about a . . . colonel?"

"Oh, did you just catch that?" Marco asked.

Erik threw up a hand. "Jesus, I still really don't get what's going on here. Are you people all *drunk?*"

"Not yet!" said Dr. Riccardi. "Though my girl could help us out on that account."

"Erik, read it—*read it.*"

"All right: '*As I take the destiny of the Medici more seriously than your idiocy, however, I have decided to honor your request. Our family Name requires it. After all, there was much wisdom to that old saying of the poet Plautus:* Nomen atque Omen—*one's name is one's omen.*' "

"A man's name is his omen." I sat very still, as the scraps of ideas blew around my mind. "A man's name," I repeated, slowly. "His *name*—"

All at once, I remembered Señor Soto-Relada's disturbing comment about the letter, from our phone conversation earlier in the evening: *And, if you are a de la Rosa, then . . . well, you'll figure it out. The de la Rosas always do.*

I looked up again at the map on the wall. It was brilliantly colored and as intricate as a mosaic. "That's the Pontormo map, right?"

"Adriana!"

"Dr. Riccardi, is that the Pontormo that Antonio—the forger— writes about? The original?"

"What, the map? Yes. Adriana!"

I could feel Marco watching me as I took the letter from Erik's grasp and studied it.

"I examined the map a year ago," he said. "But I couldn't find anything special about it."

Adriana had just entered the room. "The next course will be here directly, Dr. Riccardi. My duck in wine sauce and sour cherries."

"We need some more wine, and more of the *amuse*, dear."

"You've had quite enough."

"Stop being cheeky!" Dr. Riccardi made an expansive gesture.

"Bah—*you* stop being a nuisance." Adriana flashed her hand above her head before leaving the room.

The doctor bent toward us confidentially: "She's an immigrant. I have to be tough with her, you know . . . born in Algeria. But so intelligent. Six languages. A knack for theory. I'm paying for her education—not that she's grateful! She'd *eat* me if I let her. Savage little beast," she said wistfully.

I unfolded the letter to read out the passage that both Marco and Erik had quoted earlier:

> "*When did we last meet, before you Exiled my wife, Sofia the Dragon, and me? It was in the 1520s, I believe, just after I returned from America . . .*'"
> We feasted "*at our family's palazzo, in the dining hall with that gew-gaw I commissioned, namely Pontormo's gorgeous map of Italy.*"

"That's what he says—and then there's something else." I began to flip through the pages, carefully, until I found the closing section:

> *Included in this letter are two Ciphers that reveal the hiding places of four Clues I have scattered through your rival city-states, and that will lead you to the Fortune. One of these Ciphers is a riddle, and the other, as you see, is a map (or at least, you shall see it should you be able to look up from your feasting and banqueting, and pay nominal attention to what I am telling you).*

"Oh, God," I said.

"This is just wildness—it's these active imaginations your forgers are playing on," Dr. Riccardi said.

"How long has this map been here, Doctor?" Erik asked.

"Since 1528, thereabouts. Reframed in, what, 1912."

I said, "So it could have been here during the dinner parties he describes."

Marco quickly moved over to the map, gesturing to Blasej and Domenico that they should remain in their seats.

"Could there be codes written in here?" He squinted up at the map, its frame, its protective glass. "Something I missed?"

Short of breath, I said, "Erik—the line mentioning Pontormo. It's awkward, isn't it? We feasted *'in the dining hall and that gew-gaw I commissioned, namely Pontormo's gorgeous map of Italy.'* Namely. That's what got me thinking, when we started talking about—"

"Yes, right, your name, his name." Erik was parsing the letter over my shoulder.

"And then—look—toward the end: *'One clue is a riddle, and the other, as you see, is a map (or at least, you shall see it should you be able to look up from your feasting and banqueting, and pay* nominal *attention to what I am telling you).'* Pay *nominal* attention to what I am telling you."

"*Namely, nominal*—from, yes, the Latin—*nomen*—"

"*Nomen—nomen atque omen*. The Latin maxim: A man's name is his omen. Antonio writes that saying in the letter—he's *focused* on names and naming."

Marco reached his hand over his head, grazing the map's gilt frame with his fingertips.

"No, no, no, no touching," Dr. Riccardi ordered.

"I've gone over this a thousand times," said Marco. "But what I've never been able to understand is *why* would a man's name be his omen?"

"And which name?" Erik asked. "He calls himself the Wolf, and the slave's called—"

"*His* name," I said suddenly. "His *name*."

From the table, I slowly lifted the last translucent page of the letter, with its strange, wide, curling signature: Antonio Beato Cagliostro Medici.

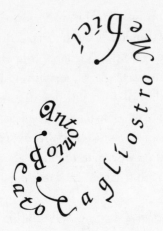

Erik's eyebrows skittered up his forehead as he looked at the wall. "Okay, I'm still getting up to speed here, but—that's *interesting.*"

"*Erik.*"

"Do you think—"

"Maybe. Can you—"

"Yes—"

"*Lift* me—"

We both stood up and practically ran over to the wall. Erik hip-butted Marco out of the way before crouching like an intra-mural wrestler, pulling down his straining jacket and extending his arms so that I could clamber on.

"One, two, three, *huff!*" He hoisted me onto his shoulders.

"Oh, dear Jesus Christ and Mary in Heaven," Dr. Riccardi flamed, "you're going to break something, you frightful idiots."

I reached up and placed the signature leaf onto the map. It fit the dimensions perfectly.

"It's like a transparency," I cried. "And the signature, it's tracing something—a route or some kind of diagram."

"Preposterous," Dr. Riccardi thundered, then, looking at the map sideways, was less sure. "What do you mean, diagram?"

"I can't—*see* what it marks through the glass."

"Blasej, what does it look like out there?" Marco muttered.

"Just a couple old farts, picking up pensions. One or two nobodies in the library."

"Good. Help me with this—also, give me a knife."

A glitter in the lamplight, as the blade was thrown through the air. Blasej loped toward Erik and me.

"Help you with what?" Dr. Riccardi asked, as Erik lowered me to the ground. "Why would you need a knife?"

The two brutes yanked the map off the wall before flipping it over to reveal its canvas and paper backing. Marco brought down the knife to tear the frame open with a great, loud *rip*.

"Even if you were right, which is impossible! This would be a matter for *experts—conservationists*," Dr. Riccardi squawked. "Good God, you cretin, *hands off—Adriana!*"

Marco pulled the map out of its frame, but with great care and delicacy. "Domenico, clear off a space on the table."

Erik's ruddy face twisted. "The lady said not to do that."

Marco did not so much as look at him. I still clutched the letter's signature page as a terrible, voluptuous anticipation began to tingle through me.

"Yes, Marco, stop it," I managed to say.

He looked at me over his shoulder. "I see *you*. Don't make me laugh." He carried the map over to the dining table, placing it down gingerly. He briefly touched the vellum, the reddish gold leaf, as if admiring the workmanship. "And Dr. Riccardi, you can't tell me you're not curious."

"This isn't the way we do things here—thuggishly—you of

all people should know that, Marco, you're a man of taste, of finesse—"

"Qualities that I have been heroically suppressing in order to withstand the constant sound of your chatter, Doctor—"

Their voices faded in my ears, as my concentration narrowed with such an intensity that my vision seemed reflected in a convex mirror.

The map glimmered on the table, its irresistible, half-visible ciphers of gold, woad blue, and crimson waiting to be changed by me.

I walked over to it in a fever.

The onionskin page shone like a fragment of light in my hand. I pressed it to the map, fitting the opal text to its intended lineaments.

This is what we saw:

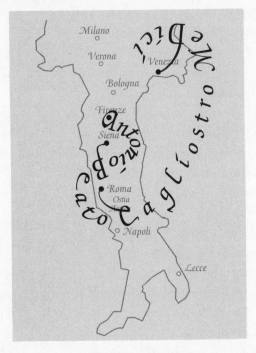

10

It's the four cities," I shouted through the room. "The ones in the rhyme."

"*A* in Antonio corresponds to Florence." Erik glared down at the table over my shoulder. "The *B* in—"

"Beato!" Dr. Riccardi butted her face against the other side of my head.

"Marks Siena," I said. "The *C* in Cagliostro is Rome, and . . . here, the *D* in Medici is for Venice. This gives us an itinerary. He's telling us—or, rather, Cosimo—to search the cities in this order."

"Oh, my, oh, no, you horrible children—*but* let me see that riddle again," Dr. Riccardi breathed all over the pages. "I do have to say, the letter *does* make more sense with this information. What's the second stanza— *In City One find a tomb? Where upon a Fool*— What was it?"

"*In City One find a Tomb / Where upon a Fool worms feed / One hand holds the Toy of doom / The other grips your first Lead*," Marco recited from memory.

"Yes. Don't you see how we need to bring in my experts? This is of critical importance. I *must* get the letter authenticated. City One must be *A*—that is *here*—in Florence. There was that crypt I was speaking to you about, Cappella dei Principi at the

Basilica di San Lorenzo, where Antonio interred his slave—the Fool."

"I wish you could have told me Antonio called him that name *before*, Isabel," said Marco. "This whole year I've been digging around the university's medical school, trying to find any records of the burial sites of the imbeciles young Antonio used for his human experiments. It hasn't been the easiest job."

"Wrong fools," she said.

"Why didn't I know that? I thought I studied all the important records."

The doctor flicked her eyes at me. "Perhaps you missed something."

"You know what this could mean?" I asked, just as Adriana walked in through the door, saying, "I forgot to ask if our guests like their duck rare or—*my God!*"

A look of scholastic ecstasy passed over Erik's face. "What could it mean? We could find Montezuma's gold, the Aztec idols, the calendars, the lost druidical gold books."

Dr. Riccardi had two bright spots on her cheeks. "Cellini, in his autobiography, wrote of rumors that Antonio brought back so much treasure it nearly sank his ship."

"Mary Magdalene, I told you people to behave yourselves— what happened to the Pontormo?" cried Adriana.

Marco smiled as he reached down to the table, where I had placed Antonio's signature page over the Pontormo map. With a twirl of his long pickpocket fingers, he spirited up the paper, and then slid the remainder of the leaves from the grasp of Dr. Riccardi, who blurted: "Hey, hold on. Give that back—"

"Marco, what's going on?" Adriana asked.

"They've gone crazy," Dr. Riccardi shouted, as most everyone began switching to manic Italian. "Signor, you must know that letter has to stay here!"

"Sorry," Marco said. "It's time that my friends and I took our leave."

"I'm afraid—that's not—possible." Dr. Riccardi's voice wavered into a banshee-like caterwaul as she snatched at the letter. "You must let me study it—if you only knew how valuable this could possibly be—"

"No—no—let go."

"You're going to *rip* it—"

"Give the doctor what she wants," Adriana ordered in a mortally serious voice.

Dr. Riccardi had her hands on Marco's shoulders, tugging at them with surprising strength. Marco yanked himself away, but she clung to him like a barnacle, her red hair waving over her shoulders.

"Let go of her, Moreno!" Adriana yelled.

"What the hell are you doing, man?" Erik thundered at Marco.

"Domenico," Marco spat.

The blond immediately sprinted over to the doctor, lifted her off his employer, and threw her splay-legged to the ground, as Marco said, "It really didn't have to come to this, you yappering old bird. But if you continue shrieking like that, I might just have to break your beak. And Adriana—for hell's sake—stop scampering around—"

Adriana did not hesitate. She sprang forward and began to expertly and brutally stab her sharp thin fingers into Domenico's thorax in a shocking display of self-help. "Dr. Riccardi—Dr. Riccardi—"

"My girl," the older woman cried, "get out of here!"

At my side, I heard Erik mutter, "Moreno," just as I saw Marco step backward from the women and open his jacket to reveal a dark steel pistol stuck in his inner pocket.

Instantly, all of us grew very still and open-mouthed.

He did not point it at anyone, only saying, softly: "Seriously, stop making a fuss, girls—yes, no screaming. We don't want those antediluvian guards to drag their walkers in here, do we? We can still all stagger out of here in relatively decent shape."

"Shit! Fuck!" Domenico was gagging.

"Except for poor Dom, I suppose."

Blasej ran over and smacked Adriana's face before examining Domenico's throat. "Moreno—man, stop blabbing and give it to her."

Marco grimaced, gave a short laugh. I was just barely able to translate his next words, muttered in a combination of Spanish and Czech: "I don't think you're a very good influence on me, Blasej. You know that? I think you're a bastard."

"Go on—you *fucking* talker!"

Erik had gone stiff with recognition. He stood next to me with huge eyes, his face shining with sweat. "Marco Moreno. That's his name. Lola—he's not related to that—no, no,—he's not connected with that other man—"

"Yes—he's Moreno's son."

"The colonel who tried to kill us—the one Estrada ripped up—in the jungle—"

"Marco," I seethed, *"put that gun away."*

"Hello—could it be in here . . . ?"

A stranger had just stumbled into our red-faced, arguing circle. I half-registered the noble-looking scholar who had been reading in the library, and had this minute wandered into the dining hall as if from another dimension. His dark pageboy flapped around his ears and his shiny spectacles tilted on his nose as he tiptoed in, squinting and murmuring to himself, with that large bronze magnifying glass in his hand.

With an air of supreme abstraction, the scholar blundered among us, in his houndstooth suit, his glossy shoes mincing in little steps as he skittered around the perimeter of the room. He gazed at the art on the walls through his bronze-handled glass, while chattering in Italian: "I say, I was told I could find a copy of Boccaccio in the athenaeum—but this doesn't look right. *Is* this the athenaeum? Or did I take a left turn when I should have taken a right—or a *right* when I should have taken the left?" He observed our little party for the first time. "Oh, cheers—am I interrupting something? I must have wandered into the wrong bloody room." He raised his magnifying glass, so his face swelled and dented and revealed his sudden attack of fright. "My, that wouldn't be a . . . gun . . . that you're holding, is it? Oh!"

This distraction was not wasted. Adriana pulled the doctor from the floor. The two women raced over to a section of the gilded friezes opposite the empty space that had held the map, pressing three different spots hidden between the beautiful golden ladies' faces staring out from the panel. A small door opened in the wall; they disappeared into the dark aperture and the door shut swiftly behind them.

Marco swore violently, as Erik gripped me and rasped, "How did he find you?"

"I don't know. He just showed up at the store."

"*Why?*"

"He thinks I can help him—"

"Well, you just did!"

Blasej kicked at the wall. "*Where'd they go?*"

"Bitches," growled Marco. "I stayed here a month, and the old woman never said a word about any secret doors—"

The scholar, in his panic, had wandered directly in front of Marco, hysterically waving the magnifying glass in the air. With both hands he suddenly grasped very hard and rather insanely onto the wrist and the hand with which Marco held his gun. "Oh, my, I do seem to have stuck my foot in it—you're not actually going to *use* that horrid thing on me, are you? I'm nothing but a poorly paid specialist in fifteenth-century majolica. I'm really just the most inconsequential person you could ever hope to meet, I assure you." The bronze magnifying glass clacked against the gun as he manhandled Marco.

"Shut up." Blasej yanked the scholar away from his boss, who sneered, "I thought you had a handle on the externals."

"I've got it handled, just let me do him—"

"'Do' me? *'Do'* me—whatever do you mean?" shrieked the scholar, who did not wait around to find out the answer to that question, as he hugged himself and ran haphazardly out the dining room's back door.

Domenico, still grasping his throat, grunted, "I'll get him."

"What about these other two?" Blasej rapped out.

"Erik knows more than I do, Marco," I keened. "He's better at code-breaking than I am."

"Sorry, what are you going to do, *shoot me with a magnifying glass?*" Erik barked.

Marco's face drained pale when he looked down to see that he now clutched the bronze magnifying glass instead of the gun—a cheap magic trick of the scholar's that I could barely comprehend with my ever-diminishing faculties. "How the hell did he do that?" He threw the glass so it shattered on the floor, then gestured at Domenico, who had turned back at the door.

"Give me your piece."

Domenico tossed a weapon and ran out. Marco pointed the pistol at Erik's tight-mouthed face. I fell to the ground, begging, "No, no, not him—not him."

"Quiet down for Christ's sake!"

"*Let Lola go.*" Erik remained standing, rumpled and heavily sweating, his voice suddenly whittled down to flat syllables. "You don't need her. I'll help you. You don't need two of us." His eyes were very steady and crazily observant, in a bizarre contradiction to the rest of his body, which began to tremble loosely in his navy suit as if he were having a seizure.

Marco took a long look at him, then me.

"Too many variables—" Blasej said.

Marco raised a finger, just as Domenico reappeared, breathing hard.

"Did he come back here?"

"What?"

"That guy. I can't find him anywhere. There's only like two rooms back there—"

"Forget him," Marco said. "We're leaving. And Blasej, move him out. We're taking him—she'll be no use otherwise."

Blasej spat, but said, "Fine. Where to now?"

But I already knew the answer to that question. I ran over to Erik and clutched him, shrilling, "Yes, just put that thing *away*. We're going. Where Antonio buried his Fool, the slave. The Cappella dei Principi at the Basilica di San Lorenzo. We're going to the crypt."

Rough hands clapped down on us. Erik and I were forced out of the dining room, upstairs, then made to wait while our captors took a short detour to gather some bags and supplies. After that came the long and silent march beneath the storm of gold lining the halls of the palazzo, beneath the barely cognizant gaze of security guards who were either so inured to Dr. Riccardi's dramatics or so deaf that they had not been alarmed by our stifled shouts. While we moved down the halls, back out the foyer, they mechanically nodded their greetings to us and our captors, as we were all the doctor's esteemed visitors, and so beyond suspicion, and help.

II

We hurried out into the dark city streets, navigating the cobblestones of the northward-reaching Via Camillo Cavour, to the Piazza San Lorenzo with its late-hour kiosks and Pisa figurine displays. Marco and the other two backpack-laden men walked behind us, and always I had the image of that weapon pointed through Marco's pocket at Erik's spine. For his part, Erik strode by my side, not looking at me, his expression struggling as we moved in a large half-arc toward our destination. He was not as panicked as before. He was not shaking anymore. But he did not look good—or even much like the same sweet goofball who had come blustering into the palazzo hours before, blathering about whiskey and standby flights. Sweat-stained, patchy-pale, his mouth moved silently. He also appeared so determined I would have sworn he had begun to plot something.

"This is it, the chapel," he said in a scratchy voice, when we'd reached a crossroads fifteen minutes away from the palazzo.

"*Good*, Erik." Marco gazed up. "You do know your Italian architecture, at least."

Above us loomed a four-story church, built of thick mustard-colored stones, its rotunda capped with a little red-tiled dome.

Barred by a spiked iron gate, its left side was obscured by towering metal scaffolds much like those we'd seen at the palazzo. Unbarred arched windows glinted on the third level. Marco, Blasej,
and Domenico quickly decided that these undefended windows
would be the best route to the crypt, though I could not yet tell
how we would reach them, even as they yanked us along. "Come
on." "Hurry up." "Move the legs." They waited for tourists to me-
ander down the street before pushing Erik and me toward the
gate's left side, to look at the scaffolding that wrapped around
the church: constructed of silver metal bars and wooden plat-
forms, the scaffold had been covered on its bottom third portion
by green serrated aluminum siding to keep troublemakers from
climbing up the framework.

I looked up: The sky was a rich shining black, and cloudless, though not empty. Tonight it hosted a large bright moon,
nearly full, and as white as fangs. In the presence of that witch-
ing *luna* and this ancient, haunted grave house, I had no trouble
imagining a caped *nosferatu* in the shadows. The evening's dinner
tales hideously filled my mind with a horror film of tomb-robbers
stretched out in a cold crypt, as thin as fish because they had
been drained of blood.

"Jump over the gate," Marco ordered. Domenico and Blasej
scrambled over the its sharp iron staffs, then dissolved into the
penumbra toward the scaffolding, so that I understood the plan.
"Now," Marco pressed me.

Erik also remained in shadow, and he was thinking hard; I
could feel it.

"How are we going to get in there?" he asked, in a queer,
dead-sounding voice.

"By climbing," said Marco.

"Climbing what?"

I removed my heels. "The scaffolding."

Erik and I bungled the effort, heaving and grunting before finally managing to hurl ourselves over the gate.

Marco light-footed over, pushing us forward through the moon mist.

As the bottom third of the scaffolding was covered by aluminum siding, Blasej and Domenico had already begun slicing up this metal skin with shears pulled from the backpacks. Quickly, they made a little door at its base. The cut metal flaps tweaked outward, leaving just enough space for a large man to crawl beneath, as they did, vanishing inside—and minutes later, I could hear the clanking of more tools; they were performing some sort of mechanical operation on the structure.

"Snipping the wires," Erik said. "These things are alarmed."

"Good to go." The unseen Blasej's voice echoed off the metal skin that enclosed him.

"You next." Marco showed us the gun again.

Erik ducked into the aluminum shell. I crawled beneath the metal sheet, Marco following after. Within the scaffolding, it was dark, cold, and claustrophobic. It *felt* forbidden. Above us rose a metal cage, ascending perhaps one hundred feet in the air and swaying back and forth as Blasej and Domenico capered up its ledges like acrobats.

The three of us stared up at that scaffolding in perfect fearful silence.

Then, without another word, we began to slip up the dark tower, toward the crypt that held a slave's ancient, deadly grave.

12

The scaffolding's metal cage ascended three hundred feet into the sky. In the night air, Erik appeared an unearthly, night-colored figure above me as he scrabbled up the metal bars.

I hoisted myself up one bar, then two, passing the scaffolding's first wooden platform as the muscles in my neck and arms burned. Far above us, Blasej and Domenico spoke in low bursts, before there came the faint sound of shattering glass. I kept moving. The cage was unsteady and wobbled and creaked. We climbed above the aluminum wrapper, scaling halfway up the scaffolding, until we overtook a second story of barred windows. Below us was the stony street and its few pedestrians who could not see us for the dark.

"Do you think you can make it?" I whispered. We had just passed a second platform.

"It's getting high." Erik croaked and pulled himself up another bar.

"Don't look down," Marco demanded below me.

We climbed another level, then another, until we reached a death-height. My palms slid like grease on the bars. Sweat dripped down my neck.

Erik tottered just below the top window, then his feet skipped, tripped. He scrambled on the bars, as if he were running on a rolling log. From his throat came a low terrified wheeze.

"Erik!"

He slipped. He hung from his sweating fists. All I could see were his shadowed feet jerking. I clawed my way up with a hellish speed, possessed by a hallucination of his heavy body cartwheeling past the chapel's delicate tracery, the golden stone, then smashing dead on the ground.

"Don't touch me!"

"He's right—all three of us could go." Marco reached up and grasped my naked foot.

"You're going to *fall!*"

I snatched hold of Erik's pant leg so that he hung limp, and very still, from the high bar. Slowly, he touched his toes down, easing his feet completely onto the bar directly below him. He clung to the scaffold and ground his teeth.

I listened to his rough breathing.

And then, without speaking again, he began to climb once more.

Marco and I followed. We dragged ourselves up the scaffolding's next level, toward the top, unbarred window, which we could see had already been smashed open.

Erik eased one leg into the window, then another. He held out his hand, hauling me into the open circle framed by glass teeth, which gave me an instant image of passing through the mouth of a fierce supernatural beast as I landed on the top floor of the Medici chapel.

We crumpled to the cold floor, gasping and pressing our hands to our hearts.

"Um, okay! Guess what. We are *never* going do that again," Erik said after a minute.

I hugged him. "Are you all right?"

"My neck's not broken." He kissed my mouth.

I kissed back, but then put my hand up at the sound of thumping, a voice. "Ssssshhh—do you hear something?"

"Oh, God, I don't know!" He leaned his head back on the wall.

"Do you hear something?"

"Yes." Marco came sliding up toward us through the cool halls.

From around the corner were the concussions and echoes of a struggle between men, as Marco padded past us on silent feet. This left Erik and me suddenly, briefly, on our own—we looked at each other by the light of the window-framed moon.

"Come on," I whispered. "We'll climb back down."

"Move your butt!"

But just here, in the dark distance of the crypt, we heard a man begging for mercy in a thin, hooting voice.

"Please, please, I didn't see anything. I have two kids, mister, I have two kids, I have a wife, I have, just don't—don't—"

Over this, like a percussion, another person was making a gargling, gagging noise.

I stopped. "Oh, no. They've got someone—"

"Damn." Erik's face contorted, even as he ran toward the sound.

On the landing of the chapel's moon-frosted staircase, I saw that Domenico and Blasej had cornered two guards. Blasej held on to an elderly man in a gray suit. This victim's face was loose and slick and shaking as the Czech unbelievably sawed back and forth on his throat with a long knife. Another man, sandy-haired, his age obscured by the frenzied twisting of his features, crouched by the balustrade as he shrilled his pleas to Domenico, who hovered over him, grim and all business. Marco observed the murder with his back turned toward me; I couldn't see his expression while he silently watched Blasej perform his gruesome work.

As Blasej's arm joggled up and down to cut the throat, the dead man's arms dangled at his sides. His mouth hung open in a melancholic gape, the eyes thrust blindly from their sockets. Black blood streamed down the quivering, white-shirted chest to the ground as the body was hacked and hacked.

"Sssssssh!" Blasej hissed, darting back, holding up one hand.

Domenico leaned forward, croaking, "What?"

"Nothing. Cut myself on the knife."

"You're in such a hurry you don't ask me first?" Marco's voice was low and clipped.

"This kid got antsy."

"Idiot. Ass! *God*—get rid of it!"

Blasej pushed the corpse over the balcony. It hurtled to the lower ground with a dreadful liquid crunch.

"Now what?" Blasej turned and his face was mother-of-pearl; his thin eyes fixed with great attention on Marco, as the remaining guard continued to cry, nearly singing: "Jesus, God, Mary, Jesus God, Mary, Jesus God—"

"Marco," Blasej said. "We're here now. This is it, you've got the gun. If this goes wrong, I don't want Dom and me to be the only boys with a problem—"

"Let me assure you," Marco replied in a voice so hoarse he was nearly mute. "No one will cut me a break."

"Just to *make* sure—"

Marco removed the gun from his pocket and fiddled with it

for a second, but then shook his head. *"I told you to wait for me before you did anything—"*

Blasej grabbed the pistol. "Agh—fine. I'll do it. But this is *it*—"

"No, no, no, no," Erik and I both screamed.

Blasej quickly aimed the gun at the crying man, and a soft, silenced *pop* issued forth.

The man's gray jacket seemed to open out, as if lifted by spirit fingers. His chest moved, jumped. That was all, just that little tremble, that little shiver. His head rolled over, the mouth kissing the air. There were two more pops, two more quiverings. Still the man lay on the ground, breathing, or hiccupping, his severed lungs unable to give air to his screams.

Marco wavered slightly, before Blasej accurately shot the man's head, which opened up into a living monstrosity made of black and red flesh and white bone.

"You have such a light touch, Blasej," Marco said hysterically. "You have *such* finesse. You gorilla. You fool!"

Blasej tucked the gun into his belt. "Well. Now there're two less problems."

Erik and I were dead quiet. I was on the floor, twisting in horror. Domenico pushed this second guard's body over the balcony, tipping it legs over head. When I scrabbled toward the balustrade, I could see the crypt's carved marble flooring. Dead men's names had been delicately chiseled into the stone, the dates of their short lives incised in Roman numerals, their piety marked by the engraving of the Latin cross.

But now these markings were obscured by encroaching blood. Below us, the two dead men were suspended within this gruesome velvety-liquid frame. The moon flooded down on the corpses, turning their red blood charcoal and their stunned faces paper white.

Erik was shaking violently again, but he said to me, steadily, "Are you hurt?"

"*Oh no, oh, no, oh, no—*"

"Lola. Calm down—right now!"

"Get them up." Marco's words came out in a shocked jumble as he wiped his clean hands off on his pants, his arms, nearly clawing himself. "Okay. Fine. We have to do this. Oh—people will be here soon."

"You just *killed him.*" I nearly passed out in gross physical fear as Blasej shoved me away from the balcony into the recesses of the chapel. We all stumbled past the sight of the bodies, the stairs, more unlit chambers, and turned twice, right.

"Lola, be quiet," Erik said. "Seriously, shut your mouth."

I did. I was panting, but I clamped down, watching him. Erik walked more swiftly now, and I had trouble reading his almost weirdly fierce expression. I didn't understand what he was thinking or planning.

Erik held up his hand as the men turned around a corner. "No, that's not the way." He said this to Marco in that hard-edged stranger's voice.

Marco stopped. "What—what do you mean?"

Erik showed his teeth. "Do you even know where you're going?"

"I thought the crypt was here—"

"No, let's get this over with. And tell your friends to get out their flashlights."

Within the space of a few seconds, Erik had taken over the lead. He assuredly brought us into a raven-black hall swept with the stars of Blasej's and Domenico's Maglites. The air grew cold and moist as we felt our way to the threshold of a stone room. The Cappella dei Principi was high-ceilinged and night-veiled.

Glorious mosaics glistened over the walls of the sepulcher. Made of richly colored Italian hard stone, the panels had been cut into the forms of lions, fleurs-de-lis, coats of arms, griffins, crosses, and urns.

Erik moved in first, pointing where Domenico's and Blasej's flashlights should lead, so that for a moment he looked like a magician, directing diamond-colored ghosts who flitted back and forth above their graves.

He crouched down.

"Oh, God help me, did you find it?" Marco called out.

"Here. This is it. This must be it. Lola, tell me the riddle again."

"I can't," I wailed. I kept on seeing the man's throat being sawed by the knife. "I can't remember. I can't remember."

Marco took the letter from his jacket pocket and fumbled with the pages, blinking at them. "I can't—*read* this." He pressed his hand to his eyes. "I can't think—"

"Give it to me."

Erik gently took the papers, and read out:

IN CITY ONE FIND A TOMB

WHERE UPON A FOOL WORMS FEED

ONE HAND HOLDS THE TOY OF DOOM

THE OTHER GRIPS YOUR FIRST LEAD.

Marco recaptured the letter from Erik, who, from his hunkering position, brought up his hand to touch one of the colored mosaic panels. Domenico's flashlight concentrated immediately on this object in a white, clear rush.

Crafted into the shape of a lozenge, the panel was alabaster white. In its center glimmered a black sickle moon.

Erik swung his head over and with large, watchful eyes homed in on Marco as if he were looking for a target hidden on the man's body.

"The Fool you're looking for is buried here."

Erik was *tempting* him. I could hear it. I knew this soft voice of his, which was a ghost's version of the irresistible one he used with me when he glamoured me with stories or lured me during sex.

Marco stared at my lover. Slowly, his features sharpened.

He couldn't help but take the bait.

13

The walls of the crypt were covered with hundreds of mosaics. A square panel displayed a porphyry griffin nestled next to an obsidian eagle, then a turquoise snake. At the bottom of the wall shone this black-and-white moon sign.

Marco bent into Domenico's and Blasej's flashlight beams, revealing his tear-shining, greedy face.

"Remember what Dr. Riccardi said." Erik tapped the icon. "The slave—the *Fool*—is buried behind the sign of the moon."

The symbol swam into my view and I fixed my madness on it. "The sign of the Moor."

"Perhaps," Marco grunted, having managed to regain some control. "All right then. Let's do this. Boys, break it open."

Blasej extracted from the backpacks long ropes, pulleys, and two small axes, which the men heaved powerfully and hideously at the mosaics, crushing and destroying them.

Then, there it was: Behind the shattered stones, interred within the wall, rested a plain black coffin.

"You were right," Marco breathed.

Blasej and Domenico worked quickly to haul it out by the ropes and pulleys. They grunted; they strained. They pulled the coffin from the wall with so much force that the rope peeled back skin from their palms, until it crashed to the floor.

It was huge, made of tremendous slabs of onyx marble, now cracked and covered with dust.

"Open it."

They couldn't at first. Blasej and Domenico leaned over the casket, kicking at its immense stone lid, which had slid several inches but not completely off. They gripped it with their fingers and pressed with the heels of their hands.

"Hurry it *up*," Marco demanded in a shaking and acid Italian.

"It's heavier than it looks," said Domenico.

"Cool out, Marco, it won't be a problem." Blasej sucked on his hand. "Come on, Domenico. Let's do this."

Domenico bent back down and lugged. "Okay, okay. It's heavy as a—"

Blasej remained standing. "Remember what I taught you—use your legs."

"I'm trying—"

"Try harder."

"*Help* me."

"I'm busy thinking—"

"Don't start with that."

"What, I'm planning this job—"

"You *always* say that."

"I'm always the one who looks after you, Domenico—and besides, I cut my fingers, that guy put up a fight." Blasej lifted his right, blood-gloved hand. This was the injury he'd received when he'd assassinated the first old guard.

Marco slapped the hand away. "Everybody, *push*! I need to see what's in there!"

As did I. I am not proud to admit it. I was still sick from the violence I had just witnessed. But I was so damnably curious that it didn't stop me from walking right up to the coffin and pressing against that slab of marble hard enough that the veins flared out of my arms and my eyes rolled back in my head.

"We've got it." Blasej skidded away as the tumbling cover sent up a white cloud of dust.

Erik bent down to me, hissing, "Be careful. If the stories I've read about this thing are true—"

"What could happen?"

"I don't know yet. Some kind of—"

"Excellent!" Marco blurted. "Look—*look*."

The dust billowed, lightened, cleared. We all inched forward to stare into the coffin.

This dead man had been tortured and starved, it was true. The brittle, twisted skeleton, some of which remained preserved in the coolness of its tomb, had its skull trapped by a large, glittering, red-gold helmet. From beneath its caul of dust and webs, this hideous egg-shaped cage covered the entire face, leaving only slits for the eyes and the nose. A wide gold band completely covered the mouth. This was the Tantalus mask of Dr. Riccardi's dinnertime story: The helmet obscured the victim's entire face, leaving only eye and nose slits so that he could have seen and smelled the fragrant dishes paraded before him in his Venetian cell while he shriveled to death.

"Oh! The Virgin!" Domenico blurted, taking several steps back and crossing himself.

"That gold thing must be worth a lot," Blasej said. "How do you get it off?"

Marco said, "Just take off the head—but not yet. There's something else in here that we need." He looked at me: "What should I be looking for?"

As Erik gripped the sides of the coffin, his eyes searching and scavenging the body for clues, I turned to Marco, spitting, "You're doing all this because you want to fund another war? They were just two old men, Marco. The guards—what the *hell* is wrong with you? *Warrior-aristocrats*, I heard you at dinner. You're as crazy as your father!"

"Watch it, Lola."

"And all it got him was *dead*!"

Marco's cheeks trembled. "Yes, you would know all about that, wouldn't you?"

"He died like a fool—"

"It's true"—he took a step toward me, then another—"Daddy's wasn't quite the hero's exit."

"Stay away from her, Moreno," Erik said in a low voice.

But Marco wrapped his arm around my waist and squeezed. "Yes, it's *much* better to go out like Antonio, all flashing and blazing on the Siena battlefield—using that weapon of his—what was it again? Some sort of witchcraft. It's worth looking into; I must check up on that. Because a man's method of dying is the best evidence of the way he lived. Don't you agree?"

"In the colonel's case, yes."

"And in your father's too."

"What do you mean?"

"Oh, Lola, de la Rosa died like a dog, here in Italy. It was humiliating. He went out like a filthy beggar."

I forced myself not to react.

"It didn't surprise me at all, though." Marco stroked my cheek and mouth in a tender, shocking gesture. "As the colonel explained to me after my cousin was killed, only cowards plant bombs, then dash away. It's less personal that way. Less—intimate."

"*Don't touch her again—*"

I jerked my face away to see Erik's eyes and lips stretching out in horrible, almost deforming fury.

Marco taunted him by running his fingers through my hair before pushing me away. "Ugh. Control him. And get them to tell us what they know."

Domenico and Blasej snagged hold of our necks to thrust our faces deep into the coffin. Our noses and lips hovered less than an inch away from the grisly remains, so we inhaled the dust floating up from the time-eaten hands of the slave. Each hand held an object, just as Antonio's riddle hinted: *In City One Find a Tomb / Where upon a Fool worms feed / One hand holds the Toy of doom / The other grips your first Lead.* Immediately, I saw there *was* a dangerous either/or choice to be made: One of the skeleton's tight claws, turned palm-side up, clutched a large, green jewel, a thick clog of grime nearly obscuring its delicate carvings. The other bony hand was also clenched but turned down. It held something round and metallic that I could not make out.

Erik squeezed his eyes shut, whispering in so sparse a voice I could just hear, "Don't touch anything, don't touch anything."

Louder was Domenico's breathing above me. High and quick and shallow. All at once I remembered his soft-brained reaction to the dinnertime tales of vampires and werewolves. And he'd crossed himself in panic at the sight of the corpse. He had an Achilles' heel. Yes. He was *superstitious.*

"Look at the body, Domenico." I squalled at him like a witch. "Did it just move? They say vampires wake when their coffins are disturbed—do you really want to do this?"

"Shut up."

"Look at the mask. No wonder there were stories about *nosferatu* haunting the crypt. Whoever thought this up was a monster. Do you think those rumors about bloodsuckers are true?

I heard there's something in this place that attacks you on the neck, like a bat."

"Blasej." Domenico shifted his weight from side to side.

"You're fine, man."

"Have you heard about the man they found in here," I shrilled, "with no blood in his veins? Attacked by some kind of ghoul."

"Blasej, she's giving me the creeps."

Marco ordered: "Enough of this!"

"No problem, boss." Blasej still had one hand on Erik's neck, and with his free fingers, he slipped his bloody, long knife from his belt. "Domenico, relax, *odpočívej!* Don't I always watch after you? You just keep by me, and this'll be fast money." He flipped the glinting knife in his hand, with an amazing agility that turned the blade into a pinwheel, a star. He carved at Erik's neck, so blood flashed down his collar.

"*AAAAAGHHH,*" I screamed.

"WAIT— I'VE GOT IT. I'VE GOT IT," Erik blared, holding his hands up in surrender.

"What?"

"Ugh." Erik gripped his neck, the blood seeping through his fingers. "There. Look at that. What do you see?"

"Nothing."

"Look closer." Erik pointed down to the slave's powdering hand bones, the upturned claw with the green stone darkly glinting in the one-time palm.

"What's that?" Blasej bent closer to the corpse, shining the flashlight. "Is that an emerald?"

Marco barked: "What is that thing? Don't touch that."

But Blasej had let go of Erik and reached down into the box. "It is. It's *carved.*"

Erik narrowed his eyes. "It looks valuable. And it's just moldering away in here—"

"Don't get jerked around by this guy, Blasej," Domenico warned.

"I've almost . . . *got* it." Blasej tugged at the bones to get at the emerald. He touched the jewel with both hands, twisting the skeleton, snatching it from the slave's hand. "It feels funny." He stepped away from the coffin, his back to me.

"Blasej." Domenico had me by the shoulders. "What are you doing? Let's hurry up."

Erik stood up, facing me. He stared at Blasej, whose head I could see bent over his treasure. A look of satisfaction passed over Erik's face.

"Blasej. *Blasej.* Let me see." Domenico released me and went to his friend.

Erik ripped off his jacket, moving quickly and viciously over to Marco, who thrust his hand into his jacket for the gun. But Erik raised his fists and brought them down on Marco's face, smashing his eyes and his cheeks as if he would kill him.

I was running. I was electric-brained and screaming. My hands were outstretched. Erik hauled back and hit him again as Marco tried to shield his face with his arms.

Marco sprang away. With his left hand he landed a precise crushing punch on Erik's neck, sending him colliding to the ground. I grappled my arms around Marco's back and with spasmodic jerks worked to wrench his right arm around his back. I clawed my other hand around his paper-crackling chest. The letter and gun were in his jacket pocket—I scratched at him to get the weapon out, but with his left hand he easily slid out the gun and neatly swung it up toward my face in a rotating crosswise maneuver that was as lucid and unexpected as a baseball player's pitch. The sharp metal cudgeled me hard, high on the forehead, and a spray of pure watery light blew into my eyes. I heard another metallic *clang*, and then felt a bright, cold agony as the floor rushed up to my face.

I shook my senses clear to see a flash of dark limbs. From the men's squirming bodies came the dim *pop* of a silenced shot— mosaics on the other side of the room exploded. I heard a viscous thwack before Marco rolled away from Erik. And I saw then that something desperately wrong was happening to him, to Erik. He had been somehow *replaced*. His eyes puffed and his lips clenched back over his teeth like a snake's.

"Erik!"

He only glared at Marco, who had a bite mark on his cheek that throbbed blood down his face, and the gun was free and pointed straight at the head of my lover.

"Blasej. Domenico! Help me out! What am I paying you for?"

Even as he brayed out those words, Marco jerked his head toward the gold-masked bones. He scuttled backward, the gun useless in his shaking hand. His eyes jutted from his skull.

From behind us, Erik and I could hear a moist and thick gurgling.

Domenico was screaming.

Blasej stood before the coffin, staring into the distance as if he had gone blind. He was choking, drowning. Tears streamed from his eyes as his mouth inflated with agony. His face twisted and paled. His cheeks sank into his head. The cut fingers that had touched the emerald were shriveled black, as a crimson line dripped from his lips. The blood ran down his chin, his chest. His body shuddered in a horrifying, elbow-flailing dance of death until his knees collapsed. He was still making the wet sounds in his throat when he fell onto his side.

With a heave and a spirt of blood, the noises ceased.

"Blasej!" Domenico blundered toward the corpse, dropping his flashlight. Blasej's face had shrunk and his hand had withered into a blackened claw. Domenico crouched over his friend, gagging as he sobbed. Though I'd thought him the weaker-brained of the crew, he proved intelligent enough not to touch the tainted body. Nor would he linger in this booby-trapped tomb any longer. He shook his head in a rage, still crying, scowling over at Erik. But he was done for now.

"Marco."

No reply. Marco raised his hand and nervously bit at his finger. He looked ill.

"Marco." Domenico spat out the words. "Time to go."

I crawled over to Erik in a daze. Half of Marco's face shone with dark blood, giving him a hideous resemblance to a harlequin.

"Why are you doing this to us?" I demanded.

"I want— I want—"

"*What?*"

"My . . . family . . . *back!*"

"I can't give that to you."

"Let's go!" Domenico shouted. He picked up a backpack before running from the room with fast crashing steps.

The crypt went utterly silent as Marco, Erik, and I stared at one another.

"What should I do now?" Marco murmured to himself in the hush. He still held the gun.

"You should make peace with me," I said, shocking myself.

His eyes were on me, fixed and bloodshot. "Peace."

"I mean it. I'm serious. Make peace with me, Marco. At the palazzo you said you'd give me a chance—remember? So do it. Let's forget all this."

He smiled or sneered or wept at me, his mouth distending. "Forget my father? Do you know what I saw in his coffin, stitched up, ugly—*That wasn't him!* How can I get him out of my head? Like this?" He began violently beating at his forehead with his hand. Then he hit his own temple with his gun. "Like *that*? How can I, how can I, how can I?"

"What you should *do* is get out of here," Erik threatened. He was crouched on all fours, his eye bleeding.

Marco touched his gashed cheek, stared down blankly at the gun. He looked over again at Blasej, jerked his head away, and squeezed his eyes shut. "Yes, right," he said after a long time, standing up. "That's the better idea." His teeth were bloodstained. "This is your day, isn't it? I've had enough, and you're lucky, lucky, lucky, lucky, lucky, lucky."

And then Marco simply left us. He wrapped his arms around himself and walked backward, disappearing into the shadows. We listened as his steps broke into a run, dashing down the echoing corridors of the crypt, shouting after his lackey. They smashed their way out of the church through another window.

"You stay away!" Erik's mouth tore open, and his face was red and wet.

But there was no one there anymore.

The flashlights scattered on the chapel floor. Dropped on the ground, their beams haloed around us. Erik and I stayed on the ground, shaking, pressing our mouths together in mad kisses.

"Okay, okay, okay, okay, okay, okay, okay." Erik stopped the kissing to start hugging me convulsively tight, trying to calm himself down. "You all in one piece?"

"Yeah."

"Am I all in one piece?"

"I think so."

"Oh man, oh man, oh man. I was going to *kill* his ass."

"I know. You looked—for a minute—you seemed—"

He began shaking his hands in the air, hooting, "Oh my God. Yes. I got—mad. Agh. Oh, Lord!"

"Like an *animal*."

He ran his shaking fingers under his eyes. But he looked more like himself. "I need a drink. I need a Campari. I need an ibuprofen. I'm out of my mind." He touched his temples. "Those guards outside are dead!"

"Yes."

"I killed him." He turned to peek at Blasej's corpse, and stared. "I whacked that guy. Blasej. I totaled him. I saw it— I saw the things— The green stone. The emerald. I'd read about those other robbers—of this grave—like Dr. Riccardi and I were talking about. They'd touched jewels. And died. I was hoping—and then it did. He did."

"Thank God!"

Erik pressed his cheeks. "I thought we were going to die. Oh, oh, oh, thank you, Princeton. Thank you, Princeton graduate seminar on the Medici." He turned toward the door where Marco and Domenico had disappeared. *"Don't fuck with my woman, motherfucker!* I'm dangerous! I've got . . ." he began laughing and crying. "A Ph.D. Christ!"

"Erik, Marco got away with the letter," I finally said.

"Okay, but I'm not going to run after him and ask for it back. Because punching and biting people and . . . assassinating them make me feel really *hideously* gruesome."

"And there's something else in the coffin besides the emerald."

He was quiet for several seconds, but then looked at me from under his lashes. "Oh, you think I didn't see that?"

"Just pointing it out."

The silence crystallized between us. Our eyes locked. Even

as we were bleeding, wild, and in the awful presence of that dead red-haired man, we were both thinking of it.

"It's in the skeleton's other hand," I whispered.

We eased apart. The room felt colder than before. The destroyed fragments of griffins and lions shivered across the gaudy walls. Slowly, we craned our heads around to look at the black stone box and the motionless figure lying next to it.

The first clue was still secreted in the coffin.

14

Erik and I approached the helmeted slave. Blasej had tumbled to the flag floor before us, impeding the way. One of the flashlights focused hot silver light upon his leather shoes, and the right foot's was untied. This miniature negligence somehow made the body more human to me, more pathetic. The corpse's head lolled from the white collar, freakishly marred by the mouth that had collapsed inside the jaw. The face looked shattered and the open eyes sunk into the skull. The hand clutching the emerald looked like twigs charred black by a fire.

Erik kneeled by the body. "It does look as if he's lost blood." He shook his head. "Yes, you sure are *dead*, Monsieur. Blagh—vile. You look terrible."

"Those stories you were telling at dinner—about demons bearing deadly gifts—"

He looked up at me and nodded. "Were a warning. This is your toy of doom. It must have poison smeared on it. Blasej's fingers were cut—whatever it was, it got into the blood."

We circled the remains, careful to avoid the contaminated hand. Erik picked up the flashlight and drew near the opened tomb.

For one moment I was pained, first with a vision of the dead old men outside, who then quickly metamorphosed into a murky image of Tomas de la Rosa lying in a similar box somewhere in this country, with his eyes closed, his hands crossed over his chest. *He died like a dog,* Marco had said. *Like a filthy beggar.* But I had never met the man, or even seen a clear photo of him, and so could not hold the picture—and then everything faded away when a shadow passed over the vivid remnants at my feet. It quavered over the skeleton, which appeared to jump and twitch like an animated puppet or a bedeviled effigy.

"What?"

We wheeled around. But we saw only the jet-wreathed walls, the shimmering colors of the stone mosaics.

"It's nothing—it's nothing," I said.

Erik stared back for a long time, pale and menacing. But then he relaxed. "No. It's not them. They're gone. It's no one."

At our feet, the skeleton remained unmoved in its bier, its bones tweaked and dented from Blasej's rummagings. The slave's gold torture mask gleamed beneath a lace of spiderwebs, and would have resembled the helmets of the Homeric Greeks but for the bars across the mouth. The ribs of the body had crumbled into splinters. The hand that had clutched the emerald had disintegrated into powder.

"There's a piece of metal in the skeleton's other hand," I said.

"It's some sort of— What's this?" He hunched down. "It's some sort of *coin.* What was the riddle—

IN CITY ONE FIND A TOMB

WHERE UPON A FOOL WORMS FEED

ONE HAND HOLDS THE TOY OF DOOM

THE OTHER GRIPS YOUR FIRST LEAD.

I followed these grim directions, leaning down, beginning to pry apart the slave's fragile fingers using my dress hem as a skin guard. The complex knots of the knucklebones softened into ash at my touch.

"Hold on. I've got it—some of the bones are still—stiff."

"Be careful, Lola!"

"Here!"

I pulled the brilliant gold disk loose. It spanned my palm; its carved surface shedding sparks of red-amber light. I'd seen a similar color of metal only in one sacrificial gold bowl installed in a Mexican archaeological museum. It was pure, soft, touched with pink. And it had hallmarks engraved within it.

"It's a medal," I said, stunned.

Erik gripped his head with both hands. *"A talisman."*

Marks that resembled an abstract flower swirled in the center of the massive coin. I had been expecting an Aztec or Mayan symbol, and so had trouble interpreting the medal's elaborate and curving lines. Finally I realized with a throbbing detective joy that I was looking at a European character written in densely foliated high-Gothic calligraphy.

In that death house, Erik and I pressed close together to read Antonio Medici's first clue.

15

A n *L*!" Dr. Riccardi hissed excitedly two hours later in the police-packed sitting room of the Palazzo Medici Riccardi. She perched on the edge of a black leather sofa between Erik and me, surreptitiously examining the gold medal she held in her hands. Adriana sat across from her with an exhausted if satisfied look on her reddened face. "That's delicious—it's going to spell some sort of password, yes? What *could* it be, do you think? There are only a thousand words that start with *L* in Italian: *lazo, loto, leva, luce, lido* . . ."

I shook my head. "It's probably not going to start with *L*. Antonio said the ciphers were out of order. Remember, they have to be recombined after they're all recovered."

"So delightfully *tricky*."

Adriana leaned forward to squint at the traceries of vines and blooming roses obscuring the medal's legibility. "Here, let me see it. How can you even tell what it is?"

"When I first looked at it, I thought I was having that special amnesia that strikes you after traumatic episodes," a blasted-looking Erik answered. "You know, aphasia. When you can't read anymore? But then I realized it was just that the letter was so ornately carved."

Erik and I had returned to the palazzo from the crypt three hours before, but our trauma remained evident in our faces' burst blood vessels, as well as the confusedly multilingual manner in which we had answered police interrogations about Marco Moreno, dead bodies, guns, and poisonous gems. Now surrounded by six officers, all standing sentinel in response to Dr. Riccardi's earlier shrieking emergency call, we had not had a chance to talk since our reappearance. We'd been peppered not only with official queries but also the doctor's extremely enthusiastic response to our recovery of Antonio's first clue, a "fabulous find," which she encouraged us not to share, just yet, with our protectors.

"Yes, it's beautiful work." She covered the medal with her other hand and looked up at a police officer standing by a lamp several feet away. He blinked his eyes so slowly that he seemed to fall momentarily asleep whenever they closed.

"Doctor." Adriana huffed at the concealment of the artifact. "What are you doing?"

"Well, I do think it's best if we keep this discovery among ourselves. What if that detective scurrying around here thinks it's evidence? My God! We won't see it again for sixteen years! They're keeping us up half the night with these interviews as it is—it's already midnight."

"It's lasting this long because of how much you talk," the younger woman said happily.

Dr. Riccardi touched a red raised spot on her protégé's cheek, the welt marking where Blasej had struck her. "Did I tell you how clever Adriana was? Saving me like that. Rushing me over to the frieze, then pressing the secret button!"

"It was incredible," I agreed, as we all looked over to the gilt striping the walls.

"Actually, I was kind of wondering why you didn't take *us* with you, to the secret special hiding place," Erik asked.

"All I can say is *thank God* the Medici were such filthy paranoiacs," said Adriana.

"She just *hurled* me through the secret passageway—it winds all through the house—"

"They never could have found us, even if they'd tried."

"Even if they'd tried! And we just ran away, laughing, really, at their stupidity."

"To try and mess with us."

"And now if they try to get back into the palazzo, my friends here will kill them." Dr. Riccardi fluttered a hand at the police officers before looking back down at the medal. "Though that Blasej person is already dead, isn't he?"

"Dead as a stuffed moose," Erik said.

"As you could have been too—look at your head." Dr. Riccardi pointed at the gauze that not only covered up the wound in my hairline but also clashed with the chic black slacks, flats, and ballet-necked sweater Adriana had lent me. "And all for this medal—though it *is* a charming bauble. I wish that we could go galloping around the country with you, researching this mystery."

Erik widened his eyes, touching the bandage a medic had stuck on his neck. "Yes, I suppose that's what we're going to do now, isn't it? I hadn't thought that far ahead. We're going to go limping all over Italy to find booby traps designed to really painfully kill Cosimo—"

Dr. Riccardi hallooed: "Of course you're pressing onward—Lord, if you don't go, then who's going to go scrambling after that fiendish imposter? Marco. I thought he was my friend. Oh, no, you're *going*. Let him get away with this? Police will take ages to catch him—and you have to get the letter back from him, after

all. It's imperative! I can't, you see! There's so much work to do
here. The Pontormo, after all—what a disaster!"

"It didn't seem that badly damaged," Adriana said.

"It's practically ruined! And then Adriana here is going to
have to do a complete inventory. Who knows what that Marco
creature has been stealing while my back was turned?"

Adriana's face readjusted completely to its former expression
of pestered acquiescence.

"Still, this is too exciting." Dr. Riccardi gave me back the
medal. "You're going to have to go do Siena, my dears. Immediately. Don't let anyone intimidate you—there's no other choice.
Listen: I still do think that the letter's a forgery. But now, obviously, I don't have the document to send to Rome, and there's no
time with those maniacs at large to send this medal out for study,
either. So you two *have* to pursue it, the sooner the better."

"Marco doesn't seem like the type to waste time," I acknowl-
edged.

"And you'll have to *tell me everything you find*. Let's see. Lola, tell
me that you memorized the riddle. I can't seem to recall any of
it—I've been through such a shock."

"Not *all* of it—"

"But some, yes? Yes, good. At least that's a start. *And* we know
where you'll have to go look. What was the order again? A, B,
C, and D: Florence, you've done. Siena, next. After that, Rome
and Venice. And as to Siena, there was that mention—in the letter—of the She-Wolf and Dragons. Remember? You'll have to
read Sofia's diary to understand, the entry from their last day in
the city—you saw the book in the library. I think Antonio might
have been influenced by it, and Marco never bothered to look at
the thing."

"Sofia's diaries, last day in Siena," I stammered.

Dr. Riccardi looked up, just as one of the uniformed police officers gestured at her from the doorway. "Oh my, am I needed again?"

"Yes, ma'am," the officer said. "Another interview."

The room was much quieter after she and Adriana bundled out. I propped my head in my hands, trying to fend off the voices in my ear—

He went out like a filthy beggar

I want my family back

—and the visions of the guards' gray, slack faces.

"This is a mess, Erik," I finally said.

He nodded. "Those poor old boys."

"How are you doing about Blasej?"

Opening his mouth, he wagged his jaw. He was very, very pale. "I don't know. I might be in shock. Maybe I'm in denial. Maybe I need a huge amount of alcohol. I don't really feel much of anything. I mean . . . I *do*, but when I think about it I want to pass out. Or scream, a very high-pitched scream. So then I think that maybe it's better if I don't focus on it too much." He closed his eyes, then opened them back up. "Did I *bite* Marco?"

"Yes, you did."

"That was weird. *Lord.* Who knew I was so flamingly dangerous?"

"Not me, honestly."

"I know!" He made a sour mouth, as a tear suddenly welled up in his left eye and ran down his cheek. "Except that he was a bastard and I'm also glad that Blasej is dead."

"Erik, are you crying?"

"Hmmm?" He wiped off his face and looked at the tears on his fingers. "Oh! I guess a little. Ach. Maybe we should . . . just stay here and cooperate with the police and then bolt home as soon as possible."

I clutched the medal tight. "Maybe."

"Except—*what* exactly is the law on self-defense in Italy? I mean, are they going to fling me into jail with a gaggle of mafiosos?"

"No. They'd better not!" I opened my hand, moving the medal back and forth beneath the lamp glow. The coin glistened gold and rose, its hues shot through with crimson shades. "We should probably give them this, and just get out of here. We could just forget about—"

"Right, going to Siena, Rome, spectacular Venice." Erik glared down at the medal. "But . . . Here—make sure they don't see it, Lola. And look at the *color* of the gold. Did you notice it?"

"I did. It's a kind of red gold. Strawberry gold, some call it. Viking gold was that color. And also . . ." I looked up at him, unable to stop a smile. "Aztec gold."

"Isn't that a coincidence?"

"I've read about it. In the histories. Aztec gold was supposed to have this reddish cast."

"Hmmmm. Okay. Stop it. You're just trying to get me all excited."

"No I'm not! I'm not saying. I mean, Marco got away—and he knows where we'd be going. It's obvious that we shouldn't look any more into this—"

"Obviously."

But it was precisely because we were seriously considering the mad prospect that we both began convulsively and silently laughing, hunching over and spasming the way people do after getting their hands slammed into a door or surviving a plane crash.

"And there's the matter, too, of Tomas?" Erik gasped, his eyes still wet. "I heard your monstrous pal Marco gurgle something about the way that Tomas died."

"Yes, actually, he *did*."

"And his grave is supposed to be here, isn't it? Not that you're really *interested* in scallywagging around Italy in search of mythic gold and your long-lost pops—"

"Not at all."

"Not that you aren't *completely* bats and are so curious it probably amounts to a medical compulsion—"

"So. It's decided. We'll just stay in Florence for questioning, and forget all about treasure-hunting."

"Yes, and when they give me life for murder, you can bring me biscotti in jail."

We both glanced up, and I tucked the medal into Erik's pants pocket. A nearby standing clump of police officers had just begun to undulate and part a path for one of their superiors, who'd been roaming the palazzo's halls.

"Is this them?" the man asked in an official, if weary, voice.

"Yes, sir," came the reply.

Erik and I wiped our faces before standing to greet the detective. He wore a navy suit, and a flat tweed cap was perched on his head. He was small, with blue eyes and short grizzled hair poking out from under the cap.

"Hello, I am Officer Gnoli," he said in good English. "I need to ask you some questions about the unsightly dead man we found in the crypt tonight."

"Yes, certainly."

"So, you two, sir and young lady. Sorry if you are repeating yourselves—I think you have given this story many times already. Regardless. Tonight you saw these bad men with the gun?"

"Something terrible happened in the Medici chapel . . . , " I began.

"Yes, I see, so they ran away, but one of them was dead, the one we found," the officer said after he'd pressed us for a clearer description of Marco Moreno and Domenico. "So the boys with the red and the yellow hair. They were friends of this black-haired one."

"The black-haired one—we know him," Erik said. "Sort of."

"At least, my family—my father knew his father."

As I had twice before that evening, I tried to briefly describe the civil war and my family history, though my account quickly got complicated.

Officer Gnoli stopped scribbling. *"Guatemala?"*

"Well, I'm half Mexican, actually, my mother's from Chihuahua, but my biological father—"

"Yes, yes, yes, we'll need to interview you more. This much I can tell. But first, I must see after this dead boy in the chapel. And, there are fingerprints to take—from that Luger we discovered—"

"What's that?"

"A weapon, it was left behind here, in the dining room. All I know is that one of the palazzo's janitors found a professor holding a veritable cannon between his thumb and forefinger and blithering about majolica."

"Oh, *right*." The noble-looking scholar. "I *forgot* about him. He was— He did this magic trick thing. *Where* is he?"

"He went darting out of here as if his tail had been set on fire, apparently." Officer Gnoli tugged at the brim of his cap. "But you—you will have to stay here in town, yes? Whatever your arrangements. So that I may send my men to you to make a report. You in particular, Signor Gomara, as you were saying you had a *struggle* with one of the victims. You may be here days, perhaps. Weeks. It's impossible to say."

"We could be here weeks?" Erik asked.

"It's impossible to say?" I added.

"Yes, you can never tell how long these things will take. Yet we are finished for now," Officer Gnoli muttered. "I understand that you were guests at the palazzo, but no one may sleep here tonight. So if you please, you will go and find yourself a hotel. If you please also, call me at this number in the morning, not too early." He handed a card to me. "Okay?" He popped his jaw at us. "Yes? Or, is there a problem I should know of?"

I shook my head, just as I felt Erik sneak his warm hand into mine.

"No, not at all," we said to Officer Gnoli, very gravely, very soberly. "Yes sir, we'll be sure to do that."

An hour later, we sat on a train. The midnight sky was just visible through the windows. A hard, fast rain smacked crystals upon the glass.

I rested my head on Erik's chest. He was petting my hair and chatting breathlessly about emeralds, Renaissance burial rituals, and long-lasting *cinquecento* poisons.

I squeezed him in a hug and closed my eyes, half-listening. It was true that I wanted to hunt after the ghost of my genetic father. And I did want to dig up the buried, bloodied treasure of my ancestral Aztecs. But I knew, too, that one of the reasons I was racing through Italy like some half-crazed heroine out of Jules Verne was that I'd fallen in love with Erik Gomara.

The train raced through the dark, under the stars, toward the medieval town of Siena.

BOOK TWO

THE SHE-WOLF

16

At eleven a.m. the next morning, a considerably strung-out Erik and I stood within the splendor of Siena's Piazza del Campo, a fan-shaped courtyard made of rust-colored brick: It extends from a turreted gray-and-red Palazzo Pubblico, or city hall, which is ringed all around by cafés, a medieval cathedral, and the nimbus of the remarkable Sienese sun. The rapturously morbid St. Catherine lived here in the fourteenth century. In 1348, the Black Death swept away three-quarters of the kingdom's citizens, leaving behind only the phobic penitent. Yet the city's golden warmth drew Erik and me away from our Florentine death thoughts, as it evoked less those dour citizens than its happier mythological founders, Senius and Aschius, the Bacchus-worshiping sons of Remus.

" 'Romulus and Remus were abandoned in the forest by their father,' " I read out loud from a book, *Italy: Land of the Lycanthrop* by Sir Sigurd Nussbaum, that I had purchased from a musty little shop just that morning, " 'and were cared for by a She-Wolf, who suckled the twins as if they were part of her own litter.' " I looked up. "It's a sort of early werewolf tale—especially when you consider the mayhem that happened afterward—"

Still wearing his navy suit from the night before, Erik sat down to sun himself on the *campo*, where purple, hood-shaped flowers bloomed between the cracks. "Right—this was when Romulus and Remus became the founders of Rome, and Romulus decided he didn't want to share any of the glory, so he bashed poor Remus's head in with the jawbone of an ass—or did he pour poison in his ear? I might be mixing up my mythologies—"

"You've got the basic point. But *before* Romulus killed Remus, Remus had just enough time to conduct a little romance, and the girl gave birth to a set of twins: Senius and Aschius. Once they got the picture that Romulus was about to chop them into bits too, they snatched an effigy of the she-wolf and raced away to Tuscany. They planted said effigy in an olive grove, founding Siena there, in order to, let's see here . . ." I consulted the book again. "Ah, '*to finish their dead father's work.*' "

Erik opened one eye when he heard my voice pitch strangely. "You were saying that Tomas might have been hunting down this gold business when he died."

"Marco said that, yes."

"So, finishing off a dead father's work? See? You're not the only crazy one."

"It's very comforting to know I'm as neurotic as the ancient Romans. And Marco Moreno, come to think of it—"

"Oh, angel. On you, crazy is *very* attractive."

"And on Marco?"

"Not so much. But let's just hope he's still in Florence, preferably captured and writhing under Officer Gnoli's exquisitely painful and possibly unconstitutional thumbscrews—and that Mr. Domenico has picturesquely drowned in a vat of Super Tuscan wine, or some such—"

"While we safely look for Antonio's she-wolf."

"Exactly. Which brings us to the riddle—how much of the third stanza do you remember?"

"The first three lines, but not the last one."

"Okay, then, let's hear it again."

I recited:

> IN A SHRINE AT CITY TWO
>
> A SHE-WOLF TELLS MORE THAN I
>
> FOUR DRAGONS GUARD THE NEXT CUE . . .

"And then—that's all we've got to go on," Erik said.

I shut my eyes, concentrating. "I think the last line has a name in it. Maybe . . . *Matthew*—agh, I just can't remember. But what we *do* know is that the riddle mentions a *shrine*—what does that mean, exactly? Shrine. A church, most likely—"

"Any place of worship, I'd think. But there wasn't really anything like a separation between church and state back then. So, a shrine could be practically any building in the city."

"So, fine, keeping it at basics. We're looking for a she-wolf—in a shrine—"

"Which would be any kind of important structure that might have been considered holy in the sixteenth century." Erik peered around the *campo*, softly singing the riddle. " 'In a shrine *at City Two . . . A She-Wolf* tells *more than I . . .*' "

Before us sparkled the Palazzo Pubblico's famous fourteenth-century Gothic façade, built of pink, white, and gray bricks. Its imposing tower loomed over marble sculptures and pale friezes carved with images of a fantastical forest menagerie.

"*Oh no.*" We grasped each other's hands. "Damn." "Good God." "They're *everywhere.*"

It was as if they had suddenly sprung out at us from their plain-sight hiding places: The predominant beast in this zoo-adorned city hall was the she-wolf, or *lupa*. We saw her snarling in bronze at the top of a marble column; two of her sisters were carved into the white stone of the façade; two more wolf mothers peeked at us from under pointed arches; and at least one glowered down from the highest parapets.

It was here that we remembered the terrible fact: "We're looking for a she-wolf in Siena?" I asked. "The she-wolf is Siena's *emblem*."

"Yes."

"It's like a practical joke."

"A very good one. On us."

"We've got our work cut out. This place is going to be *full* of wolves."

We began to walk away from the *campo*, toward the shining, rose-gold city, with its chiaroscuro of cobblestone streets and ebony alleyways.

"Let's just hope these wolves are the kind that don't bite," Erik muttered.

His were words that I would later remember as prophetic.

"I think I've counted four hundred and twenty-two separate sightings of she-wolves today," Erik babbled seven hours later as we staggered back to a twilit Piazza del Campo.

We approached the courtyard's cafés, chugging on water bottles and famished from our wanderings through the city's ambiguous forest of signs. Our investigations, though taxing, had nevertheless passed without any breath of trouble from the likes of Marco Moreno. We began to believe that the villain *might* have been subjected to Officer Gnoli's internationally disapproved interrogation techniques, or at least that he had been sufficiently admonished by Erik's cheek bite to keep his distance from us. So we did not have to run for our lives that afternoon, yet we faced a dilemma far subtler than our own possible murders. All that day, among Siena's frescoed magical hydras, tapestried lambs, the bird-footed women, there were the *wolves*. We saw canines suckling, howling, heraldic, scratched into walls, and crafted from bronze. They were sculpted into fountains and gracing the tops of pillars that occupy the centers of Siena's little piazzas. But despite Erik's and my Sherlockian study of them, none of these curs had yielded up anything that could be remotely taken for a clue.

Nor had our inspections of the Duomo proven any more fruitful. This, Siena's most famous shrine, throngs with gold-leafed saints gazing piously at a ceiling sanctified with red-gold stars. Down below, on the richly decorated floor, shine round inlaid mosaics. These black, terra-cotta, and white-colored stone picture circles lead up all the way up the nave. We could not make all of these out, as several had been covered by Masonite sheets, for protection and to designate them for cleaning. Still, we did see a panel showing scenes from the terrifying *Slaughter of the Innocents*, as well as curiously pagan images of female sybils.

"Yes, yes, it was beautiful, but there wasn't any sign of Antonio in that place—*any* place," Erik said, as we sat outside at L'Osteria del Bigelli, on the perimeter of the quickly darkening *campo*. Several couples occupied nearby tables, and at the far edge of L'Osteria's dining area relaxed one man who arrived after the waiter took our orders. This solitary diner was wreathed by shadows and the server brought him a large dish of whitefish, which he ate in silence. Erik and I drank Chianti and tasted linguini puttanesca by the light of our table's large candle, which was set in a very heavy red glass votive. This light flared just brightly enough to let me read the *Diario Intimo* of Sofia Medici (pocketed the night before from the library at the Palazzo Medici Riccardi) that I yanked from a purse already distended with water bottles, matches, wallets, and other bulbous necessaries.

"But Erik, Antonio and Sofia *did* live here. In Siena. Remember what Dr. Riccardi was saying about their last day in the city? I read some of her journal on the train. They moved here after he first returned from Mexico, and she and Antonio were finally married."

"They had a hugely long engagement, didn't they? Something like ten years. Sofia kept on putting off the wedding, saying that she'd rather drown in the Arno than become a Medici wife—and *actually*, that reminds me of something that is maybe even as important!" Erik reached out and fiddled with my engagement ring. "*We're* getting married in eleven days now."

I bit my lip. "I know. We're going to have to hurry up this Aztec gold-hunting so we can make it home in time."

"There are still tons of things to do! Your mother was throwing these cummerbunds at me a couple nights ago and I thought I was going to crawl out the window and run away. And we still haven't decided on the music. When you stood me up two nights ago, we were going to settle on a DJ. For the rehearsal dinner. You wanted an eighties theme; I wanted seventies."

"I didn't stand you up! I was kidnapped. Sort of. At first."

"*Kidnapped*. Come on, Lola. You got right on that plane with Marco. You didn't yell out for security or anything."

I pressed my hands to my head. "It was complicated."

"I'll bet that Marco just flapped that letter at you and you went *racing* after him."

"Kind of —but—yes. Oh—wait—*on* the subject of the DJ? I

still want eighties. Eighties or Mozart. Or classical Brazilian. Or thirties jazz. Or Elizabethan."

"Um—*no*. You have to dance at these rehearsal things. I'm talking seventies. Disco. Donna. Sly and the Family Stone."

"*So* over."

"Oh, something else. You know how you want your sister to lead a scavenger hunt for the wedding party?"

"Ye-es."

"She doesn't want to do that."

"*Why?*"

"She thinks it's too stupid. She says she'd had enough of doing stunts for her family—something about how Tomas used to make her track all by herself in the jungle when she was just a kid—"

"Ugh. Yes. He'd dump her in the rain forest without any food or water, point her north, and say bye, only to pop back up a week later when he was satisfied with her performance. He was always putting her through these tests, making her prove herself to him."

"That's nice. Well. She says she's a real tracker and not a side show."

"Okay, no problem. I thought she'd like it. You know, give her something fun to do, have her track all around Long Beach—"

"Yolanda's still so depressed about Tomas passing away that she'd probably just lead the bridesmaids into a golf course sand pit, bury them up to their necks, and leave them to die."

"I hope she can get over it." I held up Sofia's journal. "I mean—like Sofia. *She* was able to start a completely new life—"

Erik laughed. "Ahh, yes. It's easier to talk about neurotic historical figures than annoyingly alive family members."

"Precisely! So let's do *that*."

"All right."

"Okay. Good. *As* I was saying—"

"As you were saying—"

"Sofia and Antonio had this very long engagement. Because she hated him when they were first betrothed."

"Yes, yes. But then she changed her mind."

"Uh-huh. She gave in to her father's demands when Antonio returned from Mexico. After the expedition with Cortés, Antonio was so traumatized, or something, that he started being nice to her. So that's when she agreed to the ceremony."

"Not that it helped Sofia's house gain any points with the Medici, because Cosimo the First pretty quickly afterward cut Antonio off from the family."

"That's right. Florence became dangerous, so they came to Siena in the fifteen thirties, living here for about five years in some kind of safe house attached to the Duomo."

Erik spread out his hands. "The safe house—that could be where the she-wolf is. Though, I have to say, I'm going to need a *lot* more pasta before I haul my panties around any more of these blasted museums—"

"They lived—I'm not exactly sure where, but I do know they began having trouble with the locals . . . what was I reading?" I flipped the pages of the *Diario Intimo*. A few of the couples had just stood up to leave, but I saw that the man eating fish raised his head to listen to me. I paid him no mind, continuing to turn through the book. "Here, I've found it. This is from the year they left Siena— their last night. They'd had to leave town very quickly. . . ."

December 3, 1538

We have just nearly been driven from the city by a band of peasants who have no liking for wolves or witches.

And to think, I'd had such hopeful plans for this evening.

One year ago, Antonio gave Siena's Council two trunks of pure gold with which to restore their crumbling Duomo, in return for their agreement to shelter us and our books from the Medici in the cathedral's cold womb. Yet despite their need for the metal with which they might make the repairs, the city's craftsmen refused at first to lay hands on our Treasure. I worried they had heard what happened in America, and that Antonio was a *Versipellis*, for only after the Council threatened the knaves with flogging did they mix the reddish gold with Spanish copper, and then paint the Duomo into its former splendor.

Sadly, my fears, and their suspicions, have all been confirmed tonight. We have been repaid for our gift not with protection, but with violence, and during our most vulnerable hour:

This eve, a round white Moon shone in the sky, a dangerous time for my lord, but also the most auspicious hour to administer the Cure to the Condition. Though Antonio claims his Disorder is born of Mysterious causes, I think his *nom de guerre* fits him well: The Black Wolf, *il Lupo Tetro*, a dark and moody beast—for I agree with those philosophers who call the torment of the *Versipellis* a *melancholia canina* that changes Men into howling Dogs, and can be corrected only by administering to the patient a philter in the first few moments that he stands directly beneath the full moon—precisely before he commences his great Alteration.

It was in our search for his Remedy that we planned to travel to the Woods on the outskirts of the city. We went equipped with our flask of the Experimental Universal Medicine mixed of Gold and the Alchemical Elements, and two weapons to guard against any Enemies of the Wolf. The first was a sprig of the ubiquitous Fruit of Love, Belladonna. My second Defense was a candlestick—one of the deadly Tapers that Antonio and I have crafted within our Laboratory. Then off we hurried, to reach the silvered Forest before he felt the Luna's effects.

Even as we had been walking not sixty paces, however, I could tell at once that his spirit had suddenly grown as dim as that sky's silver Orb was bright.

"I am guilty of great Crimes, Sofia," he said, his face darkening, already Shifting. "In Timbuktu, America, Florence. I starved a man, tortured him. I am a murderer. And yellow is the color of my courage!"

I brought my hands to my hips. "You killed a Slave, darling, which was no crime. The death of that Fool was in his cards, after all. I should know—I read them! In the Tarot, the Fool is the sign either of Dead End or Fresh Starts. It was his destiny. You are not to blame."

"I will be punished. I am being punished—by the Condition."

"Nonsense."

"Is it? Do you fear nothing?"

"I am made of the strongest mettle when I am in your company."

"And do you think we will always be together, my little Dragon?"

"Always, Antonio."

"You are a liar. This Medicine will fail, and we will both of us die, and thus be eternally separated. That will be the worst penance of all."

I said nothing, for I could not answer his morbid mood, which deepened as we walked through the shadows. I could hear his breathing change. His Features transformed even further. So I treated him as a good wife must, and began to drag him by his leash.

But it was already too late: the torches of the Mob could even now be seen, so in a twinkling peasants descended upon us, their twisted faces stained red in the fire.

My husband pawed at the ground; he barked and roared and bared his fangs.

"The Wolf," one of the villeins hissed.

"The Black Wolf," another cried, as the men beat Antonio, breaking his right hand.

"Vixen of the Devil!" a third bitch yelled.

"And who do you think you are?" I screamed back.

"We are the Salt of the earth," the Banshee cried, as she and her sisters began hurling at me handfuls of just that white, stinging stuff, which they kept in little burlap sacks tied to their ugly skirts. On account of their Christian Gospels, they believe pure Salt repels devils—or Dragons—such as me. They heaved the bitter grains much as superstitious crones will toss spilled salt over their left shoulders in order to blind the Beelzebub they believe is always lurking behind them.

"Well, then, you are salt that has lost its taste." I pointed at their unfashionable clothes—for I can quote Scripture just as well as they.

"Harlot! Serpent-Sorceress!"

"You are right to call me by my true name." I gestured at the cowering furred form of my husband. "Love has transformed me into a creature powerful & terrible. So look, and fear what has been Created!"

I lifted my Taper to one the men's torches, summoning the Candle-crafting Power of the Goddess.

"Raaassshhhhhh!" I cried in the secret language of Fire as a torrent of flame rushed toward the horde. Six men fell at my feet, their faces bubbling, their eyes smoking coals.

"Shhhhhsssshhhhh!" I uttered the mysterious tongue of the Wind as I threw the belladonna on the blaze. A noisome Fume floated into the air. Ten of the women collapsed in a heap, a vile yellow fluid issuing from their crying mouths.

But I could not kill them all, I found, not even with my most powerful Magic.

And so this is when Antonio and I fled. To Sanctuary. To the Duomo!

Down the campo we ran, and my galloping husband could no longer call my name with a human voice. To the cathedral we raced, reaching its stone steps, the large portal. Yet, despite the law of Sanctuary, the frantic priests tried to bar the door when they saw the mob behind us.

We took care to remind them that we had fitted the Cathedral out of our own pocket, and funded many of its restorations.

And when this did not work, my husband convinced them by performing his Trick.

He used all his might, and then the Wolf turned clockwise round, and round again. And a third time.

Thus my werewolf Love protected us from all harm.

All last night, we huddled in the Duomo's Den and prepared for our escape. We have only the time to pack our Treasure, and our rarest books—*the Prophecy of Sappho, The Emerald Tablet*—and the embroidered jacket worn by his doppelgänger in Gozzoli's *Procession of the Three Magi*.

For we must leave Siena this morning, and strive to make friends in Rome. With my Candle-craft, my Tarot, my knowledge of the stars and precious stones and the secrets of Hecate—I know that I will be able to discover a way to sweeten that city, to convince it that Antonio and I are not just a wolf and witch, but friends.

For we are homeless. We will never come back here again.

"Well, here are some things that make sense." I pointed to the lovers' conversation about Antonio's crimes. " *'The death of that Fool was in his cards, after all.'* This is why Dr. Riccardi knew that Antonio called his slave a Fool, because she'd read this diary. The nickname fits too: In the tarot, the Fool is the sign of dead ends."

"And fresh starts." Erik brought his head close to mine. "But this—what does it say? I'm drawing a blank."

He pointed out a sentence, which I translated again: " *'Though Antonio claims his disorder is born of Mysterious causes, I think his nom de guerre fits him well: The Black Wolf, il Lupo Tetro.' "*

"*Tetro* means . . . ?"

"It's Italian for sad, gloomy, dark. It's the word for a depressive, basically."

"He certainly was that. Not too cheerful with the death obsession. And—did you get this? The mob broke his hand." We had ordered espresso by now. Erik twirled the dark liquid in a porcelain cup. "You told me that at the palazzo you compared Marco's letter with another letter Antonio had written in Africa?"

"Yes. He wrote it from Timbuktu—while he was conducting a raid of an alchemy lab, and was almost burned to death by some sort of chemical. The writing in the two documents wasn't the same."

"Maybe the reason the writing was different is this fight with the mob. After they broke his right hand, he might have had to write with his left. So what we're talking about here is a—"

"Southpaw *Versipellis!*"

"Exactly. A southpaw—*Skin-changer, or skin-shifter,* in Latin. The word they used for werewolf."

"Mmm-hmmm. *Versi* means 'change,' *pellis* is 'skin'."

"And that's precisely what Antonio was supposed to have achieved: Skin-changing, or shape-shifting."

"It sounds like he did have some type of epileptic fit—"

"She's clearly got an imagination, though she wasn't the only Italian with superstitions about Antonio."

"Meaning . . . ?"

"You see here, at the beginning of the entry, she writes, '*I worried they had heard what happened in America.*' Lola, remember how Dr. Riccardi and I talked about this in the palazzo, the myth of Antonio's demon possession?"

"What, about when he performed experiments on peasants in Florence?"

Erik pinched the space between his eyes, concentrating. "No. Hold on, let me get the timeline straight. First Antonio was in Florence, acting like a crazy person—then he sailed over to Timbuktu, burning alchemy labs, taking at least one slave. But his reputation took a *real* beating when he later went with Cortés to the Americas. That's what Sofia's writing about. I've read that something fantastically bloody *did* happen before Antonio sailed back from Tenochtitlán to here, Italy—Venice, actually.

"There was a massacre of Cortés's sailors over Montezuma's gold. It began with a fight among the men, for the shares of the treasure, and Antonio's African slave apparently attacked him in the confusion. After that, Antonio is said to have lost his *mind*, really. He disemboweled about half his soldiers and drank their blood, that sort of thing. Some of the survivors who made it back to Europe ranted to everyone who would listen about his having been cursed by Montezuma and turned into some sort of dog-monster."

I felt my bravery dissolving with all this ghoulish talk. Next to us remained the shadowed man eating fish, then the black *campo* beyond. The waxing moon was barely visible through a spooky, ragged layer of cloud, though a shaft of light struck the stones of the courtyard, so I had a sudden vivid image of the humped and growling Antonio standing beneath its rays. I also easily called to mind the innumerable bronze and marble she-wolves tucked into the crevices of Siena, as if ready to pounce. Then came even more disturbing visions from the past two days.

"I'm glad I don't believe in fiends or ogres or devils," I said, my voice wavering.

"Lola."

"I'm glad I know all those *thousands* of stories I've read about man-eating werewolves were just the projections of dipsomaniacs and sexually repressed schizophrenics—"

"You're starting to make the hairs stand up on my arms."

"It's not me—it's the *place*. With all these wolves, the stories, the moon—"

Erik's wonderful face glowed coral from the candlelight. "Why don't we talk instead about how *I'm* the only wolf you have to worry about, and how when we get a hotel room, I'll show you my big ears, and my big teeth, and my *huge* though muscular belly—"

I grabbed his hand. "Yes, yes, that's a much better plan."

"Good. So, look—we'll leave off on the hunt until tomorrow. I'll go inside, use the facilities. Then I'll get you a pensione and . . . massage your feet."

"*Excellent.*"

Erik kissed me on the lips before disappearing into the trattoria.

I picked up my book, turning a few pages. Still, I remained uneasy. I closed the *Diario* to tuck it back into my purse. I began observing again the scene around me.

The city seemed too shrouded, too secret. Most of the laughing couples had departed. A very few others entwined and cooed in far-off corners. The waiter had just collected the fish dish from our neighbor, and was nowhere to be seen.

But all at once I could swear that the man seated close to our table focused his eyes upon me. I could not see his face for the darkness, though the sputtering candle before him illumined his cheek, then a shaded eye.

He sat in three-quarters profile, touching the rim of his wineglass. His voice drifted toward me like smoke.

"You are right to believe in monsters, Lola," he said.

17

The candlelight continued to burn up from the heavy red glass holder. It loosened a faint light that escaped onto my hands and the oilcloth before me. It slipped across the shadow-cloaked man two tables away. I stared at the figure, though I could not see his face.

The man had spoken to me in a cowboy-toned Italian. The accent was pure Tuscan, which branded him as a native. Also, I discerned no Marco-variety of mischief in his voice. I must have misheard his saying my name, or he heard Erik saying it.

"Excuse me, sir?"

"You were talking about the brigand Antonio Medici?"

"Yes."

"I overheard. Sorry to disturb you."

I hesitated. "Oh, no problem."

"He *was* a monster, you know. At least according to the old wives. Seems to me that you and your friend haven't heard the whole story."

I peered closer but still saw only the man's rose mouth, gold cheek, that shadowed eye.

"The story that he was . . . a killer?"

"That he was a werewolf," came the soft low voice toward me in the dark.

The man remained seated at his table, tasting his wine, smoking a cigarette. "The legend of the *loupgarou* is an ancient one, little girl. Even Queen Cleopatra knew about the men bitten by beasts, who became half-human, half-hellhound. Pliny thumbed his nose at the myths, since he was a reasonable man. Cornelius Agrippa, on the other hand, did not. These days, most folks with enough IQ to spell their own names will have themselves a good belly laugh at the stories of thinking animals. But on a night like tonight, with a full moon like this, and when the church bells ring through the square, even the most godless heathen of a skeptic crosses himself."

As he spoke, my skin began to sparkle with dread—and curiosity.

"It's said that old Antonio Medici was one such foul fiend," he continued. "That he capered off to America in the form of Dr. Frankenstein, but then came back as his miserable creature, if you understand my meaning. The man returned to Italy a shape-shifter, a skin-changer—it was a jungle sickness he'd brought home along with a heap of gold stored in an explosive safe. But no gold, no matter how well guarded, could cure him of his disease." The man paused. "I can tell that I have your attention. You've gone quiet as a mackerel! So I'll tell you just a little bit more: There're unofficial histories, *highly* discounted, which claim that he contracted the Condition one night, in the year 1526, when Cortés's men had themselves a brawl over the gold. The angry Aztec gods saw their chance during the melee, and sprang upon the soldiers unawares, so that Antonio was somehow . . . contaminated."

"How did it happen?" I murmured.

"Oh, no one really knows. Or no one likes to *say*. There are only whispers of rumors, an echo of an echo of a tale . . . of Montezuma's curse . . . unholy acts . . . of Antonio drowning in his own blood only to be raised again in a grisly spectacle. . . . Later, the story descends into your Hans Christian Andersen–type of were-wolf bedtime story. Tattle of slaughtered women, infants snatched from their beds, et cetera. Though Antonio's biography does pick up toward the end of his life. They say the last time Antonio got himself moonstruck was on a battlefield. He killed squadrons of men with some sort of witch fire, before being struck down himself. The catastrophe occurred here, actually. In Siena."

The man stopped talking. He finished his cigarette, turning his large, shadow-puppet head to blow white fumes over his shoulder. I still hoped for more of this story as my hands nervously gripped the glass votive, so the candlelight glowed through my fingers.

But a moment passed, then another. It seemed very silent in the square.

All at once, I had the distinct feeling that I had not met this man by accident.

"Are you a visitor to Siena?" I asked.

"I've only recently arrived, Miss."

"You seem to know a great deal about Antonio Medici."

"I've been researching this angle of Italian history for . . . friends of mine."

"Are you an academic?"

"Once, a goodly long while ago, when I was just a tadpole like yourself."

"And now?"

"And now . . . . who can say? I don't think they have names for what I am today. Not respectable ones, anyway."

Grasping the votive, I could feel my heart beating faster.

"Who are you?"

The dark figure shifted, leisurely. "Nobody."

I leaned forward. "Sir, what is your name?"

"Not one that you want to know," the man said, standing up.

This is when the light hit his face. And it was almost as if he changed shape before my eyes.

From his accent I had believed him to be a country Italian. I had been so convinced of this that when his features first emerged in the light, his face appeared to me as a kind of shock. It seemed to shift from the round, Roman visage of my imaginings—for the man caught by the candle was not Mediterranean. I read his face: He had the telltale sharp cheekbones, the tilted eyes, the rough, bronze skin. A long ponytail trailed down his back. Gold earrings shone in his ears. Blue and red tattoos of snakes and Maya hieroglyphs serpentined down his neck. He was not young. But he was Guatemalan and so with Marco Moreno. *I've been researching this angle of Italian history for . . . friends of mine.*

He loomed over me, close enough so that I could hear his breath.

In the next second, he reached out and touched my cheek, my mouth, with a horrible and frightening tenderness.

I stumbled from my chair shouting for Erik with a dreamlike laryngitis, and took hold of the heavy, red glass votive while having instant, nearly psychedelic flashbacks to those guards' bloody bodies in the Florentine crypt. The man floated a few steps away from me, telling me to wise up, in sudden streetwise Spanish. With antic spasms of my legs, I knocked over chairs, scuttling over them. How had Adriana stabbed Domenico's thorax with her fingers? I could not remember—I held up the votive and thrashed it back and forth in an ungainly threat. "Go away, go away!" The man reached for me in the shadows. I swung again, more savagely. His large hand lightly grasped the arm that was not carrying the votive. In a delicate maneuver like a magician's, he painlessly folded it back on my spine.

"That should hold you until you cool your hot head down," he said.

I am not a natural fighter. But I am able to learn, and I took my lesson here from the tutorial I had already received from Marco Moreno in the crypt.

With a feverish whirling baseball pitch I swung myself out of the arm pin, crushing that red glass mace into his jaw with all my strength.

He dropped like a boulder, still gripping my arm, and I went down with him.

"Help, help!"

I twisted away, shuddering. There was a bursting in my head. Pain blazed in my hip. I heaved up, aimed at the man again. I stared at him. He sat upright in a wash of blue moonlight, stared back, grimacing. His teeth flashed white in the smoke-dark face.

But here I saw something I did not expect.

A glance, a flinch, an image. In the black eyes. The wide wolf mouth. What was it? An expression. It struck me, then disappeared.

I collapsed backward. Just for that second I lost all control. I thought I heard a wailing sound. It was from my own throat.

Then the man I suddenly knew to be Tomas de la Rosa unwound himself from the tangle of my attack and ran away.

18

Lola!" Erik cupped his hands on both sides of my face. "What happened?"

"Something—something—"

"Are you hurt?"

"I don't know!"

"Who was that?"

He had come racing up to me, pulled me to my feet. The space outside L'Osteria was a disaster area of splintered crockery and flung furniture. The waiter came running up, a figure in a red apron waving a receipt, and exclaiming, "Madam! Are you all right? I'm calling the police!"

"No! Don't —thank—*ugh*—I'm fine."

I snatched up my bag and glared out into Siena's starscape until I detected the faintest black lineaments of a tall figure retreating into the shadows.

I pursued him.

I tore over the brick square. My purse flew behind me like a kite. The specter vanished, reappeared. He hovered before my eyes like a mirage or a phantom within the depthless recesses of the city. I dashed through Siena's market halls, now far past the *campo*, the baptistery. Behind me, Erik gasped, "Where . . . are . . . we . . . going?"

"After . . . him."

I had to find him. I had to *be sure.* Barreling over cobblestones and street trash, my flying feet darted over the snake-thin sidewalks. Then an alleyway. This lean, cold channel, capped by the black sky, was backlit by an unseen streetlamp's phosphorus-green mist.

At its end stood the man. I saw the mammoth shoulders, the long stream of hair flicking down his back. He glanced back in my direction before melting around an ebony corner.

Careening around this bend, I found myself in a perplexity of nameless streets, which opened out into the Piazza Jacopo della Quercia. We lurched to a halt several hundred feet from the arched, Gothic, gilded Duomo, which we had come in sight of again.

Erik and I bent down, breathless.

"Where'd he go, Erik?"

"Who are we chasing?"

"Tomas de la Rosa."

A pause. "Tomas de la Rosa."

"That's what I said."

"Tomas de la Rosa, the archaeologist and your dead biological father."

"It's him—I'm *positive.*"

"That's—*cracked.* He's not alive."

Even I could see the logic was wanting, but I still said: "Yes he is!"

"Lola—"

"I swear it—"

"I thought you'd never even really seen his face, except for crappy photographs—"

"Doesn't matter—"

"If that man's your father, then why is he running away from you?"

"I hit him with a very heavy object, as hard as I could."

"That would be a good reason."

"It is very important that you believe me right now, Erik."

He looked as if he'd just been hurled through a wind tunnel. "Just . . . give me a second."

"It's him—it was his *face*—as soon as I looked at him, I saw—"

"What?"

"I don't know— *him*."

I could nearly see Erik's thoughts battering against his forehead. "Okay." He spread out all his fingers in a gesture of benevolent half-comprehension. "I get it—you saw him."

"I did."

"I believe that *you* believe it. Even if the idea is pretty much clinically nuts."

"That's good enough for me—because *there he is*."

From the darkest periphery of my eye, I'd just caught a glimpse of the shadowed figure above the Duomo's stairs. He dematerialized in the penumbras of the shrine as if he were seeking sanctuary from me.

We rushed toward the Duomo. Erik and I threw ourselves against its immense wooden doors, too hard, so they flew open. We tumbled inside the cathedral at such a calamitous pace that we would have sprinted over the steel security turnstile if only its various protuberances hadn't murderously goaded our ribs and nether regions. Our bursting entrance also came to the heart-stopping shock of the two workers within: a woman and a man who had been disinfecting the church's Midas-golden cherubs and other assorted spiritual furniture.

My purse was thrown as I bashed down onto the mosaic-glittering floor. Erik skidded crazily on the slick stone. The man and the woman jumped up and yelled incredibly violent threats at me. Then they began hitting Erik.

"No, no, good man, kind lady, please stop doing that," I heard

Erik saying in Spanish. *"Alto, alto—terminare—arrete—Aufenhalt—*
Christ, I'm forgetting my Italian."

I gaped up at the vastness of the cathedral. But there was no
sign of the man from the *campo* here.

"Where—are—you?"

This is when I looked down at the mosaic below me and understood that the tattooed stranger had somehow *led* me here.

Earlier in the day, when Erik and I entered the Duomo, our
gaze traveled up, up, up, to the Duomo's heavenly ceiling and its
gold seraphim and rose window. The ancient circular mosaics ran
across its floor—the roundlet showing the *Slaughter of the Innocents,*
others of saints and sybils. Custodians covered these with Masonite
panels to protect the tiles from the wear of foot traffic. But tonight
the church had been closed to tourists so that these workers could
clean the church's art. Thus the floors were, at this hour, naked.

I raised myself on all fours. Beneath my hands and knees lay
a large, stone ring:

IN A SHRINE AT CITY TWO

A SHE-WOLF TELLS MORE THAN I

Within this circle snarled the intricate black, porphyry, and
white mosaic of a majestic she-wolf.

❦ 19 ❧

The wolf's beautiful face glimmered inches from my own. Made of a puzzle of tricolor *pietre dure*, the central image flowered into an enclosing circle of roundlets, which displayed icons of satellite kingdoms: the rabbit of Pisa, the leopard of Lucca, the lion of Florence. . . . I transfixed on the large beast at the center of this hoop. Beneath her white belly, with its pale teats, Romulus and the doomed Remus rested and sucked. The artist had rendered her as a protective mother who furrowed her brow as she gazed down at her busy foster sons.

The six satellite icons, including the rabbit and lion, and also an elephant and a leopard, orbited in their minor circles, framed by a larger red-stone ring. This red rock was in turn bordered by a white circular band of stone, and the entire mosaic was planted within a multicolored square.

My whirlwinding father dreams reined in immediately. I homed in with a painful hypnosis on the white border ring of stone encompassing the she-wolf, running my fingers around this wheel of alabaster-colored marble. A deep ridge marked where it ended. This created a fissure, after which the multicolored square began. The circle containing the wolf seemed all of a piece, separate from the surrounding square.

"Erik."

"And what in the *hell* do you think you could be doing racing in here like that?" the cleaning lady shouted. "We are closed; you have to leave right now. *Don't you hear me?* Madam? Pietro, where are the damned guards? . . . On a break . . . cigarettes . . . They'll be back here in just one minute. . . ."

"Erik."

He had half-remembered his Italian. "I'm so terribly sorry, sir. I'm glad we can lie down now; it's just been something of a terrestrial misunderstanding . . ."

"*Out of here . . . jackass . . . we're closed . . . ,*" the janitor was ordering him.

"Erik!"

His head jerked in my direction. His gaze swerved to where I pointed. "A she-wolf—"

I stretched my arms over the length and breadth of the image, so that I hugged it. "It was covered up before—I know this is it! Sofia was writing about wolves, and the Duomo, in her diary. She said, something . . . that Antonio gave the city pure gold, remember?" I stared up at the ceiling's gold angels, red-gilt stars. "So that would mean some of Montezuma's gold was—"

"Above us." Erik raised his face to the Duomo's heights. "Though this *can't* be what we're looking for. This gold's mixed with other metals—and Antonio couldn't have expected Cosimo to lug away a whole cathedral ceiling—"

"Yes—but the second clue is probably *here*. '*In a shrine at City Two / A She-Wolf tells more than I / Four Dragons guard the next Cue. . . .*' This is a shrine; here's the wolf. And remember, they lived somewhere around here—she describes it." I ran over the floor to pick up my tumbled bag. I pulled out the *Diario Intimo* and frantically paged though it.

Erik turned and in three hyperactive strides stood before the mosaic.

"When they were running away from the mob, they came here for sanctuary. And the priests tried to bar them from coming in—"

"She wrote about how he performed his *trick*," I said.

"About how he turned . . . turned . . . good lord, what was it?"

I read: " *'My husband convinced them by performing his Trick. He used all his might, and then the Wolf turned clockwise round, and round again. And a third time. Thus my werewolf Love protected us from all harm.'* What does that mean?"

The cleaning lady and the janitor made increasingly astonishing threats about how they would assassinate us if we even scratched the mosaics, while Erik crouched down, running his fingers along the gap between the white ring and the multicolored square.

"Oh, I see," he said, after a second. "Yes, I think I might." He put his hands down carefully on the stone circle, the pale wheel that encompassed it.

"What?"

He braced himself against the floor, leaning his weight on his hands. He began to press. His cheeks bulged with the effort. An alarming shade of crimson spread over his forehead. Soon, sweat poured down his head, his cheeks, soaking his collar.

"I think I might understand," he grunted.

"What are you doing?"

"Honey, help me! Push!"

I watched what he was doing for a blank moment before I understood his idea.

"All right—all right—harder."

I bore down on the white stone round, grinding my hands

against it, crushing my fingers and the heels of my hands down so
that my neck pinched and my back burned. We heaved, our wet
hands slipping. Thrusting and shoving away at the implacable cold
rock, the strain deafened me to the battle cries of the cleaning lady.
She was trying to summon back the cigarette-smoking guards.

Nothing.

Erik and I fell back, panting.

"Again," he said.

We bore down once more on the immobile pictures, pushing—
pressing—so the skin felt as if it were being torn from my hands.

And *then the Duomo's mosaic turned.*

The circle inched to the left, clockwise, in a good, if stiff, half
rotation.

"Oh, look at these idiots, they're destroying the mosaics!" the
janitor exclaimed.

The cleaning lady's voice dropped an octave. "No, Pietro,
what *is* that they're doing?"

"Keep going," I yelled.

Erik and I pressed until the wolf circle turned once, a complete revolution. We stared at each other across the images of
Romulus and Remus, laughing like asylum inmates.

"We're doing it!" I said.

"This is it—this *is* it!"

Again the wolf turned. It turned once more.

With a huge last thrust, Erik and I pushed the stone circle
back into position for a third time, to hear a loud, unmistakable
metal *click* beneath the floor.

A great heavy creak shook the mosaic, causing dust fumes to
rise all around us. The circle opened up about ten inches off the
ground, jerking from its position on an invisible hinge. It was a
trap door.

"Ah, incredible, look at that," Erik breathed.

"They, they broke it, Carla," said the janitor.

She backed away from the chasm. "No, dearest, they found something."

Erik and I scrambled to look through the enormous hole. We gripped the thick circle at its edge and pushed it up, so it stood perpendicular to the floor. A giant green-rusted iron slide bolt, blooming whitely with spiderwebs, was affixed to its underside. The aperture gaped about five feet in diameter, exhaling stale, cool air up to our faces. Within the cleft, the air swirled blind-black, except where the light from the Duomo's lamps poured in. This illumination revealed the top of a massive wooden ladder, which led down to imperceptible earth somewhere far below.

Erik lowered to his knees again, poking his head into the dark before crouching on his haunches, his cheeks puffing. He eased one khakied leg tentatively into the chasm. Next he stepped onto the first creaking rung of the wooden ladder.

"Let me go first," I said. "Come on, hold up—"

"Forget it, Lola. *Agh*—okay. What have we got here? Yes, the ladder seems to be holding under my weight. That's a plus."

As he began to disappear down the round floor, I reached for my purse, which had been squashed at the feet of the washerwoman.

"These mosaics have been here since the fourteenth century," she spat. "They're the work of artists long dead now, with nothing left to show for their lives but these pictures. This is sacred ground, you fool! What do you think is going to be under there? *Madonna*—nothing good, so why don't you get out now? The guards are going to be here any second."

"With guns," the janitor said to Erik.

"Fascinating—and *on* the subject of death and mutilation," he replied, pitching his gaze my way. "Lola, something's just occurred to me—this is obviously where Sofia and Antonio hid from the mob, but I'm worried about something. The riddle says that the she-wolf *tells more than I*, right?"

"Yes."

He continued descending. "I think that there might be some sort of potentially *really* frightening pun going on there." The hole swallowed him up to his neck, so that he looked like a ruddy, voluble, disembodied head. "*Tell*—that's not Italian. It's an Arabic word. Tells were artificial markers—rocks, hills, mounds. They were found in what used to be ancient Babylonia, to designate underground sepulchers, or buried ruins that were still *haunted by its genies*. People back then didn't regard them as you and I would. You know, as more or less invitations to go scavenging under to see what we might find." His head vanished; he was only a voice. "They regarded a tell as a *warning*, you see—a kind of antique *keep away* sign—so that you didn't fall into the buried area and meet up with the inhabitant ghosts and demons, who would subject you to the everlasting tortures of hellfire, thumbscrews, defenestrations, other nasty— *Kabunk-agh*—"

Mid-sentence came a bad downward-tripping sound echoing up from the chasm. I heard the unmistakable bone-whacking racket of a body's thud.

"Erik— Erik!"

I scrambled over to the edge of the abyss.

"Erik!" I put my foot on the top rung of the ladder and began hurrying down it.

"Where have you been? We've got nutjobs over here!" the cleaning lady was hollering, in the sudden rush of male voices.

"Heard something about a fight in the *campo*, signora, and reports of noise—"

The cleaning lady blared: "And who's *this* guy?"

"We're closed, for Mary's sake!" the janitor added. "Who are all these people!"

The frosty air of the Duomo's basement closed in on my legs as I dropped into the black space. But in the moment before my head dipped below the cathedral's floor, I glanced up. In the doorway of the church I saw a trio of blue-capped police officers, one of them still smoking. As we had fled Florence less than twenty-four hours before, Officer Gnoli had not yet broadcast our names to the authorities. Yet these police officers were sufficiently freaked by our apparent destruction of one of the most important mosaics in the whole world to consider arresting or torturing us on the spot. They began to whirligig their arms around their heads so violently it almost seemed as if they were experimenting with the possibilities of human flight.

"What the hell are you doing? Why's there a hole in the floor? Where's that girl going?"

And in the midst of their hubbub, I saw another person peering at me.

Ponytailed, Olmec-faced, stained-glass colors running down his neck: It was the tattooed man.

"My, my look at that," he muttered admiringly, his leather jacket rustling as he slipped between the police. "You cracked it, Lola."

Whatever familiar signs I had seen in his face before had been erased. I could not read him, except for the excitement in his dark eyes and the red welt on his cheek from my bashing. But I was certain now it was Tomas. I'd heard all the tales about how he had donned disguises and faked disappearances to sabotage the

Guatemalan army, and how as a young man he easily picked up accentless German, Nahuatl, and, yes, *Italian*, by seducing foreign ladies. And I'd heard, too, of how his eccentric, mercenary personality took its toll on my sister, Yolanda, when she was growing up. He'd pulled stunts and reappearing acts like this on her many times before.

"Why are you here?" I hissed in Spanish. "What is this all about?"

"So you know who I am?"

"Yes. You're *dead*!"

He only smiled.

"What are you doing?"

"I heard this rumor that I had a kid who was a hell of a lot like me. I thought I'd come out of hiding to check it out."

"Get out of the floor, Miss," one of the policemen ordered. "You're damaging this monument."

But I just blurted to Tomas's damned amused face: "You must be crazy. Do you know what you've put Yolanda through? Stay away from my family!"

"Not before I give you this." He chuckled, pulling a little silver phone from his pants pocket and tossing it to me, soft and easy.

Instinctively, spastically, I raised my hand and caught it in the air.

"Get out of there, Miss!" the police yelled again, one of them laying hands on Tomas.

"Text me if you have any questions, sweets," he said in this growling, happy voice. "I'll get out of this fix easy enough. But I think you'd better slip out of here, quick."

"Aggggghhh!"

Staring at him, and with all my strength, I pulled down on

the door's slide lock so the stone ring slammed with a deafening echoing *ring* back into the floor—now my ceiling. I rammed the bolt into an unseen hole.

Then I stumbled, yelling Erik's name, into the darkness of the church's secret bowels.

20

I fell under the earth. Dropping free into a black chilly space, my hands breaking loose from the crumbling ladder, my eyes strained through the darkness as I turned through the rushing air. All at once I landed hard on a soft, quivering chest.

"Agh—"

"Erik— Erik!"

We rolled over on a cold, dusty floor, gripping each other and crying out assurances before falling apart.

"Where are we?" I asked.

"Some sort of hallway—I could see a little bit before you closed the door. And—um—*why* the hell did you do that?"

"I don't know. I lost my temper."

"Because I nearly broke my neck?"

"Because I saw—*him* again. He was in the cathedral, right when you fell."

"Him, meaning de la Rosa."

"Yes. Didn't you hear me talking to him?"

"I heard a whole lot of hollering, that's about it."

"That was us having a conversation."

"I see. So, I am to assume that your argumentative dead father

has somehow pulled a Lazarus and is even now shaking the tomb
dust out of the creases of his trousers and the formaldehyde out
of his hair—"

"He gave me a phone. Where is it—I dropped it—"

"*Even* assuming that to be true, you thought this was a good
time to lock us down here?"

I blindly cuffed at the ground until I found the phone and
stuck it in my pants' pocket, blithering, "Well, also, these police
showed up and they looked like they wanted to beat us to death."

"Ah! I see! Excellently argued. . . . So. Fantastic! I guess the
only thing to do now is figure out where we are." He grunted and
shuffled around. "I still can't make out anything—"

"Lord, it's dark in here."

"But there was something I saw, just before—"

"What?"

"A torch, maybe—on the wall. Can you get the matches from
your purse?"

From somewhere in the blindness, I heard the sound of
screeching metal. After a few moments of rustling, and Erik's
cursing, I saw a spark flare and die.

He began to softly murmur an encouragement to the fire.

"Light, light—*burn*."

A spray of gold lit the leaden air.

Erik suddenly appeared above me, incomparably beautiful,
with a stream of copper-colored fire streaming from his right
hand and bathing him in its light. The torch he'd pulled from
the wall was not made of iron, but of a roughly beaten red-gold,
forged into the shape of a cone fitted with a bronze-banded bone
handle so long and thick I might have taken it as the relic of a
man's arm. The cone had been filled with some sort of ancient,
scentless tar, which could still take almost too readily to a flame.

Its increasingly violent light showed Erik's delighted face jerking away from the fire.

"Oh, look where we *are*," I said.

The torch burnished the nebulous floor beneath us. The ground billowed with centuries of pallid otherworldly dust. Up went the light, skimming the long black corridor. Furred creatures with fleshy pink tails slithered away from our legs. From the ceiling, the walls, streamed ragged white webs that looked like the shredded gowns of a lady wraith. In the air revolved the silver spirals of dust lifting up from the floor, disturbed by our feet. Mine kicked up a fair amount also when I scampered away from the trembling haunches of a rat, who escaped with his brethren into the murk.

"Ooooo, *come on*," Erik said.

Creeping forward in the fire's advancing circle, we observed that the web-draped walls had once been brightly painted, and led into the blackness of the hallway's vanishing point. Erik and I stared at each other with open mouths. I reached my hand out to the velvet layers of spider-floss and dust, peeling them back with the tips of my fingers. Behind this appalling caul glinted a damaged fresco. Half-erased nymphs worshipped an earth goddess with a fearsome, mingle-blooded face. Next came the lascivious, red-and-blue portrait of Cernunnus, the Celtic horned god, mythological precursor of Lucifer. Then we saw a fair, beautiful woman with a long curling dragon's tail. Her consort—a smaller figure, a black wolf—lapped wine or water from a golden cup.

Erik moved past the fresco, his torch's pitch burning with a curious green intensity. The images were revealed, then abandoned, by the progressing luminescence.

Then the light stopped.

The hairs on my arms spiked. Erik's moving lips mutely spoke my name.

"It's an entrance to—somewhere," he whispered.

In the halo of light towered an impenetrable-looking oaken door, perhaps ten feet high and six feet wide. At the center of its enormous breadth faintly glowed a round bronze instrument obscured behind a veil of webs. Sweeping these away, we saw that the bronze fixture was massive, about twice the circumference and weight of an iron manhole cover. Within its center were three thick dials. Crusted with the detritus of an age, each wheel bore multiple carved images of medieval people and mystical wildlife running up and down its face.

"A combination lock," I said.

"With images from the tarot."

The fire reflected hotly off the bronze as Erik and I rubbed grime off the metal. We pushed these wheels hard enough to make them slowly, and very stiffly, rotate, so as get a plainer view of the glyphs.

"Here's the Fool," Erik said, "the Queen of Cups, the Wheel of Fortune."

"A horned moon."

Next came a delicate image of a plumed serpent breathing fumes of curling, nearly floral-looking fire. "Lola—a *dragon*."

"Yes. Yes—the Riddle—what can I remember:

'In a shrine at City Two

A She-Wolf tells more than I

Four Dragons guard the next cue. . . .' "

I nudged the first dial all the way up, revealing the complete image of a serpent-dragon. "This could be it!" I nudged the second dial, calling up the Worm's twin. "But it says *four* dragons guard the second clue—this would be only three."

"Try it anyway."

The third dial budged into place. A trio of dragons blew flame in a line.

Nothing happened. All was gloom and silence, except for the *tick-tack* of the grisly rats tangling themselves outside the perimeter of the firelight.

"Lola—"

From behind the door now came a slow, grinding noise of metal gnashing on metal.

With a heavy creak, the immense door opened onto a thin ebony slit.

We breathlessly pressed our faces together to peer within. A frigid breeze curled out from the black room beyond, bringing with it the remnants of dead perfumes, a memory of mortal flesh, the ancient spirits of rot and decay.

"I guess the fourth dragon's waiting for us in there."

Erik's hot and shining eyes made him look half-wild when he said that.

"Let's go meet her," I said, kissing him before I grabbed his arm and we plunged inside.

21

The creaking door was so heavy we could barely push it open. We crept into the stifling, hidden room, as the door swiftly and shockingly banged shut behind us. Erik and I ran back, tried to force our way out.

"It's locked from the outside!"

"And there's no handle."

We pounded and scratched at the thing, yelling, but it was no use.

"God, we're going to have to find another way," I said.

"There'd better be one."

We turned around, our panic first ebbing, then slowly shifting into a spellbound calm as we saw the lair that had been disclosed by the torch.

Erik moved forward alongside me. "What is this place?"

His flame burnished a long table set with an astrolabe and crystal bottles that dimly glittered among contorted iron implements. Our eyes blurred, adjusted. A fireplace yawned at the far end of the room. In front of its gigantic iron firedogs sat a graceful reading table, paired with a disintegrating leather chair. A book in a gold clamshell cover rested in the place where the seated reader would turn its pages. In the left corner, standing before a thin mirrored door, towered a mammoth candle on a bronze pedestal. An iron furnace presided to the right of the fireplace. Before it had been deposited three tremendous leather chests tooled or burned with shamanic designs.

Erik sputtered, "It doesn't look like anyone's been here—"

"For centuries. How come no one's found it?"

"It actually happens all the time—control-freak restorers don't want the site disturbed; digs aren't permitted—in ninety-three a German found a hidden door in the Giza pyramid, and we don't even know what's behind it yet. *Agh!*"

While chattering, Erik had moved the torch directly to our left, and both of us gasped: The fire glow washed clear over a white, once-polished skull, with eyes made of carved rubies and a grinning, emerald-studded maw that laughed crazily at us from a low shelf.

"That used to be a person's head," I gabbled.

"Now it's a—book end."

From the left side of the room shone the spines of rat-chewed books: St. Augustine's *City of God*, a much-worn copy of Copernicus's *Means of Transmuting the Human Form Through Use of Starlight*. Propping up these occult and holy tomes, as a kind of ethnographic *memento mori*, were carved human femurs inlaid with ebony and silver. These, along with the ornamental skull, we recognized immediately as examples of the ancient Aztec art.

"This is a Renaissance alchemy lab," Erik croaked. "We've got a still, beakers— Look at these reference books."

"I know—here's *The Occult Teachings of Hypatia*—"

"The bones are from the Americas." Erik anxiously inspected his white-handled torch. "I'm starting to get a very bad feeling this thing has been *recycled*—"

"Antonio was an alchemist, so what would he be doing here—"

"*Ai*, trying to transform gold into the Universal Medicine, and transmute lead into gold."

We began to make our way carefully to the long table set in the center of the room, which was laden with dusty red-crystal crucibles and a bowl of crushed pearls. A mummified lizard with sapphires for eyes stared out next to a pair of lead scorifiers and thick iron pincers. Within the vessels, melted gold had hardened like gilt wax.

"Supposedly he was looking for some kind of cure," I said. "To the Condition."

"He would have been using the three primal elements: sulfur, salt, and—mercury."

"What is that?"

I made toward the reading table at the room's end. Brushing away the silt, I saw its massive bible. The book's gold cover was worked with the jeweled image of a Byzantine Mary, and cinched with a crimson ribbon that shivered into powder at my touch.

Inside, the book's text block was made of large pages of foxed parchment tattooed with Gothic print describing the ancient genealogy of holy men: *Liber generationist Iesu Christi filii David filii Abraham, Abraham genuit Isaac Isaac autem genuit Iacob. . . .*

"It's a copy of the Gospels," I said. In the Vulgate, the Latin. It's so *beautiful.*"

Erik stepped back from the desk. "What are we looking for here—another dragon? And then—*what is that last line* of the riddle?"

I gripped my forehead. "Okay, hold on, hold on: '*In a shrine at City Two / A She-Wolf tells more than I / Four Dragons guard the next Cue . . . Read*' . . . something, something that rhymes with I . . .

Erik— It's *'Matthew or die'! 'A She-Wolf tells more than I . . . Read . . .*
Matthew or die.' I'm missing a word or two, but I think that's the
gist of it."

Still guided by his torch, Erik moved to the room's left corner, with its bronze pillar, candle, and looking-glass door.

"Read . . . Matthew or die." I repeated the words as an idea formed
in my mind. "Erik—wait a second. Look at this Bible again."

But he did not seem to have heard me.

"Lola."

"Do you think maybe the riddle's talking about the Gospels?
The book of Matthew—"

"Lola!"

I jerked away from the book. "What?"

"I've got it."

"What—you remembered the line?"

"No, *I think I found the second clue.*"

He had been drawn to the massive candle before the tall
mirrored door. The lit mirror reflected back our bloodless faces
and the huge, web-shrouded taper. Erik had already scraped off
a portion of the spider fluff, and I peered close as he peeled back
the rest.

An object had been suspended deep inside the tawny wax.
It had a round, metallic shape made plainly visible by the torchlight. It also appeared to bear occult carved markings.

"Erik— Erik!"

"I know—it *looks* like the other medal—"

"Can you read it?"

"No, not in there."

"We've got to get it out."

"Take the light."

Erik found a dull, short knife on a table, and the next few

minutes were spent trying to hack away at the candle, which had petrified into the hardness and clarity of amber.

His face dripped sweat. "What is this stuff?"

"I don't know—it's just old."

His arm dropped. "I can't get it out of there."

The longer I held the torch close to the taper, the more its paraffin or tallow began to glisten. The gold coin locked within absorbed the firelight. Through the amber medium I could just spy an etched line here, a curling swash there.

"Erik, I'll just light the candle. It'll soften the wax—"

"I know, so that we can *see*."

After a weirdly long time, we heard the hissing of centuries of webs and their imprisoned tiny skeletons. The amber mass was less wax than some sort of crystalline resin that proved resistant to heat. But as I pressed the fire close to it, inflaming the wick, I heard the dripping sound of resin sliding, melting. There was a bubbling, something dribbling.

A hot red flash curled up instantly toward the ceiling, nearly knocking us backward. "It's eating the wax—the tallow—"

"Whatever it is."

The candle burned down remarkably fast.

In mere seconds, it melted to the metal circle inside the wax.

"Oh—that's hot. Watch out—hold on, there were pincers on the table."

Erik ran back to retrieve the iron tongs, then extracted the drenched, red-gold coin. I covered my hand with my sweater to grasp it, but in a few moments I could touch it with my bare skin. The wax felt strange on my fingers—thin and almost antiseptic. I wiped it off with my shirt, quickly, before raising the second clue to the firelight.

"It's a—let's see—a *P*!"

"First *L*, then *P*. *L—P*," I stuttered. "We're probably looking for four characters. What would that spell?"

"Pole. Lope. Opal. Liposuction. Opaque."

"No, not in English."

"*Pala*, which is the Italian for 'blade.'"

"I can't think. Palazzo."

"Polenta. Lapse. Lapsed Catholic. Lapland."

"Are any of those Italian?"

"I don't know."

"You're fantastic!" I laughed, my excitement apparently giving me some sort of hot flash, so that suddenly even my fingers felt very warm. "I just love you."

"Jesus, after all this, you'd better."

"Is it hot in here?"

He smiled. "Are you suggesting something— *Wah!!!!*"

All at once he ripped the torch out of my hand. He threw his torso onto mine and smothered me with his arms.

"Help me put it out!" he yelled.

"What are you doing?"

"*You're on fire, Lola!*"

I screamed to see my waxy fingers ablaze like candles on a cannibal's cake. A swift, hot ring of white flame rapidly expanded on the sweater I had borrowed/stolen from Adriana. I swatted at myself with a terror of fire, and so savagely that I would find bruises on my chest later. My fingers were blackened. My sweater had been eaten through.

"The wax . . . ?" I said, questioning.

I should have known, but still did not realize what kind of beast I had just touched. I looked up to see a strange blood-pink corona fringing Erik's head. The torch that burned on the ground next to us dimmed now in comparison to the volcanic light streaming from the amber puddle of the candle.

I took a step back. "That fire's getting out of control."

"I'll put it out. Snuff it with my jacket."

Both of us talked in rapid panicked breaths.

"No, just hold on—we'll douse it," I said. "The water in my bag." I threw it to him.

"Good thinking—"

He ripped off the little plastic cap on the bottle with his teeth. A fast nozzle of water hit the blazing tongues.

The incandescence crouched down, nodding. But in the next second, it shot a hot wild tentacle of flame to the ceiling.

"Lola."

"This couldn't be—"

"No—"

"God—"

"The fourth dragon?"

"I summoned the Candle-crafting Power of the Sorceress," Sofia had written in her diary, of how she had torched the mob that attacked her and her husband. *"I remembered to carry along one of the Tapers that Antonio and I have crafted in our laboratory. A torrent of flame rushed toward the horde. Six men fell at my feet, their faces bubbling, their eyes smoking coals."*

The candle's wick sparkled, as it would on a stick of dynamite. The amber substance melting off the bronze pillar in a thick gold spiral had become agitated by the water. The fire reared up its snaky green-eyed head, breathing fire.

Then it burst into flame like a bomb.

22

The water from Erik's bottle had glazed the pale points of fire, but instead of weakening their force, the tendrils shot out and wrapped around our feet and legs before condensing into the darkest gold. An oily smoke detonated. The flames ran fast across the floor, up the walls, eating the books, crawling up the long mirrored door in a deadly barrier. The fire blocked any possible way out through that passage.

I just killed us, I thought.

"Lola, get down!"

We fell to our knees. A tower of scorching heat flared before us, radiating off in silver spikes and stars to the place where we crouched.

Erik and I shielded our heads as we ran toward the now-locked front door we'd come in through. My hands tore on the wood, my fingers scraped and bleeding. But it still wouldn't open.

Hunkering, we covered our heads with our arms, trying to suck in the air close to the ground. A malignant whirlpool of black smoke coiled toward the ceiling. The room was still so bright I could see every corner of the room, every object in it.

Erik shielded his eyes. "Let's just make a run through that door, the mirrored one—"

"No, it's already covered by fire!"

"There's no other way out!"

I was gasping. "The riddle—the riddle, what's in it? Repeat it to me."

"You said, '*In a Shrine at City Two—*' "

"Not that part!"

" '*A She-Wolf tells more than I / Four Dragons guard the next Cue . . .*' "

" '*Four Dragons guard the next cue,*' " I repeated. " . . . '*Read*' . . . something . . . '*Matthew . . . or die.*' Matthew—Matthew."

He grabbed my arm. "You were talking about that book—the Gospels."

"Yes!" I launched forward toward the desk and knocked the Bible off onto the ground.

" '*Read the*' . . . something . . . '*Matthew or die.*' " I repeated the line while crawling with the tome across the floor.

I turned to the first book, the Book of Matthew.

My eyes jolted over the story of the birth of Jesus, of Herod, of John the Baptist, the Fast. But the fire crawled up the bookshelves, whipping out long deadly tails on the ground.

"Matthew . . . Matthew," I murmured.

"We have to get out of here." Erik yelled at me over the roaring sound of the flames. "We're going to run through that fire—I don't care!"

"Okay—okay . . ." He was right—even though I didn't think we'd make it alive through the door. Still, better to try that than just roasting here while I nattered away at a text!

But it was just then that terror of hot death was answered by my mind with an almost mystical surge of memory. I touched the pages of the glimmering book, the Roman numerals that made up each of the chapters. I, II, III, IV . . . Instantly, it came it me:

> " 'IN A SHRINE AT CITY TWO
> A SHE-WOLF TELLS MORE THAN I
> FOUR DRAGONS GUARD THE NEXT CUE
> READ THE FIFTH MATTHEW OR DIE.' "

"The Fifth Matthew. *'Read the Fifth Matthew or die.'* Matthew Five!" I cuffed the leaves until I reached the chapter reciting the Sermon on the Mount. I raked my eyes down the page. Then I saw something I recognized, in Matthew 5:13:

Vos estis sal terrae quod si sal evanuerit in quo sallietur ad nihilum valet ultra nisi ut mittatur foras et conculcetur ab hominibus.

I bellowed out the translation: "'You are the salt of the earth; but if salt has lost its taste, how shall its saltness be restored? It is no longer good for anything except to be thrown out and trodden under foot by men.'

"Sofia wrote about this quote—in her diary," I yelled. "Antonio used the diary as a blueprint for the trap.

"'We are the salt of the earth, the Banshee cried . . . they hurled at me handfuls of that white stinging stuff . . . They believe pure salt repels devils—or Dragons—such as me.'"

Erik nodded, spraying sweat. "When those women threw salt at her—salt is what you throw at demons—at witches"—his eyes flashed—"and certain kinds of *fire*—"

I was already crawling over the floor, coughing under the blanket of smoke, searching the room for the substance I knew would save us. Trivia flooded my mind: of Alexander the Great, who'd vanquished the Persians with an unstoppable holocaust of

Greek fire, which was inflamed by water; of the oozing incendiary weapon of the ancient Indians, which had to be smothered
by earth or salt; of the modern sodium used by firefighters. I
half-recalled Antonio's letter to Giovanni de' Medici that we'd
read at the Palazzo Medici Riccardi. In that missive, Antonio had
recounted his invasion of Timbuktu, his raid of the Africans' alchemy lab. The resisting Moors set him on fire with some sort of
potion. He had killed the old wizard who assailed him, but was
saved by his son, the future slave-Fool:

> . . . the Savage's potion was not doused by water, but instead incensed.
> I tore off my clothes, rolling on the floor, as the Wizard's son hurried to
> sprinkle upon me a thick layer of salt. It was only by the Charity of that
> Moor that I did not die a Martyr's death. . . .

"This isn't regular fire, Erik. This is *naphtha*. Coal-tar fuel."
"That's why water inflames it—"
"But dirt or *salt* snuffs it out. So that quote, the bible—"
"It means that salt is somewhere in this room. '*But if salt has
lost its taste, how shall its saltness be restored? It is no longer good for anything except to be thrown out and trodden under foot by men.*' And we're
supposed to throw it to the ground, stamp it with our feet—"
Erik bugged his eyes at the lab, its three leather boxes. "The
chests—"

We jolted toward the three gargantuan trunks. Their owner
meant them to be opened by whoever found them, for he had
not padlocked them, instead wrapping them with crumbling
knotted rope. The leather covering the lids of the trunks had
been burned with those mysterious designs; I cuffed the dust off
the third.

"Hold on, stop."

He was already grappling with the first. "We don't have *time!*"

"We don't know what's in here."

"Salt and—who *cares?*"

"They're marked—branded." I knew these signs, even as I drowned on the foul black fog. "I think they're—warnings."

Erik scraped off the dust on the trunks' humped covers. These were their marks:

"They're alchemical symbols," I said. "Of the alchemist's elements."

Erik's eyes were running with water and blood-red. "Oh, hell—"

"We have to be careful."

"The elements—salt puts out fire, but mercury and sulfur can kill you." His throat made a rattling sound. "Lola—get down. You're inhaling too much smoke."

Erik tried to shield me from the blaze with his body, and my mind was shuddering to retrieve the rest of the contents of Antonio's letter to Giovanni de' Medici describing his attack of the alchemists in Timbuktu:

> I set light to the Quicksilver . . . sixty souls fell dead, quivering, green-faced from their own infernal Poison. Close by, there were two additional barrels, each marked with different signs. One was for sulfur. . .

The other was for the salt that the Moor had used to save me....

Wheezing, I pointed to the first chest, its burned Satan-like mark. "That's Mercury—which makes this—poison—a gas—if you expose it to fire."

"Any mercury—would have evaporated by now."

"But these other two"—I pointed to the second, square-headed mark—"that's sulfur."

He edged away from the trunks. "Sulfur's no joke—it explodes."

"Salt!" I ripped at the rope knots on the chest bearing the mark of a circle cut through with a bar. The loops loosened until I was able to slide the fetters off the box.

But I had made a perilous error in my detection. This was not because I had falsely remembered the alchemical signs.

I had not considered the possibility that Antonio would lie.

I tore off the rope on the salt-marked chest. The air-tight cover lifted after I ripped at its hinge, but I found no salt: instead, a drift of pure, deadly, marigold-bright sulfur appeared beneath the lid. A beautiful haze of this powder floated easily from its surface, spreading like oxygen or light in the air.

"Dammit," Erik roared.

"Close it!"

Together we slammed down the lid, hard. Too hard.

Air had gathered in a pocket in the long-locked chest, and when we smashed it back shut, the air rushed out, carrying with it a thick breath of brimstone. Around us sparkled a thick mist of fairy particles, sizzling like stars. They landed on our faces and arms, singeing the skin.

We were burning, shrieking. The fire rose, a hellish gold wall. Circling our faces were deadly gold-red flowers of erupting flame.

Erik grabbed the water bottle, soaking us. "Water puts out sulfur fire!"

I was half-blind as I flung open the lid of the first chest, but inside I could make out a white crystal bank. And something else: Half-buried in its center like a vivid fossil was *another letter*, this one also Wolf-sealed, but in a blood-red envelope.

Stuffing this message into my shirt, I clawed my hands into the salt and flung a white storm of it into the air.

We hurled the bitter crystals on the barricade of flame that had eaten half a wall of books. I hurled bowlfuls of it on the bronze pillar, which still bled the diabolical amber wax. It was a hard war against the strength of the fire. The blaze shrank slowly, then finally snuffed under the white mineral. Salt spread over the lake of fire that had been the floor. A pale sheet covered the scorched Aztec skull, the blackened tomes on alchemy, the charred *Hypatia's Oracle*, and the gold-bound Gospels. Before we smothered all the light in the room, I ripped off a shred of my sweater, using it to hold the bone handle of the torch Erik had thrown to the floor.

"Is there any more salt?" He was breathing heavily.

"No. I think we've done it."

We looked around. The room gleamed white and black now, lit with a few dying spits of white-gold kindling. I snatched up my purse that I could barely see for the smoke. The filthy clouds had only grown thicker.

"The air—" I said.

He had his arm over his mouth. "Not—enough—in here."

"The door. The mirrored door."

"Can you find it?"

"Can't see—"

"Oh, the *books*, *Erik*, they're burned!"

"Better them than us."

We pushed through the smoke clouds, stumbling over furniture until my hand touched the glass. The torchlight parted the black. The mirror doubled our wretched, gap-mouthed expressions.

Erik wrapped his shirt around his hand and turned the white-hot handle of the door.

It barely budged. Centuries of dust had lodged in its lock. We pressed and threw our bodies onto it, cracking the mirror.

It gave. Clear, cold oxygen rushed back in, onto our faces.

I drank that air like holy water as we stumbled out of that poisoned tomb. Most of all I felt sick over those horrible, dead books, the sight of which could make a girl like me go numb. But I didn't have time to react to everything that had happened yet, stranded as Erik and I were in that dismal hell beneath the Duomo.

We still had to get out of there.

23

E rik, can you walk?"

"I can run." He gripped the torch. *"Really* far from here—wherever that is."

The torchlight revealed only a glimpse of another corridor extending before us.

"Let's move."

Despite our burning lungs, we raced through a surreal kaleidoscope, as the torch's red and green flashes battered against the walls. The corridor led us into an ascending spiral that drew us stumbling into a series of stone switchbacks. The ceiling dropped suddenly; we had to scuttle like crabs until we hit a thick stone wall, and a narrow upward passage composed of small stone steps.

"What's this?" Erik asked, coughing hard.

Rats scattered in our wake, scampering up the ancient, half-pulverized staircase.

"It's a way *out.*"

At the top of the steps glinted a long stone-paved landing. Its low ceiling had been fitted with a large wooden trap door, from which dangled a massive pull handle forged of iron.

Erik beamed at me. With his shock of hair and his soot-streaked face he had turned into a savage Pict.

"I think the old Sanchez luck just kicked in."

"Let's hope."

He took hold of the iron ring, grunting as he pulled. The door budged and creaked. It swung down.

We stared up in mute horror at what had been revealed: a slab of marble lodged into the space over the escape door, entombing us.

"Tell me again about that Sanchez luck?" I croaked.

"It works like a charm, Lola," he said, in a graveled voice.

"Right—*no problem.* So we're going to have to . . . let's see here . . . just try to *move* this stone. Get up through the door."

"That's it."

We shoved our hands against the white stone blocking the door. We pushed. We *smashed* our weight against that square of solid rock. But it remained fast. Neither of us said a word. We were too frightened even to look at each other. The other access out was smog-choked *and* locked from the outside. We began to wildly thrash ourselves against the barricade, leaving blood on the pale rock from our shredding hands.

"Okay, I'm starting to have a heart attack now," Erik yelled.

"No, no—hold on—don't you feel it?"

Here came a screeching sound, the grinding of stone against stone.

It moved. We heaved it, slowly, off.

I buckled over with insane, hacking laughter. Erik was crying. A wedge of black air became visible, as the rock barrier shifted away from the door.

"It goes through."

Hauling away the rock, bleeding and sweating, we cleared the large hatch. I crawled through first, hoisting myself onto a floor as cold as lead. Next came the bright fingers of the torch through the portal. Erik heaved himself up, landing with a thud.

"Where are we?"

"It's attached to the church. Hold the light higher."

The torchlight wavered over a tall vaulted ceiling. Above us radiated frescoes of Christ on the cross, and placid-faced angels who celebrated a Christian version of the pagan saturnalia painted along the hidden corridor beneath the cathedral—later, Erik and I would learn that we had been in Siena's Battistero di San Giovanni. Below us spread a network of graves. These were the tombs of Siena's royalty, marked with Latin crosses. One stone had been carved with the bereavement *Patris est filius* below a beautiful etching of a beardless knight holding his sword.

"We came out of a coffin," said Erik.

The stone we had knocked aside was the cover of a false tomb, designed to look like the others, with the etchings of a cross and a fish. Yet when we inspected it closer, we saw it bore the name *Antonio Beato Cagliostro Medici*.

I put my purse down. "He had an evil sense of humor."

"Well, whatever message he was trying to send with this treasure hunt, I think I'm getting it. And it's not very friendly. God, did he *hate* Cosimo."

I kneeled on the floor, ignoring the false grave. I hovered over the tombstone etched with the smooth-cheeked knight. The Latin inscription *Patris est filius* unfurled beneath his feet.

"Lola?"

I did not answer him.

Patris est filius means "Like father, like son." My fingers glided over the engraved words.

"Look at this," I finally said, staring at the carvings with a kind of fish-eyed intensity.

"What?"

"Erik, I just remembered my *dad*."

Patris est filia. I, too, had a father whom I took after, though one whom I had not thought of much in the tumult of the last days. He is a small, skinny, book-mad, and *very* sensitive curator, my adopted pop, Manuel Alvarez. Suddenly missing him terribly, I recalled Manuel's bulging eyes, his faint wisps of hair, his chattering and kisses. Then I saw again the other man's face in the Duomo; I remembered his leaf-shaped eyes and the Chagall colors of his tattoos.

"Your dad. Who, Tomas?"

"No, Manuel. I don't want him to know about de la Rosa, Erik. He *hates* him—and he's worried that my mom still loves him. Even though Tomas is supposedly—"

"Pushing up the daisies, as it were—"

"And he *won't* like the idea of Tomas following me around—"

"Yes, if you tell him a dead de la Rosa is trying to meet you for drinks, he'll certainly freak, but not *as much as I am now*. So, come on, honey. Let's go. We'll talk about this later."

I let Erik take my hand and we moved through the baptistery, under the angels, above the long-dead Tuscan soldiers. Our footsteps rang out on the stone. Moving over to the modern front door, we slammed down its metal push-down bar, instantly ducking at the sight of four police officers quarreling so violently about a soccer match we were able to creep away.

The air that met our faces and ruptured lungs was fresh, cool, and free. The onyx and silver Sienese night shimmered in front of us like benediction, or like a fantasy covering up the horrid truth beneath the ground.

Into it, we fled.

~ 24 ~

"You know, if Antonio Medici were suffering from a disease he probably would turn to alchemy," Erik said between bites of a near-midnight snack, three hours after our flight from the cathedral. He and I were repairing the evening's damages in our pension's suite, on a large oak tester bed draped with a red silk canopy. "Particularly if he were under some kind of delusion that he was a werewolf —a *Versipellis*—because the alchemists were completely obsessed with the idea of transmutation, transformations of any kind, and particularly those from the supposedly baser to higher levels. See what I mean? Lead to gold, old age to youth, sickness to health—"

"Moody werewolves into well-adjusted Italians." I held a letter opener and slipped it under the wolf-shaped seal of the red letter I'd retrieved from the laboratory's salt chest.

"Precisely. And mortality into immortality. Which, quite possibly, may explain the reason that, despite the fact that two years ago Colonel Moreno had his militia bump off Tomas de la Rosa for the murder of Serjei Moreno and then buried his poor old carcass in Central American swamps—you saw him prancing around a Sienese caffè tonight."

I broke into a brief asthmatic fit from smoke inhalation. "You know what? You were right before about dropping the dad subject. Though I'm sure that I'm going to be able to find a *very good explanation* for—for—"

He gently whopped my back. "The reason Tomas de la Rosa escaped from Hades? Apparently with the sole aim of driving you crazy and making Manuel's life miserable?"

"Yes."

He rolled over, looking intently at what I was doing.

"So, if we're not going to talk about that, then *let's read this letter.*"

"The seal, I'm just trying to be careful."

"I'm very itchy to see it."

"I know, I want to tear it open with my teeth. But just *wait—*"

"Fine. Tell me if you want some more ravioli."

I sat cross-legged next to him on the bed, scraping at the wax signet. During the last hours, I had been waiting for us to return to some level of lucidity before I opened this epistle, since we hadn't arrived at this pension in very good shape. Despite the fact that Officer Gnoli could at any moment send out a Mediterranean APB on our hides, and police were probably dragnetting for two suspicious mestizos, our escape-from-Siena plan had consisted of little more than limping to this little hotel sited on the outskirts of the city. Checking in around eleven p.m., we had just stood in the lobby, coughing like Keats and throwing cash at the manager, a small, wizened creature with extremely furry earlobes. Erik did not look quite as shaken as he had in the crypt, but like me he was afflicted with a ghostly pallor and generally incapable of linear thought.

Even so, our evening had improved.

The manager, for one, needed no instruction in how to receive payment. Better yet, he cooked like a warlock and possessed a wine cellar full of amber-red vin santo. Escorted up the stairs, supplied with the first of many glasses, Erik and I had bathed together in the iron tub four doors down from our room, in between scrubbings accomplishing a delicious inventory of our various scrapes, stings, cuts, burns, and bruises. Once back in our room we both arrived wordlessly at the same conclusion—that we had better make love immediately. This we accomplished, sweetly but also carefully, like porcupines. It *greatly* restored our moods. Now resting on the bed's crimson blanket, nude but for thick white towels, we dipped into dishes of butter-dripping polenta with meat sauce and *ravioli en brodo*, which tasted of sage, salt, and wine. And as I worked on the gold seal of Antonio's letter, my lover had begun talking again.

The knife slowly slid under the gold wax wolf, snapping it off. "I've got it."

"He was a weird old bird, wasn't he? Antonio. I mean, leaving that letter in that chest."

"Among other reasons."

"Let's look—what the hell *does* he write in this thing?"

"I don't think we should be eating while reading this."

I coaxed a page from the red envelope. Pure white, the paper was illuminated with botanical watercolors of purple flowers, as well as Antonio Medici's elaborate italic script.

"That's always my problem." Erik took another sip of the vin santo before he put all the plates onto the bed's side table. "I always want to bathe, drink, read, and eat at the same time. It's not very good for the books, but it is—"

"Heaven."

"Exactly." Pink flushed his cheeks; he wagged his tail like a Saint Bernard. "Hey. Hey you. Lola."

"What?"

"I was just thinking . . . you know what I also feel like doing?"

"We just did that."

"*No*, not that. I feel like getting married."

I smiled at him, not understanding. "We *are*, in—uh—it's not *eleven* days now, is it?"

"At the stroke of midnight, make that ten."

"Oh, God! We still have to figure out seventies, or eighties, fish or beef, scavenger hunt or no scavenger hunt—"

"No scavenger hunt. And let's just forget all that. Let's do it now. Here, in Siena."

"Ah, I see."

"We'll *elope*—"

"But don't you *want* to marry a woman dressed up like a cupcake in a Long Beach Hilton, while all your aunts get sloppy drunk?"

"Despite the fact that my lungs have been kebbabed and I need a good stiff shot of Paxil, I'm getting hot right now just hearing you talk about it—"

"Really?"

"*No*. Look, I don't want to wait anymore—I just got my ass burned off, and am probably on the pope's most wanted list, and it's making me a little sentimental. You know? I *love* you. Pretty desperately, as might be obvious by now! I'd like to get the old 'you may now kiss your lawfully wedded wife' business taken care of before I get blown up by antique Molotov cocktails or yanked off to an Italian gulag."

"I know it's been a rough couple of days—"

"Rough is not exactly how I'd describe it. I just think it'd be more romantic if we got a priest to do the wedding, here, tomorrow."

I couldn't help but laugh. "You are *not* the man I met two years ago—"

"What, when I had all those shiny undergraduates hanging all over me? When I was a womanizer and so ridiculously cheerful?"

"Don't remind me."

"Yes . . . All that tacky sex—was *definitely* overrated. In retrospect." He flopped onto his back and flung out his arms. "And, of course, I'm *not* the same obnoxious pinhead I used to be. Remember what I told Dr. Riccardi in Florence. Love changes you for the better." He deepened his voice, mock-serious. "You, my lovely Mexican, my goddess, my punishment for bad behavior—yes, you, Lola Sanchez, have made me a better . . . man—egads."

"Oh, Erik!" I cackled, but tears sprang into my eyes at these words—even as he leaned up on an elbow, mumbling, "And plus *another* advantage is that if we get married now, I think it would hideously annoy Señor Orestes."

I blinked, blinked again. "Who?"

"Orestes? From Euripides' play—*Orestes?* Come on, you remember—the avenger of his father? Having a crack-up because of the Furies? Marco Moreno, I mean."

"How does that play turn out again?"

"Orestes kills Clytemnestra for killing his father. Except that's matricide. So after he does his duty, it's time for *his* punishment— he winds up going bonkers from his persecution by the Furies. Happily Apollo sweeps down and saves him just in time. *El* deus ex machina. Most everybody else gets creamed, though."

"Your point is?"

"Remember when Marco was pawing you *far* too much in the crypt and giving me such a seizure? I think he has a Charles Manson–sort of crush on you."

"Okay, enough." I put up my hands, palms first. "First, we're getting married in Long Beach so that Manuel can give me away, and I can watch Yolanda clothesline all the boys who get too close to her on the dance floor. Second, we're going to get back to the matter at hand."

"You mean the letter."

"That's right." I looked down at the page shining on the bed. "I'm dying to read it."

"All right, woman—we'll table the elopement talk. But you can't do a cartwheel in Italy without kicking a bishop, and I'm sure that plenty of these *padres* would be very happy to do us the honors—"

"Erik—"

He nodded energetically and pointed at the page. "Yes, my darling. Yes, my bossy love! Subject closed. Read, read, read. No more dallying."

We both stared down at the handwritten paper.

Erik rubbed his hands together. "This *is* pretty exciting."

I squinted at the script. "This looks like the first letter I saw— Marco's letter."

"It looks to me as if it has the same writing as the letter you showed me at the palazzo."

"Which would mean it was written after he broke his hand."

"Lola, you do it, your Italian's better than mine."

"Okay. So, Antonio, what do we have here. . . ."

My Dear Nephew Cosimo,

If you are reading this missive, then you succeeded in escaping the symbol of my Beloved Sofia, the Dragon, as well as my naughtily shifted Elemental symbols.

Congratulations! Having survived to take up the challenges of City Three, you have earned that many additional hints, which will help you find the Treasure—but before I give you this Trinity of new Clues, nephew, allow me one more indulgence: I'd like to amuse you with a brief history of your long-sought Prize.

You already know that after my scientific career in Florence, and my ventures in Timbuktu, I helped Hernán Cortés vanquish Tenochtitlán in '24. Like the other soldiers, I expected compensation—imagine my surprise when thirteen months after King Montezuma had handed us the Treasure, that measly, pox-ridden, beef-headed General commanded that a third part of his lucre be returned.

That terrible night was pierced by a full moon, I recall, and a bonfire had been lit, around which I, my Moorish slave-man, and the rest of the men took our ease with pulque. Cortés arrived to our little party with his pet Montezuma in tow, and at the sight of this Indian we grew instantly sober, for the half-dead man was dressed in rags, and his once-beautiful hair knotted in mats, if not ripped from his scalp by his captor or himself.

"You see what I can make a man into if it is my will?" Cortés lazily poked the Aztec with his sword so that the Indian danced, and shuffled, and whined.

No one dared answer, except for my slave, who muttered: "Repulsive."

"Sssshhhh!" I hissed.

Cortés continued to bellow: "Do you all see how I may transform even a great Emperor into a shambling fool?"

"Yes, my Lord," one or two men finally admitted, the rest of us grumbling as Montezuma whispered prayers to his gods.

"Then hand over your gold, which is mine, by King Charles's right as well as Christ's," Cortés ordered. "Or this Savage's fate will also be your own."

It took far more threats than these, but after much swinging about of his sword, the men feigned obedience. One complaining soldier after another tossed by the fire their red-gold Coins, Calendars, and ingenious Torture masks. They also handed over the Holy idols of the Aztecs' fearsome dragon-Lord Quetzalcoatl, and those in the form of the half-man, half-dog Rain God of the Underworld, Xolotl.

Soon there was a magnificent pile and Cortés threw himself on top of it, caressing it with his hands, slobbering in victory.

You have heard two stories of what happened after this: One is that the men mutinied, and that after the blood-spree, hundreds of fleeing soldiers drowned in the rivers, their pockets filled with heavy deathly gold. In this version, Cortés is said to have escaped only with his life, whereas the largest portion of Montezuma's treasure has been lost forever.

In the second version of the Tale, however, something quite more horrible came to pass.

It is said that as Cortés pawed the Indians' golden idols of their Dragon-God Quetzalcoatl, and Were-Dog God Xolotl, King Montezuma rolled his eyes to the heavens and sang out an unearthly word, which could only have been a prayer summoning those devils.

"Mocuepa! Mocuepa!"

This cry filled me with a cold premonition, and I looked to see my Moorish Slave man instantly bathed by a solitary ray of the blood-Moon. His face turned up to the silver sky, while his mettle changed from that of a yellow-bellied Moor to Quetzalcoatl's dragon-Vampyr:

"Aaaaaiiii!" he screamed.

Fangs grew from his jaws; his skin turned moth-pale; his fingers curled and sharpened like claws; filthy wings grew from his shoulders. Upon the completion of his metamorphosis he turned to me and roared:

"DIE!"

Rising in the air, Satan-quick, he sailed back down to bite me on the Neck. The Moor had long protested his enslavement. In his moonstruck Power, he sought to kill me in Retribution! But the germ he transferred made me stronger, whilst he weakened with the other fiend's gift.

Thus I was infected. My body trembled, convulsed, and grew to the Freakish hairy dimensions of Xolotl the Dog-God. I lowered my Wolverine's gaze to the helpless Spaniards, whom I commenced to kill in an ecstasy. Only the shrieking & nimbly fleeing Cortés escaped.

In the morning, I found my restored form now cauled in thick blood. The camp was littered with Gold & Gore, abandoned by all other living creatures save for my sun-crippled Slave (for the Nosferatu have an allergy to Light), who begged me:

"Have mercy! Have mercy upon me!"

But I did not. I hastened the Treasure back to my Italian ship, which I had hidden from Cortés's famous burning. First I clapped one of the Aztec's gold Torture masks upon his face, as it would allow me to slowly starve the man whilst also guarding him from any energizing Moon. Then, months later, I landed in Venice; here my slave-man died in the dungeons. It was with both a jubilant heart, and the vampire-Moor's gilded remains that I began the parlous journey back to Florence, buried the Slave in a plot by our crypt . . . only to then be exiled again by you.

Which of the Tales is true? You know the Answer, Cosimo, as you have called me Versipellis, having recognized me as a man who has shape-shifted into an Aztec Monster.

And so ends my letter, filled as it is with Tricks & Clues. Only if you study my words, and what lies beneath them, will you discover the Key to the mystery that waits for you in Rome. If so, your mettle will prove cleverer, and much less yellow than I supposed.

But in my Wolf heart, by the beating of my Wyvern's blood, I hope you die on this next Quest.

Sincerely yours
Il Noioso Lupo Retto,
otherwise known as
Antonio.

25

Antonio says there are three clues in here, Erik—'*having survived to take up the challenges of City Three, you have earned that many additional hints*'—but I don't see any." He and I were closely inspecting this bizarre letter. "There's something going on with these flowers, the illuminations. They form some kind of design." We squinted down at them.

Erik's eyes drooped slightly; he had begun to tire. As had I. "I don't know what that is. But—look at this. It's strange."

He pointed to the letter's closing lines:

> "*Sincerely yours*
> **Il Noioso Lupo Retto,**
> *otherwise known as*
> Antonio."

" 'Il Noioso Lupo Retto.' There's something funny about it. . . ."

I wrapped one of my legs around his. "It means, 'The Righteous, Tiresome Wolf.' "

"*Lupo* means 'Wolf.' *Retto*—that's 'righteous.' "

"And then *noioso* means 'boring' or 'tiresome.' I think from the Latin *nausea*."

"That's weird."

"That's etymology for you."

"No—I mean the phrasing of it. Calling himself that. It *sounds* weird. It doesn't sound like the rest of the letter—even the line's script is different."

I looked closer. "You're right."

Erik deftly opened the side table's drawer while remaining entangled with me. He extracted a pen and paper, and commenced scribbling.

"What are you doing?"

"I think it might be scrambled."

"A word puzzle?"

"Yes. A palindrome—or an anagram. Because Antonio was an alchemist, his wife a spiritualist or witch. Right? Renaissance occultists were crazy as *loons* about acrostics. And Witches were supposed to compose these palindrome prayers—kind of early versions of the Beatles records—read from the front, they'd be homilies to Christ, but then, backward, they'd be invocations to the Devil. When I was younger, I went through a manic little anagram phase myself—I formed them out of my name all the time. *Erik Gomara* turns nicely into *Karma Ergo I*—sounds vaguely like a yoga position—and *I'm a Keg Roar,* which reminds me of some parties I attended in my youth. But the best one I ever thought up was O *magik rear,* which I thought sounded like a Wiccan description of my posterior region."

"O *magik rear?*"

He yawned. "It's so bad it's good. But—before I pass out— help me out with the literal translation, here."

Erik scratched his pen over the paper, writing Antonio's closing and its English conversion:

Il	Noioso	Lupo	Retto
The	*Wolf [who is]*	*Tiresomely*	*Righteous*

In short order, he nimbly scrambled the letters until he came up with this:

Il Noioso Lupo Retto =
Io Sono il Lupo Tetro

The resolved anagram, translated literally, is

Io	Sono	il	Lupo Tetro
I	*am a*	*Wolf Dark & Sad*	

Or

I am a Sad & Dark Wolf

I slapped my hand on the bed. "That's it! That's it, Erik!"

"*Tetro.*" Erik rested his head on a cushion. "That means 'sad and dark, or gloomy, melancholy,' like we were talking about before."

"Yes."

I read it again, and again, until something disgruntingly obvious occurred to me.

"But we already *knew* that. Antonio was a depressive. I don't see how this is supposed to be any kind of clue."

Erik's eyes had just closed. His head sank down farther into the comforter.

"Erik."

His eyes half-opened. "Yes."

"Let's figure this out."

He crawled under the covers with lumbering lunges. "You just come here, snuggle up—you talk, and I'll meditate on it."

In the next minute, his mouth opened and he had splayed dramatically all over the bed.

I, on the other hand, continued to obsess over the letter.

Il Noioso Lupo Retto:
The Righteous and Tiresome Wolf
Io Sono il Lupo Tetro:
I am the Dark and Sad Wolf

For the next few hours, until just before dawn began to break, I alternately napped alongside Erik and leafed through the epistle in search of the *"Three Hints"* that Antonio promised were secreted in the letter. His story about the gold did seem to contain occluded meanings, but there were not any I could interpret; I also could not begin to fathom a treasure clue from the unscrambled lament concerning his dark sadness.

I glared out the still-black window of our room while I pondered the Wolf's strange life and death. The letter that Marco Moreno had dragged me to Italy to study had been written by Antonio on the eve of the Florentine's 1554 battle against the Sienese. History told that the fight had gone well for the Florentines but not for Antonio. As I had explained to Marco days before in the Red Lion—and as the tattooed man/father/freakshow had briefly recounted for me before our scuffle at the caffè—Antonio had becóme fatally confused during the skirmish against the Sienese. No book on the Medici history is complete without

this colorful story of his demise: Antonio had been in the possession of some extraordinarily powerful weapon (which many
attributed to his alchemical experiments, and others to Sofia the
Dragon's magic), but somehow his horse had turned the wrong
way on the battlefield, and before he had been cut down, he had
killed many men in a catastrophic sixteenth-century version of
"friendly fire."

A man's method of dying is the best evidence of the way he lived—

Marco Moreno's voice echoed in my mind. Those were
the words he said to me in the Medici tomb, moments before he described Tomas de la Rosa's supposed ignominious
death.

*It's much better to go out like Antonio, don't you think? All flashing
and blazing on the Siena battlefield, using that weapon of his—What was it
again? Some sort of witchcraft. It's worth looking into—*

I rubbed my eyes. Perhaps we were missing some key that
could be found only in Antonio's last days. The melancholy Wolf
had fought and been executed on the Tuscan battleground of . . .
I couldn't remember.

Slipping off the bed, I made for the stack of books I had
purchased that morning in Siena's shops. Though I hadn't found
any in-depth studies of Renaissance Tuscan mayhem, I did
stumble on a little capitalist self-help gem called *How to Crush
the Competition Like a Medici: Learn from the First Cosa Nostra's Battles
to Achieve Global Corporate Domination.* Paging through this brutal
little guidebook's many maps, I found the spot where Antonio
fell in the '54 war.

There it was, in the south of Tuscany:

Marciano-Scannagallo. *How to Crush the Competition's* atlas indi-
cated that the battleground was not so very far away from where

we were. But what exactly had happened in the theater—at that hour? And why had Antonio become confused and killed the wrong men before being cut down himself?

I checked my wristwatch: four in the morning. A perfect time to wake up.

Erik lay in an immobile heap on the bed. I began to jostle his arm until I saw that his eyes were already open, and his skin was pale and moist.

"Erik— Erik, honey."

"Ye-es."

"Why are you awake?"

"Because sleeping's so overrated."

"What are you thinking about? What happened in the crypt?"

"Nonsense."

"Want to talk about it?"

"I don't think that's a very good idea."

"Why?"

"Because I *am* thinking about how those poor old guys died, and Blasej . . . and I'd rather forget the whole business as soon as is humanly possible."

"Well. If you're sure you *don't* want to talk."

"Very."

"Then, sorry." I began tossing him around again. "You have to get up—"

"Um—*no*. I want a drink. Or you could just crush up a bottle of Ambien and sprinkle it over some gelato for me."

"No, no, no. Come on, lovey—come on, sexy—"

"I'm really not joking—"

"On your feet. I'm going to talk to the manager—see if we can rent his car. We're going to make a little trip."

"Oh, right, a trip—*where?*"

"Marciano."

"What? Why?"

"To find out how Antonio died."

26

"Dad—are you there?" I was fumbling with the cell phone that the tattooed man had tossed me in the Duomo. "Can you hear me now?"

"Monster? Where *are you?* Why haven't you called us?"

"Ah—Pops—how's the world's greatest father, and most macho Mexican—"

"Lola, what's going on? You—you—you ran away!"

"Er, um, yeah, I'm in Italy."

"Good Lord! A few nights ago Erik calls us gibbering about Aztecs, the Medici, some Lothario whisking you off to Europe, and—gag—I can barely *say* it—something about de la Rosa's grave. The next thing we knew, he'd sped off to Rome. And then your *sister* . . ."

"Yolanda—what do you mean?"

"Darling, you know I love you. You are my angel and I adore you from the tips of your toes to that little zany brain of yours, and I would slay dragons to protect you—even though you suddenly appear to have gone as witless as the seven hundred pounds of poultry your wedding caterer is even now transforming into tacos for your wedding reception!"

"Dad—"

"Lo-la. I understand you went to Italy because you might find
Tomas there? I *do* know that your miserable excuse for a biological father cut quite the dashing figure—after all, I nearly lost
your mother to his gassy charisma decades ago, which I cannot
completely regret, obviously, since it gave me *you* . . . but let's
get past all that, can't we? He is *dead now*! And I thought that
might mean that I could *finally* get some peace of mind—but no!
First your mother gallops off to the jungle to find his tomb and
nearly gets squashed to bits in the jungle—and then you! Racing
off without a single whit of notice, and practically on the eve of
your wedding." Manuel Alvarez took a big breath and blew it out.
"Though I must say that I *am* so glad to hear from you, Creature.
I do adore you so much that I can't really be very upset (though
your mother has been a raving *animal*) even if it means that I have
to share your affection with of course the eternally damned ghost
of that scoundrel de la Rosa. . . ."

While Manuel gasped into my ear, Erik and I drove in our
manager's rented car, a silver Fiat. It smelled like cigarettes and
guzzled gas, but we'd stocked it with books and provisions Erik
thought we'd need to barrel over the thirty southeast miles extending from Siena to Marciano della Chiana. We headed to the
bucolic countryside that once was the battlefield where Antonio
had died. It was not quite dawn. The region's groves and twisted,
dark trees diffused the early lavender light. The scene's Zen-like
beauty, however, stood in harsh contrast to the jangling voice of
Manuel Alvarez, Ph.D.—my adopted father, the long-unmarried
lover of Juana, and the Guatemalan curator whose secret stores of
bravery helped us face down Colonel Moreno two years ago and
to locate my mother in the jungle.

"Okay, Pops, listen. First off, I'm definitely not here looking
for de la Rosa—de la Rosa's *grave*," I assured him with this very
incomplete truth.

"You're not?" he asked in his high, scratchy voice. "No? Oh. Well! Then why in the world was everyone howling that Tomas died in Italy?"

"That's just a rumor, it's not true. And I need you to focus on something else now."

"First Tomas is dead in Guatemala. Then he's dead in Italy. Then he's nowhere. And *still* he is able to drive us all absolutely bats—"

"Dad, listen to me."

"Um . . . okay! All ears, darling."

"Right now, we're in Siena—actually, almost at Marciano della Chiana."

"We're practically there," yawned Erik. He was simultaneously driving and blinking at the map. "Just looks like vineyards. Grapes. Farmhouses. Good. Nothing that could kill you." He squinted at my silver cell. "Where'd you get that phone, by the way?"

"Ssss—*him*," I mouthed.

"Oh, right, the Ghost of Christmas Past—"

"Was that Erik?" my father asked.

"Yes, he's here."

"So he found you? Before he left, he said you scampered off with some sort of *man*."

"I did—I'm here because someone showed up at the Lion with this document, Dad. His name's Marco Moreno. We sort of . . . know him. Remember Colonel Moreno? Victor Moreno?"

"Marco Moreno? Mmmm, no bells. Wait—did you say Colonel *Moreno*? From the jungle? The *dead* one? The one who tried to shoot us and was smashed to pieces?"

"Marco is his son."

"*Is that her?!*" I heard my mother exclaim in the background.

"The *son*," my father said. "That's not good, is it?"

"Well, he's gone, now. He went off, after Erik . . . talked to him and his friends."

"Yeah, that's what happened," Erik muttered next to me. "We just hugged it out, and then they all teleported away."

My voice pitched: "But this letter he brought me—it was written by Antonio Medici."

"I'd rather talk about this Marco fellow—"

"*Dad*, Antonio Medici? Do you know about him? The con-quistatore?"

"Agh, yes, yes. I attended a panel on him in Morocco, where we all *foamed* about these beastly colonials. Antonio Medici, al-chemist, werewolf, soldier of Cortés, mass murderer—"

"In his letter, we found a map, kind of. It's amazing—it could lead us to Aztec treasure."

"Well, there *was* that old rumor, of Antonio having stolen some sort of Mexican stash. Never been substantiated. So, I see. You are trying to find old Montezuma's gold? *That's* interesting—but, wait— Honey— *Juana*—calm down, gagh—*I'm talking to her*—"

My mother is a silver-haired, Mexican-born world expert on Mayan iconography, who began booming out in the loud, dan-gerous voice that terrified her underlings at UCLA, where she headed the archaeology department: "So? What'd she say? Is she shacked up with some guy?"

"It doesn't sound like that, dear."

"Then what's she doing? I'm playing Wanda the wedding planner over here, and I've got a dozen bridesmaids coming over any minute to slap a tiara on her head and get her wasted—"

I blurted: "*Dad*—we're looking for this place where Antonio died. Go with me on this."

"I know where Antonio was killed, Lola. Used to be called Scannagallo, a valley—"

"We're driving to it now." I explained to Manuel that I needed whatever details he could muster about the Florentines' conflict with the Sienese, and Antonio's last battle.

"Fine. All right. Let me try to collect my thoughts—though I'm starting to feel very queasy about this Moreno person . . . ah, let's see . . . Siena was a pawn in Franco-Italian tensions in the sixteenth century. In the so-called Italian wars. The city wanted independence from Spain—Charles V had Spanish garrisons there—and the Medici also wanted it for themselves."

"Good, good, what else?"

"Cosimo aligned himself with Charles to fight against the French, who were protecting the Sienese rebels. A soldier named Pietro Strozzi, an enemy of Cosimo's, defended the Sienese. In, what, 1554, his infantry went rampaging around the countryside, pillaging and whatnot, also very cheerfully disemboweling Imperial supporters. But the decisive battle happened during the summer. That's when the Medici forces arrived."

Erik pressed harder on the gas. "The map says we're going to pull up around it soon."

I looked up as he drove the car off the main road, bumping over dirt roads until he pulled up directly west to a valley. The lifting light revealed a long dip in the countryside, filled with wild-looking sycamores, and from this vantage I could just detect a man on the other side of the valley. He wore a shirt that looked dark gray in the predawn. This would be a farmer or a vintner. He was too far away to see in any detail, but I could discern that he walked alone among the trees, squatting on his haunches as if to examine the grass.

"Who was fighting with the Medici?" I asked into the phone as Erik parked the car.

"It would be mercenaries mostly."

Erik rested his head on the seat and rolled his eyes back into his head from exhaustion.

"They had about five thousand men under the marquess of Marignano," Manuel went on. "Give or take. Both sides were made up of hired guns—except the Sienese were weaker. Their army had been decimated a few months before, in another skirmish against the emperor's men, and the survivors were tired and injured, as you'd expect. The two armies faced off there for months—until early August. Antonio was in the Imperial camp by that time—it was his money that paid for at least a third of the men who were fighting more for Cosimo than Charles. And then, there was the battle—something happened. There was bad weather, I believe. In any event, he became confused. Antonio began killing Florentines, not Sienese, and then was killed himself, by some mysterious explosive device—"

"Dad, I had a book in the library—it's a history of the war. *God Loves the Mighty.*"

"The Gregorio Albertini, yes. I *love* that book. Deathless propaganda! Here—let me go get it—I actually remember that Albertini had a curious description of the fight—"

This is when I heard my mother clatter onto the phone: "Lola."

"Hi, Mom."

"*I'm* not upset."

"Good."

"It's your *father* who's upset. What did you just tell him? Do you know he looks like he's about to faint?"

"I just—"

"And that your wedding shower is in an hour? And because you don't have any friends but your sister and your boyfriend, I had to invite all *my* pals over here to play pin the tail on the stripper—"

"Oh —agh—*right.*"

"*And* that Yolanda has gone running off to find you?"

"What, what, what do you mean running off—"

"You can't yell like that in the car," Erik grumbled. "Your voice is boomeranging off the windows."

"She's gone off, Terrible Creature," my mother said. "She read some news on a blog yesterday about two or three unidentified and unstable Latins breaking into the Sienese Duomo, and she had this ridiculous theory about how it must be *you,* and she was already so edgy about the mariachi tryouts in the living room, and the butterfly motif of the bridesmaids' dresses. . . ." Her voice lowered into a gravely whisper. "And *also* about that craziness Erik nattered about. You know, *Tomas?* About where he was buried? In *Europe?* Despite the fact that I nearly got my head caved in digging around for him in the jungle? Because I was under some misimpression that I still *loved that old dead houndog?!* Well! Humph! I—that is, *she,* your sister, just couldn't take it anymore—she's been trying to call you, couldn't get a hold—and finally just went racing off. You know how she is!"

"That's not good," I said, thinking about the tattooed man. Ever since Tomas had disappeared, my half sister had fended off a serious depression. My sister is a very . . . *special* person, and I knew that if she learned de la Rosa faked his death and deserted her, all of her beautiful melancholy would flower into a devilish head-spinning rage that might be great in my Criterion copy of *The Exorcist* but heinous in real life.

"Who's coming here?" Erik asked.

"Yolanda," I said.

"Your sister? That will be so cozy—"

"She's there now," my mother went on, "landed in Rome a few hours ago. Monster, she said she'd track you down. And Tomas's grave, if she could. And I heard your father saying something about Montezuma's gold?"

"Yes, there's maybe a possibility that we could find it here, but—"

"*How?* Do you have any good leads? Yes? Hmmm, you'll probably need me to figure that out. But it *does* seem intriguing! Manuel and I tried to find that gold ourselves, in Brazil, in eighty-three. UCLA gave me a grant, but I have to admit that we spent most of our time streaking drunk through Rio. I think Tomas hunted around for old Montezuma's cache, too. . . . So! Italy *does* sound nice. Around here, it's all taffeta and canceled scavenger hunts—and bridesmaids who look like dogs in their dresses, by the way. Where do you think you'll be in the next few days?"

I could barely concentrate on what she was saying. "What?"

"I'm asking *where you'll be?*"

"I don't know, Mom— It could be anywhere. *When did Yolanda leave?*"

"Yesterday. Look—I'm asking you a question."

"Oh—I don't know. Maybe Venice if we're lucky."

"Venice. Perfect. Pop in, nose around, see what we find. Pop back in time, get you hitched. Though I suppose it will be cutting things rather close—"

"You're not thinking about coming here?" I flabbered. If my sister would be Linda Blair at the sight of the resurrected Tomas, Juana would be Grendel's *mami.* I looked out onto the green and gold paradise. "The weather here is so disgusting."

"Since when did that ever stop me?"

"And . . . there's been an outbreak of plague."

Another clattering noise. "I've got it," my father said. "Hello again, dear. Your mother's turning a terrible shade of pink. *But* you'll be happy to know I found the book!"

I pressed the ball of my left hand against my right eye, as if trying to keep the contents of my head from spilling out all over the car. "Let's hear what it says."

Over the line came the sound of pages being turned. "*This* is the passage I was thinking of," Manuel said. "It's awkwardly written."

"Erik." I lifted the phone. "Honey. Come hear this—it might be important."

"Mmmm? What is it?"

"It's from *God Loves the Mighty*—"

❦ 27 ❦

My father's voice crackled over the phone line as he read out this portion of Gregorio Albertini's history:

It was on August 2 that the Florentines won their great victory against the Kingdom of Siena, under the aegis of my Lord Cosimo I. In the hours before daybreak, the two armies faced off together on either side of the valley at Scannagallo, and the torches held by both armies revealed Siena's black-and-white flag fluttering at the east end. Antonio Medici, the elderly Uncle of our Lord Cosimo, took his position at the Florentine vanguard, warning the gendarmes not to move before his command.

In the silence, we could hear nothing but the rattling of the pikemen's staffs, and the snorting of the horses, the coughs of a few of the Swiss.

The next thing we knew, Antonio broke ranks.

It was already a warm morning, such as one will find on any ordinary day in late Summer, and so, even as the sun began to raise her golden head I could see quite clearly (from my position on the top of a very high hill, as I scribbled down my notes at Cosimo's

*order), Sir Antonio rear his shrieking horse as if it were a Beast of
the Devil.*

*The gleaming Steed charged down the valley's cup. Antonio
was the first into the Breach, wielding his halberd, hacking off many
a Sienese head. From his Wallet he took a handful of amber Mud (a
powerful and secret Weapon he had learned to craft in his days spent
among the Moors), lit it with a Spill, and from these two Elements
conjured a Ball of Fire as powerful as a Star.*

*But at this instant, just as he had raised his Rocket against the
Sienese, a miscalculation occurred. It nearly lost us the war.*

*My Patron, the Lord Cosimo, wishes that I make clear in this
History that all morning, the valley's Battlefield had been plagued
with a thick & hazy Grimpen Mist, for there have been various rumors
surrounding The Error. My Lord instructs us, Dear Readers, that it
was only on account of the terrific Fog that Antonio did not correct his
wild horse, which turned around, away from the Enemy. So blinded
was he by the Murk, he began to throw these Fiery missiles at Our
own Men, killing nearly three hundred before a brave Florentine threw
a pike, and struck the Wolf in the chest, causing him to fall dead.*

"It sounds like he was using naphtha," said Erik, when my
father had finished. He and I were hunkered together in the car,
sharing the earpiece.

"That's a very interesting theory," my father said. "Hmmm.
Naphtha."

"Not just a theory," I muttered, still stinking of the ancient
petrol that had nearly souffléd us beneath the Duomo.

"What?" my father asked.

"Nothing—just saying it's a gruesome story."

"Yes, it's not very charming," my father agreed. "And, like I
said, confusingly written. But does it help?"

I looked out the car's windshield. The sky had brightened considerably. "I don't know, I don't even know what we're looking for. But we're there now—at the field. We're going to poke around, see if there's anything interesting here."

"Fine—my heavens—but *call us later*—"

"See you later!" I heard my mother hollering.

"And remember that we—that *I*—love you," Manuel said.

"Me too, Pops—"

He clicked off.

My fingers formed a miniature tepee over my nose. "That didn't go very well."

"Lola," Erik said.

"My father . . . and my *mother*. She's not going to stay put. She's going to come flying down here, like those flying monkeys in *The Wizard of Oz*—"

"Lola, *look* how beautiful it is."

I hushed and looked.

From far off, beneath the opening sky, pale blue hills captured the first hues of the sun. In front of these lay the valley, painted by foliage in shades of green that varied from a nearly white lime to a chocolate-ivy. A recent rain had fallen and there remained still a glistening layer of dew upon the landscape. Wet-black dirt paths threaded through the vale; this part of the territory was a vineyard. Upon the descending hills struggled very dark, gnarled trees. These were more numerously planted in a small grove to the east. I glanced back and forth along the far edge of the vista, but could no longer see the farmer or vintner whom I had seen meandering through the grass when we'd first pulled the car up to the valley.

"A little sleepwalking will do us good," yawned Erik.

He tossed the keys onto the front seat, also grabbing a bundle of foodstuffs before walking away from the car across a stretch of grass. Moving to the right, we spent the next twenty minutes heading down a sloping path that skirted around the rim of the declension, then into the valley, with its expanses of purple-black flowers and wild trees.

"Are you holding up?" I asked.

We had reached the west side of the ravine, as the sun continued to rise behind us.

"Yes, I'm awake now. It's *nippy*. But I brought along some coffee—that manager man was nice enough to make a giant portion of *macchiato*—steamed milk and everything—and there's cookies—little amaretti—and a couple of slices of orange cake—"

We ate these in a companionable huddle. The glen stretched visibly to the other side, where we saw a lemon-yellow car parked.

"Another Fiat," Erik said.

"Can you see that from here?" I asked.

"My eyes are good. I can even see the spoiler. And anyway, that's practically all the Italians drive."

Below us extended a slope, covered with crystal-tipped grasses and fat scrubby bushes. The descent slipped into a small copse of sycamores. We half-walked, half-slid down the mud path while snagging our pant legs on the brambles. The decline was fairly steep.

"Let's see," I said, "the Florentines would have been flanked here. We're on the west—"

"Right—the Sienese were on the east side. I'm trying to remember Renaissance battle tactics—the vanguard would have been made up of footsoldiers, pikemen, artillery, and cannons."

We approached the dusky copse of trees.

"Albertini said the front line was commanded by Antonio, on horseback," I said.

"Then—over *there*—to our far right, and to our left, would have been the light cavalry."

We entered the grove. It broadened much more than it had appeared to from the car, though it had not been thickly planted. The sunlight fell like water from the trees down to the grass and scatterings of dark purple, hooded-petaled blossoms.

"But he—Antonio—charged out first, without giving a signal to his troops," I said.

"And he would do that because . . . ?"

"Some kind of battle madness?"

"But he didn't even believe in the war with Siena." Erik shielded his eyes against the strengthening sun. "What's missing here?"

"Missing?"

"I was expecting something else—I've read about the battle before, and I saw it the way that Albertini described it. There's something about this place that isn't . . . quite . . . *right*."

"Albertini wrote—What?—'*it was already a warm morning*'—something like that—'*the kind one will find on an ordinary day in late Summer.*' And he wrote that he had a good view of the battle, too—from far up on a hill—just like you saw the Fiat so clearly—"

"But *then* he wrote something else—about the weather—"

"That there was a mist," I said slowly.

"That's it—*that's* what's missing. He contradicted himself."

I stopped walking. "And this is a colder morning than it would have been in August."

"And—don't you remember what your dad quoted to us? What did Albertini say? That Cosimo wanted him *to make clear*—something—"

" '*That all morning, the valley's Battlefield had been plagued with a thick & hazy Grimpen Mist*'—something—'*there have been rumors surrounding The Error.*' "

"That's right—it sounds almost as if he were lying."

"To keep Cosimo happy. Revisionist history, to avoid a scandal."

"Because if there were *no mist*—I mean, it's impossible to know. It depends on the weather patterns of the fifteen hundreds—but still, Albertini doesn't sound like he's giving us the whole story. And if there *wasn't* mist, then that would have meant—it's just possible—"

"That Antonio killed the Florentines on purpose."

"That he wasn't mistaken." Erik thinned his eyes at the copse that stretched farther in front of us. "He could see his—"

"That *he could see his victims.*" I finished the thought. "He knew whom he was killing."

Erik did not respond. He kept his eyes fixed ahead, toward the vanishing point of the grove of trees.

I followed his gaze. I saw the gold leaves on the ground, the black-purple buds among the sycamores. I noticed a flicker of red from behind one of the trees.

Perhaps half an hour earlier, in the dawn's half-light, I had thought the man was a vintner or farmer, wearing a gray shirt. But here I spied a red sleeve, a red shoulder. A royal blue back-pack sat on the ground, next to the tree.

A red-shirted man leaned against one of the trees, facing away from us, writing in a leather-bound notepad while reading from a hardback book. We had disturbed him.

He turned around, gazing at us from behind the bole of the tree. We saw his black hair, dusky cheek, his dark and expanding eyes. We knew them.

He had not followed us. We had surprised Marco Moreno in this valley. And for a second, as we stared back at him, I saw that he looked almost pleased.

∼ 28 ∼

Shining leaves spiraled down upon the three of us. Marco rose quickly from his position at the base of the tree, his shirt a flash of blood against the transparent air. I saw with X-ray clarity the bite-bruise Erik had left on his cheek, and his black, deep-set eyes, which had extraordinarily dark shadows beneath them. He still held his notebook and pen. The open hardback book rested on a small plaid square of rubberized cloth—a mackintosh square—so as to protect the binding from the ground's moisture. Not far from it, the royal blue rucksack, dented and stuffed, lay in the purple-flowering grass.

I walked toward him, while Erik chattered: "He's the yellow Fiat. Let's go. Go go go."

"He's got the letter—"

"Oh, damn—*right*. And you don't remember the rest of the riddle?"

"The last time I tried out the old photographic memory—"

"We were screaming and surrounded by fire." Erik's eyes were huge. "Right. Okay. At the moment, though, I'm having trouble coming up with a plan for both getting the letter *and* sprinting away without getting shivved by Mr. Personality. So why don't we just say sayonara get the f—"

"I *thought* you might come ferreting down here, Lola," Marco sang out, much calmer than I would have thought. "Though I admit I didn't expect you so soon." He darted his eyes at the dripping grove behind us. About one hundred feet away, Domenico squatted by a pit he'd dug in the ground; he worked to kindle a campfire with a lighter attached to his keyring. His face was flat and very pale as he gazed up. "Look who's here, Dom," Marco said in Italian.

"Yes, I see," answered the blond man, his hands shaking so the keys jangled.

"I suggested that he drive me to this valley for a little fresh air." Marco waved at the scenery with his notepad. "Neither of us is doing very well, unfortunately."

I could just make out that the notepad's visible page contained a passage of sepia handwriting. The rest of the leaf was filled with what appeared to be a beautiful cross-hatched architectural sketch of Siena's Duomo.

"Does he know why you're really here?" I asked.

"Domenico? All he knows is that his friend is dead."

"Because of that emerald." Domenico's grief-stained eyes swung from me to Erik as he crouched over smoking twigs.

Marco took a step toward the backpack. I saw no gun, and he made no menacing gestures—yet. "Do you know? Why I'm here."

"I know you're smart," I said carefully. "I know you've figured something out."

"I think you might be trying to flatter me, Lola."

"Not really. What's in the rucksack?"

"Your favorite—secrets."

"Are you being *charming*?"

"Do you like it?"

"Not really. It doesn't suit you."

"I don't think you mean *that*—"

"Well, I like it better than watching your friends kill people."

He gestured at Erik, who moved forward to stand between us. "Yes, *or* watching Chewbacca poison Blasej to death—"

"Your friend got himself into trouble," Erik was saying to Domenico in slow and precise Italian during this exchange.

"I heard what you said to Blasej." Domenico pointed at Erik so that his keys jangled again in his hand. "You said it looked valuable. The emerald. You wanted him to touch it. You knew there was something wrong with it."

Marco took a step toward the rucksack, then another. "Poor Blasej. I've known him for years—when I first came over to Europe from Guatemala, I bribed him and our dear Domenico here off their armies, to be my bodyguards—more like drinking companions. They became awfully close."

"I heard you left Guatemala before the end of the war," I said.

"It was a sabbatical, let's say—from myself! Or my father—it was so difficult to tell the difference between us two, sometimes. But my time away wasn't altogether successful. Even here, unfortunately, they read the papers, and Colonel Moreno's international press was not . . . very good. Domenico and Blasej hoped they were attaching themselves to some barbarian grandee, didn't you, Domenico?"

But Domenico was mouthing something at Erik.

"Oh—stop that growling," Marco barked.

"I want you to go to our car," Erik whispered to me. "Maybe I can get to theirs—steal it—then they can't follow us. We'll have to split up—opposite sides of the valley—"

"*What?*"

"Relax, *relax*," Marco was saying to Domenico.

"Why should I?"

"Because—I want them to stay—I haven't said confession in so long. And who better to absolve me of my sins than a pretty girl? You see, Lola, my association with the boys has unfortunately *not* been very good for their health, particularly Blasej's. Nor did it benefit their reputations. The Italians call them turncoats, but I prefer to call them, or rather, now, just Domenico—"

"A *Versipellis?*"

Marco hovered over the backpack, the shadows beneath his eyes spreading down to his cheeks. "Aha, *Versipellis*—skin-shifter. That's very clever. How metaphorical of you."

"Thank you."

"Much better than my word for him. I was simply going to call him practical."

Erik stared at me over his shoulder. "What are you doing?"

"She's *playing*," Marco answered. "She thinks she has figured me out. My weaknesses. And what's interesting is that she is . . . partially . . . right."

"You're here researching Antonio," I said.

"Rather obvious, isn't it?" He gestured toward the book on the ground, amid the vivid blossoms. "What do *you* think happened here?"

"He killed his men on purpose."

"*Yes.* Very good. *Very*, very quick. The question is why?" He bent farther down, but did not snatch at the backpack yet. Instead, he plucked up one of the stalks of purple flowers, with the bell-shaped petals and dangles of black berries, and waved it at me. "Careful, careful, careful, *pretty lady*," he said.

I looked at the darkly glimmering flowers. I recognized them but said nothing.

"Ah, and *this* pretty lady sees, she remembers—something?"
Marco threw the blooms to the ground. "But let's not get ahead
of ourselves. First things first—the she-wolf, that is—"

"If you know so much, then where were you all day yesterday?" I asked. "We didn't see you."

"Oh, well if you had, then I wouldn't be much good for anything, would I? I gave Domenico a little sleeping powder in the
morning. He wouldn't stop crying. And I wanted to go hunting
for you by myself, and worm into your findings like the good
little weevil I am."

Domenico snapped his head toward his employer and cursed,
as he apparently understood more Spanish than I'd believed. He
stood up.

"I wound up following you around for *hours* until I grew so
bored I thought I'd die!" said Marco. "By the way, did you ever
find that blasted wolf?"

"No." Erik stepped away from me, toward the campfire. He
began to work his way toward Domenico.

"So, I'm assuming *yes*."

"Erik, hold on, don't mess with him," I said. But Erik didn't
acknowledge me.

"Straining on his leash a bit, isn't he?" Marco purred.

I thrust my chin at him. "Why didn't *you* find it? The She-
Wolf?"

He shrugged. "My research was interrupted. I became . . .
tired."

"Tired?"

"Having trouble with the euphemism? By tired, I meant *depressed*. Sick. Sad. Suicidal. What do you think I mean? *My father's
dead. And* my cousin's dead. *And* Estrada—who was my *friend*. I'm
supposed to punish *you*—and what I'm doing instead is hobbling

about Italy, digging through books, looking for I don't know what, and getting back into some old sticky messes that I had sworn I'd given up."

"The guards."

"Yes. I had hoped to avoid such ugliness." His voice sounded shredded. "But apparently that's not possible for me."

At his feet I saw the volume he had placed so carefully on the mackintosh square. I crouched before the backpack that I *knew* contained Antonio's letter, but it was the book I picked up: it was an old, fine, early edition of Jacob Burckhardt's *Die Kultur der Renaissance in Italien*, an amazing history full of art and murder.

"This is a good book." I handed it back to him.

"A classic." He ran his hand over the opened pages before closing it.

"I don't think you're here because of your father, Marco."

"Ah—"

"I think you're trying to solve this puzzle because you're *good* at it. You knew the clue about the map was planted in the letter. And you know something happened in this valley—"

"You've seen what I'm good at." He swallowed. "In the crypt."

"You weren't good at all. I saw you. Blasej and Domenico killed those men. You just stood there—crying."

"Unfortunately, you're wrong. Because I'm very, very, very talented. I was better than he was, in the war—I was better than my father."

"At what—fighting?"

"Fighting." Marco tormented the shape of his mouth while saying the word; apparently it was another euphemism. "That's why I left Guatemala! What a joke! Now I'm here, looking for this money, bumping off old men, because I'm just like the old colonel, and *I can't change.*"

"So now you want to be—what—a dictator?"

"You don't even know the meaning of the words you're using. My father had a beautiful vision for the country: as a place of light, of learning, of beauty, of order—a dream far greater than Pinochet's—and we wouldn't require all the rigor of Miloševic. Only after a few reorganizations, and sufficient *funds*, ours could be a country that would leave Cuba, North Korea, even your United States in the shade—"

"It's so *stupid*. If you weren't so messed up, you'd be a scholar!"

He looked at me, bemused for a moment. "A scholar . . ." But then he shook his head. "No, *that* was Tomas de la Rosa."

"De la Rosa. You're obsessed."

"As I said. I'm like my father. You'd just better hope you're not like yours."

"Why?"

"Because he *killed* himself, Lola. I've been waiting for the right time to tell you! He committed suicide, here, in Italy. Out of guilt. Out of his guilt." Marco picked up the backpack and shook it at me. "I can prove it. I'm going to show you. I've got papers in here—a death certificate—that records how he died. You'll see *he* was as much of an animal as me."

"Suicide?"

"Yes—he was mad—"

"That's not possible. . . ."

But I would have been insane to tell him anything about my brush with the tattooed stranger. I instead took hold of the rucksack's strap, as Marco pulled it back, slowly, forcefully. I planted my feet, breathing harder.

"Tug of war?" he asked.

"I know the letter's in here! I want it." I pulled and yanked and tugged.

"You're kidding, right? You're *hilarious.*"

"Just—give—it—to—me—"

"For someone so short, you're awfully grabby—"

"Don't you dare grin at me," I heard Domenico suddenly order Erik, who now stood face to face with him.

"Oh, I swear, this is *nervous* laughter. That wouldn't be a gun, would it?"

"Boss doesn't think I should carry one in my—condition, that's what he calls it. But this works pretty well, doesn't it?" Domenico slipped out a long silver knife from his pocket, cradling it in the hand that did not carry the keys. He twirled the blade so that it glittered like tinsel, and then with two fast swipes ripped the flesh on Erik's right arm.

"Erik!!"

Erik gripped his bleeding bicep, scowling—no, I saw his face: He was *laughing.* His dark, red, twisting expression suddenly lit up like a madly happy version of the beast-face I saw briefly in the crypt. Buoyed by a Satanic playfulness, he began to dart around Domenico, dancing, bobbing, howling, shaking his arms like a tap dancer as he taunted him with Spanish curses, a terrifying sight as his face was streaked with his own blood. Domenico watched him, waiting. Erik swiftly crouched and picked up a rock.

"Hey *batter, batter, batter,*" he called madly. "Swing batter. *Catch, idiot!*"

The rock flew through the air; Domenico instinctually grabbed it. The keys fell to the ground.

"Car— Lola—"

"What? What are you doing?"

"CAR!"

Erik swung down his arm like a bowler and snatched up the keys as he stampeded to the far side of the wood, Domenico bolting after. "Sorry, boys, did you need these?"

I suddenly understood that Erik was going to steal their vehicle so they would be stranded; I would take our manager's Fiat.

Grabbing the rucksack from Marco, I raced like hell in the other direction.

Through the woods. Past the dripping sycamores and the perfect lucid light, through the twirling curtains of orange leaves falling through the glassine air. The trees seemed to multiply in front of me, blocking my path. Branches whipped over my face, hands, and arms as I ran by the sycamores. The cool air blasted against my eyeballs. The forest was transformed into a kaleidoscope made up of a thousand broken pieces because of the impact of my feet against the ground, juddering my head on my neck, shattering my vision.

Past the trees, the incline began, out of the valley. The mud clung to my hands, peeled off the ground. I hurled myself up, the rucksack up—and right behind me, I could hear Marco panting and scratching his way up the incline. I raked my fingernails through more mud, leaves.

Up I scraped and mud slashed onto my face. Mud in my eyes. I heard a roaring, before feeling a hand gripping my calf, clawing up at my hip.

I twisted back.

Marco held me down, his breath coming so hard he looked as if he would eat me, and his eyes looked broken.

"You're stronger than me, Marco," I said. "Think of what you're—"

"Don't push me. Don't push me."

"Oh God!"

He glared at me with those red eyes.

"What are you going to do?"

Just the sound of breathing. But then he said: "You look just like him."

He let me go. He leaned back, lifting his hands, palms up. I grabbed the rucksack and did not stop running.

The shining silver Fiat came into view. The key jangled up from the seat, I crammed it into the ignition, the engine slammed into life.

Just as the yellow Fiat appeared in my windshield, the green-gold landscape unfurled out my window, while my wheels turned, hit the soft ground, spinning and sliding before barreling away from the valley's cliff.

Blood-striped Erik hollered like Emiliano Zapata behind the wheel of the other car.

We sped away—we were flying from Marco, who stood stranded in the mud with his hands at his sides. Away from Domenico, who would be cursing invisibly in the forest below. The tires levitated over the humps and hunks of grass, battering down the inclines. It sounded like a cataclysm when we skidded onto unmarked pavement, me joyfully tossing out the gun I'd fetched from the stolen backpack as if it were a live bomb. The road veered up, through the hillocks, past the valley, toward anonymous fields and vineyards and cow-mooing pastures. But we knew where it was leading.

Rome.

BOOK THREE

THE
INVISIBLE CITY

29

I think I've figured out the next step," I said excitedly to Erik several hours later, around four o'clock in the afternoon.

He and I were waiting at the miniature, cluttered, espresso-and-brioche-fragrant Bar Pasquino, an establishment tucked into a corner of Rome's Piazza Navona. Bar Pasquino is identical to perhaps five hundred thousand other caffès in the Eternal City, all resplendent with their flashes of brass, purple-belled flowers in pottery vases, and little zinc tables over which giant flat-screened TVs play blindingly violent soccer matches. After our hectic flight from Marco and Domenico, and our rapid three-hour passage into the city, we had been instructed to patronize this particular locale during a traumatic cell phone chat with my mother. Having by now learned from Manuel about Marco Moreno's blood ties to the genocidal colonel, Juana was in a manic frame of mind. Beyond explaining to me in an inner-ear-damaging staccato that I was just as bad, reckless, and nuts as my bio-dad, she'd also said this was the place just-arrived Yolanda intended to use as a message-trading center. I had tried to put the bulk of that conversation into a deep dark pit at the back of my brain, and for the past twenty minutes had been impatiently attending to the bar manager, who was about to return with the note my half sister left only a few hours before.

While waiting, I first glanced up at the billboard-size boob tube. The machine's high-def HDTV whatchamacallit was so godlike in its resolution that I found little psychological succor in an image of an Uruguayan knocking his bloody soccer-skull on a Sicilian's during an international youth tournament. I then began to bruise my thumbs sending Señor Soto-Relada text questions about Tomas's putative death, as he had claimed to know so much about the man. After that, I happily abandoned modernity to study the materials before me. On our table, cluttered already with a small purple bouquet and a jumble of silverware, I had spread Antonio's first letter, which I teased out from a thick bundle of other papers and Italian *Rough Guides* in Marco's rucksack, now in my own green backpack for safekeeping. I also had out for inspection the second, illuminated dispatch we'd snatched from the fires beneath Siena's Duomo, in addition to my increasingly thumbed copy of Sofia's *Diario Intimo*.

I had just determined that of all these documents, the last probably contained the most auspicious signs that could help us crack the third stanza of Antonio's riddle:

CITY THREE'S INVISIBLE

WITHIN THIS ROCK, FIND A BATH

BURN LOVE'S APPLE, SEE THE CLEW

THEN TRY TO FLY FROM MY WRATH.

Erik pulled out one of the purple blossoms from the table's vase while I fretted over the writings. A dark-belled, black-berried flower, it was the same kind that Marco had teased me with in the Chiana Valley and that we had been spotting throughout our stay in Italy.

"What did he call you when he gave you one of these?" He shook the plant in the air.

I barely glanced up from my studies. "What did who call me when he gave me what?"

"Marco. When he handed you one of these flowers. I heard him: He said, 'Careful, careful, careful'—and then he called you—"

"Erik, never mind that"—I pointed at the diary with both hands—"I've hit on something incredible—"

"He called you 'pretty lady,' didn't he?"

"All I remember is that there was blood all over you and that you were dancing around Domenico like a maniac. How's the bandage I put on your arm?"

"Fine—but he did. He called you that. I told you—he's getting a crush on you. He gets sweaty and glassy-eyed when he looks at you, like a kind of sweet, friendly sociopath, instead of a revolting, scary, guard-slagging—"

"Erik, he's gone."

He winked up at the televised soccer match and was briefly distracted by a failed goalie shot. "For now."

"We don't have to worry about him. They're not going to find us in the city. They don't have the diary or the second letter—they have nothing to go on."

"Madam?"

The bar manager's die-shaped face suddenly hovered above us. In his big breadloaf of a hand he held a scrap of paper.

"A note for you, signora."

I unfolded it.

Hi Lola!!!!!!

You can relax now. Yeah, I've come. Yeah, I'm here to help you in this girl detective act that's got you so into a twist that you just run off leaving me with Medusa Sanchez, who's spent the last day and a half pinning some butterfly bridesmaid's barfbag on me. By which I mean those dresses, which are beyond ugly.

So! I know you just forgot to ask me to come along to Italy, right? Huh? While Erik was slam-dancing around here right after you'd gone, I got details about you possibly fornicating with a mysterious guy and looking for Aztec gold or somesuch. And then, this morning, your ma told me on the phone that the slob you'd gone running off with is a really classy customer. Colonel Moreno's SON, was it? Juana has been keeping me updated on all the little particulars, and boy, it has been just a pleasure to have those really relaxing conversations with her. You have got to be the all-time most troublesome pain-in-the-neck half sister I ever heard of, and when your mother's not yelling, I like to tell her it's only the Mexican side of your mongrel composition that makes you such a tribulation.

I can't wait to see, you, though.

Rome's not too bad! I'm assuming you've been rolling around in libraries and found a couple things that might help us with this Aztec gold theory Manuel was filling me in on. And there was SOME-THING ELSE, if I recall, that Erik was mumbling about—Dad dying in Europe, was it? Yeah! That was interesting! What the hell is that about?! Is it true?

Okay. I'm here to find out, lucky for you. I'm sure you need my help by now, you big old pansy. So. You'll fill me in when we meet up here later—say, at 4:30? That is, if I don't see you before that, since you know what a good tracker I am.

How's that chatty big-boned know-it-all Guatemalan Romeo of yours doing? Give him a sloppy kiss for me.

Love you, Y

P.S. Oh— I hope Erik told you that you can forget my heading up
that scavenger hunt for the wedding party. You know how Dad used
to make me do those monkey stunts when I was a kid. I am retired.

"I can't believe I'm saying this, but I'm glad she's here to help
out," said Erik, taking a sniff of the flower.

I smoothed out the papers. "I just don't know what I'm going
to tell her about Tomas."

"You mean the man with the ponytail—"

"Yes."

"Maybe you shouldn't talk about him. Reading this, she
sounds almost *happy*—and you can see how excited she is to be
here—"

"She's getting to track her dad, and she hasn't tracked anything since we were in the jungle. So, yes, I think she is feeling
pretty excited."

"For the last two years, all she's been doing is stalking around
Long Beach in that big black hat like one of the villains in *High
Noon* and she's waiting for the shoot-out."

"I just wish she were already here. Because I want to get going now, after what I've just read here, in Sofia's diary."

Erik raised his eyebrows. "All right. I'm listening."

I underlined Antonio's riddle with my finger. "Okay, the riddle says,

> CITY THREE'S INVISIBLE
>
> WITHIN THIS ROCK, FIND A BATH
>
> BURN LOVE'S APPLE, SEE THE CLEW
>
> THEN TRY TO FLY FROM MY WRATH.

"Let's just start with the first line."

" *'City Three's Invisible.'* Erik, isn't *invisible city* what people used to call ruins? In the sixteenth century."

He nodded. "A lot of imaginary places were called that. St. Augustine's City of God, Plato's Atlantis, the Arthurian Avalon, Shambhalla—but yes, the colonial Spaniards came up with that nickname for the ancient cities they excavated—"

"Copán, Machu Picchu—"

"Even sections of Tenochtitlán."

"Because they were buried, underground—"

"Right. You're right—"

"They were *invisible*. That's what we're looking for."

"A ruin—in Rome."

"Just outside, actually, if I've figured this out. Like the riddle says, we'll have to find an invisible city—a ruin—and a *rock*, then some sort of *bath*. And then we have to burn *these*—"

I plucked the black-purple flower that still dangled from Erik's hand. I placed it carefully on top of the letter I'd found while getting grilled to death by naphtha fire under the Duomo.

Marco Moreno had already shown me how these flowers grow wild in Italy, when he had taken pains to draw my attention to them in the Chiana valley. I knew now that he had done so for a good, and possibly even generous reason. As I'd explained to Erik on the drive to Rome, the bloom corresponded perfectly to the floral illumination that decorated the first page of the letter, which had turned out to be, along with the anagram, the second of the three "hints" Antonio had promised were in the missive. The rebus (a code word formed out of a picture image) it formed symbolized "love apple," the name of this very common, wild, berry-dangling flower, which had a mysterious significance for Antonio Medici—and that Marco Moreno had showed me so pointedly in the valley of Chiana:

" 'Burn Love's Apple, see the Clew / Then try to Fly from my Wrath,' " I quoted, looking at the silky dark bells.

Erik admired the trick, slapping his hand on the table. "Yes, right, I get it—these flowers are *love apples*. Which apparently we're supposed to burn. And that's great, but I don't think you're paying *quite* enough attention to that last line about the *flying from his wrath* business . . ." He turned his head toward the television as his sentence trailed off.

"Oh, we can worry about that later."

He had now turned his body completely toward the TV and tilted his head, his smile fading. "Yes . . . maybe you're right. Maybe we have *just* enough on our plate at the moment."

I chattered on: "I just want to look into it *now*, you know? I wish my sister would hurry up." I looked at my watch, which said 3:59. "It's going to take her another half hour."

Erik continued to blink at the TV. "I actually think we probably should go now."

"Why?"

He gestured for me to follow his gaze. "Well, blagh, ack, *look*."

On the screen, a well-coiffed female newscaster with scarlet lipstick and a creaseless forehead smoothly cooed that international authorities were even at this moment searching for a trio of grave-robbing and murderous bandits:

The two men and woman are of Indian extraction, say authorities,
perhaps of Guatemalan or Mexican heritage. The only description
the police have disclosed is that the fugitives are "dark-skinned" and
"plump," and are believed to be hiding in Florence or Siena.

In possibly related news, two or three South Americans report-
edly broke into the Sienese Duomo yesterday evening and destroyed
the famous "she-wolf" mosaic. In a daring move, they darted into a
hidden trap door in the Duomo floor and disappeared. Experts in me-
dieval architecture restoration have been called onto the scene. . . .

Erik stood up and began to swiftly sweep all of our papers
and books into my bag, saying in a falsely calm singsong: "Oh,
dear, tra la la, let's not draw attention to ourselves, but something
tells me that we're the swarthy fatties the little newscaster lady is
blabbering about—"

"At least they think we're in Tuscany," I whispered, darting
my eyes around to the drinkers who were fixated on the television screen, where the soccer match had replaced the news an-
chor. "No one here is even looking at us funny. Their descriptions
couldn't be vaguer—or more wrong. I'm not plump. Marco's not
plump. And you're *robust*—you're . . . manly—"

"I *know*," he said, without missing a beat. "Damned racial pro-
filing—they forgot to mention my ethereal sensuality. But just
in case, I'd rather not stay around right after they've announced
our APB."

"Just one second—I have to leave a note for my sister. I just
hope she sees it here. I don't want to give it to the manager—just
in case he does get suspicious."

I scribbled a message for Yolanda on the other side of the
paper she'd left for me and left it on the table:

4:00 *Y— Gone to Ostia Antica —L*

Erik hustled me out the door, bundled us into our car, and then we sped away down the skinny Vespa-crazed streets of Rome.

"Where did you tell her we were going?"

30

"Okay, in the interests of full disclosure, I just have to say that when I met you, the idea that I would be running from Italian police was really *very* much not in my career plan," Erik told me as he hunched over the wheel of our (Sienese landlord's now basically stolen) silver Fiat and rocketed past an endless tidal wave of tourists, Peruvian street musicians, and locals cramming the art-stuffed streets. He was lavishly perspiring. "I know I came off as a big old macho buccaneer back then, but really, I *wasn't*. It was all an act. I was a poindexter. And if I'm now galloping around like Sancho Panza it's because you, woman, have corrupted me. *But*, that being said—"

"When I met you, you were having affairs with something like ten women at UCLA alone—"

"Yes, *sexually* I was very impressive but otherwise, in terms of dashing around and having adventures and searching for treasure and getting into horrid kung fu matches and poisoning Bosnian or whatever assassins with long-buried booby-trapped emeralds, and feeling my eyebrows go all crispy in towering infernos—no."

"Go left, go left again. Go right here."

In one hand, I had Marco's copy of the *Rough Guide to Rome*, and in the other, Sofia's diary, both of which I had pulled out of my bag. The car swerved and spun on the route I traced out on the guidebook map while trying not to head-bang into the dashboard.

"Erik, I know it's been awful, I'm so sorry I dragged you here!"

He blew out a big blat of air. "I think you're forgetting that I would have packed myself into a FedEx box to get the next flight to Rome. Of *course* I came to Italy! You're here! Where you are, I am. *That's* not even a debate. And let me finish—that's not what I'm saying."

"This morning, when you couldn't sleep, in the pension, in Siena—I could see that you're really struggling with—what happened."

"Look. I'll admit, ever since the whole Blasej . . . thing I've been feeling strange, or something."

"Tell me about *strange or something*."

"Uh, I'm not quite sure. Sort of terrible. Sort of like maybe I'm actually not that great of a person after all? Either that, or I'm maybe *becoming* somebody mean and violent and horrible, and maybe there's no difference between me and the Morenos, and somebody *should* probably just lock me up away somewhere—"

"*That's* not true!"

"Right. Right. I know that's right. It was self-defense? Right? I think. What I do know is that it's probably *really* better if I don't talk about that part too much, and just race along here . . . wherever we're going. Because what I'm trying to say is, I'm glad I'm here with you."

"You are?"

"Yes. I just want to tell you that before we get nabbed by Smokey. And if I work on my selective amnesia, even I can still see that this is all very weirdly amazing. With the crypts and medals and scary hidden combustible alchemy labs, and everything. It's an archaeologist's dream! Except for the depressing death part! So yes, I'm glad I'm here. Almost as glad as *you* are."

"What do you mean?"

"What do I mean. I mean that I know that you've been having an absolute blast ever since you got here, Lola—I can see it. You're having the party of your life."

I watched the manic streets whiz by. Was he onto something? Had I been having a high old time of it ever since I was abducted in the Red Lion by mercenaries?

"Oh, God, you're right," I wailed. "Except when the guards got killed."

We looked at each other with our sweaty faces and bulging eyes, and Erik started cackling.

"See what I mean? Freak!"

"Oh, my, oh, my, oh no, agh . . . ," I moaned. "It's true—I'm like the happiest I've ever been, and we're runaways, hoodlums, on the lam, delinquents, going to the dogs, up the creek, and *my father is going to wig out when he finds out about Tomas*—"

"All right, all right. Don't pitch a fit."

I squeezed my eyes shut, rubbing my forehead. I tried to work out the reasons that I was so hell-bent on solving Antonio's riddle when I could simply go home, get married, and forget all about Aztec treasure and reanimated dads. As the Fiat continued to skid down Roman roads, a familiar but still very disturbing idea that perhaps I am not normal flitted through my mind: I was thirty-three and had whiled away my best childbearing years between the pages of books, and had recently merrily skedaddled through flames to recover a letter written by a dyspeptic Medici. We already had three dead bodies in our wake and were wanted by the police. Whereas I should have been busy sneaking Erik to

safety over the French border, then dashing home to live a bal-
anced nuptial life, I instead remained fixated on . . . yes, discovering the possible site of Antonio's next clue. The medal. The third
hidden sign. The *invisible city*. From my recent research, I thought
it might be found in an ancient and totally fabulous Roman ruin
where il Lupo and his witch-wife, Sofia, had conducted secret,
magical rites: Ostia Antica.

"Lola, Lola," Erik was saying.

"Huh?"

"You're thinking about the riddle again, aren't you?"

"Ah . . . *no*. No! I think we should talk more about what you're
going through."

"I already said I don't want to; it's no good. Seriously, tell
me what you're thinking; it's better that way. Just tell me what's
next."

"If you're sure."

"Yes, whatever! I'm *sure*."

We quarreled about this for another one or two minutes before I suddenly blurted: "Okay . . . *turn left here*." The car careened
onto a highway that led out of the center of Rome. "First thing,
you've got to call out if you see anybody selling those purple
flowers we were talking about. Or if you see them growing on
the side of the road."

"*Where* are we going?"

I rustled the books in my hands. "Well, you see, I *was* reading—"

"Ye-es."

"Sofia's diary. And I think I figured out where the invisible
city is. Let me read you the passage. . . . I was looking at in the
bar before—"

"We showed up on *Italy's Most Wanted*."

"Yes."

I paged through the journal, until I found the cunning entry I had in mind. This described a scandalous witchcraft ceremony in the deep lair of a ruined Roman village called Ostia Antica. The account contained, as well, a treasure hoard of codes, cues, and signs that I had just now interpreted in a hot—and perhaps too hasty—passion.

"Just listen to *this*:

Rome, April 1540

Tonight, I held the Holy Rite of Naming, wherein witch-acolytes receive their Secret magical names in what is supposed to be a very beautiful sacrament, complete with dancing, conjuring, and the ecstasies of the Strega's Flying Charm.

I orchestrated the ritual in one of the most powerful pagan sites I have ever set foot upon. It is at Ostia Antica, the old miller's town on the outskirts of Rome. In the months that Antonio and I have lived here, I have assembled a Sacred Circle of Baronesses, Judges, Infantas, Midas-wealthy merchants—and even one Cardinal Pietro Borodoni, who has permitted us to indulge in the Old Religion only after paying over Six Chests full of Antonio's Gold, with which the Church is to gild the Colossus that Michelangelo will soon work upon, the tomb of St. Peter.

Five of us crept beneath Ostia Antica's surface, to the underground bathhouse of Mithras, the Sun God who the Persians claim created the world by killing a sacred Bull. Antonio was in a rare jolly mood, dressing for the occasion in his green, gold-embroidered coat; I had him take this expensive article off when he kindled for us a small fire, upon which I threw the sorcerous blooms that give witches the Power of Flight.

Around the sparks the coven danced, laughing.

"Before we begin, we must thank our good Cardinal Pietro," said I, gesturing toward the priest. "For it is only by the virtue of his Grace that the Old Ways may still be observed in Rome."

"Am I the Rock upon which you build your church, my dear?" the Cardinal asked.

"Is that not blasphemy?" inquired cheery Signora Canova, a wealthy merchant's wife.

"It is merely a double pun upon the Cardinal's name, Pietro," Antonio offered. "And of puns, I always approve."

"No, you ninny—I'm talking about the Bible," Signora Canova chattered. "I learned it when I was a tot! About the Saint! Diddle, daddle, what was it? Something about Christ saying Peter was like a rock, or that a rock was like Peter, or anyhow that they had a great deal in common, I can't remember—"

"That's Matthew 16," the Cardinal began twattling. " 'And I say also to thee, That thoust art Peter, and upon this Rock I will build my church; and the gates of hell shall not prevail against it.' "

"Do shut up," said the Baron Modigliani, who was anxious for Fornication state of the Ritual to begin, so that he might sink his own Word into that of Signora Canova. "Signora Medici, please begin."

I stood before the flames and unfurled a parchment. This paper looked quite empty—but, upon my incantation, it would reveal Signs most Secret and Dangerous.

"Arise, arise!" cried I. "My Witches Fair! Your true names are written upon the fires. Take your New Title and ascend the Air!"

The parchment glowed before the flame; my patrons stood before it, mesmerized.

Then one by one the mysterious Ciphers appeared on the page.

"Black-eyed Hecate," I shrieked, reading out the witch-name of Signora Cavona, who was swooning from rapture.

"Actaeon of the Hounds," I shouted, branding our troublesome Cardinal, as a way of Warning what he might expect should his greed wax too great.

"Lusty Pan," I sang, finding a singularly accurate moniker for a promiscuous Baron.

"Most excellent," he replied.

The drugs worked: Within minutes, our feet had lifted from the ground.

We danced as pixies in the aerosphere, whilst the firelight danced upon the Bath's red and blue water.

"How utterly amusing, my darling," Antonio chortled, flapping his arms, as merry as I'd ever seen him.

But then my magick turned against me.

I should have foreseen it. A Sudden understanding of Reality is one of the gifts of the Flying Charm, and whilst my witches gazed upon my chuckling husband, their senses cleared to the degree of Revelation: in that instant they knew Antonio the Wolf's most secret, most lethal Name, which I never would have dared to write upon that parchment.

"You beast!" they cried. "You _____ !"

They screamed foul profanities at him. The words entered my husband's ears like poisoned darts, infecting him with perilous melancholy.

His metal began to transform.

His claws extended; his face shadowed; his fangs bared; he wept & roared like a Creature from the underworld. We came tumbling to the ground.

When we rose to our feet, my witches would not meet my eyes.

"It matters not at all," they stuttered, while he shivered before them. "I had heard, anyway, that Antonio was somewhat odd." "We'll remain friends, of course! We will not think any less of him, certainly." "This is a mere inconvenience; it changes nothing, my dear Sofia."

I did not show them my own terror, and laughed along.

Tonight, I have already begun to gather together what precious belongings we can easily carry should we need to travel, to Spain, perhaps, or Venice: These are our most costly clothes, books, the Cartoons & paintings & idols, along with the Treasure. The rest will be picked over by vultures & scattered.

My Witches now know Antonio's Secret and over us it will give them an extraordinary power.

Yes, with such knowledge, they could as good as kill us. . . .

31

E rik and I exited our Fiat, wandering into the tumble-down ruin of the southwest Roman town described by Sofia in her diary, which was sited off the green mouth of the Tiber. Millers and craftsmen raised Ostia Antica in the fifth century B.C. Today its pink brick buildings had eroded into the softness of old bones, surrounded by sun-struck grasses, marigolds, and poppies.

"The book says it was a popular site in the sixteenth century." Erik paged through our copy of *Rick Steves' Italy*. "Fortune hunters dug around here. Aristocrats held séances and debauches in the mineral baths."

"This has to be it—it has a bath; in her journal, she writes about how she held fire ceremonies here. Okay, here's the riddle:

> "CITY THREE'S INVISIBLE
> WITHIN THIS ROCK, FIND A BATH
> BURN LOVE'S APPLE, SEE THE CLEW
> THEN TRY TO FLY FROM MY WRATH.

"Okay. '*Within this Rock, find a Bath*'—there were mineral baths here, though I don't know about the '*Rock*' . . . it just must mean the stone buildings."

He looked up from the guide, hoisting the green rucksack on his back. "It says they have a little museum on the premises. The next medal could be there."

Upon paying a few euros, we were admitted into a gallery galactically less impressive than the ruins themselves. It did not take us long to pick through the displays. These were filled with dusty fractions of petroglyphs and reconstructed marble figures of naked athletes blessed with extraordinary musculature. They were also absolutely innocent of anything that could be remotely taken for Antonio Medici's third clue.

After we exited the museum, however, Erik did find something.

Little mud roads networked through the ruins. They were marked with red-lettered modern signs. We had examined several of these, but Erik eventually stopped before one of the buildings, looking up to see the designation:

VIA DELLE TERME DEL MITRA

"The Road of the Baths of Mithras," he said. "That's the Persian god Sofia was writing about—the Bull-Killer, who created the world. This could be that mineral bath—where she performed that Rite of Naming for her coven."

"Let's go look."

We moved down a pathway lined with grass; it led between two separate apartments made of that same rose stone. They had open-air, though steel-barred, doors cut into the walls, leading down to steps of more crumbling stones: curators had barred access to the ruins' bottom levels.

Erik and I peered hungrily down between a door's bars to the damp, mossy stairs on the other side. They descended into shadow. And there were no other tourists in sight.

"Let's go in," I said.

We slipped between the bars, Erik pushing and grunting

past. We stumbled on the downward stone steps, which led into a half-shadowed network of destroyed rooms built of ancient, dusty brick. The ground was filmed with a layer of incandescent green moss growing up the pocked stone walls, blooming out into sprays of wild grass. Erik walked ahead of me, his rucksack-humped body now gloomed by the murky air, now awash in a strobe of white brilliance falling through sun windows cut into the ceiling. He turned around a corner, disappeared from sight.

I followed him. At the end of this corridor, Erik found a tall, ruined, marble statue of a young man. Half of the figure's arm was missing, and before him lay the figure of a straining bull. The vanished part of the man's arm had once been poised to slit the animal's throat.

"Mithras," I said.

Erik hovered before the figure. " *'City Three's Invisible / Within this Rock, find a Bath / Burn Love's Apple, see the Clew / Then Try to Fly from my Wrath.'* This place is certainly *made* of *Rock*—bricks. But I don't see a *Bath*."

"No, let's turn around."

We backtracked, turned left, circled through black-shadowed passages that only increased our confusion. Ducking through a low-slung door that looked as if it might cave in at any moment, we found ourselves in another very dark, tumble-down space. A rounded arch of bricks formed the ceiling above us. To our left, a small window was half-barricaded by the earth, the level of which had risen since the Roman era; it was overgrown with vines. Leaf-green light flowed through the window, glinting on a small, black pool filling the hollow in the center of the room.

We crouched down, staring at the water.

Erik ran his hand through the wet. "Is this the *Rock* he was talking about? Is this even where we're supposed to be?"

"I don't know. And is this a bath—or just *flooding*? There's no way to know if we're in the right place."

He slipped off his rucksack. Digging past Marco's papers and the desiccating purple bouquet of love apples we'd picked earlier, he found a Maglite we'd taken from the Florentine Crypt. A blade of light moved through the shadows.

I took a breath. "All right, this is all we have. The riddle, the diary. We might as well start here."

The Maglite's beam skidded onto the skin of the ambiguous pond. We could spy only the blind vegetation fringing the water and toadstools palely shining. Some of the fallen ivy floated over the water that remained as obscure as black veils.

I stood up, slipped off my shoes, my pants, and my black sweater, which was still half-gnarled from the Duomo fire.

"What are you doing?"

"Going in."

"Let me—"

"Whoa, whoa, whoa, Mark Spitz. No way you're going into dark creepy pools where I don't know *what* could be in there. Besides, I'm the better swimmer."

As Erik reminded me of his dogpaddling skills, I stepped into the water, letting it close around my body.

It was a shock, like freezing. I plunged down, headfirst, to find the pool as fresh and clean as it was perfectly black. I surfaced, breathed, dove deeper.

But even after nearly an hour of roaming the water, I could not find anything like the gold medals we had found in the crypt or the alchemist's lab.

I dragged myself back up the bank. Erik dried me with his shirt, gently rubbing my flanks, my stomach, my neck.

"None of this is any good." I uselessly bounced on the balls of my feet for warmth. "But maybe that's because we're not following the instructions."

"What—the riddle? That business about *love's apples*. The flowers. Burning them."

"Yes."

"But how could setting flowers on fire help us find anything in here?"

"I can't tell you. I'm out of ideas."

"It sounds sneaky. Think about it: You *know* how witches were always concocting nice little drugs and poisons out of buttercups and wormwort and things like that. *'Burn Love's Apple, see the Clew'*? The whole thing's too pharmaceutical for me. These flowers were probably supposed to kill Cosimo. What else would? And that means they'd kill *us*."

While I tugged my clothes back on, I gazed at the shadows, listening to the lapping of the water.

"We could just *try* it."

He beamed the Maglite on the rucksack; the purple tips of the half-crushed flowers peeked from its mouth.

"Well . . . there is a window. That's ventilation. And if something went wrong, we could just leave, I guess. Run out, do a nice, screaming, four-hundred-yard dash. But even just saying that, I can hear how *crazy* it sounds."

Two minutes later, we piled the purple flowers by the bank.

A snap, then a match scraped against graphite. An aureole of gold flushed onto Erik's cheeks. Troubled specters seemed to cast their shadows against the green-growing walls, awoken after centuries by our pantomime of Sofia's Rite of Naming.

"Witchcraft," I murmured into that spark of flame, as if to summon the third clue.

But I did not realize what spirits I called up.

∾ 32 ∾

It took a while for the flowers to burn, on account of the damp, but soon the series of struck matches began to crisp the petals black. Erik squatted before the twiggy blooms, blowing on the threads of flame as I beamed the Maglite.

"It's catching," he said.

A tendril of smoke lifted from the stems. It smelled of something sharp; I did not yet notice the red and raised patches of skin on my wrists and fingers, where I had touched the flowers while gathering them.

The black smoke continued to lift into the air. It filtered into the cave's green light, disappeared over the black water.

"Can you see anything?" Erik asked.

"No."

"I'm telling you, I don't understand how this could *help*."

The air wavered in front of our eyes. And it was already too late.

A light, lovely, warm feeling enveloped me as the purple bells, one by one, caught fire. I looked over at Erik, and time curled in, just like the smoke. The emerald air covered us in a halo. The shadows seemed to splinter, then surround us like butterflies.

I opened my eyes; I had been dreaming. I was on the ground. My cheek rested on the moss, bathed in the cool water. I had dropped the flashlight; it shot an arrow of light over the floor. Across the kindling, Erik's eyes were shut. He whispered something to me. My name.

"Lola."

His voice was full of longing. And then, somehow, I wasn't on the ground anymore. I lifted above the water and the burning flowers, and my body began circling the black pond. I was suspended in the air, laughing, as witches do. Fragments, mosaics, glittering scenes appeared in my mind, of Erik's lovely body, and of his hands, from all angles, all sides. No, it was more than that.

I saw—*everything*.

I saw Erik radiant, iridescent, out of time. I saw all the incarnations of him. I saw Erik as a baby, a snail-small fetus, as a boy. I saw him as an old man with scars and wrinkles on his face. I saw him choking with rage in the jungle at the same time as I saw him leaning over my naked body in a golden Long Beach morning. I saw him in knee socks, reading from a big book; I saw him floating in his mother's womb, curled like a seahorse, with large alien eyes. I saw him embittered, unkind. There were lines beneath his eyes; his hair was tangled; he was half-mad, bleeding from inexhaustible wounds. I saw him morph from the smiling countenance I had fallen in love with to the animal face I had seen him wear in the crypt when he killed Blasej. I saw this face, too, change into the red, nearly demonic expression that had flickered across his features in the Chiana valley. For a moment in that drug-time, I thought that these transmutations were particularly important . . . but then I saw others that were more beautiful, more beguiling. I saw his face become my face. I saw his face transform into Marco Moreno's sly, sharp-boned face, and Yolanda's, Manuel's, my mother's. I saw him

straining during sex, with purple veins in his throat. I saw him lying peacefully in his coffin. And I saw him being born. I was dying
from drugs as something holy and perfect was happening to me.
I shouted out this terrible love I had for him, though it came out
blitheringly.

From far off, I could hear Erik roaring. I heard myself coughing and gagging.

My feet jerked and fluttered as I continued to fly in my hap-
piness across the room. But this was in fact my body convulsing
within the black-blue pool into which I'd fallen.

Time passed.

I was dragged out into the daylight. A face flashed above
me. It was beautiful and familiar and encircled by a black halo. A
black hat. I saw Erik huddled on the grass outside, gasping for air.
His face was ashen and his eyelids had swollen into plums.

A woman said my name now. My half sister, Yolanda, was
screaming it.

Then after that, for hours and hours that I couldn't count,
there was nothing.

33

A pallid wall and then only thoughts, fractions of thoughts. Images of my dark-eyed and lanky sister, the sounds of names; the images of letters written in deep black on a page, the ink-jet characters sinking into the depths of paper as pale as the hospital around me.

My dreams were made mostly of language. In my hallucinations I could sculpt words like clay. I conjured them, so their letters hung in the atmosphere of my imagination, and I made them combine, change shape, as a magician will marry a rose with a silk scarf and create from this alchemy a live dove.

Sam Soto-Relada. The fence's name floated to the top of my submerged mind.

But now someone was talking to me.

Today, I know why the color of the afterlife in hallucinations and movies is white—because that is the color of the hospital walls and the fluorescent bulbs jittering above you as you lie in your cold cot, in spirit flying into the shining paleness and then dipping back into your dark body like an ocean diver. White is the color of Heaven because that is the last color a great many of us will see.

So I was in the hospital for two days, fed intravenously for the first twenty-four hours while I pondered the mysterious transmutation of words and speculated on the interior design of the underworld.

And the entire time an angel sat beside me.

This angel wore a large, night-black Stetson tilted way back on her head. She had black glossy hair spilling over her shoulders and eyes so blackly dark that there was no differentiation between her pupils, which were dilated by fear, as they glared down on the shivering, drug-blasted form of yours truly.

I opened my eyes and saw her there. Wide cheeks, wide mouth, blue jade necklace, long pretty body.

"Love's Apple is another name for belladonna, or deadly nightshade, you *absolute* ass," the angel admonished me, at a rather violently high decibel despite her hysterical sobs and accompanying hiccups.

"That would explain it," I whispered. "Belladonna. Pretty lady. He called me pretty lady."

"You're not making any sense. Look at you. You're out of my sight not even a week and you nearly get yourself bone-dead."

"Yolanda, where's Erik?"

"I had to find you an apartment, then treat him there with castor oil and morphine I lifted from this place—and it was a real party, let me tell you. But he made out better than you did from that little experiment of yours, and I couldn't let these docs see you together now that you're so *famous*—"

"Oh. Right. The police—"

"Don't worry, you look more like a dead dog than the little sketch they just started showing on TV. And I told the nurses here that you're a semi-retarded Peruvian didgeridoo player named Maria Juarez, no papers, smoked the flowers by accident.

They bought the story. For the time being. Though I really do recommend that you try to get out of here as soon as you can before they deport your *brainless* butt back to Cuzco. . . ."

She began a litany of criticisms about the numbing weaknesses in my intelligence, ferociously pounding her knees and continuing to weep in between verbal abuses.

I closed my eyes again.

```
i think we need to talk senor relada

                    . ' .

where r u

                 . ' . '

right now in an apt off piazza navona

                . ' . ' .

u been alright havent heard from u

                . ' . ' .

wel i guess i almost died

                . ' . ' .

sory to hear that but did u find the gold
dear

                . ' .

thnx for the sympathy btw i know u havent
told me evrything about my dad

                . ' .

like what

                . ' .

that he was such a [expletive]

                . ' .
```

```
temper temper

                  .  .  .  .

[expletive expletive]
```

After two days spent alternately in psychic delirium, mute revelation, and text-message-sending frenzies, at six a.m. on June 9 I sat up and drank coffee in a small third-floor apartment off the Piazza Navona that my extremely resourceful half sister had rented after rescuing us from the death-pit of Ostia Antica.

Yolanda de la Rosa, thirty-five years old, the legitimate heir of Tomas and a now long-dead wife named Marisa (car accident), had been well trained by her father in the art of shelter seeking. She wore a black Stetson in memory of the ten-gallon that he had affected, but that was only one of the resemblances between them, as he had whipped her into an adventurer's shape tough enough to deserve the famous family name. At the age of twelve, he famously set her loose, and alone, in the Petén forest in Guatemala. She had tracked through the jaguar-happy swamps and defiles for thirteen days, until she discovered him waiting for her in a remote Quiche village, where he had ordered local chefs to prepare a fourteen-course feast celebrating her survival. Other equally difficult tests continued to punctuate her young life: tracking girl-eating puma in the Amazon, maniacal wildebeests in Patagonia. These Herculean labors had made her into a hard-muscled, wily, melancholic woman with deep shadows beneath her eyes, who had been living uncomfortably with us in Long Beach ever since her father's "death." But though her schooling had given her the equanimity necessary to face down equatorial cougars and South American vamp bats, it did *not* prevent her from presently dissecting my stupidity in a machine-gun stutter, though I was still tottering green-faced about the apartment.

"So, love apples are nothing more than belladonna, and *that* was used as a main ingredient in the 'flying balms' of Renaissance witches," Yolanda boomed at me. Now hatless, wearing a scarlet poncho, as well as her ever-present blue jade necklace, she sat drinking her *macchiato* across from Erik and me as we sat at a tiny table in the kitchen. "Back in Guatemala, I'd heard about *brujas* who still use it, when they try to go into trances. They mix it in with pig lard, and then spread it all over their bodies. It gives them this, I don't know, vertiginous feeling—but you'd be able to describe it better than I would now, wouldn't you, fool?"

"That we would, I'm sorry to say," Erik muttered. His eyes remained rosy from the gassing, his cheeks resembled copy paper, and he still wore the navy slacks and shirt of his now-scrofulous suit. "For God's sake, I thought I had these big fuzzy wings and was flapping them all around like a happy pterodactyl. Until I realized that I was blind and near paralyzed and I could hear Lola choking next to me. And then—you came. And pushed me out of the Mithras bath."

"Only reason it didn't wind up being any worse is because I saw a little smoke coming out of those ruins, and when I ran in—when I came in I saw . . . what I thought was a corpse. *Why* did you burn that stuff? Didn't you have any idea?"

"Yes," I said. Erik and I looked at each other.

"We thought we could scamper away if things grew . . . tricky," he said.

She shook her head. "They've got names for that kind of thinking, Gomara, and most of them are obscene."

"I know, I know!" grunted Erik. "You don't have to tell me! I was a moron—*ape*-stupid! If I get any dumber—"

"It was my fault," I murmured. "It was my idea."

"I'll devolve into a caveman with a monobrow as big as a freaking Frisbee—"

"Erik."

I put my cup down. Still unsteady, I had no idea how to broach the subject on my mind. I simply flung it at him. "Erik—honey—when we were—you know—underground—did you *see* anything in there?"

"See anything?"

"Feel anything? Anything strange? Or even—"

"Besides hallucinating that I was a big bird and worrying that you were going to die? No." His mouth dragged down his face.

I reached over to squeeze him. "Honey, it's okay. Everything's fine now."

But this is when I knew I was the only one who had that mystical vision of love in the Mithras ruins.

Yolanda crossed her long legs at the ankles. "Ah, I told you she'd be all right, Gomara, you old panda. Look at her—she's peachy. And you've got to buck up. You haven't eaten anything in like two days."

"Haven't been hungry. Too upset."

"Nah, that was just morphine I gave you. Say, why don't you try to choke something down? I went shopping. You should be hungry now; I hear that belly of yours bubbling. There's plenty of calzone in the fridge."

"There *is*?"

"Sure."

He kissed my head and unclasped me. "Hmmmm. Oh. Maybe . . . I could give food a try, I guess. I'll be right back."

As Erik quickly ambled off, Yolanda pulled her hair back into a ponytail and regarded me with her leaf-shaped eyes. "He was like that the whole time you were gone. A real handful. I had to dope him, *bug* him—though all that didn't work as well as when I distracted him with that thing you were looking for—that clue, the medal—"

"Did you see the ones we found? With the letters stamped into them?"

"Sure did. And I'll admit, that's some interesting stuff. I got him busy writing down everything he knew about that riddle—the invisible city, Antonio il Lupo, Cosimo, this Sofia woman. And he came up with something about a hint you might have missed. The third hint in the letter, is that what he said? Something like that."

"What hint?"

She sighed. "I don't *know,* Lola! I've had some other things on my mind, too—like you croaking, and your koala in the kitchen there having a nervous flip-out, and then this business everybody's been yelling about Marco Moreno."

"He's the one who got me over here, Yo," I said.

She leaned back in her chair. "Aw, damn! So, it's true. Marco 'the snake' Moreno, come to see my little sister."

"Marco 'the snake'?"

"Yeah, that was his nickname back at home. That kid's a chip off the old colonel's block, and I had the bad luck to run into him more than a few times. In the war, man, he was a serial killer. That dude's not even human."

"What did he do?"

"Why don't I tell you all about that when *you're* not half-dead? I had some hopes that he'd stay under the radar 'cause I heard he had some sort of psycho breakdown in Paris. Which was no surprise. He was always sort of freakish, you know? A real dork. No friends, reading a lot—when he wasn't cleansing the fatherland of untouchables. But he didn't change his stripes, judging by the company he's keeping. Erik told me that some Eastern European friend of his got creamed, but an Italian didn't, and this Italian boy wants to punch Erik to death."

"More or less, yes."

"Oh, too bad it's true. I was hoping it was the morphine talking."

"No."

"Not the best news. So why's he here? Why's he following you around?"

"Gold. Blood vendetta—"

"The regular stuff. My question is—does he really know *where Dad died?*"

"No. He doesn't."

"Are you sure?"

"*Yes.*"

"Why?"

I didn't answer, and not only because I was anxious about her reaction. Still in the midst of my spiritual convulsion that had begun in Sofia's cave, I must have had the benign and unhinged air of a saint about me when I suddenly fell forward and threw myself into her arms. "Aw, I *love* you, Yolanda, you know that? Really, I really completely awfully do. I'm so glad you're here."

"Stop it—you're getting mushy," she grunted, but I saw tears form in her eyes as she roughly petted my hair. "And I lied. You *do* look terrible. Ya look like Jack Nicholson, kid."

"I feel wonderful. I feel like I have been baptized."

"What?"

"Nothing. Or, actually, I do have to tell you something. I know that Marco was wrong about our dad because . . . I saw Tomas."

Her hand paused as she stroked my hair. "Did you just say you thought you saw Tomas?"

"That's it."

"Tomas—as in our father, Tomas. As in Tomas de la Rosa."

"Yes."

"As in the Tomas de la Rosa who possibly left Guatemala for some unknown reason and is now dead."

"*Yes*—except that he's not. I'm sure of it. He's alive. I saw him in Siena."

She continued to touch my hair. "Oh, Sissy, Honey-Bunny. Don't you think I saw him for weeks and weeks after I'd heard he'd died?"

"It's not like that. And there's more—this fence person, Soto-Relada, this man I talked to—you've got to hear this whole story: He said Tomas *owned* Antonio's letter before Marco and that he was on the trail for the gold, and then I started texting him—"

She frowned. "Blah, blah, blah, blah—I'm not listening to any of this malarkey. Because it *is* like that. I know what you're talking about. It's like Daddy's a ghost, and he comes back, and you're seeing him. But you're *not*. I used to follow these strangers around for hours, *positive* it was him, and that all of this was just another test—like how he'd show up in the jungle after I'd been tracking alone for days? That's what I thought would happen *all the time*. But then these strangers, they'd turn around, and I'd see, pfffft. It was just me going bananas—and on that subject, you understand I'm not doing that damned scavenger hunt—"

"Yeah, I got that. But listen—I swear I *saw* him—"

"Tomas de la Rosa is buried in the ground. And I have got to find out where that is, so I can say my good-byes, goddammit."

"I saw him—he had a ponytail and tattoos—"

"*Stop saying that, Lola.*"

"What are you two yelling about?"

Erik had emerged from the kitchen to stand in the doorway, looking white and boneless, as he clutched a calzone in both hands.

"Um . . . nothing," I said, giving him a good, long look. "You're pale, sweets. Are you okay?"

"Well. *No*."

"I told you," Yolanda muttered, also calming down. "Your boy needs some fresh air or something."

"Why are you guys fighting?"

"We're not—we're not. She was telling me . . . right—that you have a theory, baby."

Yolanda nodded. "Yeah—okay, let's talk about *that*. Gomara, that idea you worked out in the hospital, the third hint handed down by our Lupo. I know you came up with something good, buddy. Let us have it. Because hell, after all—you guys are on some treasure hunt, and I know I wouldn't mind tracking down some nice Aztec gold doubloonies. Besides, if that Moreno does know anything about Tomas dying here—"

"Which he doesn't—" I said.

"I'll bet he'd be interested in trading on information. So let's get with it."

Munching the calzone, Erik glanced at my sister. "Oh, about the letter."

"About burning the letter," she said.

"I did come up with an amazing theory," he said. "But I think we should probably do that later. You know, because I'm feeling a little"—he made a wobbly gesture with one hand—"schizo-phrenic."

"You're going to burn a letter?" I asked.

"Yes," said Yolanda.

"No," he corrected. "We're going to *heat* it up. But just not now—"

"Actually, this could be good. I'll go get it." My sister banged off to the bedroom.

Erik sat back down at the table, squeezing the calzone so hard it dented. "Lola, go back to bed."

"No, no, no. I feel fine. What did you figure out?"

"You won't be any good if you're sick."

"I'm great."

"Look in the *mirror.*"

"Here." Yolanda raced back into the room with Antonio's second, illuminated letter and a cigarette lighter. "How did you say you were supposed to do it? Like this?"

She removed the epistle from its red envelope, brandishing the papers before our eyes so the purple-black painted flowers glittered dimly under the apartment's electric lights. Antonio's script blazoned across the blond paper, telling the story of the march on Tenochtitlán, Montezuma's curse, and the wolfman's bloodbath under the moon.

Yolanda flicked on the lighter and held it up to the last page, which contained the passage:

And so ends my letter, filled as it is with Tricks & Clues. Only if you study my words, and what lies beneath them, will you discover the Key to the mystery that waits for you in Rome. If so, your mettle will prove cleverer, and much less yellow than I supposed.

But in my Wolf heart, by the beating of my Wyvern's blood, I hope you die on this next Quest.

Sincerely yours
Il Noioso Lupo Retto,
otherwise known as
Antonio.

"Oh she's gone insane," I shouted when I smelled carbon. "You're going to burn it! You're holding the lighter too close."

"Don't worry. I had Erik make two copies of the text the day before yesterday."

"Yolanda, stop that—*that's a very valuable piece of paper.*"

"Fine—fine—God, you *women,*" said Erik. "And she's right about you, you pyromaniac, give it to me."

"What's the theory?" I asked.

"Erik showed me the journal—Sofia talks about waving a banner in front of a fire—"

"Lola, remember the Rite of Naming? What did she write . . . something like . . . *'I stood before the flames and unfurled a parchment. This paper looked quite empty—but, as the parchment glowed before the flame, mysterious Ciphers appeared on the page.'* It doesn't matter—just have a little patience."

"I really don't think that's possible under the circumstances."

Erik held the little flame a short distance beneath the missive; I could hear its gentle smoldering, the light sound of crackling.

"Oh, whatever you're doing, I can't watch," I said, staring.

"It may not work," said Erik. "The ink's probably already evaporated. My only hope is that the salt preserved it."

"What ink?"

The paper shimmered beneath our eyes. The tiny flame beneath it sent up a bloomlet of rich light, which haloed the letters with green and gold.

"Nothing's happening," Yolanda said.

"*Wait.*"

After more than a minute, a red shadow appeared on the paper. This penumbra was formed of fine, curving lines. They broadened, ramified, like molten iron poured into a sword's mold.

"There's a shape," hissed Yolanda. "There's a pattern here— some kind of insignia."

I reached out and traced the specter on the page, which was as warm as skin.

"It's a note written in invisible ink," I breathed.

We leaned our three dark heads together and read the ancient message.

~ 34 ~

"CIVITAS DEI"

It says *Civitas Dei*," I rasped.

"Oh, oh, oh! There's the third hint—it *worked*." Erik began nervously dancing around the room. "I can't believe it worked. Invisible ink—I can't tell you the chances of our being able to read this. The words must have been spelled out in, I don't know—vinegar, urine, lemon juice. Maybe allum—"

"How did you know to do this?" I asked, as Yolanda ran over and snatched the paper from Erik.

"Sofia played this trick for her coven in the Mithras baths. Remember the journal?"

"In the Rite of Naming—when she waved the paper in front of the fire—"

"Ciphers appeared, with their Witch-names."

"And then they started feeling the effects of the drug."

"Yes, but here, look at this—at the way Antonio signs the letter.

"'So ends my letter, filled as it is with Tricks & Clues. Only if you study my words, and what lies beneath them, will you discover the Key to the mystery that waits for you in Rome.'"

"Invisible ink was a *huge* trend among sixteenth-century cryptographers. And then Antonio tells us to look for an invisible city? I thought, well, invisible *ink*—"

" '*Only if you study my words, and what lies beneath them,*' " I cheered. "Talk about a subtext."

"*Civitas Dei*—that means 'City of God,' " Yolanda translated, rapid-fire. "Ugh . . . what's that—Augustine."

"St. Augustine," I said. "Christian writer. Fifth century."

"That's the title of his major book," Erik added. "Antonio uses it as a double pun—the cipher's invisible, and the City of God's invisible, too, because it's in Heaven."

"Well, not just in Heaven, right?" Yolanda shut her eyes tight. "The invisible city? That's the whole point of the church. To make the invisible *visible*."

"The *church*," I jabbered. "It's the icon of the invisible city."

"Best guess," my sister said, "is that what we're snooping around for is a cathedral, a chapel, a basilica—"

"Ohhh . . . but wait." Erik stopped dancing and held up his hands. "This is exciting and everything, *but* I do think it's time for us to take a break now. We should just take our Vicodin and sleep for another twelve—"

"Which one, though?" Yolanda asked me.

"God, which church," I said. "In Rome. More churches here than Starbucks."

"I'm actually not kidding about this," said Erik.

" '*City Three's Invisible,*' " quoted Yolanda. " '*Within this Rock, find a Bath / Burn Love's Apple, see the Clew / Then Fly from my Wrath*' . . . Okay we're looking for a church—but what's the *Rock*?"

"I don't know," I replied. "But maybe the *Bath*'s a baptismal font."

"Could be right—"

"And we already know about the *Love's Apple* and *Wrath* business and don't have to repeat that."

"Okay then, you ready to go, Lola? You look strong enough. I want to get started. I've been going nuts sitting on my keister around here—"

"Let me just get some Advil. And did you bring some jeans I could borrow? And a shirt?"

"Yes, oops, watch out. Gomara's having a fit."

"Dammit!"

Both of us looked at Erik. He remained as pale as a sport sock, and anxiety clenched his features as he blustered: "I just think we should *take a minute.* I mean, sure: Would I *like* to flop around in a big mountain of Aztec gold that my genius has rescued from the sands of time? Yes. Do I *want* all of my colleagues to get asthma attacks from jealousy because I'm on the cover of *National Geographic? Yeah!* But if I have to get my tits burned off, Indian wrestle with contract killers, or deal with the possible death of my fiancée just one more time, I might just go totally, flamingly *whacked*, girls—seriously."

But we did not heed this warning.

"My oh my, Erik, you are getting into a state," my sister drawled. "Though I'll admit you've got a point. I mean, finding Montezuma's stolen gold? Psssshhht. No one's ever done that, right? And how we supposed to do it? Using some old clues left to us by a Renaissance crackpot, we have to find one little gold medal in a church, in a city that's busting with gold-stuffed churches? While hoping that we don't get bumped off by some booby trap or cross paths with the Blues Brothers?"

"That's the size of it."

Yolanda walked quickly over to the bureau, where she'd put her Stetson, which looked big enough to sail back to Long Beach in.

Keeping her eyes on him, she put the hat on, taking care to wickedly tilt it over one eye. "Look. *Gom-a-ra.* I've led twenty-eight linguists through the malarial Guatemalan swamps where there was no road, no path, no *nothing* but the scent of eucalyptus to guide me, and I found them the last known living soul who still spoke fluent Xinca. And I was once hired to track a band of wild pygmies that no Spanish-speaker had ever seen, and for sixteen days I wandered through that rain forest full of giant cats and enough mosquitoes to give you epilepsy, before sitting down with the little folks to a nice cup of hashish tea. So you see, what you're talking about here—it's just music to my ears. So come on. Get your carcass up. Take your Ritalin, or whatever. There's no time for you to have a conniption, man! Let's *go* rampaging."

And when that didn't work, she said: "Fine. Lola, you get the arms; I'll get the feet."

"Okay."

A small sumo match ensued. As the battle waged between two of de la Rosa's daughters against my one darling, Erik did not face the fairest odds.

Eventually, and inevitably, through the use of kisses, squeezes, threats from Yolanda, and an eloquence of assurances from me, we were able to persuade Erik to help haul my dilapidated bones out the front door. Soon, out we excitedly raced, or, rather, enthusiastically staggered, into the Eternal City's wilderness of churches—a glorious temple to God and art that I now, in cold retrospect, wish I had never heard of, stepped foot in, or seen.

The early morning sun glittered like the finest jewel in the Vatican's collection as we hurled ourselves into a gold-tastic dream called Rome. Centuries ago, Antonio had plotted his murder of Cosimo I within these walls, laying down his breadcrumb trails, his traps. But since that time the city had shifted shape around his scheme, perhaps irrevocably burying the clue that he had hidden here.

"Thirty-eight cathedrals in the city, and most of them rehabbed by the pope's interior decorators in the past couple hundred years. Not much of a chance of actually finding what we're looking for," Yolanda gleefully complained as we set out to search all of the cathedrals—aka, *Civitas Dei*. We had just exited the eastward-situated St. Peter in Chains, having found nothing there but the shocking perfection of Michelangelo's *Moses*. From this church, we were to brave the infinite arts of the Vatican and St. Peter's Basilica. "Though *all* of this is just a side business to finding where Pop's buried. Because, what if Moreno *isn't* lying? What if he's right, and Dad's here—"

"Oh, well, yes, Tomas *is* here," I answered.

"Because, you know, it never made sense to me that we couldn't find his body in the jungle. And I was thinking—maybe he just came over here and got into trouble, couldn't get in touch with me. Like, once, he woke me up in the middle of the night; he was calling me from the Sahara, I didn't even know he was gone. I'm like, *where the* hell *are you, ya old buzzard?* He said that he'd been on the trail of this sixth-century gold diadem, ancient Libya, belonging to some Princess Badar al-Budur. He'd been buried up to his neck in a sandstorm, nearly died. Maybe something like that happened here. Except, he couldn't get out of his fix this time."

"No, I'm sorry, but it didn't—"

"You'd better drop that line about Dad still being alive. Because do you even understand what you're saying, munchkin? If he's alive, the only reason I wouldn't have seen him is because he abandoned me." Though she was talking about such grim matters, she seemed cheerful enough, even slapping me on the back. "And the old dads, well, he promised he'd never leave me high and dry."

I hitched down the red nylon top my sister had lent me. "He is alive, Yo. I can prove it."

"Told you to *can it*—"

"Wait. Wasn't there something we heard about that?" Erik asked me, hiking up his backpack.

We both looked at him. "Something we heard?"

"Something we heard about Tomas—"

"We've been hearing a lot of things . . ."

"Was it about Dad dying?" Yolanda asked.

"Yes. There was some kind of—some kind of . . . ," he mumbled. "It'll come to me."

"Sounds like a belladonna flashback," Yolanda concluded after giving Erik a close eyeballing. "Or maybe Gomara really is schizing. Whatever it is, wish I had a camcorder."

I watched as she hacked her arm like a machete through the

crowd in front of us, which is how she savagely cleared out any obstructions lying in her path in the rain forest. The breeze that she whipped up with her velocity made her hair flutter around her shoulders, and her face shone like an impatient saint's beneath the brim of the Stetson.

"Look at you," I said. "You're so happy."

"Guess you could call it that."

"I've been wanting you to look like this ever since you moved home."

"Home."

"That's right."

"Long Beach, California, is the *home* of the Quik-E-Mart and the ninety-nine-cent store and the chicken fajita wrap."

"There's also this really nice bookstore there, I've heard—"

"What I'm saying is, Long Beach is for suckers. It's got nothing but softball and Christians, and your mother sewing me up some bridesmaid's dress that makes me look like a trannie. We should all move."

"Where?"

"New York, São Paulo, Caracas. Here."

"You want to move to Caracas?"

"Maybe."

"Slow down. Jesus, you're killing me," sputtered Erik.

"You shouldn't have brought your groom-to-be, L," she said, looking at him over her shoulder. "He looks like a dug-up dead rat."

"That would be the effect of the poison and the excruciating vomiting, Yolanda," said Erik. "Though I appreciate the concern."

"You know what I mean, and you're welcome for the concern. I just want you to keep your eyes sharp."

"One thing," I said. "Most of the churches have gold fixtures. Watch out for gold that looks red—it's likely to be in a church that Antonio had ties with."

"What?"

As we pressed deeper into the city, I explained: "We think that the gold's going to be reddish. It's described that way in some of the colonial histories. And it's the color of the medals."

"*Red*-gold? All right. But what you're really saying is the nobility fat cats got Montezuma's wampum after all." Yolanda's legs and arms swung as she swatted her invisible machete once again through Rome's crowds; tourists and locals alike fell like jungle vines as she cleared our path. "I could have told you *that*."

She was leading us to the Vatican, straight west, where the crush of people was at its most intense. Fashionable women in impossible heels floated in and out of streets made deadly by whizzing Vespas. We passed the Trevi Fountain, the Spanish Steps (Keats, Shelley), and dove in and out of the Pantheon (with Raphael's remains). Dark and pale faces hurled toward us, then vanished. An assembly line of tourists' shoulders knocked at my skull; foreign hips swayed around us in perilous patterns.

Half a mile from the papal palaces, a toffee-colored woman bumbled into me before turning a hard left into another battalion of tourists. As she cleared from my view, I had a glimpse of something—someone—in the crowd.

And that sight dipped me in ice: I saw the hard-etched, blue-eyed, golden-haired, horrible face of Domenico. Massive shoulders, gorilla neck. Slitted eyes combing the crowd. He did not look back at me but at the swarm.

I ducked my head.

Then he was sucked back into the mob.

"*Ooooohhh!*" I hissed.

"What?" Erik and Yolanda both asked.

"Let's go, *let's go.*"

I grabbed their shirts, running and dragging them with me. We had just come in sight of the gigantic Vatican and its museum. Here there was an even denser agglutination of people. Pushing rudely into a long line, I led our too-ponderous shuffling way up to a doorway, so we could hide inside. I had seen Domenico. I *had* seen him. I was sure. But an anonymous sea of humanity crushed afore and aft, and I couldn't spot the likes of him in the mob waiting to get into John Paul II's house.

"Oh my God my God *my God.*"

"What the hell is going on?"

"Marco."

Erik bunched his mouth. *"Right."*

"Right?" I asked, barely paying attention

"Marco—"

"What—*Do you see him?*"

"No. Huh? Remember? What I was trying to remember about Tomas. In Siena, in the valley, Marco told us . . . he said something about . . . proof. He was talking about showing you proof that Tomas . . . and it must be in the stash from his rucksack, what we put in our bag. We haven't looked through all of it yet—"

"Proof that Tomas what?" Yolanda asked.

"Oh. That. Yes," I said, remembering Marco's words in the Chiana valley, and how he'd shaken the rucksack at me: He'd said that in the bag was evidence that Tomas had killed himself. "Why don't we just hold off on that right now while we—agh—try to get inside." The line for entrance to the Vatican museums moved at a funereal pace even as I continued to press my shoulders really rudely against the people ahead of me. "Let's go, let's go, guys, get a move on."

"Proof that Tomas what?" Yolanda asked.

"Oh, ah, well." Erik remembered the delicate nature of this ersatz "proof." "It's not good, Yolanda."

I forced my way through the line, simultaneously apologizing and coughing like an escapee from a tubercular ward so as to forestall the other pilgrims' foreseeable ravening reactions. "Agh, gag, gag, oh, *sorry— blagh.*" Erik was attempting a hesitant description of what Marco had told us about the supposed suicide, while Yolanda, now on the scent, yanked the backpack off his shoulders and began to dig through it.

"What do you *have* in here?" she sputtered, thrusting her entire arm into the bag.

"Book . . . papers . . . maps . . . some food—" Erik said.

"These are all folded up, and crushed up at the bottom."

"No, no, *no*—don't look at anything in there. Keep walking." I pulled them through the door. After more delays, ticket purchases, and a lackadaisical weapons search the likes of which would become extinct in the coming September, we were allowed inside the white anteroom of the Vatican museums. Here, lines serpentined up and down stairs that led into and back out of the building.

Yolanda continued rattling her hands around inside the backpack.

I kept my eyes on the tourists and the guards and still did not see signs of Domenico or Marco.

"Wait," Erik said. "What's that?"

Yolanda had a handful of crushed and crumpled pages. She extracted one sheet from that crackling paper bush.

"Oh," she said. She smoothed it out, held it up, and read it. In large Gothic letters, I saw the words *DEATH CERTIFICATE.* And she said again, *"Oh."*

"What does it say?" Erik said.

I yanked at her wrist. "No, don't read it. Whatever it is—I don't care what it says—it's just—*lies.*"

Yolanda tensed, as if she were not so much scanning the text as bodily absorbing it; her lips formed the words on the page. Her eyes filled with tears.

She raised the sheet of paper up to our faces. It shivered in her hand.

Upon that certificate was the hard proof that Tomas de la Rosa had killed himself in Italy.

CERTIFICATO DI MORTE

VENEZIA, ITALIA

(*Translated*)

This is to Certify that our records show <u>TOMAS DE LA ROSA</u> *died in Venice, Italy.*

Month: <u>MARCH</u> *day:* <u>23</u> *year:* <u>1998</u> *hour:* <u>NOT LISTED</u>

Age of death: <u>63 YEARS</u> *Sex:* <u>MALE</u> *Race:* <u>HISPANIC</u>

married or single: <u>UNKNOWN</u>

Primary cause of death given was: <u>SUICIDE BY DROWNING</u>

Signed by <u>Dr. Rosate Modalas</u>

physician, health officer, or coroner

Place of burial or removal: <u>N/A</u>

Date of burial: <u>N/A</u>

Funeral Home address

SEAL

Signed   <u>Dr. Rosate Modalas</u>

          <u>Health Officer</u>

address   <u>Venice, Italy</u>

date   <u>March 26, 1998</u>

Record Filed: <u>MARCH 28, 1998</u>   *Certificate Number:* <u>4</u>

❦ 36 ❦

I gaped at the death certificate. Yolanda was oblivious to the sultry humanity pressing us up the stairs and ever forward into the Vatican's sanctum. Erik took the document from her and read it closely.

"It looks real," he said, sadly.

"Oh. Oh, Dad."

I felt electrocuted. "That's not—that's not right."

"What does 'n/a' mean?" Erik asked. " 'Place of burial: n/a. Date of Burial: n/a.' Don't they know? Or is just that he wasn't buried?"

"He killed himself," Yolanda whispered, when she could finally speak. "Oh my Jesus. Daddy *did* abandon me. He left me. The old dog *left me*, Lola. He left me all by myself. In Guatemala. Surrounded by bastards! Like Colonel Moreno—"

"Seriously, Yolanda—*we have to keep moving.*"

The crowd continued to push us past turnstiles, up the spiraling stairs. At the landing, the human wave swept us left, into the first of the extraordinary papal galleries. I feverishly looked around. No sign of Domenico or Marco within this fantasia of antiques. We began rushing about, to and fro, crying and arguing. At our feet slept mummies kidnapped from Cairo; another apartment bristled with marble Apollos. I could barely see the Gallery of Maps because of my escalating anxiety attack about our AWOL switchblade-wielding Italian.

"It's not true," I wheezed. We had confusedly backtracked, and floundered in the Gallery of the Candelabra, where I think I stood next to a statue of Plato. I shut my eyes. "That paper's not authentic, Yolanda."

Tears rolled down her cheeks and she just cried and cried. Erik hovered next to a gray-and-white marble pillar, looking at her.

"It can't be real." I frantically tried to keep my eye on everything at once. "For one thing—Yolanda—Tomas wouldn't have killed himself. He wasn't the suicidal type. Mom never said anything about that."

She stood with her arms hanging down loosely, and her face glistening as she mournfully hiccupped: " 'Course he was."

"What?"

"Suicidal? Ahhhhh, *sis*. He had his rough times. Pills, drink. That's why he was always testing me, 'cause he was so screwed up. Because he was worried neither of us would survive . . . this stupid *life*. But even at his worst, goddamn! He *swore* he wouldn't do this to me!"

Now I looked at her, completely focused.

"I guess the old man just couldn't forget the things he did in the war," she said.

I knew these *things* included the murder of Serjei Moreno, and possibly other sins as well, but I didn't have time to care about Tomas's crimes, which didn't matter nearly as much as the sight of my sister's collapsing face. I pressed her hand to my cheek, kissed it. "Oh, honey."

At the entrance of the gallery, a guard with startling green eyes shook his head at us.

"No, no," he said. "Not so much noise, please."

But Yolanda only cried harder.

Amid the splendor I lamely hugged my sister. "I saw him, I swear—and I've been text messaging with this guy, Soto-Relada . . ." But though I tried to tell her, neither she nor Erik appeared to so much as hear me. As I rocked her, Erik moved toward us. His earlier expression of wariness had disappeared.

He knew the right thing to do. He knew before me.

"Yolanda," he said, in that voice full of wicked humor and even sexiness. "Yo-lan-da. My dear."

She cried just a touch softer now.

He wiped her face with his shirttail. "Yolanda, my sweetie. My darling. You can cry, that's all right. We'll wait. There's no rush. And when you feel better, we'll get back to what we came here for."

"What the hell's he—talking about?"

"You tell me. What are we doing here?"

She didn't answer.

"Yolanda, what are we doing here?" he repeated.

"I don't know!"

"We're tracking, Yolanda," he said.

After a minute, she nodded.

"We're looking for a clue, baby," he told her.

Yolanda glanced at us from under her eyelashes, let out a ragged breath.

"It's got to be around here somewhere," I said.

"A little round medal, with a letter engraved on it," said Erik. "Come on, my precious porcupine, my grumpy Guatemalan." With great finesse, he squeezed her shoulder, nudged it. "Help us find it."

It took a few more seconds, but then she forced herself to say, "You must be nuts."

"You would not be the first to make that accusation."

"It's true," I said.

She put her hand up to her hat, squashed it down. She wiped her face again with his shirt before glaring around at the crowd that slowly sweated among the pope's thousand trinkets and priceless bagatelles. "Oh, I don't know," she moaned. "How can anybody find anything in this big ol' hairy pawnshop?"

"That's what you're here for."

We led her out of the gallery, passing back again through the map room, the apartment of St. Pius V, the Sobieksi Room. We murmured encouragements, and the riddle: *City Three's Invisible / Within this Rock, find a Bath / Burn Love's Apple, see the Clew / Then Try to Fly from my Wrath.* But she was right; inside that gilded pandemonium there seemed no way of finding the riddle's *Bath* let alone a six-inch gold medal engraved with Antonio's runes. She tried, puffing her wits back into shape, squinting at artifacts with her wet eyes. She inspected a multiplication of red-gold crosses, statues, altar cloths, mosaics. Still no evidence of MM or monstrous blonds. She moved past idols, thrones, gold-leafed paintings. Still nothing.

Then we arrived at the Sistine Chapel.

We stood in the middle of that glorious human pen. As the guards hollered exasperated admonishments against the use of flash photography, we stood shoulder-to-shoulder with a crush of other peripatetics to take in the beautiful horrors of *The Last Judgement*, finished by Michelangelo in 1541.

It is one of the master's more beguiling works.

For a brief, silent, death-forgetting moment I let the fresco teach me.

At first, I saw in the *Judgement* a specific, immutable structure. This holy system is divided between high and low, with Christ at its heart. From the celestial zenith, the brawny angels of the Resurrection carry the cross-nailed Saved up to glorious Heaven. Below, the more interesting creatures, the howling damned, grimace, leering, their gorgeous round flanks distorted from the floggings they receive from surprisingly attractive demons. The damned, as we all know, include murderers, adulterers, and suicides. If everything I had learned today was true, then that would be a decent description of Tomas de la Rosa. I lifted my eyes from the writhings of these fallen, to the center of the maelstrom, or lottery. There, in the eye of this storm, floats the mother Mary, and at her side presides the great Christ.

Christ lifts his right hand, making his selections. His torso is massive, muscle-fluttering. His face turns to quarter-profile, its expression impassive.

He is surrounded not with a small rounded halo, but rather is suspended within an immense swirling zephyr made of gold light. This shining cataract shimmers and whips in the heights of the chapel. I thought that it appeared to be made of a mix of citron, white, and gold paint, just touched with a reddish hue.

I was, and remain, convinced that Michelangelo's paintbrush had been dipped in stolen gilt melted down from an Aztec deity. I thought again of Sofia's journal, dated 1540: *"Antonio's Gold is to . . . gild the Colossus that Michelangelo will soon work upon, the tomb of St. Peter."*

Five hundred years ago, Michelangelo's brush touched Christ's corona, making a sacred calligraphy. Standing there, I saw the sinister magic that the master practiced appropriately enough with this filched, Mexican, red-gold paint: The central aureole causes a miraculous confusion in the *Judgement*. It creates a circular, centripetal, whirlwind force, absolutely out of keeping with the static organization of Heaven and Hell, as it threatens to whirl the angels into the abyss and the demons into the firmament. The holy fire that surrounds Christ is more like a Buddhist prayer wheel than a halo; more like an Aztec calendar signifying the eternal return than the fixed, closed circle of the Catholics.

Michelangelo knew that there was chaos, not just in history but even in Heaven.

Around us, people wept. Yolanda was one of them. I was too. Erik stood in silence. Others raised their hands to the images, with their eyes closed and a mixture of agony and beatific joy in their faces.

"*No photo*," yelled a guard as the crowd swelled, thrust forward, trembled.

"Time to go," Erik finally said. "Yolanda's right. We're not going to find anything here."

She screwed up her face, pointed. "There's an exit this way; I saw some people take it."

I was sunk deep in my thoughts about *The Judgement* as she led us into a darkened corridor beneath the incredibly bloodthirsty fresco of David and Goliath, so that we emerged in a dazzle of light. Out here, on gray-stoned streets, there were still more crowds. Everyone made their way from the Vatican museums to the Basilica of St. Peter's that was now in sight.

Before us shone this brilliant fairy kingdom. St. Peter's is a white-and-gold mansion fronted by grand pillars, Herculean bronze doors, and capped with colossal statues of marble saints. It boasts also the pigeon-busy square where Nero crucified Peter, the spot marked today by a cross-topped Egyptian obelisk

"He died here—I want to know where Dad's *buried*, Lola," Yolanda demanded as we moved toward the monument.

I winced into the sun's glare reflecting hotly off white marble. By my side, Erik stopped walking, all at once, causing a clutch of pigeons to fly up in a squawking burst. He stretched his neck forward; I heard a sharp intake of breath. The face with which he had murmured encouragements to Yolanda in the Vatican museums had been replaced by the earlier, harsh expression. He began to move swiftly forward again.

"Erik, what are you doing?"

"Hoping that I'm hallucinating."

"Where in the hell did they *take* him?" Yolanda said, still talking about Tomas. She didn't know what was happening yet. "Why isn't it on the certificate?"

I didn't answer. My vision had just cleared.

"Who's that?" my sister asked, after a second.

In front of us, seated alone and cross-legged on the basilica's white steps like a bodhisattva, was Marco Moreno. Black hair, black eyes, white shirt. Bemused, exhausted face.

Yolanda stiffened. "Oh no—*him*. He looks exactly the same, Jesus. I'd know this clown anywhere."

Marco turned his face up to that too-bright sky, as my lover appeared ready to spring upon him and my sister began to fly toward them. But he looked past those two, as if they weren't half real. He stared straight at me and grinned.

"I knew you'd figure it out, Lola," he said.

The three of us circled the seated Marco, who looked older and thinner than the last time I'd seen him. New lines crazed around his mouth and eyes. The bite mark on his cheek had flourished into a purple bruise.

"What took you so long?" He rose from his yoga pose and walked in a right-handed diagonal down the steps, toward the feathered, bloomer-wearing Swiss Guards stationed at the metal detectors on the far southern edge of the basilica. "I've been waiting forever, from opening till closing. Let's get this done."

"Took us so long to what?" I hurried after him. "What are you doing here?"

"Biding my time like some heartsick suitor. Hoping that you're not holding a grudge over that nasty spat we had in Tuscany. Sightseeing. Waiting to see your squidgy little face again and listen to you blather on about overheated military history theories and my hypothetical scholarly gifts." Marco peered closer at me and stopped walking. "God, you look terrible."

"Love apples," Erik blurted. "She could have died!"

"I told you to be *careful* with those."

"I know."

He touched the skin under my eyes with a gentle thumb before I averted my face. "You'll be all right. Two days and you'll be fine."

"Come here." Erik reached out to grab him, but Marco slipped from his grasp like a fish and began scooting down the steps again. "I want to talk to you, sir. Yes! I want us to have a long conversation *in private*."

"No, no, no. We can't have a squabble now. These chicken-headed guards will get excited, and then we'll all get thrown into jail for international crimes, like being Central Americans in the possession of rare Italian artifacts without any paperwork. *And* killing Blasej! I could also tattle on you for stealing my car. That was quite an irritation, by the way."

"He's right," I said. "About the police. All of us here together, we match the description on TV."

"Marco Moreno." Yolanda stalked him as he approached a line of people waiting to pass through the metal detectors before they could ascend the stairs to the basilica. "In the flesh, and all grown up. Last I heard, you were drinking your way through Paris, or Stockholm—when you're not killing little old Italians! You're a real credit to the family name."

"Hello, Yolanda. Oh, you're looking a little sniffly, dear."

"I think I'm just allergic to your smell, punk. Damn, I haven't smelled that particular fragrance in a long time. And you were just getting famous when you left home. Lola—look at this guy; you'd think he was any old sort of ordinary jerk, wouldn't you? Any old sort of regular loser. But he's not. He is not. I remember, sure. You were just getting good at your war games before you left Guatemala, Marco."

"I suppose you could put it that way."

"The reports were exaggerated, though, weren't they? What you did to those farmers?"

"What did he do to what farmers?" I asked.

"Where's the other one?" demanded Erik.

"Domenico?" Marco replied calmly. "He and I parted ways. That is, I broke off our contract. He was becoming somewhat . . . unmanageable. He's very interested in speaking to *you*, though, Erik. He's around here, somewhere. He followed me here from Siena. For the past few days he's been sitting there, under the obelisk, feeding the birds, hoping that I'll lead him to you. No, he's not there now. Probably on a bathroom break. We've been having something of a staring contest. I think he's very depressed. But let's not waste our time jabbering about him when we have so much to do! Come on, then, come on, hurry up—"

"I knew it," I said.

Erik looked at me. "What?"

"No, I knew I saw Domenico, maybe half an hour ago." I gabbed out a brief explanation in his ear. "In the crowd . . . before . . . standing there . . . he disappeared. I wasn't sure, but now . . ."

Erik scanned the throng of tourists and pilgrims. "He won't keep away—will he? I tried to—to make him stop—back in the valley."

"Our fathers are dead, Marco," Yolanda interrupted. "War's over. Just go back home."

"Why don't you?"

"You know already—my *dad*—and what happened to him—"

"Yes, well. If that's the case, you'll see there's a very good reason for keeping me around." He looked at me again. "Several very good reasons."

Yolanda stared at him with a scary intensity. "I'm listening."

"I know where Tomas is buried."

"He doesn't know what he's talking about," I said.

"Sorry, but I know exactly where he is."

"Where's my father?" Yolanda demanded.

"No, no, no. Not yet." Marco put his finger to his lips.

"Oh, you'll tell me."

"First things first." He had now taken his position at the back of the line and gestured up at St. Peter's colonnade of sculpted saints. "Tell me why you took so long to get here."

I scratched my head. "Well— I, um—there was this—theory— about—ruins? I don't know— It sounded good at the time."

"My God, you *don't* know, do you?" he marveled. "About St. Peter's."

"We just know now that we're supposed to find a church," I admitted.

He touched the tips of his fingers together. "Well, then! Perfect! I think a trade's in order here. I'll tell you what *I* know, if you tell me about the clues *you've* already found. You see, I have no idea what I'm looking for."

"Forget it," Erik said.

"Don't be stubborn."

"I'm not feeling like myself today, Marco." Erik gripped his white-fingered hands together, as if to keep from striking the other man. "Honestly. I wouldn't test me."

"What are you going to do, bite me again? Even if you *are* channeling your Neanderthal forebears, I know that you will be very interested in the cards I'm holding." Marco lowered his voice. "Come *on* people—Antonio's riddle about the Third City is so intriguing . . . a little wordplay, a little Biblical history, a splash of logic, and it's actually simple. Are you sure you don't want me to tell you what I puzzled out?"

"No," said Erik, after a strangled pause. "That is, yes, of course I do, you flabbering twit, but I still want you to get the hell out of here."

"Let's just kick the info out of him, man," said Yolanda.

I was practically biting my fists.

Marco walked backward and fixed his eyes on mine as we moved forward up the line, closer to the pantaloon-wearing *Swan Lake*–looking Swiss Guards clustered together around the detectors. "Yes, I can see that *you* do, Lola. And these ballerinas around us seem not to have yet realized that they have celebrity criminals in their midst, so let's cut to the chase and just admit that we're a team. Okay. There are two secrets. One is the location of gold, the other of a grave. So that I'll tell you the second, you must help me find the first. And as to the information that led me here, I know just what you do, which is the riddle:

> " 'CITY THREE'S INVISIBLE
>
> WITHIN THIS ROCK, FIND A BATH
>
> BURN LOVE'S APPLE, SEE THE CLEW
>
> THEN TRY TO FLY FROM MY WRATH.' "

"Yes, right," I said, moving forward, as if pulled by a string. "I've got that much."

"There's only *one* rock in Rome." He walked up to a blue-coated guard who ushered him through the detector while he talked. "*Any* Catholic would know that. It's all in the name. All in the Latin! Though of course I'm purely Indian *and* a devout atheist."

"All in the name," Erik repeated now, as if despite himself. " '*Nomen atque omen.*' "

"St. Peter's Basilica," I said, not yet understanding.

"St. Peter—*Peter.*" Yolanda's eyes fixed on the bone-bright dome flashing under the sky. She began playing upon that name in Italian and Spanish. "*Pietro. Pedro.*"

"*Piedra,*" I said, murmuring the Spanish word for "rock."

And this is when I remembered. The clue to which church we were seeking had been staring at us all along. *Rock* and *bath* had nothing to do with the Mithras mineral springs in Ostia Antica, just as invisible cities did not relate to Roman ruins. *I should have known.* I had read this! Cardinal Borodino had given the idea of St. Peter to Antonio just before the Rite of Naming in the baths of Mithras. Moments before the coven had felt the effects of the flying charm, the Cardinal had pedantically quoted from the book of Matthew— a Gospel that was evidently one of the favorites of our Medici guide:

> *"Am I the Rock upon which you build your church, my dear?" The Cardinal asked.*
>
> *"Is that not blasphemy?" inquired cheery Signora Canova, a wealthy merchant's wife.*
>
> *"It is merely a double pun upon the Cardinal's name, Pietro," Antonio offered. "And of puns, I always approve."*
>
> *"No, you ninny—I'm talking about the Bible," Signora Canova chattered. "I learned it when I was a tot! About the Saint! Diddle, daddle, what was it? Something about Christ saying Peter was like a rock, or that a rock was like Peter, or anyhow that they had a great deal in common, I can't remember—"*
>
> *"That's Matthew 16," the Cardinal began twattling. . .*

" 'And I say also to thee, That thoust art Peter, and upon this Rock I will build my church; and the gates of hell shall not prevail against it.' " I quoted, grabbing Erik by the arms. "Do you remember that?"

"That's the biblical foundation for the Catholic Church," he said. "Where Christ makes Peter the first pope."

"It's Matthew 16. It's also a piece of wordplay in Mediterranean languages. But maybe not in Aramaic, though."

"What?" Yolanda barked.

"*Petros* is the Greek for 'Peter,' and *petra*, the Latin for 'rock.' Antonio's rock—and Christ's rock—is Peter—St. Peter's Basilica. *This is the Rock.*"

Erik squeezed his eyes shut. "It's a famous pun!"

"God, why didn't I see that before—it's so obvious," my sister blustered, as she passed through the metal contraption. Next was my turn. Then Erik's.

Free of the guards, Marco walked backward, up the marble steps, keeping his gaze trained on me.

"Aren't you the least bit interested in what we'll find in there?" he asked.

He turned to make his way toward St. Peter's great columns, its massive bronze holy doors. His frame looked very thin and insubstantial against that heroic architecture before he disappeared into the entrance.

We looked at one another, and then bolted after him up the stairs.

~ 38 ~

Moving up beyond the barricade of the marble columns, we passed through the great bronze doors of St. Peter's, with their staggering images of crucifixion and flesh-starved death. My shoes rang like cymbals against the floor's polished *pietre dure* medallions that lead the worshipper into Michelangelo's masterpiece.

St. Peter's is a stone and gold cosmos. Within the dome ahead there is an *oculus*, a punched-out hole, from where the sunlight thrust down like a spear made of mica. The sunshine formed walls in the massive space, carving out dark and bright rooms that obscured, then illuminated, Marco's head and shoulders as he moved ahead of us through the church.

"You said you thought Montezuma's gold had a reddish color?" Yolanda asked, pointing skyward.

The ceiling we glared up at was fashioned of pure gold, carved into baguettes and roses, and the worked ore was radiant with a suspect reddish spectrum. It was not, however, the most beautiful of St. Peter's treasures. To our right, and protected behind a thick shield of bulletproof plastic, mourned a massive sculpture of Mary. She held her dead son on her lap. This was Michelangelo's gracious *Pietà*. Ahead flourished the bronze canopy of St. Peter, which appeared less like an altar than a magical, melting house made of tasseled gold.

"The riddle says to look for a *Bath*," Marco said when we caught up to him by the canopy.

I was busy scoping. "A baptismal font. That's what makes sense in a church. Where do they perform baptisms in here?"

"That would be the baptistery," Erik said.

"That's toward the front, I think," said Marco.

"Just hold on, just hold on," Yolanda said. "Your technique stinks. This isn't how you track. You people are all running around here like turkeys."

Marco waved her off and moved back, toward the entrance, turning into a busy room off the side of the nave. We followed him into the chamber along with a rash of tourists.

"There," I said. Among the baptistery's splendid collection of mosaics and icons, a baptismal basin stood in the center of the room. Built out of a red porphyry cistern, its chiseled base and bronze furbelows were forged in a flowery style that is not quite of the Renaissance.

Erik, Marco, and I still made directly for it. We crawled our fingers through its carvings as we searched for some nook that might hide a gold medal. The two men bumped each other with their hips and sides as they worked.

"Move over," said Erik.

"There's plenty of room," Marco replied. Then, to me: "What are we looking for?"

Erik bumped him again. "My God, *go away.*"

"Why . . . are . . . you . . . so *hostile?*"

"Is he serious?"

"Will you two calm down?" I said.

"Here's an idea: Why don't you and I make a bitter little truce for the time being?" Marco waved a two-fingered peace sign in front of Erik's face.

"A truce," Erik said. "With a murderer?"

"I'm sorry to remind you that *you're* more directly responsible for Blasej's death than I am those dithering guards'. But why quibble? You must see how stupidly inefficient this treasure hunting will be if we're trying to bash in each other's brains."

"But you are *dangerous*."

"I think you have seen by now that I don't want to hurt her."

"*I don't want you here.*"

"And yet you see that I *am*."

"Oh, he's not going anywhere," Yolanda said. "I'm not finished with him."

"See?"

Erik looked at me.

"I want the families to try to come to an agreement," I said. "A truce is a good idea."

"Bah," said Yolanda.

"Aren't women wonderful?" Marco asked, diabolically.

Erik moved his mouth around his face as if a sliver of lemon had been magically pressed upon his tongue. A brief, struggling meditation. "Give me some room," he said.

"All you need." Marco magnanimously bowed and moved to the side.

"Actually, I think you're done," Yolanda said, suddenly glancing over her shoulder. "You're starting to draw some unwanted attention."

Behind us, tourists flocked and murmured:

"What they doing?"

"Someone call a guard."

"Oooo, we don't want them to do that—and I can't find anything here, anyway," I said. (Later, I would learn that the porphyry basin had been installed in the basilica in the seventeenth century; whatever *Bath* Antonio had referenced in his riddle was gone.)

Yolanda whistled and rolled her eyes to the ceiling. "You ready to let me take a look around? Now that we've brokered the Geneva Convention?"

"Yes."

"Okay. This place is a jumble sale. Knickknacks have been hurled around here since it was built. But I'll bet there were one or two persnickety types who wanted to put all the little bits into one place, where they could keep their eye on them."

She walked out of the baptistery, moving slowly into the basilica's intricacy of chambers, surreptitiously touching bejeweled icons and sculptures, until she eventually found her way to a building off the side of the main basilica: the ten-room Treasury Museum.

Inside, the walls glistened with rows of glass cabinets, which held some of the most precious rarities in the papal collection. Tourists in long pants and unaccustomed floor-length dresses stooped before these displays, squinting.

With a swipe of her hand, Yolanda parted these human barricades with such authority I barely heard a mumble of protest. She led us through the treasure vault, stopping in the fourth room. Here, she conducted a visual search of a case displaying a gold reliquary with fragments of the true cross, a gold key of St. Peter, a silver-wrapped chalice. Marco stood patiently in the midpoint of the gallery. Erik, at the doorway, kept closer watch on him than the antiquities.

But then I saw him give a jerk.

"What?"

Yolanda and I hurried over to the glass case that had caught Erik's eye.

The case was on the west wall of the room, containing miniatures not in any way remarkable compared to the rest of Peter's riches. A small emerald cut into the shape of a Celtic cross glittered next to a tiny bone sculpture of a lion. A tiny, miraculous pinecone made of crystal sparkled; a little Sphinx whittled from petrified wood stared out from its pretty prison.

There it was.

On the right-hand side, on a small Lucite stand, shone a round, thick, heavy, red-gold medal. It was elaborately etched, with roses, curling ferns, preternatural blossoms so Edenically lavish they nearly choked the cipher beyond recognition.

Erik, Yolanda, and I pressed ourselves against the glass pane.

"What?" Marco asked. He stood beside me. "What do you see?"

I did not say it out loud. Erik and I had found first an *L*, then a *P.* Now I stared at the third sign, which had been waiting for a prepared reader for more than five hundred years.

Marco followed my eyes. He saw it, the clue:

39

What is that?" Marco gasped the question in my ear.

"*U,*" Yolanda exulted.

"*U,*" Marco repeated, not understanding.

"That's it, then," Erik said. "We've got it. And we've got to know what word the clues are spelling—don't we?"

We were already whisking out of the basilica's treasury, through the sacristy, then reaching its golden-phosphorescent nave.

"*What was that?*" Marco demanded.

"I'll tell you when I find out where my father's buried," Yolanda said.

"What if I tell you that the grave, such as it is, *is* in Venice? And that I'll take you right to it when we get there."

She stopped. "What do you mean, 'such as it is'?"

"Yolanda," I said. "I told you already—"

I shut my mouth with a snap; I could not mention the tattooed man in front of Marco.

"What did you mean by that?" she asked him again.

"I'm *not telling*, yet." Marco kept moving forward. We were now following him out the doors, to the basilica's front steps.

"I know why you're doing this, Marco," she said thinly. "And it isn't just because of some scramble-headed idea about gold."

He smiled. "Your sister has that theory, too. She says that I'm pursuing this because I'm good at it. At puzzle-solving. That I have promise."

"And not because you're pathetically lonely?"

A pause. "What?"

"You heard me. You're lonely. I can see it—it's pitiful. You've *always* been a weird puppy. And now, here you are, the son of the great Colonel Moreno, following around the de la Rosas because you're such a guilty, friendless *headcase*."

Marco worked to retain his style beneath the glare of the afternoon sky. "Thank you so much for the diagnosis."

"Enough of that, Yolanda," said Erik. "Let's concentrate on what we're doing."

"It's *true*."

Marco's bitten face twisted. "Right, oh, poor me. I'm just following a squad of spelling bee contestants because of a blistering Oedipal complex and psychobabbling alienation."

"Pretty much, yeah," my sister concurred.

With a quick shift of tone, Marco then said, "Ah, well, perhaps you can leave off abusing me for the moment. More important matters present themselves. As you see: there he is."

He had turned to look across the square, toward the Egyptian obelisk.

"There who is?" Yolanda asked.

"A former friend, actually. I said he'd followed me here and was waiting for you."

Beneath the obelisk stood the mourning and gaunt-faced Domenico. His blond hair was bunged up, and he wore a crumpled suit. He carried a paper bag. From the bag he drew pellets of birdseed, scattering them for a tremendous horde of clacking, ravenous pigeons. This made him appear like an inoffensive animal lover–slash–homeless person—so much so that a tourist in a black coat and red cap came up to him and dropped a euro in his palm.

"Who *is* that?" Yolanda asked, squinting and blinking as if she didn't see quite clearly.

"Domenico. I don't believe you two have met. He's lost his mind, I'm afraid," said Marco. "It will take a couple of tricks to keep him from shooting you in the head, Erik—that's how he does it. . . . Once I saw him lose his temper in Gstaad. A mess. Don't worry, though, I made sure he didn't get a gun—"

"You know, all of sudden, I think I've just *had* it with these people, Lola," Erik broke in, the flat, dead tone I recognized from the crypt.

"Erik. Calm down."

He pulled at the skin around his eyes. "I'm feeling pretty calm, actually. I'm pretty clear, right now. I told you we should stay in the apartment. I *knew* it. And now I see that I just have to make him *stop* all this. Make him leave us alone. Because Domenico isn't interested in any bloody truce!"

"Just let me think."

"Gomara," Yolanda said. "You're getting that funny look again, all pale and squibbly. Chill the hell out."

"He's threatening my family, Yolanda," Erik stammered. "I can't have him hurting you girls. And, Lola, I just saw you—sick—I just saw you—" His eyes welled, and a tear ran down his cheek. "It was really, really bad—"

"Just give me a second. Just give me a minute. Yolanda, *keep* him here."

"Erik, stop shaking like that! Get yourself in control."

He looked at his hands, which had begun to tremble. "Oh, good Christ."

"I'm going to try something," I insisted.

"*What?*"

"The guards, they'll help."

"No, they *won't*," said Marco. "They'll just arrest us and throw us in jail. And you, Yolanda, you'll never find out about your father."

"*That* can't happen," my sister said.

"Forget it, this is over. Erik—Erik, it's all right. I'm just going to talk to the guards. They'll take care of him. . . ."

I hurried down the white steps, toward two puffy-suited men standing about twenty meters left of the obelisk, making a small island in a large gray pool of pigeons. Domenico was still casting seeds to this fluttering multiplication of flying rats.

"Signores?" I asked.

The guards turned around. One was short, with large blue eyes, and the other was tall, with a giraffe neck. Both wore the Swiss Guards' signature bloomers and vests and feathered hats. "Si, Signorina."

I pointed at Domenico and said in Italian: "That man is threatening us."

They peered over at the blond thug, who was making kissing noises at the birds. "Him?"

"Yes. He's threatened to kill my friends and me. You *have* to help us!"

"When did this happen?"

"A couple days ago."

Giving Domenico another once over, the giraffe neck said: "Perhaps you are confused. Look at him—he is harmless. For the last two days, all he does is feed the birds. He's like St. Francis of Assisi."

"Actually, he's a hired serial killer, and he's really mad at my boyfriend for . . ." *Killing his friend with a poisoned emerald, in the crypt of the Medici in Florence. And then for stealing his car in Siena.* I began stuttering: "This—um—thing he did. Agh . . . shoot . . . you have to arrest him, or question him—"

"Arrest who?" They began swiveling their heads around. "Your boyfriend?"

"No—no! No no no. Not my boyfriend. St. Francis of Assisi—this blond man."

They stared at me, muttering, "Americans."

"*Okay, Sis, that's quite enough, now,*" I heard Yolanda singing at my back.

The giraffe neck fluttered his yellow cap-feathers at me. "Carlo, have I seen this girl?"

"I don't know," the short one replied.

"Yeah. On the wire. On that fax we got. Five two, dark hair, small-built, Indian—"

Yolanda was barreling toward me. Marco, still by the steps, was trying to persuade Erik to jam out of there.

"No, yeah, I did," the giraffe neck said. "That drawing. Of the crazies in Siena."

"Or wasn't there something in the Medici crypt—"

The guards hadn't yet noticed Erik, and I began to see that I had made an error of titanic proportions. Worst-case scenario, they would detain me, doing nothing to stop a fracas between the two men. "Let me be clear: I am filing a complaint. I am asking you for help—"

The giraffe neck pressed: "Ma'am, are you that lady on the TV?"

"You're not listening—"

Marco had persuaded Erik to walk away from the Basilica,

past the obelisk. But Erik stopped to make seething eye contact with Domenico.

"You getting everything sorted out here?" My sister now stood to my right, warning me with an irritated twitch of the lips.

I looked at her and said in Spanish, "Yes, okay, *mistake*. Get me out of this."

Yolanda grabbed my shoulders and began steering me away. "Hi, boys. Never mind my sister; she's incredibly stupid."

"May we see your passport?"

We began to move away from them, through the square, nudging past tourists. "Sorry, no time, we're due at the place where naked gladiators used to axe each other—"

"Come on," I called over my shoulder to Erik.

"Carlo—get her."

"Ma'am!"

Yolanda snatched at Erik and thrust us both forward, still smiling and bubbling out, "See you later." As the guards began to move toward us, she looked down at the swarm of pigeons, making a curious clicking noise. She jumped up and stamped her boots on the ground. "Sssssssssssshhhhhht!"

The pigeons, startled by her jungle-bird call, gave a collective squawk and flew up in a blinding, charcoal swarm, obscuring us and scratching at my hair with their hundred sharp claws.

"Let's *book*, Lola."

"Agh! *Ack!!*"

We ran.

I took hold of a stiff and strange-looking Erik and we hustled through the pigeon pollution and across the square. Domenico began to follow us in a swift, long-legged stride.

We dashed faster through the sideways light falling across the square, over the bricks, snaking in between islands of map-reading nuns. Hitting the square's border, which demarcates the end of Vatican City and the beginning of Rome, I looked over my shoulder to see Domenico cutting through the throng into a muscular and incredibly fast sprint. The guards had followed us more or less toward the border at a decelerating trot, and now had their fingers in their ears as they talked and listened to a radio device affixed to their heads.

"Lola—move."

Erik bolted, taking me with him into the depths of another crowd. I bashed into priests and sweating, squalling women. Feet and legs tangled beneath me. I pushed against more bodies, shouting, but a high-pitched babble of voices speaking Italian, French, Norwegian, and Japanese snuffed out my cries.

We doglegged into a dead-end alleyway. My sister was yelling *no.* The sunlight soared in over the tops of the bordering redbrick buildings, landing on the narrow, cobbled space. Domenico appeared from behind the corner of the alley—white shirt, flapping blue jacket, white pants. A black object stuck into the waistband of the pants. The handle of a gun. I saw his blue eyes like two hollows in his veined, angled face. Erik stood between us. My lover's shoulders hunched forward and the flesh around his eyes and jaw started to swell weirdly, horribly.

Marco skidded around the bend.

"Don't be an ass!" he said to Domenico, shoving past him. "I gave you enough money so that you should be drunk in Greece."

"Time to get out of the alley now," Yolanda belted out. But Domenico's huge frame blocked our exit.

"I knew what to do with that money," Domenico said to

Marco. He gestured at his weapon now hidden by his jacket. His face was so pale as to be almost silver. "What do you think I am? That I'm not a man. I have no heart. Drinking my life away with a devil like you."

"Of course not!"

"You think you're the only one with the right. To teach them."

Marco hauled back and fiercely struck the blond man's immobile chin with his fist.

Yolanda cried out, "Oh, Jesus, who is this guy?"

"Erik! Erik!" I yelled. His back was humped over. He shuddered strangely. From his throat came a rasping sound.

Domenico had not yet taken a step toward any of us; he was not even looking at us, but only rubbing his face where Marco had hit him. Erik did not wait to see what he would decide to do next with the gun he carried. I saw his knees buckle to the ground. He jolted toward Domenico, weeping, falling forward. I did not understand what I was looking at, what was happening. I thought he had been hurt, that somehow he had collapsed in a faint.

Erik reached up, under the jacket, and grabbed a hold of that black handle sticking out of Domenico's waistband. Domenico leaned very slightly back, his mouth opening. Erik dug his hand down into the pants and grasped hold of the trigger. He pulled it.

There was a sound like a snap. Like a coin dropping on stone.

Domenico's grief-scarred face seemed to split apart. One eye dragged downward from the concussion tearing apart the lower half of his body; his mouth bloomed and fragmented, the lips skiddering wildly onto his left cheek.

Erik shot the muffle-nosed pistol once again. A great red star of blood exploded from Domenico's abdomen. The blond man's head was thrown back. He fell sideways onto the sunlit ground. A hideous fizzing noise came from his lungs, or the gaps in his body, where air was escaping.

Then Yolanda and I were flying forward, our arms stretched outward. We lifted Erik bodily from the ground, dragging him out of the alley and into a white haze of people. This was made all the harder as his body had gone soft, his neck collapsing, his head over one shoulder.

"Get him out of here; get to the train station," I heard Marco say in a hard, controlled voice as he snatched the gun, rubbed it free of prints, and stuck it in his pants. "Get the next one to Venice. I'll meet you there."

"JUST SHUT UP," I screamed.

"No, don't say that," he called out, his face agonized. "I'm helping you—I'm cleaning this up—"

Yolanda yelled "Go—go—go—go."

Our hands scratched on the cobblestones as we scrambled from the brightness of the blood and the last wheezing sounds of Domenico. We pounded down another thoroughfare in grim, panting silence, making our swift way through a hot tide of a thousand believers.

I looked back at the shivering mosaic of faces. I heard a woman shrieking. There was a rustling and buckling of the crowd several feet behind us, as people began to see the body and looky-loos streamed toward the commotion.

Then I could see one navy-suited man, with a police cap and a gun at his white belt, running through the horde, looking around frantically.

"Oh, man, we have *got* to get him out of here," Yolanda gasped, as we staggered forward.

"Did I kill him?" Erik coughed and cried out.

"Move faster!" I wept.

Yolanda barked, "Marco was right—we've got to get to the apartment *right now* and get our stuff, get to the train—"

"But how are we going to get away?"

As I looked behind me again, I glimpsed the back of some tall, thickset man who ran into the street, calling for the police's help. This arm-waving Roman wore a red knit cap over his dark hair, and a long black coat.

"Help, help," he called out. "Somebody's hurt."

The policeman stopped and grabbed the man, who talked excitedly while hopping up and down. The Roman pointed the policeman down the street in the opposite direction from us.

The policeman ran away, and the man with the red cap disappeared into the crowd.

"That's our break," I gasped.

"I think I'm in shock, honey," Erik said. "I'm numb all over. I can't feel my hands. I can't feel anything—"

"It's okay, it's okay, it's okay."

Yolanda, looking back at the freak chance we'd been given, squinted and grimaced. She pressed her hands hard over her eyes. "Jesus, I'm going crazy. Let's move it. Let's haul ass, people. We've got to disappear."

And that's precisely what we did.

40

"Madam, where to?"

Twenty-five minutes later, Yolanda, Erik, and I stood in the ticket line of Rome's airy Stazione Termini, the city's main train station. Its ceiling was formed out of curving white rafters shaped with the disturbing elegance of human ribs, and these arches descended over the luminous black floor. The minimal design was punctuated by two dark green palms whose spines and sharp leaves butted up against the bony firmament.

The three of us looked like miserable ragamuffins in the soaring heights of the station. My sister had partially obscured her appearance by taking off her Stetson and ratting out her hair so it stuck out in little stiff tufts over her eyes. She took Tomas's death certificate out of the rucksack and obsessively began to read it again. I was hiding beneath a sweatshirt hood but could see plain enough the skull lines of my face reflected in the ticket kiosk's window. Erik had killed someone. Again. I knew that Domenico had been suffering with grief and was stupid as well as bad. And Erik knew the same. He stood between us in line, with a damaged expression in his eyes, and his mouth was as flat and pale as a scar.

Marco I could not see so as to describe. After the shooting, and our flight from the police, I lost track of him during our
sweaty, flat-footed race back to the apartment. Perhaps he was
gone. Maybe he wasn't planning on "meeting us" anywhere, as he
had suggested over the still warm body of his friend. But I felt so
crazy that I could have sworn he even now was lingering in the
purlieus, and watching our movements from somewhere in the
crowd.

"Madam? Hello? Where are you traveling?"

The ticket lady's large oval eyes observed me impatiently
from behind that glass window.

Erik studied the ground as if an invisible hand had just
written a message for him there on the linoleum, the way King
Balthazar had seen the writing on the wall in the biblical story.
I thought I had a decent idea what that message said. I, also,
had my share of alarming ciphers flashing up at me from the
little liquid crystal display window on my cell phone. Yolanda
clutched the death certificate that obscurely told of her father's
burial site.

"You know where we're going," she said, flapping the paper
at me.

"Erik decides," I said. "I think we should go home. If we can
get a flight—"

She pulled both of us to the side and hissed in our ears so
the ticket lady wouldn't hear: "They won't be looking for us in
Venice, anyway. They'll ask for passports at the airport—we'll
be screwed. And we can't take your car because you stole it, so
they'll have the license plate—"

"What if they look for us on the trains? And he's in no shape
to keep running—"

"I'm in supreme shape to get the hell out of here," Erik said in a low, even voice, though looking so gray-skinned he didn't even appear like the man I knew. "For the moment anyway. I think it's adrenaline that's keeping me glued together, and keeping me from doing a Lady *fucking* Macbeth impersonation all over the station." He ran his fingers back and forth, back and forth, across his forehead, as if manually keeping his thoughts in check.

Just then, right over Yolanda's shoulder, I saw a queer little flicker in the crowd. It felt as if a fox were staring at me from the bush: an inconspicuous figure in a dark shirt had just melted away among the business folks and the *bambino*-hefting moms.

Athens, we could have picked. São Tomé. Reykjavík, where internationally wanted felons disappear into the snow drifts and survive on herring. But as if inspired by some demonic posses- sion, we hurled ourselves onward to the fourth city of the Wolf, whose lagoons promised refuge, fathers, as well the last letter of Antonio's unfinished, if perhaps obvious word.

L—U—P—[ ]

I spirited a packet of bright paper euros from my pocket, slid- ing them beneath the glass window.

"Venice," I said.

The express swept past Rome, then through the northern coun- tryside on the way up to Venice. Farmhouses and pastures stalked by lavish cows appeared and then evanesced in our dingy win- dowpanes. Erik, Yolanda, and I took our seats, Erik falling asleep immediately and atypically against the blue-and-pink upholstery, clutching my thigh with his cold hands. Yolanda spent some time fidgeting with the complimentary plastic-wrapped anise sweets and miniature espressos before abruptly losing consciousness.

I had been crying, and also vomiting in the train bathroom, until my sister shoved Sofia's journal in my face and said, "Stop that. Distract yourself. You're not helping *him*." Somehow I followed her advice, and spent the next several hours anesthetizing myself with the portion of Sofia's journal that described her life in Venice, before the sudden flashing and beeping of my cell phone diverted me from this study. While Erik and my sister were still both buried beneath train blankets, I determined it was time for me to attend to the voluminous correspondence I had been evading and vehemently exchanging in the brutal seventy-odd hours that had just passed.

There were two sets of cell-phone texts. The first set had been sent by my mother, but I had been so consumed with the latter communiqués that I had not even studied their contents. Though these missives were as highly crypted as the Egyptian hieroglyphs, I could still, unfortunately, read them, and realize what a mistake this omission had been:

m hru cu asap	MONSTER, HOW ARE YOU? CALL US AS SOON AS POSSIBLE
m cub asap	MONSTER, CALL US BACK AS SOON AS POSSIBLE
tc cb worid	TERRIBLE CREATURE, CALL BACK, WORRIED
l worid	LOLA, WORRIED
l ura pita cb	LOLA, YOU ARE A PAIN IN THE ASS, CALL BACK
l ur driving me craz	LOLA, YOU ARE DRIVING ME CRAZY
md wer cuming mt rorv	MONSTER DARLING, WE ARE COMING,

	SHOULD WE MEET YOU IN ROME OR VENICE?
l r or v	LOLA, ROME OR VENICE?
l r or v	LOLA, ROME OR VENICE? [AD INFINITUM]
ok we r flyng 2 v	OKAY, WE'RE FLYING TO VENICE
m we r in v	MONSTER, WE ARE IN VENICE
we r st8ng off s8ntms	WE ARE STAYING OFF ST. MARK'S SQUARE
l w84u2cu xox md	LOLA, WAITING FOR YOU TO CALL US, HUGS AND KISSES, MOM AND DAD

I clicked these exclamations off the liquid crystal display window and decided that I would delay my responses to my mother for a while longer yet.

The second set of text messages I could not ignore. I began this series of communications while I was still in the hospital, and the epistles were to and from the fence, Señor Sam Soto-Relada. I had been writing to him in earnest ever since I had discovered who he was. Though I had attempted to read Señor Soto-Relada's mind-tweaking disclosures to my unhearing friends before, I now judged that discretion would be the better part of sanity. I also will not publish the great bulk of these letters now, as I am ordinarily a woman of delicacy, yet I had been able to find, in my belladonna delirium, sufficient creative inspiration to transform the cell-phone pad digits into a vehicle for the most scorching of profanities.

The last communiqué, his, will suffice: L IM IN CAR 4, it read.

I quietly rose from my seat, taking care to avoid disturbing my family, and slipped through the train cars like a thief.

I read the car numbers posted on the walls; I entered the fourth. I looked down a long row of seats.

To my left there were six men, the first five identically clothed in gray suits, gorgeous Italian ties, suit coats hurled over the seat top as they unanimously attempted to do inchoate forms of business on phones and computers and out of expensive-looking briefcases.

The sixth man had a red cap on his head, a black coat, and a huge rucksack in the empty seat at his side, and was otherwise not like the rest. But he was like me.

I regarded him for some moments in silence before I said, "Hello Señor Soto-Relada."

He gazed back, kindly. "Or, angel, you could just go ahead and call me—"

I raised my hand. "Don't say it."

"Dad," insisted Tomas de la Rosa.

41

The green fields whisked by outside the train window as Tomas de la Rosa slipped off his red cap and replaced it with a night-black, piratically tilted Stetson.

I shook my head. "I'd rather call you—"

He grinned wickedly.

"I think you *know* the names I have in mind. And they're not anagrams."

(*Sam Soto-Relada =Tomas de la Rosa*)

He crossed his arms behind his head. "You wouldn't be the first woman to give me a lashing. But I'm still happy to see you didn't bring Y in here, because then we'd be having ourselves a nice little family reunion that would probably flip this damned train right over. Though you're more of a handful than I expected. In those little messages of yours? Shoot. You should learn how to watch your temper, Lola. Though I suppose you can't help yourself, being born half Sanchez and all."

His ponytail hung blackly shining beyond his shoulders, and I could see the revealed red and cobalt serpents tattooed on his neck. Gold hoop earrings glinted like eclipses against his brick skin; beneath his ink eyes flashed white teeth. He raised his hand—a large, square, neat-fingered hand—and waved it as if he were shooing away a pesky and fang-dripping Rottweiler when he growled out the word *Sanchez*. I remembered when that same hand had lightly gripped my arm like a magician's, in Siena's Piazza del Campo. I suddenly remembered, too, the scholarly fop with the silvery spectacles, bronze magnifying glass, and Umberto Eco accent who had skittled around the Palazzo Medici Riccardi's dining room before magically stealing Marco's gun like some hybrid of Gandalf and Bugsy Berkeley.

"So that was you in Florence. In the palazzo—"

"Sure it was. Wasn't going to let that nasty Moreno put a bullet in my honey."

"Honey" was one of Erik's names for me. "Don't call me that. Don't ever call me that."

"Why are you crying?"

"Everything's *ruined*."

"What's wrong?"

"I don't know. Erik—he—hurt someone!"

"Jesus, stop that. Now. *Get a hold of yourself.*" For a second, he was fierce. "You're not out of the woods. You don't know the meaning of ruined. The boy you should be focusing on is Moreno."

I clenched my jaw and wiped my face. "He's why you're here. Marco."

"You're why I'm here—"

"Why didn't he recognize you? At the palazzo? And—was that you in Rome—in the red cap?"

"He didn't recognize me for the same reason you didn't. Because I didn't want him to. I'll admit I did get a little sloppy in Siena, where you might recall we did our tango and you nearly split my brains open with a candlestick or something." Here his anger or fear subsided, and the grin slowly returned. "But all was forgiven when I saw how good you are at using your bean. With the wolf mosaic—which I led you to, don't forget. I'd figured as much after reading the riddle. But dammit, you cracked it, kid, and I wasn't sure about you then!"

"Wait a minute. Last year—*you're* the one who found the Queen Jade in the forest—before Mom got there—at the cave— that's why it was excavated—"

" 'Course it was me. I was *just about* to hoist the old girl out when the army bastards came sniffing around and I had to race away so as to keep my lambchops in working order, if you see what I'm saying. It was nice, though, when I read that your mother showed up later and tidied everything up in there—though I heard she ran into some trouble—"

"Why did you *lie* to everyone?"

"Because I didn't think a dead man would be a danger to his family. Marco's clan was going to give Yolanda a visit, just to give me a taste of my own hooch, as we say in the jungle. Then they were going to give you a call. I thought me being buried would satisfy them."

"It was the wrong move, Tomas."

Once again, his face nearly lost its Olmec aplomb. "I know it. All of it for nothing. It's the son. Marco. He was nice and alcoholic here in Europe till the day he found out his father died. Considering the mess the man left him, you'd think he would have thrown himself a panty raid. But then the boy starts really having fits. *And* feeling the pressure to pay back what I'd done to that worthless cousin of his, honor the name of the aardvark's ass who sired him, et cetera. There wasn't anything else for me to do than to come out of hiding, make you valuable to him—"

"As Soto-Relada—"

"Right, posing as a fence, throwing at him that Medici letter I'd busted my tail to get my hands on for fourteen years. Telling

him about you and your big brains. How you could help him find
the gold. How you were worth more to him healthy—and how
if he had at anybody in the family, you wouldn't lift a finger for
him."

"But you wanted me to know. About you. That's why you
made up the anagram."

"And gave you about a billion clues when we were talking on
the phone, back in Florence—not an easy task, I'll let you know,
as I was spying and scampering after those big goons of Marco's
the whole time, and racing back and forth between you all like a
Ping-Pong ball so nobody'd let on to my trick."

I held my face. "I would *really* like to black out right now—"

"But. Look. What I'm trying to tell you is that it's better you
stay far away from that Marco. That is, after today. And keep
Y away from him, too. Also that boyfriend of yours, who looks
like he got yanked out of his grave just after he'd got comfort-
able in it. But I don't want to talk about the reasons for that.
I can see it just gets you into a tizzy. And you've got bigger
chickens to fry."

"Marco. He might have followed us here."

"Yeah, and it's no mystery." Tomas stuck his thumb over his
shoulder. "He's right back there, in car number five. I'm sitting
here keeping an eye out"—I glanced to the clear glass window
on the sliding door separating the cars—"because he's crazy. Get
me? From what I've been able to tell, I think you're being a *woman*
about this, getting fuzzy-brained, thinking maybe he's not as bad
as you think? Nah. He'd hurt you very easily, Lola. Even if right
now he seems to be just a little poor puppy dog, lonely as a cloud,
all that garbage. Don't be fooled."

"I'll make up my own mind, thanks."

"I'm serious—be careful. I've been watching him. Kid's beyond help. Went into a bad depression and was close to killing himself a couple of days back. I'm familiar enough with the signs. But he didn't do it, unfortunately."

"God."

"Morenos don't stay cuddly for too long. Soon as this game plays out, he'll be another bastard entirely. Which is why I'm going to have to break one of the commandments where he's concerned."

"*Why are you here?*"

"Because I need to make sure you find the gold, without getting garroted in the process." The wrinkles deepened on his face as an ambiguous expression skated across it. "Which is really just another way of saying I was curious. I wanted to know how you'd do at this game. I needed to see."

"See what?"

"If what Juana said was right. If it was true about you."

"If what was true?"

His eyes glittered up at me impatiently. "That you are my daughter."

A racket of confusion banged and hooted inside me when he said *daughter*. "You think Mom lied to you about that?" I asked hopefully.

"Nah, course not. I mean, if you were *really* mine. You know, a tough nut who hadn't fallen far from the tree. You think I haven't romanced my share of ladies who come yelling after me about the numnuts they want me to call 'son'? Hell, I don't have time for any of them, and I certainly wouldn't for some soft-belly from the 'burbs, all sweet and fussy like that boyfriend of Juana's who went and raised you, no offense. 'Cause a kid like that, well, hell, that wouldn't work out, would it? I'm not the tender type of *papi*, you see. Better off she and I never met—"

"I've heard about you," I said. "And your *tests*—Yolanda told me. When she was twelve, in the jungle—"

"Why do you think she's so strong? A woman like that's the only kind that can survive this ashtray of a planet."

This subject was dangerous; I switched it. "They say—I read—that you—de la Rosa died here. Venice. The certificate looked real enough."

Tomas just smiled.

"What you're doing isn't *normal*."

"I know I should have stayed out of sight," he replied. "Better for Y, better for everyone. *And* it was relaxing, being stone dead, keeping tabs on Yolanda from afar the way the dead do. I found things very, very, peaceful without being hassled by all these *women*. But the thing is, our family's always had that problem. What I'm talking about is that curiosity. The wanting to know. The de la Rosas are always poking their noses where they shouldn't—though I'm sure you've already heard the stories. Your mother must have told you about the family. . . ."

I grew very quiet here, but my face betrayed me.

"Or not. I guess she didn't mention it out of kindness to old Manuel. *Nice* man. But it is a shame, you not knowing about your real kin. It would help you understand why you're so . . . strange."

I found myself holding my breath. "What do you mean?"

"What do I mean? What do *I* mean? Look at you. Cut-to-fit, dyed-to-the-bone *de la Rosa* is what you are. Even when you're bawling and honking and sniffling, darlin'. If you want, I could tell you a little about us. Show you where you got that personality of yours. What you really inherited, besides this letter. Would you like that, pee-wee?"

I did not answer.

"Sure you would. Because, Lola, you *do* remind me of your grandfather. With your books. How you went off loping into the jungle two years past. Anyway, Jose Diego de la Rosa, that was his name, your grandpa. He used to ramble around Argentina looking for this sword he swore belonged to ol' King Arthur, which was inherited and buried by a girl pal of Che Guevara. He'd go banging around Patagonia with a backpack full of sextants and thermometers, and a bunch of history books, looking for the thing. 'I think that sword's at the bottom of Laguna Negra, my boy, thrown there in disgust by the revolutionaries,' he'd say to me, sticking one of his books under my nose. He was a genius, swear to Christ, *and* right about a blade being at the bottom of the Black Lake, no surprise. But before he could study the thing, he was killed by a Peronist with six bullets. And then—girl, you look like you're going to faint, you okay?—there's one of your great-grandmothers, Ixzaluoh. Bow-legged as a circus freak, but a great warrior for Honduran independence in the 1800s. She wanted to learn the best way to a kill a man—she was fighting the Spaniards—and so she spied on the hidalgos at the encampments, hiding in the trees while they made their gunpowder down there on the ground. She memorized every secret ingredient they used, brought the recipe back home, and wound up killing eighty colonials with that brimstone before she got dead in an explosion she set off herself—"

"Stop it," I said, though even at this moment he'd hooked me. I instantly, wrongly, wanted what he was offering. An enchanted lost family taken from the pages of my favorite books. An epic pops who would explain me to myself. But I knew I couldn't take these things because that would be a betrayal of Manuel. "Stop it."

He leaned back lazily. "That's all right, Lola, I'll just tell you when you're ready." Then he said, with less languor: "It's time for us to end this conversation, anyhow."

"Why?"

" 'Cause I need you to do something. About Marco. That's why I called you out here. I've been keeping my eye on him. He's been crying and so on, playing with that gun he lifted off the stiff you guys left in Rome. He thinks you don't like him anymore, Lo-lee-ta. And he thinks you're the only girl in the whole, wide, bad world who understands him, how smart he is, how much he misses his precious daddy. But if I let him brood too long, he'll take a bad turn. I saw it happen with his father in the war—ugly sight. And I don't want to have to have a chat with him until we're away from all these businessmen and babies. So you should go and calm him down, which apparently you're not too bad at, according to his blithering. Tell him what he wants to hear. About how he'll get his hands on enough gold to make him into a baby Hitler, and how you think he's just a peachy and misunderstood sonofabitch. But you'd better do it before he has himself a fit and I have to do something unkind to him in front of a toddler."

"I don't want you to do anything to him," I said. "And he *can't* see you."

"Like you're already aware, I know how to make myself hard to spot when I want."

I pressed my fingers to my temples. "And Yolanda—"

"Don't you worry about her. I'll take care of Y; she is my love-girl. Just like I'll take care of you, L, and your mother too—"

My teeth clashed when he said that.

"You'll take care of Mom and me?"

There was a threat to Manuel in his promise. It made me want to shake Tomas by the collar, or cry *and* abuse him, or somehow ensure I'd never see him again.

Except then, I could not do any of these things: In Siena, I had read his face like a book; though I had never seen him before, I had recognized it immediately. As I glared down at the man's ugly-handsome face, I suddenly knew why. It was because I had inherited that same face, the same bones, with feminine touches. I had recognized myself in him. I looked more like that prevaricating, honey-tongued destroyer than Yolanda did; I looked more like that story-telling daughter-escaper than my mother.

Then I didn't want to know any more. I walked away from Tomas de la Rosa without another word, down the empty seats, past the businessmen.

"Careful, sweets," I heard him say.

When I turned around, he was already slipping down the aisle, the ponytail snaking down his back. He disappeared out the opposite door.

He had certainly done his job with me, offering me my weirdness dressed up as brilliance. And he had more than reminded me that Marco had wanted to erase the evidence and fruit of my family's secret history.

I steadied my breath as I entered car five.

But there was no monster waiting for me in the next car.

Tomas had his facts wrong; that war of his was old.

I opened the communicating doors upon a hollow-cheeked man meditating like a desert hermit in one of the blue upholstered seats.

Marco Moreno glanced up with his astonishing eyes and did not seem surprised when he saw me come in.

"I threw away the gun a few miles back," he said, softly. "I wiped it down. Nobody will track it to him." A pause. "I meant it when I said I'd help you."

I sat down on the seat opposite his and just looked at him, not saying anything for a long time. While I saw how his feelings had maimed his face, I thought again of how he let Blasej kill those guards, and of the hideous hint that Yolanda had given me about what he'd done to farmers back in Guatemala. I had not forgotten these details; on the contrary. And yet, I knew that here was a person in a crisis of villainy, just as Erik, six cars back, was in the throes of some kind of crisis of goodness. Marco was learning the painful lesson that he could be different.

He blinked at me, nodding, before gazing out the window at the blue radiance flying past. Not many words were required between us at this point.

"What am I going to do with you?" I finally asked.

"I don't know."

Marco reached out and patted my hand. He held it until I gently extracted myself from his grasp. He looked out the window again.

"But I know you'll love it, Lola."

"What?"

He smiled as if he was in love with me, and pointed at the view.

"Welcome to Venice," he said.

We were there: At the edge of the window frame was water, the color of cobalt mixed with sapphire and glazed with melted topaz. Farther still, as if floating above that lagoon, presided a casbah built of gold domes and white spires. Dark flying creatures—La Serenissima's famous pigeons—circled the panorama of St. Mark's Square, the pale obelisks topped by the golden winged lions that guarded this place we had run to for sanctuary.

My heart gave a painful, hopeful leap when I saw the Fourth City.

BOOK FOUR

THE
SHAPE-SHIFTING
WRETCH

❦ 42 ❧

I looked back from the approaching fairy city to Marco Moreno's lean, wrecked face. De la Rosa had told me he wanted to meet with Marco in a place empty of toddlers and businessmen; he sought privacy for his retribution against the Morenos. I would not let him have it. There would be no more deaths.

"*Venezia. Venezia.*" I heard over the speakers.

I pressed into my cell phone pad the message:

`Were here, meet S8ntMS 30 mins`

Then I said: "Come on."

"Where?" Marco asked. "Just you and me?"

"No."

I took Marco's hand and half-dragged him through the compartments, the doors sucking open and closed as we passed through. I did not see Tomas in the slender space of the train, though I expected that he saw us. The blue view through the long rectangle of windows revealed that we had nearly reached the end of the line.

"*Ultima fermata, Venezia.*"

Another door opened, shut.

Erik and my sister peeped sleepily up at us as we stood above

them, while the other passengers rose from their seats to draw
down the packs and bags stored overhead.

Erik looked at Marco through heavy-lidded and unsurprised
eyes.

"He's traveling with us."

"Yes," I said.

"I'm glad I'm getting this news when I'm a complete zom-
bie," he observed to Marco. "This numbness is really wonderful;
I hope it lasts."

"Look at you," Marco said. "You have it bad."

"I would have killed you in Florence." Erik turned his face
away. "But I don't feel like doing that anymore."

"No, you're not built for it."

"Where's my father?" Yolanda demanded. "Where's my dad
buried?"

I kept an eye on the door breathing open and shut behind
us while gathering as much luggage as I could. Outside the window, the metal-green lagoon convulsed with speed boats, and
the taffy-colored mansions thrust up from the water like mirages.
The train shivered, halted.

"Let's go, let's go, let's go," I said.

St. Mark's Square was filled with diamond and peach light, opal-
colored birds and variegated people. The Basilica di San Marco
is a pointed, gold-crested citadel crested by four massive gilt-
bronze horses that appear to madly gallop above the basilica's
jeweled doors.

I ran into the pigeon-dusted square, ahead of Erik, Yolanda,
and Marco Moreno. The piazza tossed with thousands of crane-

necked strangers glaring at the Byzantine splendors, so they resembled Michelangelo's damned who stare confusedly up at the
angelic heavens in *The Last Judgement.*

I nearly cried when I saw two smallish, dark-haired Latins in
the midst of this bedlam. They had forced the crowd to relin-
quish a large circle of space to them through the effective and
aggressive thrustings of roller bags.

"Monster!"

"Mom! Dad!"

And then my mother and father were running toward me,
salty hair flying, bald head shining, and it was a catastrophe of
weeping accusations and nearly hysterical declarations of love as
we embraced.

On the east side of the square is Caffè Florian, a eighteenth-
century institution, and once I scoped out the crowd to ensure
any raised-from-the-dead dads weren't lying in wait, I joined my
family around one of its little wicker tables.

"And Marco . . . you are who, again, just so as to confirm?"
my mother interrogated him after ordering pomegranate-red Kir
Royales and zabaglione for the table. Her silver hair was swept
up in a cylonic twist, and her coffee-colored eyes blinked rapidly
in her wrinkled, triangular face. She wore sturdy khakis, a tweed
jacket, and talked with her long-fingered hands. "Manuel was telling me something . . . disturbing . . . about your being some
sort of lunatic with whose family we've had *dealings.* And that you
kidnapped or brainwashed our daughter, then whisked her here
to Italy, now, what—seven days before her wedding? I know that
I should probably find some sledgehammer and bash you, but it

somehow seems less appropriate now that we've met. You look like a pitiful skid row person."

"He's Colonel Moreno's son," Yolanda bassooned.

My father, Manuel, has large, bulging eyes, pewter wisps of hair that float over his shining head, and a grasshopper's thinness. "To get this perfectly straight, by Colonel Moreno, we do mean that ghastly, frothing—"

Yolanda nodded. "Yes."

"Hello," Marco interrupted, holding out his hand. "Señor Manuel Alvarez, the Guatemalan curator. *And* Professor Juana Sanchez, archaeologist and discoverer of the Queen Jade. Good to finally meet you."

My mother, shaking the extended paw: "Um, hello. Dear boy, aren't you awfully unctuous. But Yolanda—isn't he *lethal?*"

"Yes," Yolanda said. "Like I told you."

"He's on . . . sabbatical from that, I think," I said.

"Sabbatical."

"It seems as if I'm having a breakdown," Marco surprisingly explained. "Right now, I'm just tagging along."

My mother took a mug shot of him with her eyes. "Well, you look *terrible*. Not going to kill or maim anyone?"

"No."

"That's good to hear. Because, get this," she began to yell. "I'm one of those murderous mother bear types. Got it? Very, very dangerous. Capable of shooting or viciously stabbing people who threaten my brood."

"Understood."

"All right."

"Calm down, Mom."

"No, stay excited, Juana," Yolanda said.

"I'll be excited when it is appropriate to be excited, Yolanda. I'm old enough to know that one may have a civilized lunch with a person, even if they are a hideous enemy. How else could I have successfully orchestrated all my jungle digs? Become dean? Survived Tomas?" she screeched. "See, that's the wisdom that you get from being a fantastic old bitch like me."

"Good." Marco laughed.

"So! Now that's settled, I can say that you *all* look half-dead. Thank God I'm here."

"Let's just get one thing straight, Lola," my sister said. "You really don't know what this guy is."

"*Who* this guy is," I corrected.

She clucked at my distinction. "The problem is, I can't worry about that right now. Because, Juana, get this: He says he knows where Tomas is buried."

"It's true. I do," Marco said nonchalantly.

Mom knocked over her champagne glass. "Smashing. I see your self-flagellation party is still in high swing. Tomas is *dead*, sweetheart. It's not like any of this will bring him back—"

My father took one of my hands, which I had just plastered anxiously to my eyes during this exchange. "It really is so good to see you again, darling."

"Dad."

He goggled gently at me, then opened up his spidery arms and wrapped me in a hug. "I was worried!" A tighter squeeze. "As soon as I heard your wonderfully bossy voice on the phone, I was all in a tizzy until we could get over here to *help*—"

"Thanks, Pop—"

"And also to drag you home in time for this incredibly expensive wedding, of course. It's in seven days! And you missed your shower! Interesting word, that, *shower*, for what essentially was a *fiesta* for a dozen screaming drunk harpies in various states of undress—though I took a lot of pictures for you to see—"

"I'm sorry, and don't worry. I'm going to get Erik there. We'll make it."

He gave me several dry, sharp little pecks on the cheek. "Good, okay. So! Now that we *are* here—how did that business in Siena work out? When you were researching how Antonio died in the war between the Sienese and the Florentines? When you were going to that valley? That is, right after you apparently made international headlines by vandalizing a priceless mosaic in the Duomo? We read about it on a blog Yolanda showed us—the reports blame either unkempt mestizos or highly disturbed Sicilian separatists. We assumed it was *you*."

"Siena—uh—yes—*ugh*—"

"I'm listening."

"Oh—well—actually! There was something. You know how in *God Loves the Mighty*, Albertini says that Antonio killed his own—"

"Men, yes. With some sort of bomb. A mistake, it was supposed to be? Because of the fog—"

"It couldn't have happened that way—we went up there—to Marciano della Chiana. And it's colder now than it was during the battle—"

"Which took place in early August."

"Yes. But it was *absolutely clear*. No fog, no clouds. I think Antonio might have had a perfect view of what he was doing. That he was killing his own men."

My father's large hot eyes burned up at me. "*Intriguing.*"

"Now I just need you to help me figure out *why*."

"First thing, you're going to show us what you've found." My mother twirled her fingers at me. "You talked enough about it on the phone—let's see. Bring it here."

Marco raised his eyebrows. He still had not heard of the other clues. Regardless of the other gaps in my knowledge about his character, I was certain that if he found the gold before us, he would steal it.

"Well, Lola?" he asked. "We're waiting?"

"I'll handle him," Yolanda said, slitting her eyes at Marco. "You know I can."

"All right."

Along with Sofia's journal, I brought out the two medals from my rucksack. The latter items I placed in my mother's mitts, as Yolanda rapidly described our discovery of the third talisman behind the locked cabinet of the treasury in St. Peter's, though omitting the detail of Erik's and my gassing and near extinction in the underworld of Ostia Antica.

"We think these are letters that are supposed to eventually spell out some sort of code word that we'll need to find Antonio's treasure."

"Incredible," Mom exclaimed. "Look at this metalwork, Manuel. So: *L, P, U.*"

"*L, P, U* ? " Marco repeated. "We're missing one letter. That has to spell *Lupo,* doesn't it? Antonio was 'the Wolf.' "

"That's the most obvious choice," I admitted. "But that makes me worried, somehow."

"Exactly—so hold on, hold on, let's not *jump,*" my father said. "What else could *L, P,* and *U* spell. *Pulce?* No, that's not very good. It means 'flea.' "

"Or *opulenza?*" my mother suggested. "Opulence—this is about treasure, after all. And then there's—what else—"

"*Opusculum,* in Latin," I said. "That's a minor literary work. And we know Antonio's well read. And, *Opulus,* that's a maple tree—um—*opuncuolo*—a kind of bird—but all of these have too many letters—"

"Or maybe it's an acronym," said Marco.

"Some kind of acrostic," my father said.

Yolanda nodded. "An anagram."

"A pun," my mother said.

"An abbreviation," I said.

"A homonym," offered Marco again.

My mother had been muttering over the shining gold disks when she looked up. "What's . . . what's missing here?"

"What do you mean?" Manuel asked.

"There's something missing, right now," she said. "Some particular *noise*—some—constant bothersome rattling on—"

"Rattling on?"

"Yes, usually, in these situations, isn't there some kind of incessant, interrupting, *rambling*—"

"It's Erik," I said miserably.

My mother tucked her chin into her chest and peered at him. "You're right. That's it. Good God in Heaven, Erik's not talking."

The entire time we had been at the table, Erik had sat silently, studying his untouched crimson drink and half-listening to us with the abused air of a prison inmate.

"What's wrong, man?" Manuel asked.

"What's that?" Erik just now tuned in to the conversation.

My mother reached out, grabbed his face, and squeezed his cheeks. "What on earth have you done to him? What happened? He looks horrendous!! Is it a head injury?"

"Oh—" I struggled. *He shot someone yesterday.* "He's tired—"

"He's never tired. Even when he didn't sleep for three weeks after proposing to you, he never stopped talking."

"What happened was—well, have you heard anything about us?" I asked. "On the news?"

"Only about the Duomo—why, what happened?"

"It's just that—"

"There was this—" said Yolanda.

"Terrible—"

"*No,*" Erik said to me in a firm, clipped voice, shaking his head. *I don't want them to know what I did.*

"Agh . . . ay . . ."

"What?" my parents barked.

"There was this thing—"

"Accident—"

"*Accident?*"

"Wrong word—"

Yolanda and I froze; my parents gazed alarmedly at us.

Marco sighed, took a cigarette from his pocket, and lit it with matches from the table.

"Aw, Gomara and I had a fistfight," he rumbled. "He just feels bad because he got a little too rough with me."

"A fight over *what?*"

Marco squinted sideways at Erik, deciding something. The bruise on his cheek was still very bad; the stress lines around his eyes looked as they had been etched there by a knife.

"Lola," he said, grinning nefariously at Erik through the cigarette's haze.

"Lola?"

"Yes, do I have to go into the details? It's embarrassing, after all."

My mother asked, "Erik, you didn't have some sort of romantic prenuptial shoving match with this—*man?*"

"Oh, Jesus." Erik rasped at his eyes with the heels of his hands.

"He did," Marco said.

"Erik beat the hell out of him," Yolanda said.

"He was an animal," Marco said. "I lost."

Manuel frowned. "Is this true?"

"Ask Erik, Dad," I said.

Erik eased his gaze over to me and shrugged. "What can I say? I *was* an animal. But it was for love."

"Lola, what's wrong with your eyes—are you *crying?*" my mother demanded.

"No, no, no."

Erik glared out at the lucent square beneath his black eyebrows for a long Munch-faced moment. He blinked, twisted his mouth, and then downed his drink as if it were made of opium instead of champagne. "Well. Juana, of *course* I'm broody. We're in Venice! Thomas Mann, bad weather, pollution, decay . . . a mass murderer is trying to get my girl, and—I'm just about to step over the precipice and lose my freedom forever."

"Is he talking about the wedding?" my father asked.

"Yes, I can hear the prison doors slamming in on me! Literally! It's a shock that I haven't drunk myself into an absolute cracking coma! Which I just might! In fact, it sounds like an excellent idea! But before that happens, we should get back on topic, don't you think?"

"No, I think this is fascinating—" Mom tried to interrupt.

Erik forced himself to chatter at his customary full speed. "Because instead of wasting our time blathering about how much I am just *wigging out,* we should be trying to find the fourth medal. There are only about six thousand places where Antonio could have hidden the thing. Venice is famous for its secret crannies. Things *disappear* here—Casanova from the dungeons, victims of the Inquisition from their homes, even the streets are supposed to vanish and then remanifest in entirely different locations. It's as easy to get lost in this city at high noon as it is to lose your way in the rain forest when you've lost your flashlight."

"Well, at least he's talking again," said my mother.

"Speak for yourself about the rain forest," cautioned Yolanda.

"Yolanda excepted. Lola, what's the riddle's last stanza?"

I squeezed his hands. *"Erik—"*

He leaned over, kissing me. "Come on, honey." Then he whispered: "Lola, please just give me a nice little problem to solve before I get completely bent."

"Okay."

"What's the fourth stanza?"

And so I recited it:

> "'Four holds a saint from the East,
> A neighing, shape-shifting wretch.
> Once he was called Nero's beast—
> Hear his Word and meet your Fetch'"

"Fine, getting down to business." Manuel clapped his hands together. "We at least know who *the saint from the East* is." He looked up at the Basilica di San Marco.

"San Marco—St. Mark," Erik said.

"Yes. Mark's body was brought here in the Middle Ages—or, rather, stolen, then imported here, to Venice. They brought it from Egypt in a box filled with pickled pork and hams, to disgust the Muslims and prevent them from searching the container. But—what does Antonio mean by *'Nero's Beast'?"*

"That he was martyred?" my mother said. "Like Peter—and most of the saints."

"No. Nero didn't martyr Mark. We don't know even if he was killed. There are all sorts of theories of how he died. And then, *'Hear his Word'*—from the riddle—that's a funny puzzler."

"'Hear my Word and meet your Fetch.' What's a fetch?" Yolanda asked.

"It's a harbinger of death," Marco said, still smoking—and, I noticed, slipping the medals from the table into his pockets while giving me a "just keeping them safe" wink. "A vision of your own ghost or that of a relative. It's the sign of your doom."

I felt another wave of dread as I confirmed his definition. "Yes, that's it. And I know that only because Sofia met *her* fetch here, in Venice." I opened up the journal on my lap, whose last entries I had read on the train.

"Sofia?" Erik asked. "What do you mean?"

"She died here." I showed them the last pages in the journal. "And she says that she saw ghosts before she passed away. She writes about the basilica, too, and other things I can't quite understand. But I know that Antonio *must* have read this journal after she was gone, and used it to help him with these traps. In particular the one waiting for us here. It sounds like he might have been going mad. . . ."

They all leaned in close to hear.

December 13, 1552
Venice

Tonight I indulged in the witch's worst vice, being curiosity, and gave myself a reading. Yet I did not need to draw the Tarot's Death card to know that I will soon be parted from my husband: The Spirit world has already sent my Harbinger, as one week ago I saw my own Death Doom.

Seven days past, I lay here in my sickbed, when there appeared to me a dark, gleaming horse, riderless. By her stood a pale mare, upon which sat my long-dead Mother, transmuted into an angel, with her feet backward in the stirrups. These, her reversed feet, were the surest signs that she was a spirit who would lead me to Tartarus upon my black and long-maned Fetch.

Antonio refused to believe this Omen. He said that I am a silly girl, and that I will not die. Though I knew he lied because of his frantic laborings to concoct his Cure, this evening I had a Terrible hope that it was all a delusion. Thus, before he brought me this evening's vial of Aqua Vita, I teased one card from my pack. I placed it on the counterpane covering my legs.

But no: It was card 13.

Just then Antonio burst into the room. "This will heal you, my darling," he said, holding a philter made of gold & amber. He paled in horror when he saw the card, and threw himself to his knees, kissing my hands. "Ah! Thirteen is a blessed number for witches, sweet."

"There is no more time for lies," I replied. "You know as well as I that is the number of Doom. So embrace me. Whisper love-thoughts to me. While we still can."

He would not, however, but rather fled back to his alchemy lab to recommence his fruitless, waning work.

There is little of our treasure left, after so many experiments, and after paying so much ransom. Years back, after his return from the Americas, Antonio rewarded a tremendous portion to the Doge as payment for the use of his Dungeons; that is where the vampiric Slave was rendered harmless by a Gold masquerade, which some have called a Moon-shield and others a Torture mask.

Today, we still pay for the Doge's protection. This has cost us sixteen additional chests of gold, which is used to restore the Basilica and the Torcello cathedral to their former twelfth-century glories. Even without our lucre, what a marvel is this Venetian church: Not only does it possess the stolen body of St. Mark but also the four bronze Horses, which were once displayed in Nero's Domus Aurea, as a marker of his evil Power; now they represent Christ's Four for the pleasure of the Venetians.

Antonio marvels at these much-translated Horses. He says that these uses of Art & Men are their own, terrible form of Alchemy.

In years past, he never would have compared such robberies to his own Great Art. I think he is losing faith in his craft.

[illegible scrawl]

And it is just as well, I see, suddenly.

Yes, it is time for him to abandon his labors.

Neither he nor his Alchemy can help me any longer. For my Fetch has just appeared to me again, here in this room:

My mother's ghost-face is monstrously livid as she waits upon her mare. Her feet are reversed in her stirrups. My large black horse waits for me; it will ride me to another world.

"Darling, darling, darling," I just cried out, with my last strength.

Antonio emerges from his laboratory. His hands are covered in gold; his face is streaked and shining with gold. To me he is very beautiful. The moonlight eases through the window, turning these marks into platinum stripes upon his cheek, like the stripes of a supernatural beast.

He does not see the ghosts who wait. Nor does he need to. He collapses into a chair when he reads the final truth in my face. The moon & melancholy grip him.

He is beginning to change.

"I have failed," he says, or I think he says, for he cannot speak in human tongues any more. His beautiful face is o'ertaken. He humps and scrapes and he bays to the sky.

I will put down my pen. He will curl onto the bed, here, so that we lay side by side.

One more night is all I ask of the Goddess, so that I might hear his breathing just a little longer. If I could only take some warm atom from him, and hide it in my breast, for comfort in this cold season that awaits me.

Here: I will press my heart to his heart. I will try to take some memory of him. I will try to print his love upon me.

The backward walking spirit watches me.

One more night.

And then I think that will be all.

Manuel sat up straight and pressed his palms together when I had finished the entry.

We were all gaunt at the sadness of the writing. But he smiled like a fox and stood up.

"That explains a great deal," he said.

"What? What does it explain?"

He tossed some coins on the table and picked up the handle of his luggage.

"*Very* informative. Okay, off we go. It's only—what—five o'clock. The basilica should be open for at least another half hour."

"*What is it?*"

"See if you can keep up, my lovelies."

Manuel sprinted off, his roller bag flying behind him. A thick bulb of pigeons burst in the air as if exploding. All of us dabbed our eyes and blinked confusedly before snatching our rucksacks together, and then ran after him as he plunged into the deepening shadows of the square, making straight for the mysteries of the stolen saint's basilica.

❧ 43 ❧

We ran into a cave filled with red-gold light.

That is what I first saw of the Basilica di San Marco, when we at last detached ourselves from the long line creeping to its door, and made our way beneath the four triumphal gilt-bronze horses steeplechasing above the high portal: Inside, it was all red-gold luminescence blazing up to the sky like a biblical fire.

Built in 828, repository of Mark's bones since at least 1094, the high interior of the basilica is covered with vast, nectarine-gold mosaics of Christ and the apostles. Tourists wandered below this miraculous sky, and I saw that some religious women were actually *raising their hands* to the shine of the gold, the way evangelical Christians pray with their eyes closed and their palms upraised. Standing within that sphere of color, I was also staggered nearly beyond my rational wits as I fended off a panoply of images: Of Red Riding Hood in the glittering red belly of the wolf; of the silver and ivory Heaven of John's Revelations; of the Ninth Hell of the Aztecs, where the Mexicans believed they would be able to travel with their worldly treasure strapped to their spirit backs if they survived the journey—that is, until that treasure was used to pave this European church instead, as Sofia herself had noted:

*In exchange for his protection, we have given sixteen additional
chests of gold to the Doge, which is used to restore the Basilica and
the Torcello cathedral to their former twelfth-century glories.*

I was jolted out of this revelation by the sound of my father's
voice, as he rattled his roller bag behind him (again, we were
three months from the day of the Twin Towers and its weapons-
checking terrors). He hurried through the solar-colored nave, toward the transept and its altar room, searching for one particular
item as he speedily talked: "As I already mentioned, St. Mark was
literally *translated* here from Alexandria to this church in the late
eleventh century. The Venetians responded to their possession of
Mark with a euphoria that expressed itself mostly in the form of
interior design, as they began to overdecorate the basilica with
as many apostolic symbols as they could buy—or *steal*, often in
the form of pagan sculpture or painting that had some sort of
quadrumvirate formation, a group of four, you know, which was
the Gnostics' symbol of the sacred elements and the seasons,
though here Christianized. So that—right here—there's Christ
sitting up on a very pretty rainbow being held up by four angels,
which are only reconstituted Sirens, and who represent the four
apostles—and *outside* the church there is a porphyry sculpture
of four Byzantine Moors, which are stand-ins also for Matthew,
Mark, Luke, and John. And *all* of this is designed to communicate
to the old hoi polloi that *yes, dears,* we *really do have him,* one of the
Four, he's right here, sleeping quite soundly until the trumpet
sounds—the very *Saint from the East* whom Antonio claims is capable of showing us the final clue, providing that we aren't somehow mashed to screaming pieces in the process, if I understand
his threat correctly."

Manuel had led us through the iconostasis (a stone screen

made up of saint figures) and up through the densely populated altar room. After Yolanda and my mother had somehow intimidated the surrounding exhausted-faced tourists to give us space, he pointed down to a massive emerald-marble carved box that bore a titanic lock and sat below the solid gold altar.

"There was the original article."

"That's an urn," my mother said excitedly. "A sarcophagus."

"Precisely." Manuel began to gaze around, preoccupied again. "It's Mark's reliquarium. His bone house."

"Is this where the clue is?" Marco rapped out.

"Do we have to break into this grave?" I asked.

"It's completely guarded," said Erik, motioning at the sleepy-eyed sentries sprinkled all around. "The lock's as big as my thigh. We'll have to pick it while there's a distraction."

Yolanda yanked down her Stetson's brim. "I can do it. Somebody get me a screwdriver."

My mother nodded. "And, Lola, pretend to have a fit."

"What kind, psychological or epileptic?"

"Psychological."

"Oh, then I'm the man for the job," Marco said. "I'm so out of my mind right now that I can start foaming without even going into character—"

"No, no, no, no, *no*, people," Manuel said. "The clue isn't in *here*—at least I hope not! Reportedly Mark was whisked back to Egypt in sixty-eight amid pomp and apologies—if Antonio hid anything in the urn, it would have been discovered, and probably removed then."

"So where is it?" we all gasped.

"That's what I'm getting to—I'm still looking for it; it's somewhere around here, just can't quite recall . . . oh! All right, follow me out." Manuel retraced his steps back down the nave. "I had my idea when Lola read to us from that diary, and I connected the entry to the riddle."

He padded up toward the basilica's entrance hall, making his way to a separate miniature access on an upward staircase; this had a separate toll-gate staffed by a Venetian with a thousand-yard stare.

Manuel asked to see Sofia's journal after we had received our change.

"I think that Lola's right, and that Antonio *was* inspired by the writings of his wife. First, see how Sofia describes her fetch to the Underworld, as '*a dark, gleaming horse.*' Then—look here—she mentions '*the four bronze horses*'—and goes on to say that they were '*once displayed in Nero's Domus Aurea . . . now they represent Christ's Four for the pleasure of the Venetians.*' The Domus Aurea, remember, was Nero's private palace."

We had made our way to the top of the stairs, which led to a second story. This level extended to a balcony hosting the four dramatic gilt-bronze horses we had seen from the square, and, on the interior, a small museum displaying various artifacts and sculptures.

"The last thing to consider," Manuel went on, as he entered the museum area and began to pace past a rood screen and show-cased musical manuscripts, "is the riddle itself":

[CITY] FOUR HOLDS A SAINT FROM THE EAST

A NEIGHING, SHAPE-SHIFTING WRETCH.

ONCE HE WAS CALLED NERO'S BEAST—

HEAR HIS WORD AND MEET YOUR FETCH.

He stopped before an exhibit of four colossal, gilt-bronze horses identical to the ones on the exterior balcony. Placed on brick and marble supports against the museum's farthest wall, they stood over seven feet tall, and were caught in rippling mid-stride with snorting nostrils and flaming manes. A nearby placard said they were the original *Horses of San Marco* that were carried off from Byzantium during the Fourth Crusade, whereas the ones gracing the balcony façade are modern copies.

"So, do you see what I mean?" Manuel exulted, raising his arms to the statuary. "It's all perfectly clear."

"No, we don't see at *all*."

"Ha ha ha ha ha ha," my mother cackled, her hair flying like an electrical storm as she suddenly waltzed me back and forth. "The only thing *I* was thinking about these big old stallions is that during the Enlightenment people swore they were *cursed*. But *you* hit it, Manuel. I knew there must be a reason I keep letting you seduce me."

"There are several, darling." He smiled. "Anyway—as Sofia recalls, the horses were once 'Nero's Beasts.' But they were taken to Venice during the Crusades, as Christian symbols, which is why Antonio calls them '*neighing shape-shifters*.' Remember how the churches recycled pagan symbols and emphasized the sacred number four—these are original sculptures, which represented Matthew, Mark, Luke, and John. They were brought in from the balcony only a decade ago, to be replaced with copies. One of *these* horses, then, represented Mark to the Renaissance eye. He *was*, for symbological purposes, *the saint from the East*."

At this point, my father's rapturous face began to take a quiz-zical cast as he stared up at the bronze animals.

"So the clue that you're looking for, I think, will be here. Once you read it in this light, the riddle is astonishingly lucid. The fourth medal will probably be hidden inside one of these horses, though apparently it has been fitted with some sort of booby trap that is designed to stab or shoot or bomb or flay or otherwise unpleasantly dispatch us all to our miserable deaths."

With that, Manuel had given his pronouncement. He let it sink in. His anxiously dancing hands now descended protectively upon his breast, which shuddered as he took a long breath.

44

Standing in a pool of people, we stared up at the tall gilt-bronze horses. They have long broad necks and tiny flat ears, and are rendered in such fine detail that wrinkles pucker softly around their nervous open lips and horse teeth.

Manuel sufficiently collected himself to tap dance past a last layer of tourists barricading us from the horses. He pointed at one of the bronze beasts.

"Lovely work. It's a miracle they weren't melted down for cannons during the Crusades."

"Yes, or the Napoleonic wars." My mother brought out one of her typically obscure guidebooks from her purse. "Except that, actually, Napoleon would never have had them destroyed—he was such a classics nut. You know, molding himself after the great Roman emperors, even Nero."

Yolanda tilted her Stetson back on her head to better examine the horse on the extreme left-hand side. "Where do you think? The clue's got to be in the belly of one of these guys."

Marco knocked on the horse's metal ribs. "So what do you say we cut into it with a buzz saw? After hours? This place is almost closed. I could break in—"

"No—wait—" I began to say.

"You will do *no such thing*—" my mother said.

"An abomination," Manuel said.

"But efficient," Yolanda said.

The crowd attempting to admire the horses steadily fixed its gaze upon us.

"True," said my mother.

"We're talking about finding Montezuma's gold, after all," Marco said.

"Which apparently is spread out all over this basilica anyway," said Yolanda. "Brought here by thieves and hijackers! Look at the reddish color—and you read as much in Sofia's journal."

My mother muttered, "It *would* save us all kinds of trouble . . . what am I saying? You two are terrible!"

"It's just that—here, listen, hold on," I said.

"The *riddle*—" Erik raised his eyebrows at me. "It gives you instructions for how to retrieve the clue."

"*Right*—but also—what was that business about the horses being cursed during the Enlightenment?" I asked.

"Yolanda, cutting relics open with buzz saws? Your father *never talked like that*," my mother said.

My sister touched her blue jade necklace. "I know, thank God he's not around to hear it."

"Let's not talk about him right now," I yapped. "Mom, what did you just say about the horses being *cursed*?"

"Oh, right." My mother held up the book she'd brought out, which was Dorothy W. Sayer's *Intriguing Methods of Murder in Venice*. "The horses developed a bad reputation after they were temporarily stolen again in the nineteenth century. I was talking about Napoleon? In 1797, he invaded Venice, and ordered them to be ripped from the basilica and installed in the Tuilleries. But as the *gendarmes* were carrying the statues across the square, out to their ship, something nasty happened . . . here, I'll read it:

> *"The myth of the Horses' supernatural malignancy was first gener-*
> *ated when Phillipe Boudin, one of Napoleon's more scurrilous lieu-*
> *tenants, heard a rattling around in the belly of the bronze figure*
> *now called 'Horse A.' Boudin ordered the soldiers carrying the horse*
> *across the Piazza to put it down, for further inspection, believing*
> *that the Doge had secreted treasure inside. He peered up inside the*
> *creature's bent head, into the opened jaws. Within the aperture, he*
> *descried a curious contraption that remains a well-guarded secret of*
> *the always taciturn Venetians. What the historian does know from*
> *contemporary records is that, with his diminutive hand, Boudin*
> *reached into the bronze mouth, and was thereby struck in the throat*
> *by a miniature poisoned dart. His death was not instantaneous, it*
> *is said."*

Now all six of us were staring at the mouths of the horses.

" 'Four holds a saint from the East / A neighing, shape-shifting wretch. / Once he was called Nero's Beast— / Hear his Word and meet your Fetch,' " Erik and I said simultaneously.

"The talking animal," Marco said.

" 'Hear his Word.' The medal's inside the mouth, inside the jaws," said my mother.

"Dad, you are amazing."

Manuel gently pinched me. "We have to keep in mind that these horses must have been restored, X-rayed, taken apart, and put back together—"

"Dozens of times, at least," Erik elaborated.

"But any *responsible* restorer would have kept the thing exactly as it was originally—"

"All right, but stop screaming," my mother said. "People are already staring at us like we've just escaped from Bellevue."

"Which one is horse A?" Yolanda asked.

I shook my head. "No idea."

My sister said, "It *could* be gone by now. The clue."

"There could be a second dart in there," said Erik.

"Or remnants of poison, or even simply something sharp, that would be bad—" offered Manuel.

While we were talking, Marco detached himself from our pack and hopped over a little glass barrier surrounding the horses. Lightly stepping up on the marble and brick bases the sculptures stood on, he simply shoved his hand up inside the third horse's open mouth as the rest of us let out a collective and panicked *"Agh!"*

"Nothing," Marco said, keeping his eyes on me while his fingers searched inside the dark hole. Even as we continued squirming and shouting out cautions, he moved to the last horse, rummaged in its tighter jaws, but shook his head. "Nothing."

Behind us, the crowd had thickened even more and rigidified into a buzzing half-circle.

"What the hell is going on? . . . Why are they messing around with those? . . . I thought you weren't allowed to touch anything here—"

"Nothing," said Marco once more, before sidling over to the first beast in the row, a beautiful, oxidized, mournful-looking animal that had a feisty open mouth. He gingerly inserted his fingers into its bronze jaw. "Something. *Something, yes!* But I can't get my hand in deep enough. There's a chain. It seems to be attached to some sort of *spring*—but it feels empty. I'm pulling on it." He laughed. "And, as you can see, I'm not dead."

"Here, here, here." Yolanda jumped the glass barrier and stood on a marble base.

Yolanda fit her slender fingers past the animal's massive teeth. She thrust them down deeper into the throat, wincing.

"I'm touching something," she said. "Lola, it's a chain. Going down the throat, past some kind of lever."

"Careful!"

"Got it!"

As what I imagined to be a miniature crossbow twanged hollowly inside the long bronze throat, she tugged out a length of chain made of heavy red-gold links. From deep within the creature we heard a metallic clanking, a rattling.

She pulled and pulled. The crowd behind us grew as loud as the pigeons shrilling in St. Mark's Square.

I saw a glitter in the black hollow. There came a sound like a coin in a well.

My sister slowly teased out a red-gold medal from the horse's mouth.

"Look— look—"

Even as the noises from the crowd before us raised to a Greek-chorus keening, we all smashed around her to greedily read the beautiful, complex old sign on its long leash:

"Lola—the other letters, they were *U, P,* and *L,*" Yolanda roared. "And this is *O.*"

"Yes."

"It is *lupo,*" everyone but me breathed.

As if by instinct, Marco said, "Turn it around."

Yolanda flipped the medal, and etched on the other side we saw (translated):

To find my yellow mettle put pressure on the unlucky man
in Santa Maria Assunta

"That's a church," my mother called out. "Santa Maria Assunta—another basilica."

"On an island around here," both Marco and my father said in short high bursts. "Torcello."

"That's what it's called."

"We'll need a boat," said Erik.

In that instant, Yolanda flinched like a sprayed cat. Her head suddenly snapped up; her face changed beneath the black brim of her hat. She paled. It appeared as if she had just been struck in the throat or the face, and I was sure from her livid cheek that she had contracted some death agent from the chain or the coin.

But then I turned around and followed her eyes over to the crowd.

A presence like a shadow among the humid horde. An identical black hat.

There stood Tomas.

45

Tomas de la Rosa stood six deep back in the crowd. He was dressed in his black coat, his Stetson. I saw the dark eyes beneath the hat, and the look of deeply exhausted melancholy that he fixed on his eldest daughter. Tomas had manifested from the ether looking like one of Wim Wender's angels in *Wings of Desire*.

I felt something terrible here, something I did not understand. Perhaps I should have checked to see if his feet were backward.

He swerved his gaze over to Marco, who stared at the gold medal with a frightening severity. Tomas looked back to Yolanda, and then me. With a gesture of his left hand he gave us a grim warning.

"Yolanda, dearest, what's wrong?" Manuel asked.

"What's happening? Are you sick?" Erik hissed. "Jesus, *is* there poison?"

"Sit down," my mother ordered. "Let's get her some water."

"Nah, I'm peachy," she grunted when she could. "It's just—the excitement."

When I looked back, de la Rosa was gone. In a snap. Marco stood awkwardly to the side, still clinging tightly to the medal on its chain. He had not seen the black-coated specter.

"But I think it's time—to—*go*," Yolanda said, pointing her chin back up.

Where Tomas had briefly shimmered in the crowd, a bulbous-faced security officer materialized. He was attempting to press his way through the tourists in order to have a probably unpleasant conversation with us about our methods of appreciating art.

"Yes, very, very, *very* good idea," Erik said.

"Had enough sightseeing," Marco acquiesced.

"Haul your cans," said my mother. "Split up. This is no time to get deported."

"Meet outside," my father ordered.

Marco released his grasp of the chained clue, and we all began to thread speedily through the throng in separate directions

That is, they did. I followed my sister.

"Yolanda, Yolanda."

"Hurry up, or else the Italians will mess with us and we'll never get out of here."

"What did you see?"

"No one." Her face was red and tight and she looked like she was about to burst.

"Listen, he's been following us since Rome, and he wants to get to Marco because he thinks that he'll hurt us."

She shook her head but didn't slow down. "That's just precious—he says *Marco's* gonna hurt us—"

"Yo, we have to talk about this—"

"About *what*?!"

"Tomas!"

She gave a bitter, angry smile as she pushed aside pilgrims. "It's bad luck to speak ill of the dead, L, don't you know that? Yeah. It is some *bad* ju-ju to call a ghost a punk-ass 'cause he up and left you in the rotting jungle with nothing but psychos bred out from the war."

"What are you going to do?"

Tears began flying down her face. "Well, you know how I said I was done with those scavenger monkey stunt hunts? I guess it turns out I'm not! So, hell! Sign me back up for the wedding games, Lola! 'Cause I am a gooooood monkey, even when I don't know it. But even though I am *so* dumb I should have a tail twitching on me, I know I've got to play out this little comedy before I can start *kicking his ass.* And *he* can tell your parents the truth to their faces, because I'm not being the messenger on this one. Neither should you—you say anything to Juana right now, what with Marco here, this powder keg will just go boom. So, what am I going to do? What I'm supposed to. And that's to take you to see *the unlucky man* in Torcello." She caught hold of me, and began barreling forward. "Pick up the pace."

The unreal firmament glowed and flamed above me like another hallucination as I was roughly dragged past the jewels, gems, tourists like the living dead, converted pagans, and the alchemical gods and monsters of the basilica.

No further possibly ectoplasmic fathers appeared in the piazza, where my agitated parents, a solemn Erik, and a suddenly broodful Marco had assembled beneath the gathering dusk. I worried that Marco, in particular, would take a turn for the horrifyingly worse if the spectral Tomas appeared to him as he had us. With the waning aid of my common sense, I attempted to devise tactics for a peace treaty, a psychiatric intervention session with my rigid mouthed sister, backup plans in the events of attempted grand thefts or reciprocal assassinations or arrests, and another backup plan in the expectation that gruesome torture-traps awaited us in the island church where the last treasure of the mighty Aztecs could be found.

And all the time, the red-gold question was murmuring in my head: *L—P—U—O?*

What did these ciphers spell: *Lupo?* Or some other shibboleth?

Curiosity is terrible. The promise of *pressuring the unlucky man in Santa Maria Assunta* seemed to drive us all bodily forward toward the edge of Venice and a gondola-rustling lagoon that had absorbed the blood color of the sky.

Toward nine o'clock, we were on our way to the haunted isle of Torcello.

46

The boat motored softly through the black and pewter water. This craft that would sail us to the Dark Age island of Torcello was not one of the fine old turquoise gondolas clacking by the quays: we were on a sleek white job nimbly negotiated from a rich sailor through the freebooter's arts possessed by both Marco and my sister.

Yolanda steered its nose through the farther reaches of the lagoon, her stiff cowboy silhouette fading as the darkness spilled down into the air. I did not know what horrors or rationalizations darted through her mind; she had not yet spoken six words during the entire journey.

The rest of us stood on the deck. I hovered in the far back of the boat. The others arrowed toward the prow, their shadowed figures illuminated by a cloud-shrouded moon.

I approached Marco and Erik, who stood a few feet from each other and could not see me in the penumbra.

"I know what you're thinking," I heard Erik say softly.

"About the money?" Marco asked.

"About Lola."

"Yes, that too."

"You'd better give it up. You're no different than in Florence."

"*You'd* better hope that's not true."

Erik did not answer.

"The truth is I don't know what I'm going to do anymore. Gold—well, that's always useful, isn't it?" Marco went on. "But, maybe I can just wish the colonel a cheery R.I.P. and be done with it—hell, I have no idea. You see, I might even *like* you, Gomara. You nervous wreck. I do have to tell you, friend, you're not looking very well ever since . . . *you know*."

"What I did was a mistake," Erik said in a barely audible voice. "I wish I had—I could have—I don't know if he would have—"

"Nonsense. Domenico *would* have whacked you. And her. I didn't like it much, but certainly you did the right thing. And besides, you'll find, with time, that you can always come up with a *thousand* good reasons for your crimes, and make yourself feel much better. You see in me the most marvelous proof of that theory! What are you doing, anyway, nursing a little depression, bipolar disorder, alcoholism, agoraphobia? You're losing ground, boy! Are you thinking about doing something incredibly stupid?"

"Crazy's *your* racket."

"I'll just tell you, it wouldn't be worth it." Marco sighed. "Listen to me: Forget about all that. Domenico. Right *now's* the shocker. It's wonderful. Anything could happen."

"Marco," I said, so they looked quickly down.

"Give me a stroke—didn't even hear you creep up—"

"I want to ask you something."

"Listening—"

"What would you do if Tomas were alive?"

"Lola," said Erik. "Come on, *no*. No, no, no. Enough with that."

"Alive?" I could hear Marco's distaste at the idea. "Well, he's *not*."

"I want to know."

As Marco considered my question, I felt Erik's warm body right by my shoulder, my chest. Marco was wrong about Erik losing ground; he was solid as the earth. I swore to myself that first thing tomorrow morning, I'd hire him a battalion of lawyers, get the hell out of here, get married, and do whatever it took to get him safe and feeling fine.

"What would I do if de la Rosa were alive?" Marco finally responded. "Something disgusting, probably. The good thing is, we never have to find out. That rose got pruned, and isn't going to grow back, if you know what I mean. And I am *considering* taking a breather from the gardening business to dabble in . . . what you were chattering about . . . my flair for scholarship or somesuch! Because everyone involved in the old war's dead and gone. Aren't they? Even *him*? You must know this by now, don't you? That Tomas died *here*, Lola. Somewhere in the lagoon."

"I read the papers in your rucksack."

"Yes—I figured you would. Well, you had to find out. Tomas filled his pockets with stones and sank under. The loser. I found out when I was in Siena. And I was sent—you've seen it—the proof. They couldn't dredge up the body and that's why there's no marked grave. But he's not missing. There's no mystery. He"— Marco gestured at the lagoon, with a grim face—"drowned, here. So, I'm sorry for you. Not sorry for me. That's how it is."

"Who did you get that death certificate from?"

"The fence—Soto-Relada—the one who got me Antonio's letter in the first place."

"Creature, darling, what did he say?" My mother's disembodied voice thrust at us in the blackness.

"Mom—"

"We're there," Yolanda suddenly said in a high, strained tone.

"We're what?"

"We're there. At the island. Look."

My sister pointed to the sky. Barely visible through sea-haze like pounded chalk, we saw salt flats and low hills. No houses were visible beyond the dock, only the pitch and lonely slope of the deserted-looking isle that shrugged itself from the stillness of the lagoon. Deeper within its pale would be the old church.

Marco sank back into himself as he regarded the de la Rosa—drowning waters with satisfaction. But though the dismal sight deterred further conversation, my mind was ticking double-time.

Query: Two men want to kill each other—How to prevent them?

Answer: Give them a third enemy.

And who was that? Antonio Beatro Cagliostro Medici. More specifically: his *puzzle.*

I had to figure its answer out before Tomas and Marco did. I knew Manuel had been right when he warned against making too hasty a judgment about the cipher Antonio had left us. I was sure there was *something* we had all been missing, beyond even the yet obscure question of the identity of the *unlucky man in Santa Maria Assunta.* Somehow, we were supposed to use the word spelled out by the four medals to discover the gold on Torcello. We thought that this word was now obvious. But would Antonio have gone through so much trouble to hand over such a ham-fisted code as *lupo,* his famous name? It's like the dolts who use *password* for their password. And Antonio was no dolt. I'd have to tease out the last and probably disastrous trick that I *was sure* remained for us. And then I would use my detective arts against Tomas and Marco to somehow double-cross them into peaceable submission.

The ultimate clue was locked in the four letters we had re-trieved:

"U—O—L—P," I whispered to myself. "L—U—P—O. O—P—U—L. U—L—P—O. L—O—P—U. *'Nomen atque Omen.'* "

Yolanda tied the boat to the quay and rifled through Manuel's supplies-packed roller bag for a Maglite. We disembarked in the webbed darkness, up the shore that had been climbed by Roman legionnaires and monks of the Middle Ages. Marco stumbled be-hind, my parents ahead. I could not see my path for the black magic mist and the ferocity of my intrigues.

"Hang on, sweetie," Erik murmured to me.

We moved up a lengthy path bordered by flowers that scented the air with rose or bergamot. A charcoal-rubbing of fog drifted ahead. At length, a holy dome appeared from the tangles and ivied fingers of briar bush: the church of Santa Maria Assunta.

Antonio's treasure chest of a cathedral loomed before us, its bricked arches filled with midnight vapors so that they were white, like blind eyes staring out at us in the dark.

47

We walked toward the cathedral on a path of sand, where pale shoots of grass curled around our feet with such tugging insistence I thought of the long white fingers of the dead. The domed building before us was all hulk and shadow but for those pallid-eyed windows. The moon just now clearing above the crucifix shuddered its blue light down upon us; Renaissance astrologers knew this as the dangerous midsummer moon, what the pagans called the Mead Moon, or the goddess Ishtar's moon, which should be honored with offerings of skullcap blooms to ward off the monsters that it calls.

I looked madly at my feet, but the sandy earth stretched below me blameless of any witch herbs that might keep away the dark man who surely followed close by.

My family was silent and silver-colored. They moved forward as if tractor-beamed toward the church by Yolanda's swirling flashlight, which did not reveal any guards prowling about this nearly vacant island village. This omission made much more sense to us when she illuminated Santa Maria Assunta's formidably barricaded entrance.

"Let me look," Marco said.

He crouched in front of the church's massive and shadowed

front double doors, running his fingers down their carvings. A coat of arms, and little else, graced this entrance.

Yolanda hunched down next to him.

"There's no lock to be picked," he said to her.

"This isn't the way in," she murmured back. "Damn. I don't want to just be lingering out here, where any idiot can come along and give us trouble."

"Maybe we're not even supposed to be on the inside," I said.

Yolanda agreed. "Maybe Antonio's *unlucky man* was a person who was alive in the sixteenth century. What did the clue say? *'To find my yellow mettle put pressure on the unlucky man in Santa Maria Assunta.'* Maybe he's someone that Cosimo had to interrogate—to put pressure on him—and they were supposed to meet outside, on the salt flats, and duke it out—"

"No, there's something waiting for us in there," Erik said.

My mother peered up at him. "How do you know?"

"I just know how *he* thinks, now. How he thought. He wanted the killing to be intimate—an assassination of this kind has to be. Antonio wouldn't have hired a mercenary to do his own work. He *was* crazy. But the kind of crazy that people become when they—they—begin to see the world in a different light."

"What do you mean?" I asked.

Marco said with some relish: "He means that Antonio went *cracked* after he buried Sofia. You know, when he figured out the truth? That there's no hope! That human beings are nothing but animals in high heels, *and* we're all one day going to die, *and* events spin out of one's control and nothing ever stays put, except for one's own miserable self."

"Not even that," said Erik.

"Yes, right, that is bad," my father answered. "But that's why the universe invented daughters and impossible women like Juana, to console one against the inevitable despair of living—"

"Metaphysics later," my mother said abruptly. "I think you're right, Erik. I'll bet there's something in the church. We just have to get inside. Manuel! Remember Beijing?"

"Beijing . . ."

"When we smuggled the Olmec totems?"

"Oh, right—yes—out of the Forbidden City. Oh, kids, Juana here had the most *outlandish* theory about Pangea, and the genetic relations between the Chinese and the pre-Columbians—and there was that *palace*—"

"Forbidden City?" Yolanda grunted.

"He decoded seventy-two locks, all with passwords from the Qing dynasty—I learned that day that Manuel is a *terrific* fortress breaker," my mother was saying, over the others' insistent voices, though not my own, as I was focusing again with a nearly catatonic sharpness on the last and crucial piece of the puzzle I believed Antonio had hidden from view. "No, come on—enough talk, let's go. No, not *you* two. Monster, you and Erik stand guard."

Their torch's light evaporated into the indigo air as they all slipped behind the church. Erik and I were left to stand sentry against whatever fiends might come hurtling at us from the shores of the black lagoon. After a few moments, he and I silently reached out to hold hands. We did not think to extract our own flashlight from our rucksack, and together we watched the dank, star-struck air swirl into uncanny shapes amid the surrounding brush.

A good patch of time passed here. My mind continued to perform an obsessive quilt work with Antonio's various writings, despite the occasional and alarming bursts of sound that I could hear my parents making at the back of the cathedral:

In Marco's letter, Antonio had written, "*Cosimo, I do own a vast, bloodstained, and secret treasure, which I bartered for my soul in Tenochtitlán, and have kept hidden from the world all these years. I leave it to you. I bequeath my Yellow Mettle with a condition, however. . . .*

"*. . . . I am made of the strongest mettle when I am in your company,*" Sofia had promised her husband on the eve of their escape from Rome. And I recalled a mishmash of text fragments:

"*. . . . Yellow is the color of my courage. . . . You idiotically mispronounced my Secret Name. . . . Some call you il Lupo, but I see you for what you really are. Darken not my door again,* Versipellis."

"*What is your name?*" Antonio had asked the slave, after killing his father in Timbuktu.

Another ripple of sound from within the cathedral interrupted my thoughts. There came a blunt crashing noise, a violent suppression of voices.

"They're in," Erik said.

I closed my eyes, opened them again. I was sorting Antonio's secret out. An idea began to grow out of my memory of Antonio's epistles and Sofia's journals.

But then I perceived something else. In the air coursing with increasing force above the onyx bristles of the lagoon pines, I detected a thickness in the oxygen, an astral coldness. I observed also some sort of movement, of an arm, or a strangely shaped head, as if one of the silvered trees had come alive through a sudden enchantment.

"Do you think shadows are like a Rorschach test?" Erik asked in a woeful voice.

My hair had begun to swirl around my ears because of the wind. "Rorschach test?"

"The things that you can see in the dark—tricks of the imagination, making you see monsters or ghosts. In the Middle Ages,

you know, the night and the full moon were considered the devil's playground. It was said that if a guilty soul saw a dark man
approaching him through the shadows, it was the spirit of the
murdered or maybe even Beelzebub himself come to snatch you
down to Hell. And tonight—"

"Listen to me! You didn't murder Domencio. You had to do
it—he had a gun—he was insane—"

"All I can say is, tonight, that doesn't seem so much like a
fairy tale—"

"Erik, do you see something out there?"

"*Yes.* Because I'm going crazy!"

I pounded on the door. "Let us in, let us in."

"Hold on!" came Yolanda's muffled bark.

She swung the door open just as the fledgling storm gathered
power. A white dazzle of light made both Erik and me cringe as
the wind battered our bodies.

"Erik thinks he sees someone outside," I hissed to my sister,
who was grasping hold of her Stetson to keep it from flying off.

"Get in," she barked. "God, the *weather.*"

She did not otherwise respond to me except by slamming
the door back against a strengthening push of cold wind, which
convulsed the moon-stained trees. The door had a huge polished
metal bolt. This she hurled shut so that a metal *clang* ricocheted
through the strange, glowing room.

I pulled my Maglite from my rucksack. Its beam flashed
through the cathedral like a sword, and beneath it I could discern
the figures of my parents and Marco, who were illuminated not
only by the opal electricity but also a gold incandescence.

An intricate twelfth-century marvel shone above us: This was
another artist's vision of *The Last Judgement,* composed of thousands
of squares of blushing gold. The mosaic damned suffering above

us looked so nakedly pale and lonely in their cocoon of flames, and angels brandished the scales of justice before the melancholy gazes of blue-skinned demons.

So intentional, so *wicked*—I knew then with certainty that this was the place Antonio wanted to lead his nephew.

Antonio wanted Cosimo to know that *this is where you are going if you fail my final test.*

We stood before the gates of a red-gold Hell.

48

Yolanda's flashlight burned onto the faces of the hellbound who writhed within their brimstone bed. Such mosaics cover the interior of Santa Maria Assunta, and they depict with horrifying clarity the specific tortures that Satan has devised for the adulterers, the murderers, the non-Catholic. On the far wall of the cathedral sparkles this version of the judgement. Its bottom rung, that closest to our gaze, boils with sinners as naked as fetuses and who bounce along the edges of flames, while above them floats Christ and his halo-clad army.

"Are one of these the *unlucky man?*" my mother asked over the sound of the wind outside. She pointed to a series of skulls, whose eye holes housed green serpents.

"How did you get in here?" Erik asked my father.

"Oh, it was easy. Relatively open window. Some storage rooms in the back. Minimum of breakage."

"Relatively open window?"

"The old man picked a combination padlock by putting his ear to it and listening to the clicks it made when he spun the numbers around," Marco said. "It was impressive."

"I have very good hearing," Manuel said. "And then of course we had to cut a quantity of very sophisticated alarm-wiring."

Yolanda still had her flashlight trained on the mosaic, but the light began to scatter around the face of Christ.

"Are you shaking?" Marco asked.

"No," she said. "Just a little cold."

I unwrapped myself from my cardigan and threw it over Yolanda's shoulders. Manuel meanwhile began to unzip that roller bag he'd been pulling around from Venice to here. "I have other supplies. Other flashlights."

Yolanda's illumination touched down on a collection of alpinist's ropes, bottles of iodine, a compass, a snake-bite kit, assorted extra-strength Maglites.

"He wanted to come prepared," my mother explained. "There are enough flashlights for everyone."

Marco flicked on one of the Maglites so that its white triangle shone eerily below his face. "Let's go find some gold," he said, in a hoarse voice I didn't like.

No one answered him. My imagination had taken a phantasmal turn, as news-pictures of the blinding skeletal Guatemalan dead seemed to flit in the air alongside the medieval doomed. The civil war had taken many lives. And I think we all remembered the vengeance Marco had promised to visit upon our family as we moved forward slowly, fearfully, accompanied only by the shrieks of the wind.

I knew there was not much time. Antonio's words collected in my inner ear as my fear-charged memory recalled his writings about Mexico and Timbuktu: *"In Tenochtitlán, I saw my Slave man bathed by a solitary ray of the blood-Moon, which transformed his mettle from that of a yellow-bellied Moor to a dragon-Vampyr's. . . .*

"You are the opposite of me, my Lord. I am a poor alchemist but you— you are my reverse. You are an animal. You are what the Italians call il Lupo, the Wolf. . . .

"What is your name?"

Six fingers of light stretched out into the black hollow of the church, glistening on an angel's wing, a particle of text in Latin. My mother's light scribbled brightness upon a scene at the end of the nave, which I couldn't yet make out. Erik's light followed after her beam. Yolanda's torch next lined up with theirs, then did my father's, Marco's, mine.

All we could make out were partial pictures of men—saints, from the names written in Latin next to them—and some sort of altar, with a chair, below this parade.

White lightning suddenly flashed thick throughout the church, revealing the entire scene: We faced the cathedral's central apse. A miniature crescent-shaped amphitheater composed of curving stone benches occupied this space, and at its center presided a bishop's chair. At the feet of the bishop's seat was a semi-circle of stone floor, and above this arrangement, the church ended in a mosaic-covered wall. This, the apse, was filled with images of a blue-dressed Mary, holding the Infant, and below her stood the twelve apostles. Six apostles stood on one side of the wall, and six progressed across the other. Directly below the apostles, and above the bishop's seat, there was a square mosaic of a bearded male wearing a pointed hat and holding a Bible. His name had been written in black letters: *Eliodorus.*

Later, I would discover that this was a mosaic of the minor St. Eliodorus, close friend of St. Jerome, one-time bishop of Altino, and the patron saint of Torcello.

That particular identity did not concern me now: six apostles on the right, six apostles on the left. This made him number thirteen.

In the thought-world of Christianity (it is said that Judas was the thirteenth guest at the Last Supper), as well as Sofia's tarot-cosmos (that card had foretold of her death) the thirteenth man has one key feature: he is cursed.

"The unlucky man," I said.

The lightning from the windows flashed again like white horses across the wall. As my family shouted out a volley of exclamations, I gave my flashlight to Erik before slowly approaching the apse and the bishop's seat. I climbed the bleacher steps to stand upon this brick chair. I stood nearly face-to-face with the spangled visage of St. Eliodorus.

Put pressure on the unlucky man in Santa Maria Assunta.

I put my hands, gently, on the mosaic. The puzzle work looked perfect, exquisite, and relatively new. I did not let this deter me. I pushed, nervous of breaking off the gold squares. Then I pushed harder still.

The square retreated under my hands. From behind the stone wall, I heard a great, iron grinding, a clicking, a metallic thumping.

While my family and Marco began leaping around the cathedral, I looked down, below my feet.

"Down here, down here, down here," I howled.

Five strands of light flew down and converged on the one bright spot.

In the half-circle of stone floor beneath the bishop's seat had opened a dead-black trap door.

∽ 49 ∾

The storm scraped like dragon claws over the cathedral. The wind moaned and roared as the windows flared now white, now raven dark. These pulses of thunder-light splintered the gold apostles on the wall, giving the illusion that they were voodoo poppets hexed into a mad ballet. The strobe also concussed over my father, who moved in a silent film's jerks and starts as he tied the alpinist's rope to the altar, lowering it into the blackness of Antonio's trap door.

We six stood around the square opening in the floor, threading our flashlights into its maw. The flashlights sparkled in the blackness. I saw a glimmer of gold. A sparkle of silver. A scurrying, a rustling.

As if cued by a psychic Morse code, we all looked at one another over the web of light. I saw that the updraft of brightness had shaped my family's and Marco's faces into those of heavenly monsters, streaked with gold and jet, and with unnaturally beautiful eyes. But no one spoke until I tucked my flashlight into my belt and grabbed hold of the end of the rope that disappeared into the dead-fall.

"No, hold on."

"I'm going to be the one going first."

"Jesus, Lola, don't be an ass."

"We have to see *what's down there before anyone*—"

I plunged in.

The drop was long, much, much, deeper than I had supposed. I felt the darkness close around my body as I grasped my
way down the rope. I kept my eye not on the invisible ground
but on the sightless air above me, which was crisscrossed with
silver Maglite filaments and trembled with lightning. I heard, too,
a squall of voices, the persistent shrieks of advice coming from
my family.

I touched down. In soft, silty ground.

I clicked on the light.

A room had been carved out from the church's foundation,
and furnished from the last scraps of Antonio Medici's collection. The airlessness of the space had allowed just the faintest
remnants of his famous trove to survive.

A nibbled lace of Arabian carpets woven of indigo and gold
spread out across the floor, their vivid dyes obscured by dust.
To my right stood a shattered chair, once covered in velvet, and
bearing the shreds of a still-rich emerald-green fabric stitched
with gold snowflakes or flowers, perhaps even a remnant from
the coat Antonio once wore—"*the embroidered jacket that his doppelgänger wears, in Gozzoli's* Procession of the Three Magi," Sofia had
written in her Siena entry. I turned, to see at my left a fainting
couch bustling with rats. In the scurrying, whisker-busy corners
of the room crumbled wooden statues with distended, fierce
faces, pendulous breasts. These were fertility idols of the kind I
have seen from Mali and Botswana. The walls were paved with
buckling mahogany, and hung with a chewed Raphael cartoon of
the Madonna, and also what appeared to be a Botticelli of a dark-
legged woman throwing back her head while being pleasured

by her lover. Large sections of these canvases had deliquesced back into a webby sponge of *prima materia*, as had the bodies of the books. *The books.* The best-prized books Antonio had managed to take with him in his flights from Florence and Siena and Rome. These were oxblood-bound, destroyed folios that might once have been the apocryphal *Prophecy of Sappho* or *Scripture of Bathsheba*, but were now mushroom-bloomed, curled, and soft as the unborn.

No treasure in this magical parlor had lasted the annihilations of time but one.

As my family and Marco one by one slipped down the rope into the abyss, I steered my flashlight onto a strange contraption that shone in the center of the room: a massive box of iron. It stood half my height and extended three feet in width. The craftsman had etched every spare inch with Islamic calligraphy, turning the ordinary metal into an object of fantastical beauty. The center face of the chest, however, contained a strange panel, composed of seven rows of buttons or dials, forged out of copper, and each inscribed with a Gothic letter.

"A combination-lock safe." Erik approached me, shining his light up and down the designs.

"Yes," said Marco. "One of the exploding safes. Dr. Riccardi told Lola and me about these. They were one of the signatures of the Medici, how they used to safeguard their money. Benvenuto Cellini made several of them for the family—"

"I've heard of those," my mother burst out. "They were brutally dangerous. People who tried to safecrack them would be burned alive, or shot with arrows, or—"

"I recall a story about a Florentine thief being decapitated by a cunning hydraulic press when trying to break into the Medici bank," my father said.

Marco went on: "Riccardi told me that Antonio had at least two of these commissioned when he lived in Tuscany. She had made a study of them, wrote some book. She was often nattering about them. I barely even paid attention—but there's a code. You have to plug it in—"

"This is the alphabet here," I said. "The Latin alphabet."

"It's twenty-six buttons," my mother agreed. "Though the letters are difficult to read."

"It's the Gothic script," said Yolanda.

"Just like the medals," muttered Marco, removing the two amulets from his pants' back pocket. "I brought them with me."

But no one looked at the disks shining in his hand. Both my mother and Yolanda instantly pitched their faces to the ceiling's aperture, which blazed black and white from the lightning. Above us echoed a stamping of footsteps. Next we all heard an unseen man utter a low, explosive, and hilarious profanity as he admired the detection of the trap door.

My mother's face looked like a hawk's in a half-patch of light. "Who's that?"

"He's here," I said mournfully.

Marco looked up, swore. "A security guard?"

Erik and my father raised their eyes, as if in slow motion.

Down he came.

At first he was like a large dark bird against the brightness of the stormed sky, but when we lifted our flashlights to catch him in that klieg, I saw that the wings on his shoulders were made by the ballooning of the plastic tent he'd strapped to his rucksack.

Tomas de la Rosa descended the rope, those ebony-colored wings flaring behind his shoulders and his black Stetson like a diabolical halo around his head. Tomas flew swinging down on that rope just like Apollo, god of light, the deus ex machina who

once flew onto the stage in the tragic *Orestes* to miraculously re-
solve all pains and all sufferings. But de la Rosa was not any angel
of order.

"I've had it with watching you people prank around with
Marco, here," Tomas growled beneath the brim of his Stetson
as he managed his big body down. The brim lifted to reveal that
brick-colored, bullet-nosed, unredeemable, and black-eyed face.
"How am I supposed to keep hid with you cozying up to a *Moreno*—what are you all, suicides? And *you*, Y, what the hell did I
teach you? This boy's a torturer and a killer. Got a *talent* for it.
Gutted twenty tied-up farmers with a bowie knife when he was
only a nineteen-year-old army private."

A paralytic silence filled the room. Yolanda maintained the
dead heart she had developed since seeing him in the basilica.
My mother's head wavered backward from the shock. My father's chest caved in as if it had instantly been burgled of its
contents.

Marco sat down hard, before the safe, his face turned up in
disbelief. The medals rolled onto the dusty ground.

"You recognize me, Marco?" Tomas asked, in a voice that was
not his own, but spoken in the birdy tones of Señor Sam Soto-
Relada.

Marco did not answer.

Now the voice was Tomas's. "I see you do. Ah, boy, you're an
obedient cuss, aren't you? All I've got to do is dress up like a used-
car salesman and hand you a puzzle, and the next thing I know
both your bodyguards are dead, and you are wide open."

"Yes, you're very clever," Marco breathed.

"So. What do you think I'm going to do with you?"

"I think that we're both about to fulfill our obligations, Tomas," Marco replied dangerously, after a long, long pause.

I looked wildly at the ground, at the medals there. They had landed in this order:

I almost saw it then. The answer I had been looking for. The ghost-word trembled in the spaces between the two letters, nearly complete. It was a word I'd read only once, a name I had nearly forgotten.

I turned from the name half-written in the dust, to the velvet shattered chair, upon which was folded that green, inimitably gold-embroidered scrap of fabric. I had seen that embroidery before. I saw *him* wearing that jacket. This had once been a precious textile worn by a noble Medici. I saw the sixteenth-century face with a shock of remembrance.

This image tapped more whisper-fragments from the texts I
had been reading, and I heard Cosimo's voice, the Slave's, Sofia's.

The Fool is the sign either of Dead Ends or Fresh Starts.

*The swarty Magicians burned like straw men . . . save for the ash-pale
son of the Wizard. . .*

*You are the opposite of me, my Lord. You are my reverse. You are a wolf.
. . . I was impressed by the trickery of his language. . .*

. . . the jacket his doppelganger wears.

What is your name?

Opul of Timbuktu.

The answer came to me.

"I know what the code is," I said in a clear high voice.

No one looked at me but Tomas.

"It's not *lupo*," I said. "*Lupo*'s a trick. I've figured it out. It's the
only way to get inside that safe, the word *I* know. But I won't tell
you unless you promise—no violence! You two swear it!"

Tomas shook his head and spit. "If that isn't the *damnable* de la
Rosa bull-headedness already rearing up in you, L, and I haven't
been in your company more than a few minutes."

I felt my arms maniacally flap at my sides in fear and triumph.
I had performed my detection. Detection is a form of reading and
we all know that reading is a brand of art, and art is the force that
can save the world.

Except, in the next minutes, I found out the hideous lesson
that art is not as powerful as I had supposed.

Marco gave me one look, and I could not tell if it was full of
love or hate.

"Marco."

He turned around and punched a code into the alphabet
panel on the safe.

It exploded.

rik grabbed hold of me and threw me to the ground. My parents fell to the floor under a burst of white smoke. Yolanda nimbly descended to all fours like a spider landing from a web, as did Tomas. Both remained unfathomably calm and steady in their crouching positions amid the aurora borealis of gunpowder and whirling flashlights.

I did not understand what had happened until I saw blood and a litter of red-spattered lead arrows on the ground, and realized that the gore was dripping from the air.

"Marco, Marco."

From beneath Erik's chest, I looked up in shock. Marco swung and bled above us as he somehow wrangled himself up the rope. His arms had not been hit by the safe's deadly sharp arrows, but he had large wet gashes on both thighs and his left hip was soaked with blood. The strength that he had revealed in the Florentine crypt allowed him to fling himself higher toward the ceiling. He scratched his way up the aperture, wailing and shrieking with pain. He disappeared out the top of the trap door. I heard him trying to run through the cathedral.

"You—you—" my mother began screaming to Tomas. "I went looking for you in the *jungle*—I nearly *died*—you broke my heart, you bastard, you hateful—"

"It's still just us," Manuel stormed. "Juana. It's still you, me, and Lola. He has *nothing* to do with the three of us! And I've loved you for thirty years, woman! *He* doesn't matter."

Tomas still watched me. "Show us what you found out, Lola."

Erik had rolled off me and put his face in his hands. Yolanda's face was white as salt beneath the brim of her hat.

"Marco—"

"I'll talk to that boy later. You show us what there is to see now," Tomas repeated.

I felt myself floating to my feet. I do not know what my parents were saying. I do not know who was where. Soon I would find blood on my arms, which wasn't mine. I would arise in horror over the disappeared Marco, and search for him. I would see the blood spread like a calamity across the altar and the nave, and how it led to the possible scrawl of Marco's footprints on Torcello's storm-thrashed shore. But now, in the midst of my concussion, my colossal weirdness, my miscreant curiosity, I hovered across the room toward the safe. I pressed the four letters, which spelled the unknown name of a Renaissance eccentric and genius: *OPUL.*

The great iron door creaked open. Within the safe were two objects: a pair of slave's chains, marked on the cuffs with the Medici crests, and a leaf of foolscap paper.

I picked up the thick and brutal iron chains, and showed them to my family. I lifted the short letter and read it.

Cosimo

> *That you have found this means that you have remembered, at least, my real name, and know of my shame—of my mettle turned so soft and yellow from living as one of the vicious Medici all these years. Con-*

sider that your prize, along with your beautifully buried Uncle Antonio Medici.

The gold is all gone. I burned it in my laboratory. Yet my alchemical experiments are a failure. My wife is dead. I have found there is no cure for the Human Condition.

Do not tell the Priest of the manner of my death, or of the other crimes of cowardice that I performed in my life, so that I might be buried in hallowed ground, next to my Sofia.

Opul of Timubktu

"Our Antonio was the Slave," I said, shaking even harder than Yolanda as I clutched the chains. "A slave named Opul—Opul—the African alchemist—don't you see—it's so awful. The name. *What is your name?* That's what Antonio asked the Moor in Africa, after he'd killed his father in the alchemy lab. *Opul of Timbuktu.* It's like a palindrome: *Lupo* going one way, *Opul* in the opposite direction. *You are my reverse. You are a wolf.* Then in Mexico, the slave really did reverse places with Antonio Medici, when there was a riot over the gold. He probably took advantage of the confusion, stole a ship, imprisoned his master. The letter *was* a forgery. The real Antonio was dark-skinned, which is why he could pose as the Moor Balthazar, and was called il Lupo Tetro. And Opul was light—that's also why he was able to pull off the impersonation for so long, along with his use of the gold mask covering up Antonio's face, and the myth about the werewolf—what *we* thought was the Condition. *And* playing with the Italians' color prejudice—"

"*Versipellis*," Erik muttered. "Cosimo called him *skin-shifter* because he shifted from black to white. We couldn't see past it ourselves—our reading of Sofia's journal."

"Yes. But the Aztecs, the gold, the druidical books, all that's gone. The *yellow mettle* that he promised Cosimo was just this—his confession. Of his passing as Italian, living off the money stolen from the Aztecs and handed down from slave-traders. That he was a coward. At least until his death, when he killed all the Florentines, with, what—naphtha—because he blamed them for his father's death, the alchemist. And that's why his *mettle* is yellow. His character. Not the gold. The poor, poor man. What he didn't spend on protection, he burned to find the Universal Medicine—so he could stay with Sofia, who loved *him*. So he could cure the *Condition*—agh—" The image of Marco's face pressed itself with chilling insistence against my mind. "We have to go find him out there. Marco. We have to go. There's nothing here for us. No treasure, except for what's in the two medals. The rest of it's been—" I didn't know how to put it. Later I would find the word: *alchemized*.

"No treasure?" Tomas asked, his voice low and steady.

"The original gold? No. There's nothing here of value to us."

"I can't say I agree with that," he said. "Because, hell, if I didn't make a mistake keeping so far away from you, Lola." De la Rosa stared straight down at me with that ugly-handsome face, as if he were the most incredible of superheroes, gifted with X-ray eyes or psychic powers. "I thought maybe you weren't really mine, that Juana would have hammered out everything in you that she knew was from me. But now I see that wouldn't be possible. Because you are mine. You are just like me. You are root and branch, my little girl, the crazy daughter of the Indian who blew up the Spaniards, the grandbaby of the man who went searching for Excalibur in the Pampas, at the end of the damn world. You are precious to me. You are a sight. You are a *sight*. Lola de la Rosa. You are a sight for these weary old eyes."

"*Ah*—" I cried.

And here everything broke loose.

Yolanda slowly raised her hand to her head and slipped off the Stetson. She crushed it between her hands.

"What did you do?" she shrieked. "What did you do? What did you do to me?"

"Hel-lo Y," Tomas answered, imperturbable. "My tough-nut kid, my number one love-baby."

Over this my mother was yelling something, too, which was gargantuan in its anger and its profound obscenity.

But then Erik said, "Lola—your *face*."

Something had just happened to me, understand, and just that second. Something that I did not expect and that was, in its way, terrible.

Maybe I'd been preparing for this moment all my life by reading those books of mine. Maybe the Red Lion's lovingly collected anti-heroes had screwed up my psychology. But while I had been looking into the dark and strange eyes of Tomas and hearing him tell me that I was his very own, his girl, the root-and-branch grandbaby of a lost-and-found epic family, I had changed. I had *shifted*. And they could all see it.

The worst of it was when I looked up and saw the face of Manuel, and took in his expression.

"Oh," he said.

He looked down. He had read me.

I had fallen into a miraculous, heart-flinging, ocean-sized daughter-love with Tomas de la Rosa.

❧ 51 ❧

Two very difficult days passed after my transmutation.

It was now an early Venetian morning. June 11. Erik and I sat on the floor of St. Mark's Basilica. We were the first ones there; it is possible to snatch minutes of solitude even today in the greatest, and most horrible, of European churches if you cheat sleep just enough. And we had cheated sleep. We had cheated sleep for two whole days and were half demented from our waking dreams. The convulsions of history both personal and universal had continued to make their tremors felt upon our wildly expanded minds ever since we found ourselves the unlikely inheritors of the Wolf's ancient curse.

After I had gazed in love upon my biological father, who had struck both Yolanda and me with a kind of lethal Cupid's arrow as opposed to literally poisoned arrows, we had all raced from the lair beneath Santa Maria Assunta into the storm-whipped wilderness of Torcello. We tracked down the bloody path leading to the savaged shore, the missing boat with its escaped or drowned Marco, and the moon-blasted ocean. Farther down, the line of Tomas's own schooner had been cut, and the boat cast adrift, so our stranded crew was made to spend one sleep-free night beneath the pictures of hellfire and doom. The next morning found us transported back to Venice by a fisherman who navigated his craft with an amiable air that belied the Venetians' reputation for coldness. We then dragged our broken-down hides into a lovely hotel with an antique maid who fed us Bellinis and turbot, and (most of us) fell upon this repast like wyverns before staring dazedly out at the amethyst-colored canals. As Erik still didn't want my parents to know about Domenico or Blasej, Yolanda and I kept that to ourselves, trying to explain to my family all the rest of what had happened. Yet what should have been an inventory of our bereavements—love, fidelity, trust, Latino patrimony, the Aztec gold calendars, and holy Druidical books—and our gains—historical detection, triumphant reading—became instead a distraught inspection of the Lazarene Tomas de la Rosa. He drank like a whale while smilingly telling us more fables about my Arthurian-Toltec grandpa. Manuel grew white; my mother red. A bareheaded Yolanda accused him brutally with her ashen lips, even as her hands crawled over the tabletop to him, so that she touched his face and arms with an unguarded ecstasy. For my part, my fears about Erik were beginning to painfully resurface from the anodyne of my unwarranted affection for Tomas. I could also see how with every gesture, every word, de la Rosa continued to exhale chaos upon the deflated Manuel—and my mother, too—as if this deus ex machina came equipped with his own satanic censer of charisma that he swung above us.

The one person who did not figure into this ambiguous ending was my lover.

Erik was exhausted. He did not eat very much of his turbot. When he heard Tomas's story about the sword and South America, he did murmur bitterly about King Arthur being a villain and no hero, and Excalibur being the scourge of mankind, but otherwise remained silent. During even the most antic part

of my family's verbal battles, he regarded us with the benign off-
handedness of an amnesiac.

I knew the time had come to deal with our legal problems
and to try to bring my man home and make him safe. But Erik
didn't want to face all that quite yet.

"We should go back to St. Mark's Basilica, to honor the
dead—the old Aztec ancestors," Erik had suggested the night
before. "Before we go to the police and explain everything, anyway."

"No, we should go and get you a lawyer. And me one, too,
I guess. It's time we faced the trouble we're in. And see if there's
any way we can make it home in time for the wedding—it's in
five days—"

"No, just give me another day or so. And besides, we have to go
to the basilica. The gold they used to repair it is all we've got left."

"Erik—"

"Please, Lola, just don't argue."

So that last Italian morning we sat in vigil, side by side, to
stare up at St. Mark's efflorescent, stolen sky. For a long while we
did not speak, though we did hold hands.

Above us soared the central dome, which depicts the Ascen-
sion. It is a twelfth-century Renaissance masterpiece made out of
gold mosaic circles. Christ sits on his rainbow, in a wreath of sky
and stars, surrounded by a further ring of four angels or sirens.
Gold-limbed trees form a lower halo in the flaming leaves, along
with a curvature of saint-hermits and Mary-goddesses who girdle
him in a holy orbit, as well as a magic circle of Latin words that
spin *FILIUS ISTEDI IC CIVES GALLILEI* around and around like
one of Yeats's gyres.

There I was, agonized over the damage that the last days had
done to Erik, but suddenly I felt that things could still somehow

work out. Overwhelming fears of Erik's delayed nervous break-
downs and our incarcerations vanished as gold light filtered down
onto my face like a palpable blessing. And I did not care that
my brief consolation was only a delirium brought on by wish-
ful thinking, stress, the flashblack of angel dust—like hallucino-
gens, and the optical illusion caused by a trillion dollars' worth of
nectarine-colored heritage robbed from my ancestors and the
entire world.

I did not care. I stared up at gold and at history. I had been
sitting on my tailbone, straight-backed. I found myself all at once
on the floor, my shoulders on the stone mosaics, my face tilted toward the dome. I grasped Erik and brought him down next to me.
I do not know if he could see the beginnings of my rapture. Nor
could I yet see his. I could not say to him that it had started to return to me again, in a deeper and more shocking form than even
in Sofia's cave. The witch's flying potion still worked its magic
in my blood, and visited upon me this second vision, which has
been the vision of my life.

I stared up at the circles whirling above us. It made me think of
the halo around Christ in Michelangelo's *Judgement*, which creates
such pandemonium in the order of Heaven and Hell. This pandemonium or Nirvana suddenly reflected within me. I thought of
all that gold destroyed in the flash of Antonio's alchemical hopes.
I thought of the Aztecs, and the fanged idols they'd erected, replaced by the golden altars of Mary. I recalled the sight of Erik's
face when I lay there choking in the cave, and the images I had of
his childhood and his womb-life and his death. And I began again
to feel this tremendous love. I thought of the chaos of all things.
The man swinging down on a rope in the dark beneath the Torcello cathedral. A mother rising from the depths of the Central
American jungle with her silver hair like Ishtar's aura, and how

she had a switchable passion in her heart for Alvarez and de la Rosa. I thought of my two fathers. I thought of the maxim *Nomen atque omen*, and how the slave had hoped that he was the forever opposite of the Wolf, that *Lupo* was *Opul* reversed absolutely, and he intended *il Noioso Lupo Retto* to be a complete anagram: *Io Sono il Opul Tetro*, I am the dark and gloomy Opul. I thought about how dangerous the Fool's skin-shifting wordplay was, because when he changed places with Antonio, he had not only started fresh but also died. For hadn't the dark and gloomy Opul taken on some of the madness of his captor in those last moments when he burned those men on the Siena battlefield with his naphtha? Just as bad Marco showed me a face that I had also seen on Erik?

No, no, all of these people are strangers to one another, and there is such a thing as evil, but I still gazed up at heavens made of history and of gold. I looked very closely at those circles. They seemed less like the bounded confines of an antique Heaven and more like the wild halo in Michelangelo's *Last Judgement*, which spins out of control, into new shapes. An Aztec god had been destroyed to make this Mary and this Christ. And one day, too, this place would fall. Venice would sink down to the fiery, tectonic plates at the bottom of the ocean, only to rise back up in the form of a shining Chinese fish or a drop of the Indian Ocean. It would *turn and turn again*. It would take centuries, but it would perform its *trick*. And in this vision there was also no difference between the Aztec werewolf-god Xolotl and the risen Jesus Christ since they were made of the same mettle. Yes, there was no difference, either, between Montezuma and Cortés, who were brothers without knowing it. And I was made of the same stuff of Tomas and Manuel. And there really was no such thing as a forgery, because I could translate into the daughter of de la Rosa, or even Soto-Relada, while staying the authentic girl of Alvarez.

I was finally in love with the whole world, the whole, wide, hating world. There was a terrific danger in this epiphany, a heresy that threatened lives and our history. But it is a madness out of which much can be made. I had never been so happy in all my life.

"Erik, Erik," I said.

When I looked over at him, I saw that he was crying.

Large, clear, viscous tears slipped from the corners of his eyes and down his cheeks. His eyes squeezed shut, and his mouth opened wide with grief. This grief was over Domenico.

"Erik," I said.

He shook his head. I leaned over and kissed him. I kissed him again.

"Erik, remember what you said in Florence, to Dr. Riccardi?"

He shook his head again, not looking at me.

I began to feel cold. "Erik, Erik—let's get married. I don't care about the wedding. Let's find a church. Now. Like you were saying in Siena. Let's find a priest—"

He still didn't answer. Then he said: "No, no wedding. I can't anymore."

I clung to him. I grew desperate. Tourists had begun to pour into the basilica, but I didn't care.

"Erik, remember, you said that love changes you for the better."

"It doesn't." He turned his hot eyes toward me. "But I *would* let it change me, Lola. Because I love you, I love you. So I let it make me into anything, into the worst. And it did."

He would not say more. He rose to his feet; we left the basilica without giving it another look. The gold shimmered briefly behind us before we found ourselves again in the tumult of the square.

I remember the rest of that day very clearly. The light on the water shone like citrine and pearls, as if Opul-Antonio had thrown his treasure into the lagoon. The rainbow-black pigeons flew in circles above us. The warm, wet crush of travelers swarmed in Casanova's footsteps and in Titian's. I spoke to Erik twelve more times of marriage, but without avail. We passed the Bridge of Sighs, noting the shadows cast by the Doge's Palace, where the authentic Antonio Medici had starved to death in squalor but for the golden helmet that so cleverly hid his face from the world.

At night, the blue and red gondolas skimmed over the waters. Men in striped shirts sang. Erik and I had a brief dinner with my savagely quarrelsome family before retreating early to our white-linened hotel room, so that we might have a good rest before the next day's confrontation of our legal and domestic dramas.

In the morning, I woke up in a patch of sunlight. The other half of the bed was empty, Erik's side of the closet cleared. There was no note. He left only the faintest trace: a night maid had seen Signor Gomara leave the building at three o'clock in the morning, looking half-dead, she said.

Erik was gone.

BOOK FIVE

EPILOGUE; OR, THE HUMAN CONDITION

❦ 52 ❦

our months later, back in Long Beach, I sit on a folding chair in the dusk-filled and empty Red Lion.

The windows are shuttered. I would have been a bride by now, but instead, I am a single woman dressed in bulky, utilitarian clothes designed for travel. My books are in boxes or stacked in corners and waiting to be packed. The autumn atmosphere, unaided by my Tiffany lamps, is shadowed and most certainly filled with ghosts.

Outside, things do not look much better. The day of the Twin Towers has come and passed, and the newspapers are stained with the same frighteningly gorgeous red and black hues of medieval prayer books, or Mexican Day of the Dead masks.

Thus, the lessons of cataclysm taught to me by the *Versipellis Opul* of Timbuktu, and expressed so beautifully by Michelangelo in *The Last Judgement*, are facing a terrible test.

Miracles are possible: A man can change from slave to master; with the stroke of gold paint the Aztec world can fold like an exquisite corpse into the Italian and perhaps back again; Hell can transform into Heaven. And I can fall in love, like Antigone, like Electra, with the villain who is Tomas de la Rosa.

Still, the desire for chaos that so glamoured me in the Basilica di San Marco has given way, in my heart, to a longing for the twelfth-century version of a permanent and immutable eternity. Tolkien's Lothlorien! In other words, I do not want another person to die, ever, or anything more to change, except for all the dead to come stumbling out of their smoking graves to look wonderingly at the sky, and to laugh about their eternal, inextinguishable stasis.

And I would like but one more transmutation: Erik is not here. I would alchemize him back into my bed and back into my arms.

Therefore, the room is dark; the books and ephemera have been stored away. The two red-gold coins of Aztec gold (which I smuggled out of Italy, yes, which I stole like the most justifiable of bandits, despite the continued rancorous phone calls of Dr. Riccardi, and my bevy of international criminal lawyers), are locked in the store safe. Conan Doyle lurks in this pile, unread, unsold. In the next stack mumbles Verne and King alongside Sofia Medici's unbelievable-but-true *Diario Intimo*. In recent months, I have wondered if all these masters' lessons have been learned by me. I wondered, generally, if the season has come for me to put away fantastical things. The Red Lion still roars from the store front, and he will stay there for the time being. Maybe one day I will bring him, too, down.

I rise from my chair, wander over to one of these book stacks. Bram Stoker's *Dracula* and Sir Sigurd Nussbaum's *Italy: Land of the Lycanthrope* are closed tight, like shut mouths.

Perhaps this is as it should be. I have not decided yet, if we should scorn the false and absurd stories of knight-errantry, Vulcans, *nosferatu*, Italian witches, poltergeists, dragons, gods, melancholic werewolves.

But I know that I will need these tales to help me through one last adventure, at least.

There has been a rumor that has lately reached me, of a Guatemalan man who was seen on the moors of the Scottish Highlands one week ago. It is said he is bearded, and of few words. He uses a walking stick, and his face is gaunt and pale; he carries a large, roving library in a rucksack, composed, in part, of the biographies of the South American radical Che Guevara. Other parts of his collection consist of valuable medieval texts, some of which tell of a Druid named Merlin who went insane in the forest, as well as of a sword that sang like a nightingale when it swung mightily through the heathens' battlefield.

"I've got spies north of Edinburgh," Tomas de la Rosa told me last night. "Seems your boyfriend there's gone whacked, cleared out Sotheby's book collection, then raced around the British and Trinity College Libraries. He's on the trail for Arthur's sword— the one Che Guevara's said to have gotten his hands on in the fifties. But I think Marco and his sister—a low-living, hell-catting, *diabolical* shaman-witch who would've gotten burned in any other right-thinking century—might be following him. I'll tag along to make sure you don't wind up mugged in a pub and wake up with a Union Jack tattooed on your behind."

"*I* should probably go with you, dearest," Manuel interrupted, his ears turning a vibrant shade of pink.

"Well, *I'm* going with her," Yolanda and my mother said, simultaneously, while standing as far away from de la Rosa as I was close. "She'll die in the gutter without me. Creature, sweetheart, you can't even *think* of leaving without my help. . . . Lola, remember what happened in the jungle, the crypt, underneath Siena, *Rome*—you can barely even tie your own shoes for God's sake, let alone navigate the isles without a proper guide—"

"I'm going by myself," I said.

Here in the shadowed corner of my defunct Lion, I put down

Dracula and stand up. I must escape Long Beach, and quickly, before my entire clan tracks me down to London like an affectionate if more voluble version of the Furies, and makes a disaster of my mission. I walk out of the bookstore, lock the door, and do not look back. As I move down the soot-black street, I am wearing canvas pants and a leather jacket, and my rucksack is filled with necessities: a rare 1712 edition of *Lancelot du Lac*, a sixteenth-century hand-lettered copy of the *Mabinogion*, the apocryphal and very good with dust jacket *Diaries of Vivien*, and a fudgy Xerox of the letters of an unrequited sweetheart of Che Guevara. I believe Erik would have chosen these same works; being so much in love, I have learned his readerly inclinations.

There is still in me a shaken faith in these precious aids, despite their terrific failings: fantasy, adventure, the word. The word! My whole life! But even if these book gifts go wrong, even if I am left alone with no language and no other tools than my love and my many moral flaws, I can still make this incomprehensible world tell me where he is. With my quick, quick eye, I will scan its traveling borders, the fading footprints in its mud. With my keen ear I will decipher the plastic patois of its grieving denizens and detect the murderous histories that alter with each teller. This rough, whirling planet will divulge its moving meanings if I press my fingers to its hidden braille. Some text or erasure will show me the way. I will find Erik Gomara and bring him back home.

Acknowledgments

Great thanks to my husband, Andrew Brown, and also Rene Alegria, Melinda Moore, Fred MacMurray, Maggie MacMurray, Marta Van Landingham, Edward St. John, Shana Kelly, Virginia Barber, and Kirsten Dhillon.

THE HISTORY

BEHIND

THE STORY

A Conversation with
Yxta Maya Murray

Tell us about the inspiration for The King's Gold.

Throughout my writing career, I've been inspired by the tales of conquest and loss that make up Mexico's history. As most of us know, in 1519, Hernan Cortés arrived on the shores of the so-called New World, and through astonishing acts of courage and ferocity proceeded to wrest control of Tenochtitlán from Emperor Montezuma. One of the more intriguing aspects of this history is the tale of Montezuma's massive stores of gold, which he reportedly gave over to Cortés in order to prevent this Spanish, armor-clad "alien" from destroying the Mexican people.

At the beginning of *The King's Gold*, I quote from Bernal Díaz del Castillo's famous history *The Conquest of New Spain*. In that book, the author describes Cortés's fruitless efforts to lay claim on the major share of the gold, which was made impossible because of his own soldiers' thefts. I have also heard a fair number of legends whose tellers claim that gold-laden Spaniards drowned in Tenochtitlán's rivers when running away from warrior Aztecs.

In other words, most of the gold that Cortés stole from the Americas has been lost.

I was inspired to write *The King's Gold* in an effort to answer the question of where the gold wound up, and what changes it had undergone through the centuries. In the process, I found that I wasn't just writing about gold, but about history and also the larger theme of "transformation." As a consequence, all kinds of images and tropes related to transformation found their way into the plot: alchemical processes; shape-shifters like witches, vampires, and werewolves; the world-twisting effects of drugs and spiritual revelation; and the word-bending anagrammatic and etymological arts.

Are you much like Lola, the "word-mad bibliophile" protagonist of the Red Lion series?

I am. I own a rare and freakishly expensive copy of Samuel Johnson's *Dictionary*, first editions of Virginia Woolf's novels, reproduction copies of pulp-penny dreadfuls like those written by H. Rider Haggard, and count a mad-scientist librarian among my best friends. (That's Edward St. John, mentioned in the book's dedication.) In order to craft the Italian anagram in the novel, I spent thirteen hours bent over an Italian dictionary, which was a definite word-feast. I love Skeat's etymological dictionary, the works of Jorge Luis Borges, and every Saturday I visit my local branch of the Los Angeles Public Library, where I am always over limit.

Books allow me to have adventures, like Lola. After reading Marion Zimmer Bradley's *Mists of Avalon*, I bought a plane ticket and chased King Arthur through Britain's ancient castles. After finishing Euripides' *Bacchae*, I organized and hosted an authentic, all-female bacchanal, complete with poetry reading, much wine drinking, drumming, chanting, and feasting. Recently, I read Meg Bogin's fabulous book *The Women Troubadours*. So, now inspired by this Provencal history, this winter I will travel throughout Los Angeles with a group of five women poets, we'll be reciting our own poems for a score of literature lovers in the tradition of the twelfth-century itinerant troubadours that Bogin describes.

In fact, perhaps I'm a little nuttier than Lola, even.

How much hands-on travel and research was involved in the crafting of the story? Did you visit all the historical sites that the characters visit?

With my husband, Andrew Brown, I visited every site described in the book. In Florence, I tried to climb up scaffolding surrounding the Basilica di San Lorenzo. That's how I learned they were alarmed! In Siena's Duomo, I nearly did a belly-flop on the She-Wolf mosaic when I saw it and excitedly realized that it would make a perfect hidden trap door. In Rome, Andrew and I disregarded safety signs and ropes to crawl underneath the ancient Roman baths in Ostia Antica. I also grew dizzy when I saw Saint Peter's Basilica because it is both colossally beautiful and creepy. And when I stood in front of Michelangelo's *Last Judgement*, I wanted to be a magical witch like Sofia so that I could fly up above the illegally camera-snapping crowd to get a good close look at Master's grisly self-portrait. In Venice's Basilica of St. Mark, I watched people lift their hands to the massive gold mosaics as if they were somehow worshiping them, a detail that I included in my book. Then, in Torcello, I dashed around the church called Santa Maria Assunta, and yodeled in delight when I found the gold mosaic of St. Heliodorus, my "thirteenth man," who was flanked by six apostles on either side.

Also, I ate a lot of Italian food.

Were there specific visual influences in film or art that helped you set the lush tone of the story?

Horror films provided a real inspiration for *The King's Gold*, the more gothic, the better. The dark aesthetic of Francis Ford Coppola's *Dracula*, John Landis's *Werewolf in London*, and F. W. Murnau's *Nosferatu* all helped me imagine a spooky, monster-haunted Italy.

Renaissance Italian art also drove my imagery. In the happier scenes, I drew upon the lightness of Boticelli's work, and the more dreadful sections of the novel were driven by the outlandish stone art, or *pietre dure*, that I saw in Florence, as well as the death imagery found all over the Vatican, Saint Peter's Basilica, and the crumbling, gorgeous ruins of Venice.

Michelangelo was my greatest artistic inspiration, though. It was while I stood in the Sistine Chapel and looked up at *The Last Judgement* that I started to develop my own interpretations of the work. After studying medieval religious art, with its static images of heaven and hell, I was surprised how fluid *The Last Judgement* looked. As I describe in the book, I was struck by the halo that surrounds Christ in the fresco, and the energetic swirling motion that it creates in the tableau. It really does appear as if the halo is creating a kind of centrifugal force that threatens to spin the angels into hell and the damned into heaven. Moreover, the halo's antic, circular quality reminded me of gold Aztec calendars and Tibetan prayer wheels.

Michelangelo's work argues that the line dividing heaven and hell is not static but subject to radical change.

Who were the real characters from the historical sequences in the book, and who came out of your imagination?
Cosmio I, Duke of Florence, was one of the only real people I described in the novel. Antonio and Sofia Medici are figments of my imagination, though real people most certainly have undergone

the kind of shape-shifting that they do; colonialism obviously has forced people to pass, hide, and disguise themselves throughout history.

Do you pass judgment on your characters? Assign them labels of "good" or "evil" and dispense their fate from there?
Tackling concepts of "good" and "evil" turned out to be one of the main projects of *The King's Gold*.

I was influenced by two works in the writing of this book, both of which deal with the ways in which the concepts of chaos and transformation call flat labels like "good" and "evil" into question. One of these works was Jorge Luis Borges' *Aleph*, where Borges' protagonist has a mystical experience during which he witnesses the totality of experience. The event is dislocating, Sartrean, and undermining. The second book that I was inspired by was Herman Hesse's *Siddhartha*, where Siddhartha's best friend, Govinda, witnesses the totality of experience when he has a conversation with this bodhisattva. The experience, in contrast to the protagonist's in *The Aleph*, is nourishing, peaceful, and transcendent.

What I noticed from both of these descriptions, where the authors try to wrap their arms around "everything," is that binary categories like good and bad no longer exist. To Borges, this is hell, or chaos; to Hesse, this is Nirvana.

When writing about the transformations and instabilities of history, I found myself smack in the middle of this debate. On the one hand, Borges is right: The Spaniards came into the Americas, and destroyed it, but if we view this incident from a godlike vantage point, not only is such an atrocity inevitable but also it is inconsequential when compared to the giant flood of all experience. It is both good and bad, virtuous and evil; the conquest merely emerges as yet another confirmation that all things pass away and transform into something else, and that we'll all just disappear.

When viewed with Siddhartha's, or Hesse's, sympathies, however, there is something very refreshing about the Buddha's transcendent acceptance of cataclysmic events like the conquest. If we become like the Buddha or a bodhisattva, we understand that men and women contain all evil and all good inside of them, and that we are all connected. Thus, I am part of Cortés, and he is part of me; I can't claim him as a stranger any longer under this viewpoint. And an acceptance (and comprehension) of "what is" might allow us to achieve Nirvana.

I admit a predilection for Hesse's vision over Borges', but in either case, I'm also appalled that the large vision that both writers have left to us do not leave much space for judgment, or even identity.

In the end, my characters' transformations include their troubling shape-shifting from good to evil, to back again; I am playing with the idea that these labels are both meaningless and necessary.

Where is your favorite place to write?
I love this *Paris Review* question. I wrote this book on a Compaq nx9030, and my favorite place to write was in my bedroom. Though I don't have cork walls (like Proust, another famous bedwriter), I do have shooter's ear guards, those heavy duty ear muffs that people wear when they go to shooting ranges to prevent ear drum damage. I wear them when the noise from the street gets too distracting.

In addition to your career as a novelist, you are also a law professor. Do you frequently encounter academics that are as

feisty and filled with wanderlust as the characters we encounter in your books?

I have met some pretty incredible people in the academy. I have one colleague at Loyola Law School who spends his summers in a remote, rural woodland in Washington, and also, in his spare time, rewrites copyright laws in D.C. *and* conducts cancer research in San Francisco. So, he's pretty amazing. Other colleagues spend the school years advocating for the legalization of gay marriage and defendants' rights in criminal trials, and then use their spring breaks to compete in the AIDS ride or their summers to go caravanning across the United States.

I love them.

Can you tell us anything else about the next book in the series?

The third book in the Red Lion series will pick up with Erik on the nearly cold trail, as he goes searching through England, Scotland, Argentina, and possibly Paris to hunt down Excalibur. Excalibur, in my story, will have had a very interesting recent history. Rumor has it that Che Guevara somehow got his hands on the sword once owned by the Lady of the Lake (and then, King Arthur), and used it to wage his most ferocious rebellions—until it was somehow lost in the wilds of South America. Erik, devastated at the murderous events in Rome, has left Lola to purge himself with this quest. He hopes to destroy a weapon that has been used, through time, and myth, to annihilate "barbarians."

Lola, of course, tries to track her lover down, and in the process, winds up on the trail of the mythical sword as well.

Suggestions for Further Reading

I loved the following books that I read for *The King's Gold*:

William Manchester's *World Lit Only by Fire*
Dale Kent's *Cosimo D'Medici and the Florentine Renaissance*
Lucia Tongiorgio Tomasi and Gretchen A. Hirschauer's *Flowering of Florence: Botanical Art for the Medici*
Anna Rita Fantoni's *Treasures from Italy's Great Libraries*
Jacob Burckhardt's *Civilization of the Renaissance in Italy*
Lord Kinross's *Ottoman Centuries: The Rise and Fall of the Turkish Empire*
Montague Summers's *Malleus Maleficarium of Kramer and Sprenger*
Fritz Graf's *Magic in the Ancient World*
Lewis Spence's *Encyclopedia of Occultism*

The lighter side of HISTORY

✶ Look for this seal on select historical fiction titles from Harper. Books bearing it contain special bonus materials, including timelines, interviews with the author, and insights into the real-life events that inspired the book, as well as recommendations for further reading.

AND ONLY TO DECEIVE
A Novel of Suspense
by Tasha Alexander
978-0-06-114844-6 (paperback)
Discover the dangerous secrets kept by the strait-laced English of the Victorian era.

DARCY'S STORY
Pride and Prejudice Told from Whole New Perspective
by Janet Aylmer
978-0-06-114870-5 (paperback)
Read Mr. Darcy's side of the story.

PORTRAIT OF AN UNKNOWN WOMAN
A Novel
by Vanora Bennett
978-0-06-125256-3 (paperback)

Meg, adopted daughter of Sir Thomas More, narrates the tale of a famous Holbein painting and the secrets it holds.

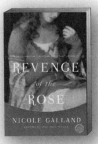

REVENGE OF THE ROSE
A Novel
by Nicole Galland
978-0-06-084179-9 (paperback)
In the court of the Holy Roman Emperor, not even a knight is safe from gossip, schemes, and secrets.

THE CANTERBURY PAPERS
by Judith Healey
978-0-06-077332-8 (paperback)

CROSSED
A Tale of the Fourth Crusade
by Nicole Galland
978-0-06-084180-5 (paperback)

ELIZABETH: THE GOLDEN AGE
by Tasha Alexander
978-0-06-143123-4 (paperback)

THE FOOL'S TALE
by Nicole Galland
978-0-06-072151-0 (paperback)

THE KING'S GOLD
by Yxta Maya Murray
978-0-06-089108-4 (paperback)

PILATE'S WIFE
A Novel of the Roman Empire
by Antoinette May
978-0-06-112866-0 (paperback)

A POISONED SEASON
A Novel of Suspense
by Tasha Alexander
978-0-06-117421-6 (paperback)

THE QUEEN OF SUBTLETIES
A Novel of Anne Boleyn
by Suzannah Dunn
978-0-06-059158-8 (paperback)

THE SIXTH WIFE
**She Survived Henry VIII to be
Betrayed by Love...**
by Suzannah Dunn
978-0-06-143156-2 (paperback)

REBECCA
**The Classic Tale of Romantic
Suspense**
by Daphne Du Maurier
978-0-380-73040-7 (paperback)

REBECCA'S TALE
by Sally Beauman
978-0-06-117467-4 (paperback)

THE SCROLL OF SEDUCTION
**A Novel of Power, Madness,
and Royalty**
by Gioconda Belli
978-0-06-083313-8 (paperback)

A SUNDIAL IN A GRAVE: 1610
**A Novel of Intrigue, Secret Societies,
and the Race to Save History**
by Mary Gentle
978-0-380-82041-2 (paperback)

THORNFIELD HALL
Jane Eyre's Hidden Story
by Emma Tennant
978-0-06-000455-2 (paperback)

TO THE TOWER BORN
A Novel of the Lost Princes
by Robin Maxwell
978-0-06-058052-0 (paperback)

THE WIDOW'S WAR
by Sally Gunning
978-0-06-079158-2 (paperback)

THE WILD IRISH
**A Novel of Elizabeth I & the
Pirate O'Malley**
by Robin Maxwell
978-0-06-009143-9
(paperback)

Available wherever books are sold, or call 1-800-331-3761 to order.